The Prince Deceiver

KIRALYNN EPICS

The Silk & Steel Saga

Book One: *The Steel Queen*
Book Two: *The Flame Priest*
Book Three: *The Skeleton King*
Book Four: *The Poison Priestess*
Book Five: *The Knight Marshal*
Book Six: *The Prince Deceiver*

Forthcoming books by Karen L Azinger

Book Seven: *The Battle Immortal*

Additional books by Karen L Azinger
The Assassin's Tear

THE
PRINCE DECEIVER

BOOK SIX OF
THE SILK & STEEL SAGA

Karen L. Azinger

KIRALYNN EPICS

Published by Kiralynn Epics L.P. 2014

Copyright © Karen L. Azinger 2014

First published in the United States of America by Kiralynn Epics 2014

Front Cover Artwork Copyright Greg Bridges © 2014

Celtic Lettering used with permission of Alfred M Graphics Art Studio

The Author asserts the moral right to be identified as the author of this work

All characters in this publication are fictitious and any resemblance to real persons living or dead, is purely coincidental.

ISBN 978-0-9910297-2-3

Library of Congress Control Number: 2014914193

For Rick

The Mordant's Domain

The haunted River

The Ghost hills

Basalt Cliffs

The Dark Citadel

The Pit

The Spires

Mer Sea

The Northern Steppes

The Dark Wall
and the Ten Gargoyle Gates

The Southern Steppes

W

E

S

Western Ocean

Holdfast Keep

Ice Tower

Dymtower

Raven Pass

Gragnoth Keep

Sword Keep

Shieldhold

Salt Tower

Dragon Spine Mountains

Castlegard

Orcnoth Islands

Navarre

The Serpentines

Domain Of Castlegard

Snowmelt River

Eye Bridge

Octagon Bridge

Navar

Snowseep

Prologue

Quintus locked the door to the healery and then shuttered the windows. For the longest time, he sat at the desk, fondling the quill, considering his words. The message needed to be short but effective. Only a few words, yet somehow he needed to make them believe. Candles melted to stubs, the pale wax puddling on his cluttered desk. With shaking hands, he wrote the coded message: *Castlegard's mage-stone walls are scarred by a wagon's wheel.* The single sentence terrified him, as if the very fabric of the world was coming unraveled. Mage-stone was thought to be everlasting, impervious to the ravages of time, weather, and war; yet a wagon's axle had marred the great castle's walls. He'd seen it with his own eyes, felt the scar with his own trembling fingers, yet he still did not believe it. Quintus prayed the masters in the monastery would heed his warning despite the lunacy of the message. Staring at the vellum, he decided to add one last word, a heartfelt plea. *Help* was the first word that came to mind, but instead he wrote, *Advise!*

Rolling the thin vellum strip into a tight scroll, he slipped it into a tube carved from bone and affixed it to the jessed leg of his frost owl. "Easy, Snowman." Tossing tidbits of chicken liver to the great white raptor, he pulled on a leather falconry glove. "Come."

White wings bated the air in a silent rush. The great owl alit on his raised glove, eager for another tidbit. Knowing the owl had far to fly, Quintus was generous with the liver.

Bracing his arm against the weight, he carried Snowman out into the castle's main courtyard. The night was cold and crisp, the north still bound by winter's lingering grasp. A half moon rode low in the cloudless night, providing just enough light to burnish Castlegard's stalwart ramparts to a glorious silver. The healer grimaced, knowing the traitorous truth. The great mage-stone walls were not as stalwart as they appeared.

Perhaps the malady can be cured.

He did not know where the thought came from, but he clung to it, praying the monastery knew the remedy. All the more reason to send his message.

Pausing at the corner, he glanced left and right, relieved to find the courtyard empty. The moon's position marked the hour as midnight, when sleep held sway and only a few guards walked the walls. Checking to make sure the message tube was secure, he fed the owl one last bite. "Fly home, Snowman. Fly home and fly fast and return with the answer to this dire riddle." With a grunt, he hefted the great owl aloft. White wings snapped open, beating the air. With a hunter's stealthy silence, the great owl gained height, soaring over the castle walls like a silvery ghost. The healer's gaze followed the owl south, his words a whispered prayer. "Hurry home, Snowman, and bring me the answers I need."

"*Home?* Where is home if not Castlegard?"

Startled, Quintus cursed himself for his carelessness. Turning, he found Otto, the master swordsmith, striding towards him. "You're late to be out."

Tall and bald and layered with bulging muscles, the big smith prowled across the courtyard like a winter-starved bear. "I've a smelt of iron ore that needs watching. What's your excuse?"

Quintus shrugged. "My frost owl hunts best at night."

"Yet you told the owl to fly home. Where's home if not Castlegard?"

He stared at the smith, a plea in his gaze, for he could not answer the question without imperiling his purpose.

"We're at war, healer, and an owl might be hunting...or it might be carrying a message of betrayal." The big smith moved close, his hands balled into massive fists, a rumble of threat in his gravelly voice. "So, I'll ask you again, where is home?"

A trickle of sweat rolled down the healer's back despite the cold. Secrets he could keep, but lies always tripped on his tongue. Quintus paled beneath the smith's iron-hard gaze. Realizing he'd get no reprieve, he made a decision. "Come, I need to show you something."

"Show me something?" Suspicion rode the smith's voice.

"Just come. I need to show someone and it might as well be you."

The smith gave him a squinty look. "This better not be a trick."

The healer implored with his gaze. "You'll not believe unless you see for yourself."

With a terse nod, the smith followed him across the courtyard to the inner gatehouse. The spiked portcullis was raised but the ironclad gates were shut for the night. Fortunately, he knew the guard on duty. "How's your stump, Harold?"

The guard raised his arm, revealing a leather-bound stump where his left hand should have been. "It pains me in this damp cold, but I'm better than most. At least I can still serve."

Still serve, such was the bravery of the maroon knights. For every hale and hearty man who served the great castle, four more were maimed or graybeards. The winter war took a grievous toll. Quintus knew the grim tally better than most, for he'd stitched their wounds and set their bones, returning many of them to service. "I'll make a poultice for you in the morning. In the meantime, can you let us through the sally port?"

"This late at night?"

"I spied a patch of mushrooms sprouting along the south wall. They're most potent if harvested by moonlight."

The guard flicked a questioning glance to the smith but Otto remained silent. Shrugging, Harold said, "I'll let you through, but don't tarry." He led them around the gatehouse to a small ironbound door. Half a dozen deadbolts held the sally port secure. One-handed, the guard wrestled with the bolts and then eased the door open on silent hinges. "Knock three times when you're ready to enter."

"Thanks." The healer slipped through the open doorway, followed by the smith. Behind them, the ironclad door eased shut, the deadbolts snapping into place with an ominous sound.

Quintus turned to confront the grim passageway. An eerie silence reigned. They stood in the killing corridor, trapped between the soaring mage-stone walls of the inner castle and the outer ramparts raised by ordinary stonemasons. Desolate of any cover, the stone-cold corridor seemed a haunted place despite the bright moonlight.

The smith leaned close, a sneer on his face. "Mushrooms? I always thought you an honest sort."

"There *are* mushrooms, and I do need them. With so many wounded, my supply of remedies grows thin."

"And you pick them by moonlight?" The smith's voice leered with sarcasm.

The healer shrugged. "An old wives' tale but a convenient excuse." He led the smith around to the south side of the inner wall to where a small patch of Donner's mushrooms pushed up through the thin snow crust. He knelt, harvesting half the crop to his deep pockets, leaving the rest to propagate.

"You brought me out here for mushrooms?"

The healer flicked a wary glance to the smith. "No, the mushrooms were just an excuse. Come." He led the smith back to the inner gate, but instead of approaching the sally port, he led him to the main gateway. "It happened two days ago, when the wagons carrying the wounded returned, but you need to see it for yourself to believe." Quintus ran his hand low along the mage-stone wall, searching for the gash, half hoping he would not find it. "Here. It's here." His voice sounded as if it came from a grave.

"What's there?" The smith sounded annoyed.

"A scar on the mage-stone."

"That's impossible."

"No, look."

And then the smith saw. He sucked air through his teeth like a hungry bellows. With a trembling hand, he touched the wall, fingering the raw scar. His jaw gaped. "How?"

"The wagoner took too tight a turn. The rear axle caught on the stone. I thought the wagon would tip...but the stone gave first."

"But...it's mage-stone!"

"I know."

"How can this be?"

The healer shrugged. "I don't know. Perhaps the castle's fallen under a Dark Curse."

The smith cringed, making the hand sign against evil. "Who have you told?"

"None save you..."

"...and the owl."

Quintus gave a cautious nod. "We need answers."

The smith scowled but he did not argue. "We need to tell the knight-captain."

"No." He grabbed the smith's arm. "Morale is all that's holding the maroon together. We dare not dash their faith in the great castle."

"But they need to know!"

"Only if an army comes calling."

"We're at war."

"All the more reason the knights' morale must not be destroyed."

The smith glared, his massive hands balled into fists, fear and uncertainty warring across his swarthy face. For half a heartbeat, the healer thought the big smith would end the argument with a punch. Standing resolute, Quintus parried the smith's brutal glare with a tally of losses. "Raven pass is fallen. The king is dead. The Octagon throne is empty. The knights battle the ravages of winter as well as the Dark horde, yet still they fight." He punched the words with conviction. "If you destroy their faith in the castle, this war could be lost."

"What does a healer know of war?"

"I know the cost! I count it every day in limbs severed, in wounds stitched, in too many lives lost to death's shroud. Morale matters, on the battlefield *and* in the healery." His voice turned hard. "I'll not give death another advantage."

They glared at each other, locked in a stalemate...till a grudging respect glinted Otto's dark gaze. A long-held sigh escaped the smith like an emptying bellows. "We'll keep it secret...for as long as we can."

They'd struck an uncertain bargain, but Quintus would take what he could get.

"But," the smith stabbed the healer's pudgy chest with a blunt finger, "if that owl brings answers, I want to know."

Rubbing his bruised chest, Quintus gave a tentative nod.

"I'll be watching you."

In silence, they trod through the muddy slush, returning to the sally port. Quintus knocked three times and the hidden door eased open. Harold ushered them through. Closing the door behind them, he rammed the bolts home. "Did you get the mushrooms?"

"Yes I did." Quintus fished one from his pocket as proof. "Picked by moonlight, they'll ease pain or induce sleep, depending on the dosage."

Harold grinned. "Well done! I'll bid you a good night."

"And to you." He turned away, following the big smith across the courtyard. A grim silence hovered between them. They were partners of sorts, partners to a terrible secret. Quintus stared up at the soaring mage-stone walls, walls he always thought were invincible. First the war and now this. Darkness stalked the maroon, like a lethal curse come calling. A shiver raced down his spine. In the depths of his heart, the healer hoped the masters of the monastery believed his message...but most of all he prayed there was a cure.

In the South

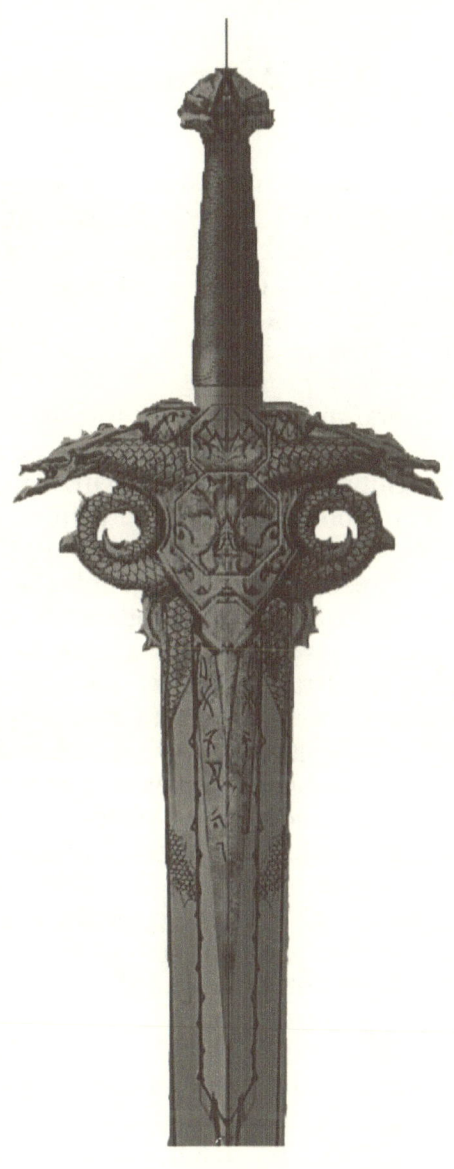

1

The Mordant

Hammers pounded against stone, a cacophony of noise announcing the queen's city. Scaffolds surrounded the outer walls, stonemasons working to convert cobbled buildings into stout battlements. *So, this is the queen's city.* The effect was laughable, like putting armor on a whore. The Mordant smiled at the feeble defense. *Mortals think mere walls can hold back Darkness. How little the queen understands her true foe.*

Under false banners, the Mordant led his entourage towards the city gates at a stately trot. Bedecked in jewels and clad in a purple surcoat, he rode a magnificent white stallion curried to a shine. Golden bells woven into the stallion's mane chimed with every prancing step, all part of the ruse. Royal banners fluttered overhead, the Great Wyrm embroidered in gold thread, proudly proclaiming a prince of Ur. His entourage was similarly attired, resplendent in purple and gold, completing the deceit. His women rode sidesaddle, tempting curves swathed in colorful silks, attracting stares like bees to honey. Behind him, a team of white oxen struggled to pull a wagon laden with treasure chests, a tease to the greedy. His cadre of assassins and dwarf-sized duegars came last, dressed as servants. Ignored and overlooked, they trailed a respectful distance behind, danger hidden in plain sight. As a final touch, a hundred Citadel guards had changed their colors, donning the purple and gold of imperial Ur. Clad in burnished armor bearing the sigil of the Great Wyrm, they surrounded his troop with a ring of potent swords. Jewels, women, and steel, his escort presented the perfect blend of pampered royalty swathed in appropriate protection.

Bells chiming, the Mordant and his escort neared the city walls.

Stares turned their way, the sound of hammers slowing to a stop. Peasants, stonemasons and passing merchants craned for a better view. The Mordant felt their envy. He watched the way they ogled his women and the wagon piled high with treasure chests. Even the queen's guards fell prey to the delusion. Leaning on their spears, soldiers in emerald tabards watched from half-finished towers, yet no alarm was raised. Unaware of the danger, the city's ironclad gates stood open like a hungry maw slavering for commerce.

His seneschal, Bishop Borgan, bellowed in a sonorous voice, "Make way for the Twelfth-fold Prince of Ur!"

Merchants and peasants scuttled to get off the road, while guards in green tabards stood to attention by the open gates.

"Make way for the Prince of Ur!"

The shadow of the gatehouse drew near. Without a single challenge, the Mordant rode through the gates of Pellanor into the queen's city.

Wide cobbled streets bustled with the noon-time crowd. Avid stares turned towards his entourage. A pathway opened through the throng, the awe-struck crowd gaped in wonder at the royal display. Many smiled, while others clapped or waved in greeting. So open and so trusting, the populous proved their naivety. Clearly, they'd never felt a tyrant's lash...but that would soon change. He'd barely entered the city and already the Mordant had the queen's measure: a weak and lenient ruler, a woman besotted with the acquisition of wealth. A smile curled his lips. He'd met thousands of her sort, all easily lured to Darkness.

His gaze roved the crowd, taking in the details. A small man clad in simple leathers slipped from the throng to approach Major Tarq. The Mordant recognized his face, one of the assassins he'd sent ahead to prepare the way. Walking next to the major, the assassin served as a guide, directing them through the tangled streets.

Signs of prosperity increased as they rode deeper into the city. Markets overflowed with goods and the people appeared well-fed and content. Scents of cinnamon, cardamom and other exotic spices wafted through the market, mingling with the enticing smells of spit-roasted meats and fresh baked breads, proving Pellanor had an abundance of food despite the recent war. Bright velvets became more common, sparkling like jewels against the commoners' homespun browns. The Mordant studied the riot of faces. Women mingled with men, the rich amongst the poor, with only a few swords in sight, evidence of a pampered city awash in too many freedoms...but all of this would soon change, for he'd come to bring ordered Darkness to all of Erdhe.

A castle thrust up from the city's sprawling center, a bright confection of airy towers and winged buttresses, bespeaking luxury instead of strength, indulgence instead of dominance. Shops grew to the very walls of the castle, negating its military value. So unlike the

Dark Citadel, it looked like a pampered palace instead of a fortress stronghold. A sneer lit the Mordant's face. Judging by the castle alone, Pellanor would be an easy conquest.

They turned off the main thoroughfare, winding through a district filled with large mansions and small manicured gardens. Servants in bright livery stood by the doors. Fountains danced in the gardens, a waste of water. The very air smelled perfumed, flowers climbing trellises and spilling from window boxes. The district reeked of pampered luxury, the perfect hiding place for lethal Darkness.

Their guide led them to a large stone manse, glittering with diamond-paned windows. A servant rushed to hold his stallion as the Mordant dismounted. A pair of tall oak doors opened, disgorging a bevy of servants in purple livery. Bowing low, they welcomed the Mordant to his mansion.

He strode through the doorway, followed by assassins, duegars and fawning servants. Sunlight streamed through diamond-paned windows illuminating a large marble entranceway. Tapestries bright with hunting scenes graced the walls, a gilded stairway climbed to a second floor. A large chandelier hung suspended overhead, glittering with crystals and golden cherubs. Gaudy and garish, the entranceway bespoke an owner with too much wealth and too little taste. Satisfied with the subterfuge, the Mordant said, "This will serve." Scanning the servants prostrate on the marble floor, he added, "You may rise."

His servants hastily stood.

Frederinko towered above the others, distinctive in his silver collar and nose chains. "Welcome to Pellanor, my lord." Bronzed from a lifetime spent beneath Ur's southern sun, the chained servant was the lone kernel of truth in the Mordant's elaborate deception. Seized by MerChanters' raiders and carried to the far north at the Mordant's bidding, he'd broken the eunuch's will in the bloody cavern beneath the Dark Citadel. Now a dedicate of Darkness, the eunuch served as the Mordant's emissary to the Rose Court. With a courteous bow, the chained servant gestured toward the gilded stairway. "Would you like to see the rest of the manse?"

"Show me the cellar."

"As you wish."

The Mordant followed the chained servant toward the rear of the house. Bishop Borgan, Major Tarq, his master assassin, Dolf, and Rollo, a snargon of the duegars, stayed close, providing a mixture of protection and service.

A doorway in a shadowy alcove opened to stairs leading down. Thick stone walls embraced the stairway with a cellar's wintery chill.

The stairs led to a small room crowded with wine casks stacked floor to ceiling.

Frederinko stepped to an enormous barrel inset in the wall. "Stonemasons worked tirelessly to complete the modifications you required."

"Have they been silenced?"

"Silent as a grave." Turning the tap on the large barrel, the eunuch tugged and the lid swung open, revealing a hidden passage.

The Mordant gestured and Dolf plumbed the passage followed by Rollo. There was no need for him to tax his powers while others lived to serve. While he waited on their inspection, the Mordant turned to Frederinko. "Tell me of the queen."

Frederinko flashed a shark's smile. "The queen toils like a drone bee, struggling to repair the ravages of the Flame War. She builds walls and rekindles commerce, but her actions prove her deepest nightmares come from the north. When Raven Pass fell, she scrambled to rebuild her army and forge a patchwork alliance. Her sole heir marches north with the Rose army, a futile attempt to delay the inevitable."

The Mordant suppressed a grin, for wars ever provided the best distractions. "What of Dominic and Castor?"

"Dressed as jesters, both were accepted as gifts and reside in the castle."

"Good. Send word that I'll meet with them on the morrow. I'll need a full report."

"As you command."

Dolf and Rollo returned, making the hand signal that all was safe.

The Mordant stepped through the opening, entering a pristine dungeon. Caged cells stretched away on either side, yet the chilled air carried nothing but the ascetic scents of mortar and fresh-cut stone.

Frederinko gestured left and right. "Cells enough to hold fifty people or more, and there are even two oubliettes if you wish to invoke the subtlest of tortures." Crossing the corridor, he unlocked an ironbound door. "This way to the sanctum."

Dolf lifted a torch from the wall, leading the way down the narrow stairs.

The Mordant followed, emerging into a large stone-cloistered chamber. Darkness arched overhead, the ceiling soaring to a corbelled vault shrouded in shadows. Torchlight flickered in the gloom, revealing a blank canvas. Bone-cold and grave-dank, the sanctum was empty of symbols save for a single great pentacle inscribed across the floor, silver inset in the dull granite. Man-high braziers stood at the five points of the pentacle. Sculpted in bronze, the twisted figures writhed like tortured souls straining for release. Simple in its design, the sanctum echoed the configuration of the Dark Citadel's bloody cavern, but it was new and unused...and devoid of power, a chapel waiting to be dedicated. The Mordant yearned to awaken the Darkness, to summon the divine Dark to the very heart of the queen's city. Striding to the pentacle, he stood in the center and closed his eyes, reaching for his god. He found the Dark God lurking at the edge of reality, slavering for worship in the heart of Lanverness. "Yes, this will do."

His eyes snapped open, his gaze fastening on Major Tarq. "Sacrifices are needed to open the gateway. Bring me orphans and pickpockets and other riffraff, people who shall not be missed. Later, we'll be more blatant in our offerings."

"As you command." The major saluted, fist to breastplate.

His gaze turned to the snargon. "Have your duegar run regular sweeps of the city streets. If the meddling monks aren't already infesting the city, they soon will be. Sniff out their magic and you'll find their bolt holes. I want reports of any magic, any monks...or knights of the Octagon found within Pellanor."

The snargon bristled, "But we can only..."

The Mordant glared. "You have eyes. Use them."

The snargon bowed low, stepping back into the shadows.

Bishop Borgan said, "Shall I send word to the queen requesting an audience?"

The Mordant's gaze snapped to the portly bishop disguised as a seneschal. "Stupid does not serve me."

The bishop blanched, a flicker of fear in his eyes.

"All of Pellanor speaks of our arrival...though they know not who I am." The simple deception amused the Mordant, wakening a fierce passion for the hunt. "The queen will seek an audience with us. The arrogant bitch will invite her own doom...and we, being obliging guests, shall accept." A thrill coursed through him, an eagerness to reach the end game. His voice crackled with power, ominous with prediction. "In this lifetime, all of my enemies shall be shattered. Let the Great Dark Dance begin."

2

Master Numar

The dark of the moon, such an ill-omened time, yet he understood why Aeroth chose it for their moon-turn meeting. Shrugging the satchel onto his back, Master Numar chose a stout staff from the stand near the door and set off from the shop at a brisk walk. Wielding his quarterstaff like a walking stick, he made his way through the cobbled streets of Pellanor.

Late at night, yet the streets were not entirely empty. A neighboring shopkeeper walked by, doffing his cap in greeting. Master Numar smiled, replying with a friendly nod. A master of the Kiralynn Order, yet he'd exchanged his midnight blue robes for the simple garb of an apothecary. He looked the part. His long white beard, brushed and carefully cultivated, drew the respect of many, a timeworn mark of a venerable elder. He could act decrepit when it suited him, but in truth, he was in robust health despite his sixty-three years.

Candlelight flickered from many windows, brightening the street. The queen's city never truly slept. Despite the ravages of the Flame War, commerce returned to Pellanor like a long lost lover. Shops were re-opened, damages repaired, and homes rebuilt. Soon the markets brimmed with goods. People flocked to the city, spending their hard-earned coin with renewed vigor. Even his small apothecary shop flourished in the wake of the war. The master was truly impressed. He'd only met the queen once, but she was a formidable ruler, truly skilled at commerce. If ever a city and its monarch deserved to be saved from Darkness, it was Pellanor and its steadfast queen. He prayed the Lords of Light protected both.

For more than the turn of an hourglass, he walked the cobbled streets, threading his way towards the tower. He kept a sharp watch for skulking shadows, for even the queen's city had its share of ill-doers, yet he was not truly worried. With a powerful focus nestled in his left pocket and his quarterstaff in his hand, there was little he feared. Perhaps it was his confidence, or the way he handled his quarterstaff, or perhaps his plain brown robes bespoke a man who was not worth robbing. Whatever the reason, he met no trouble on his late night stroll.

He turned from the street of tailors onto the street of chandlers. Wooden signs bearing painted candles hung over shop doors for those who could not read. Trade was the lifeblood of Pellanor, but the pursuit of coins sometimes seemed like a rabid religion. Some might decry the avid pursuit of commerce as a blasphemy, yet the queen's city offered more peace, prosperity and comforts than any other city in Erdhe. Pellanor's markets overflowed with everything from the ordinary to the exotic. Like a trail of tempting breadcrumbs, he followed the line of shops all the way to the tower. Torchlight beckoned at the end of the street, heralding his destination.

Rising from the clutter of commerce, the Ancestral Spire soared like a needle reaching for the very heavens. Built of polished granite, the soaring tower glittered in the torchlight, an impressive feat of stonemasonry. The master's gaze followed the spire to its lofty height, well aware of the tower's history. In times long past, the surrounding area had been a royal cemetery, but Pellanor gobbled land like a drunk swills ale. Even back then, the Rose monarchs were famed for their skill at commerce. Aware of the land's rising value, the reigning monarch ordered the Spire built and then exhumed his royal ancestors, enshrining them in the tower. Folklore said the vacated cemetery sold for a king's ransom while the tower became the most sought-after burial place in all of Erdhe. Sprawling ever outwards, the city gobbled the surrounding land, erasing all signs of the cemetery, but the tower remained as a monument to the royal line, a venerable landmark of Pellanor and the perfect place to meet Aeroth.

A pair of guards in emerald tabards stood watch by the brass doors, yet by royal decree the tower was ever open to the people. Master Numar paid a copper, the fee for admittance, and entered the arched doorway. A hushed stillness embraced him. He shivered, feeling the sudden chill of cloistered stone. The Spire was hollow, a marvel of stonemasonry rising to a lofty vault. Beneath the pinnacled vault was a small chapel. Austere yet elegant, the round chapel held a stone altar draped in shimmering cloth of gold. An oil lantern burned bright upon the altar, representing the eternal Light. A dozen braziers surrounded the altar, releasing clouds of incense. The heavenly scent wafted upwards like prayers rising to the tower's gold-leafed pinnacle.

The chapel's simplicity, coupled with the spire's soaring heights, evoked feelings of peace and humility. Master Numar bowed low in reverence to the Light, but he'd not come to worship. Instead, he took the long stairs that curled around the outer walls, spiraling upwards to the lofty pinnacle. It was here, on either side of the stairs, that the ancient royals were interred. Stone sarcophagi were inset in the walls and banister, their effigies chiseled in lustrous white marble. Kings and queens, knights and dukes, the ancient royalty crowded together, lining the walls of the spire. The early tombs showed their age, the stone-chiseled details faded by time and touch. Faces with blunt noses, folded hands without fingers, marble swords without blades, the effigies stared blind from the wall, yet he felt their presence, as if the ancestors of Lanverness kept watch. Torchlight danced across marble kings and granite knights, sparkling on the polished stone, granting a patina of warmth. Heraldic symbols of royalty were everywhere: orbs, scepters, crowns and a garden of stone roses. He read the chiseled names as he made his way up the stairs, a lesson in Pellanor's history. The tombs became more elaborate the further he climbed, the details chased with gold and silver filigree and inset with semi-precious stones. Halfway to the top, he found tombs topped with marble bards strumming lutes alongside pudgy merchants draped in jewels, proof of the tower's prestige. Fame or great wealth bought admittance to the spire, the monuments and urns of elevated commoners vying for space amongst the royals. And then, abruptly, the effigies and the fine carvings stopped, nothing but empty sarcophagi and plain walls awaiting future luminaries. Something about the blank walls made him shiver, a stark reminder that death waits for us all.

The stairs suddenly felt lonely. Master Numar hastened his steps, reaching the top of the spire. Opening the ironbound door, he stepped out onto the parapet. A night breeze snatched at his beard, lukewarm compared to the spire's stony chill. The rampart encircled the spire, offering a peerless view of the queen's city. He strolled once around the spire, making sure the rampart was empty. Satisfied, he returned to the eastern view, staring across the city's sprawling expanse. Candles, lanterns and torches lit the cobbled streets with thousands of softly glowing pinpricks, as if the city sought to rival the stars. And at the heart of it all rose Castle Tandroth, its towers rising above the city like a stone scepter. He could have stared at the view for hours, mesmerized by the lights and the bird's eye view, but he'd come to the tower with a purpose. Shrugging his satchel from his shoulders, he removed a pillar candle. He lit the candle and set it on the rampart, a signal for Aeroth, and then he sat on the stone floor, setting his back to the spire. From his satchel he removed a roasted chicken, a loaf of brown bread laden with raisins, and a flask of fine Tubor wine. Familiar with the price of magic, he knew Aeroth would be ravenous.

The spit-roasted chicken smelled mouthwatering, but he settled back to wait for his friend.

He did not have long to wait.

A frost owl circled the spire, white wings spread wide, gliding on the night breeze. Silent and seemingly effortless, the great owl circled the tower twice before alighting on the rampart.

Master Numar held his breath, always dazzled by the power of magic.

"Whooooo!" The owl gave its inquisitive cry and then blinked. Feathers ruffled, the frost owl shuddered, a faint nimbus of light surrounding it. The great owl stretched and blurred till a blue robed monk stood in its place. Unconcerned with the spire's dizzying height, Aeroth stepped down from the rampart.

The two masters clasped arms. "Well met."

Aeroth looked exhausted, dark circles shadowing his eyes. Master Numar voiced his concern. "You look tired, my friend."

"I've spent too long in the owl."

"You need rest."

"I've too many leagues to travel, too many places to watch. Much is happening in the north."

Master Numar's interest burned bright, but he gestured to the repast. "Sit and eat, and then we'll talk."

They sat cross-legged, sharing the meal. Aeroth attacked the chicken, tearing off a juicy drumstick. Master Numar cut a sliver from the breast, nibbling on the crispy skin. The chicken proved tender and tasty, seasoned with rosemary just the way he liked it, but he knew his friend's needs far exceeded his own hunger.

Aeroth finished the first leg and started on the second. "Tell me of Pellanor."

Master Numar uncorked the wineskin. "The queen's city flourishes. Commerce returns almost as if the Flame War never happened."

"And the queen?"

"A formidable monarch, she used the Order's gift of Napthos wisely. Instead of saving the hellfire to protect herself and her royal city, she used it to trap her enemy in Lingard." Master Numar swirled the wineskin. "I wonder how many kings would have made such a daring choice."

Aeroth gave him a pointed look. "So you met her?"

"It seemed necessary. With the comet low in the sky, we need to work more closely with the sovereigns of the south."

Aeroth pointed a chicken bone his way. "Yet your robes are brown."

"After Fintan's gruesome death, I'll not wear the blue below the southern mountains."

"A warning to us all." Aeroth looked distraught. "Did you learn anything of his killer?"

Master Numar frowned. "The killer lurks in the queen's castle, yet her shadowmen have no clue."

"Then we have an enemy in the city."

"Just so. That's why I suggested we meet here. The dead will keep our secret."

Aeroth reached for the wineskin. "And what of Fintan's focus?"

A chill feathered down the master's back. "Lost. After his murder, I searched his room, I searched his belongings, it was not there."

Aeroth hissed. "That focus was powerful."

"But the enemy might not be able to wield it. Magic can be stubborn, choosing the hand that wields it."

"Pray that it is so. The Order cannot afford to lose more magic, let alone have it turned against us."

Master Numar broke the bread, offering a chunk of the raisin loaf to Aeroth. "Tell me of the north."

"Raven Pass has fallen."

The breath hissed out of him, a dire stroke against the south. "How?"

"The Mordant used magic, destroying the gates. His hordes poured through the walls and then he tricked the Octagon King into single combat. The king is dead. The knights continue to fight, chewing on the enemy, but it is like a dog harrying a lion. The outcome is inevitable unless something shifts the balance."

"What of the blade bearer?"

"There is no word...but there is hope."

Master Numar pounced on the word. "Hope?"

"The king of Navarre listened to his daughter. He agreed to send the merchant fleet north to the Dark Citadel."

Master Numar's breath caught. "*The Dark Citadel!*"

Aeroth nodded. "Princess Jordan had visions that the blade bearer is there."

"In the very lair of the Mordant?"

Aeroth gave him a grim nod.

Master Numar could not imagine it. Every tale of the far north reeked of nightmares, yet, if the girl had somehow defeated the citadel, it was a victory undreamt. "And?"

"The fleet has not been seen in Navarre, so all assume it sailed north." Aeroth's voice dropped to an ominous whisper. "I tell you, Numar, finding that fleet taxed the owl to the very limits." He shook his head as if warding off a nightmare. "The owl was not meant to cross the sea. I slept for a fortnight when I reached land." He shuddered. "I pray that I never have to do that again." Aeroth leaned close. "And I'll tell you something else. I'm having dreams, dreadful night terrors, of birds bearing the faces of men...as if the two are melded together, demon-forged into one foul creature."

Master Numar hissed. "Soul magic?"

Aeroth made the hand sign against evil. "I don't know. But I tell you this, evil creeps across Erdhe, working in more ways than we know. Hold your secrets close. Take care with whom you keep company and be forewarned."

Master Numar fingered the focus nestled deep in his pocket. "I will. And you must do the same."

Both men set to eating the raisin bread. Talking of small things, they passed the wineskin back and forth. Master Numar mentioned the arrival of the Prince of Ur in the queen's city. Both men marveled that Ur would send an imperial prince all the way to Erdhe. Finished with the meal, Aeroth stood upon the rampart. "I'll see you at the next dark of the moon."

"I'll be here."

Aeroth shimmered, flaring with a soft white light, and then the frost owl stood in his place, talons balanced on the rampart. "Whoooo." Spreading its white wings wide, the owl glided from the tower, soaring over the queen's city.

Master Numar watched till the owl disappeared, swallowed by the gathering clouds. For the longest time he stared north, consumed with thoughts of the Dark Citadel. Aeroth had brought strange tidings. The Battle Immortal was a tangle of conflicts, battles wrapped in subterfuge hidden beneath ancient riddles, yet he needed to focus on Pellanor. An assassin lurked in the queen's castle, a killer of monks. He fingered the focus in his pocket, bolstered by thoughts of its magic.

Gathering up the remains of the meal, he repacked his satchel and then took up his quarterstaff. Opening the ironbound door, he slipped back inside the tower. The dank chill embraced him. Silent and pensive, he made his way back down the long spiral stairs, passing the faces of the dead. He felt as if history kept watch, waiting to see if the future would be bright or bleak.

3

The Mordant

The assassin and the duegar fell prostrate before the Mordant, their faces pressed to the jewel-colored carpet. Moon-turns ago they'd both come to Lanverness in the guise of jesters, threats hidden in bright motley. His chained servant, Frederinko, had presented them to the Rose Queen as tokens of Ur's friendship. Such gifts could hardly be refused. Accepted by the queen, the jesters served within her very castle. Now, clad in simple browns, they'd shed their false colors to answer the summons of their true lord.

The Mordant sipped brandy while seated in front of the roaring hearth. "Rise." Both men scrambled to their knees. "Time to account for your stay in the Rose Court." He gestured to the duegar. "Castor, what magic have you found in the queen's castle?"

"None, lord, save for what the monk brought."

The Mordant's interest quickened. "The monk?"

"Yes, lord." Castor flashed a jagged smile, his front teeth filed to points. "A blue-robed monk came to the Rose Court as an emissary of the Kiralynn Order. After meeting with the queen, he was given quarters within the castle. His name was Fintan and he reeked of magic."

So the monks openly meddled, how brave...and how foolish. "How did he die?"

Dominic answered, "Sting of the Assassin. I killed him in his own chambers, cut his head off, and stole his magic." He flashed a satisfied smile. "It was a particularly gruesome death, befitting a blue-robed monk. Now his magic will be yours." The assassin crept forward, his hand outstretched, a malachite coin offered on his palm.

The Mordant snatched up the coin. Rubbing it between his fingers, his senses probed for its power...but the coin remained dormant. The Mordant was unperturbed. It often took time for magical links to form with fresh-found focuses. "Do you know what it does?"

Castor answered. "No, lord, but it reeks of powerful magic...old magic."

Powerful magic...the words were like an aphrodisiac to the Mordant. He fondled the coin, dancing it between his fingers. "And how did the queen react to the monk's death?"

Dominic grinned. "She fears, my lord, for they know not how it was done."

"Fear is a good thing." He was pleased with his two servants. "And have there been more monks?"

"No, lord. None that wear blue robes and none that reek of magic," Castor hesitated, "at least none that we saw."

So, the queen does not keep her jesters close. The woman is not entirely naïve. "What else?"

"A child, my lord," the assassin answered. "The queen swelled with a bastard child."

So, the queen is still of breeding age...and she dares to birth a bastard. He had not foreseen a child, but it could weave well into his plans. "Who was the father?"

"None know, my lord."

"What became of this child?"

The assassin grinned. "Tansy in the queen's tea. She birthed a stillborn daughter."

A cold rage flashed through the Mordant. "You dared to poison the queen?"

The assassin cringed to the floor. "Only the child, my lord, not the queen." He abased himself, pressing his face to the carpet.

"I gave orders the queen was not to be harmed."

"She's not, my lord, only the child was harmed, flushed from her body."

The Mordant stared at his assassin. In truth, it was a brilliant move, for the best way to unsettle a mere woman was to attack the product of her womb. "I'll spare you, but only because the queen still lives...and because the dead babe will enhance my plans."

Pale-faced, the quaking assassin dared to kneel. "Thank you, my lord."

"Does the queen know she was poisoned?"

The assassin flicked a glance at the duegar. "Word of the stillborn birth was smothered by her own shadowmen, as if it never happened. But Castor heard the queen rant that it was poison."

"So she knows...or at least suspects." The Mordant smiled, considering the delicious possibilities. "Her own suspicions will keep her off-balance." He fondled the malachite coin. "What of the queen's heirs?"

"The queen's second son, Prince Danly, died a traitor in Lingard, a casualty of the Flame War. Her firstborn son and only heir, Prince Stewart, rides to war to confront the army of the Pentacle."

So, her sole heir is at risk. The Mordant would confirm every detail once he gazed into the queen's eyes, once he raped her soul and peered through her memories. He'd plumb her mind, reading her like an open scroll, but it did no harm to be forewarned. "Women are always undone by their wombs. One of the many reasons they are not fit to rule." The Mordant flashed a sharp smile. "Anything else?"

"No, lord."

"You've done well. Return to the castle, don your motley and remain vigilant."

"Yes, lord."

He waved dismissal, but the assassin hesitated.

"Dread lord, might I ask a question?" The assassin cringed, waiting.

The Mordant relented. "One."

"Instead of tansy in the queen's tea, I could have added nightshade, or any other poison. Yet you ordered me *not* to kill her. Why, lord, when I could save you all this trouble and hand you her crown?"

The Mordant stiffened, staring at the assassin through narrowed eyes. "Your order stands. You are *not* to kill the queen."

The assassin flinched as if lashed. "Yes, lord, but why?"

The Mordant let a hundred heartbeats pass, a sure sign of his displeasure, but then he relented, offering a reply lest his servant become overzealous. "Killing is easy. Taking life pleases the Dark Lord, but it garners the least of his favors. Our god favors those who have a long reach, those who steer the future to a dark path while muddying the brightest memories of the past. Kill the queen while Lanverness prospers and she becomes a martyr, a saint to her people, a shining beacon of hope. Instead, we shall sully her name and muddy her legacy, corrupting the queen from within. Her abject failure will keep future women from any throne, enforcing the Great Dark Divide." A smile hovered at his lips, a rush of Dark power flowing through him. He stood, throwing a daunting shadow across the room. "In this lifetime, I've come to change the past as well the future. I've come to wield the power of a god."

The assassin and the duegar both cringed low, staring wide-eyed in awe.

"Return to the queen and await my summons."

Bowing, they scuttled from the chamber.

Dark power burned through him. His shadow diminished, leaving him mortal once more. The Mordant sat alone before the crackling fire, flicking the malachite coin between his fingers. After a thousand years of life, he stood on the brink of true immortality. Corrupt the queen and so much would change, bending the past as well as the future. He flicked the coin with his thumb, watching it rotate as it tumbled upwards...and then he spied the engraving. Catching the coin, he held it towards the firelight. Engraved on the face was a shield, worn but still faintly visible, two crescents flanking a full moon...the ancient symbol of Azreal. The Mordant stilled. *Azreal*...the city of his first great triumph. Ancient memories flooded his mind. He remembered her face, her tender touch, so lovely...so trusting. In that first life, he'd corrupted a sorceress instead of a queen and started the Great Dark Divide, earning many lifetimes. And now this coin found its way to his hand. Perhaps the distant past came calling. He'd lived too long to believe in omens. The Mordant stared at the coin, amazed that it had survived so many centuries...but it would serve him, just as surely as this new queen would be corrupted to Darkness, twisted by his deceptions. Deceive, divide, corrupt and destroy. All the pieces were in motion for the Great Dark Dance. Soon the power of the gods would be within his grasp.

4

Liandra

Scrolls littered the queen's solar, the details of running a kingdom. Reports came from high and from low, from shadowmen, stonemasons, tax collectors, courtiers, merchants, military advisors, princes and even kings, a web of information flowing to the Spider Queen. No detail was too small. Liandra waded through the correspondence, considering the nuances. Plucking precious insights from the mountain of dross, she took the measure of Erdhe. Like gazing into a crystal ball, she saw what was and what could be. The answers both pleased and frightened her. In the south, her kingdom rebounded from the Flame War. Commerce flowed again, sluggish at first, but her careful prods and incentives had begun to bear fruit. Her farmers returned to the land and merchants plied the roads with trade goods. Beef, wine and grain came from Tubor, venison and furs from Wyeth, exotic goods from the Delta. Her roadways thrummed with the trundle of wagons bearing trade, the lifeblood of her kingdom. Her markets bustled, her royal treasury was full, and her people were content. But, in the north, the army of the Mordant threatened everything. A barbaric horde had taken Raven Pass, routing the Octagon Knights. The queen shuddered at the grim thought. She'd always thought the Octagon Knights invincible, a stalwart shield against the north...but now that shield was broken. Forming a hasty alliance with Navarre and Wyeth, she'd sent her only remaining son and her army north...but she did not like the odds. The two armies had yet to clash, but no matter how many times she read the dispatches and studied the maps, her conclusions were always bleak. Darkness reached for Erdhe and she had yet to find the foil.

"Majesty, it's nearly time." Lady Sarah hovered at the door to the queen's inner chambers, bearing a reminder of a pleasant distraction.

Weary from reading, the queen set aside the mountain of scrolls. "Yes, we must look our best for our royal guest."

The Prince of Ur had come to Pellanor. A royal emissary from a fabled land, he'd made a showy entrance to her city. Her shadowmen delivered a full report. Surrounded by guards in purple tabards, he brought a wagon piled high with treasure chests and three women swathed in silks. The prince rode a magnificent white stallion beribboned with gold bells in its mane. The bells struck the queen as an odd, almost effeminate, detail. Or, perhaps the bells were merely an expression of cultural differences. Ur was such a distant land and such an extravagantly wealthy trading partner, the empire garnered mystery like a bard garnered songs. All the more reason Liandra was keen to meet the prince. As to the man himself, her shadowmen described the prince as tall, young, and fair of face, with shoulder-length blond hair and a neatly trimmed mustache. They said he had neither the wide shoulders of an archer nor the swarthy arms of a swordsman, so perhaps the prince was a scrollish man. That might explain the gift of a chess set and the request for a private audience...yet why make such a showy entrance to her city? All of Pellanor whispered of nothing else. Her people were enthralled and the queen confessed herself intrigued. The prince posed an interesting riddle, one Liandra intended to solve.

She'd given him a few days to get settled, and then sent a courtier with a royal invitation to meet across the chessboard. With the invitation served, the queen set out to make every detail perfect.

After much consideration, the queen chose a crushed velvet gown of deep emerald green with dagged sleeves lined in gold and a vee neckline that showed just enough cleavage to be tempting, while maintaining a mysterious allure. A diamond tiara sparkled against her raven-dark hair, while a rope of emeralds accented her slender neck and plunging bosom. Adding a dab of rose oil for a beguiling scent, the queen contemplated the mirror. Regal beauty bedecked in confident wealth, her image struck the perfect tone for their first meeting.

Liandra returned to her solar to find the mountain of scrolls banished, safely tucked away for another day. Carefully arranging the folds of her gown, she settled on a throne-carved chair set before the warmth of the fireplace. A fire blazed in the hearth, juniper and pine logs releasing a pleasing scent. The prince's gift, the exquisite chess set carved of onyx and malachite, sat on a small table between the two chairs. Heroic figures arrayed for an epic battle, she looked forward to the game. Liandra reveled in the chance to test her wits against a fresh opponent.

"Will you have a glass of wine, majesty?" Lady Sarah fluttered around the solar seeing to last minute details.

"No, we shall wait for our guest."

A flagon of the royal cellar's best merlot breathed on a side table along with a platter of cheese and dried fruits. Lady Sarah would serve the repast, another pair of trusted eyes and ears to assess the prince, while Sir Durnheart would provide the protection. Clad in mirror-bright armor, her knight-protector stood statue-still just beyond the firelight's reach, only a sword-length away.

If only Robert were here. Liandra missed her shadowmaster, her confidant, her lover...but he was away in Lingard, serving the needs of the kingdom. She would just have to remember every detail for his return.

Satisfied with the preparations, the queen gestured to Lady Sarah. "Admit our guest."

The queen remained seated, her gaze fixed upon the oak door. The prince had come to her castle escorted by a portly seneschal and six guards, yet he'd made it plain the others were to wait in her antechamber. *A private audience for a first meeting with a prince from a distant land,* how rare, how unexpected...how intriguing. She found herself flush with anticipation.

Lady Sarah opened the door and then dropped to a deep curtsy. "Welcome, my lord."

He strode into her solar, giving her barely a glance.

Her first impression was confidence...perhaps even arrogance. Tall, blond, and fair of face with a neatly trimmed beard...the queen found her shadowmen's description accurate yet woefully inadequate. The difference lay in the way he moved. Striding into her solar, he carried an air of command, his steps bold, his eyes sharp, his face regal and proud, almost arrogant. But this was not the brash arrogance of a pampered young royal, she'd seen that many times before. Instead, he exuded a sense of self-contained power and a cloak of experience far beyond his twenty-some years. Not a word had been spoken, yet the riddle deepened and the queen found herself drawn into a web of questions.

The prince stopped before her, but he did not bow, or even nod. Instead, he gazed upon her as if taking her measure. "So, this is the queen so many speak of."

Such an odd opening...she gave him a gracious smile. "Welcome to our court. We are pleased to host a prince from distant Ur."

For twenty heartbeats he said nothing. Such a surprising silence, like a lull before the storm, but then he gave her a half nod and said, "Distant in leagues but close in trade. Commerce connects us." His smile deepened. "Trading powers should meet, don't you think?"

"Trading *powers,* not trading *partners,* what an interesting turn of phrase."

"Nothing but the truth." He flashed a smile she could not read. "Lanverness dominates the trade of Erdhe, as Ur dominates trade across the southern seas, hence, my interest in your kingdom. We are both trading *powers.*"

"And are you attracted to power?"

"Always."

The single word conveyed a voracious hunger. A warning shivered in the queen's mind, yet she found herself falling into his stare. Blue eyes, young eyes, yet they held unexpected depths...fascinating depths, fathomless depths, layers of blue, layers of darkness, an infinite darkness, full of questions, full of commands, full of power. *No!* A white-hot anger blazed through her, blindingly bright. She jerked her gaze away as if burnt.

Her heartbeat thundered as if she'd fled from the deepest dungeon. Puzzled by her own reaction, she flicked her gaze towards him but avoided his stare. He stood statue-still, a sword's length away, yet she felt strangely...violated.

"Will you have some wine?" Lady Sarah broke the silence.

The queen startled, confused by the strength of her reaction. A headache throbbed at the back of her eyes.

"Will you have some wine, my lord?" Lady Sarah asked again and the strange moment shattered.

The prince answered, "Yes, I will."

Liandra thought she heard a whiplash of anger in his voice, but his face showed no sign of it. Confused, she watched him, struggling to recover from the strange incident.

He flicked a glance towards Sir Durnheart. "A blue steel sword."

The queen was pleased he'd noticed. "So, you've heard of blue steel?"

"Even in Ur we have heard of such swords." Accepting a goblet of rich red merlot, he took a chair on the far side of the chessboard. "I see you got my gift."

The queen sensed something had shifted between them, some strange intangible balance of power, yet she did not understand, as if she played a game with unexplained rules. Unsettled and strangely ill at ease, Liandra struggled to marshal her thoughts, sensing this encounter was somehow of dire importance. "An exquisite gift, we thank you for it."

"Chess is such an ancient game, a game of kings, a game of power. You can learn so much about an opponent through a single game of chess, don't you think?"

"Your thoughts echo our own."

"I doubt that." He smiled like a fox about to eat a chicken. "Shall we let our armies clash?"

Such a simple question, yet it took her breath away, as if menace lurked in the very air between them. Liandra shook her head, confused and troubled by the premonition of dread. The prince was a riddle, full of challenges and unexpected contradictions, nothing more. Surely this strange sense of foreboding was uncalled for. The queen stared at the prince, trying to peel back the layers beneath his comely facade. She told herself this was just an audience, a first meeting with a foreign prince...yet Liandra felt as if she swam in an ocean with limitless depths...an ocean full of dangerous monsters. Perhaps the chessboard would provide the answers. Liandra fingered a malachite pawn. The game of chess was both a strength and a familiar refuge. She set her mind on winning the game. "Yes, let's play."

5

The Mordant

The door opened and the Mordant strode into the queen's solar for their first meeting. Luxury surrounded him, plush carpets beneath his boots, exquisite tapestries gracing the walls, a room bejeweled with gilded furniture and stunning works of art, but the setting mattered not. He'd come for the woman ensconced at the heart of the royal trappings. Stopping a sword's length away, he paused to take her measure. "So, this is the queen so many speak of." The words purred out of him as he took in the details. Petite with a buxom figure, her waist was hourglass trim yet the crows-feet at her eyes betrayed her age. Powders and rouge, no matter how skillfully applied, could not hide the truth. A woman of middling years, the queen of Lanverness wore jewels and velvets like armor, but beneath the royal glamour, the bloom had nearly gone off the rose. A few more years and she would pass beyond child-bearing age, the last of her beauty fading to gray, her armor dissolving with age. Glorying in his own stolen youth, the Mordant struggled to keep a smug smile from his face...but he had not come to gloat. Hungry to begin, he breathed deep, searching for the taint of Darkness in her soul. *Ambition laden with pride,* the queen reeked of ambition despite being a mere woman. Ambition was ever fertile ground for Darkness.

The queen smiled. "Welcome to our court. We are pleased to host a prince from distant Ur."

He gave her a half nod. "Distant in leagues but close in trade. Commerce connects us." He deliberately deepened his smile, a hunter sighting prey. "Trading powers should meet, don't you think?"

"Trading *powers,* not trading *partners,* what an interesting turn of phrase."

"Nothing but the truth." *How he enjoyed weaving a good lie, one of the simple pleasures of dealing with mere mortals.* "Lanverness dominates the trade of Erdhe, as Ur dominates trade across the southern seas, hence, my interest in your kingdom. We are both trading *powers.*"

"And are you attracted to power?"

"Always."

He drilled her with his stare, silently compelling her to meet his gaze. As if in answer, she complied. Their stares locked. *Ambition is the key to her soul.* The Mordant longed to make it rape, to delve the queen and pith her soul like a fly pinned to parchment...but he had witnesses. A knight with a blue steel sword stood vigil in the shadows, so this would have to be done delicately. Restraining his power, the Mordant sought a painless conquest. His gaze lanced hers, demanding entry. His will pressed inwards, seeking to follow the strands of ambition. He sought to plumb her soul, to seduce her with Darkness...and met a wall of blazing Light. Pain pierced him. His own power rebounded on him, a terrible backlash that stabbed his mind. Fury flamed through him, *how dare you!* Incandescent with rage, he nearly reached for the gem of pain, intending to blast the queen to her knees...but he fought the urge. *Destroy her now and history will not be changed.* His own ambition rescued him. Rage had nearly undone him. Taking a deep breath, he bridled his anger, forcing calculated reason to reign.

Shuttering his gaze, the Mordant considered what he'd learned. Souls like hers were rare, yet over the ages he'd encountered a few others with shields of Light. Ambition that truly served the greater good became a potent shield against the Dark. Such souls often posed stumbling blocks to his plans. He hadn't expected to find such soul-strength in a mere woman. She reminded him of someone else, a dark-haired sorceress, an ancient conquest from his very first lifetime. The Mordant supposed he would have to do this the old-fashioned way. The thought brought a sense of mild amusement. Having lived for over a thousand years, he'd assumed many different roles in many different lifetimes, but the Deceiver was ever the guise he most enjoyed, the role that most profited the Dark Lord. Ensorcelling mortals with lies was a game he'd come to love.

"Will you have some wine?" The frumpy maid intruded.

The Mordant blinked, shuttering the Darkness of his soul.

"Will you have some wine, my lord?"

Annoyed, he made a mental note to have one of his assassins kill the wretched woman. "Yes, I will." Accepting a goblet of dark red wine, the Mordant flicked a glance toward the guardian knight. Standing statue-still in the flickering firelight, he seemed unaware that anything had transpired. "A blue steel sword."

The queen gave him a feeble smile. "So you've heard of blue steel?"

The Mordant kept to his disguise, a congenial smile on his face. "Even in Ur we have heard of such swords." He took a chair on the far side of the chessboard. The dark army already arrayed against her emerald green. "I see you got my gift."

She seemed distracted, wounded by his mental assault. "An exquisite gift, we thank you for it."

"Chess is such an ancient game, a game of kings, a game of power. You can learn so much about an opponent through a single game of chess, don't you think?"

"Your thoughts echo our own."

"I doubt that." He cursed her within his mind. *I bring you Despair! Your precious kingdom shall fall to my lash, your people shall be corrupted, your deeds shall be sullied, your memory despoiled, and your very name shall become a foul curse. Your downfall shall seal the fate of future queens. Forevermore, women shall be forbidden power in Erdhe because of you. The Great Dark Divide shall be strengthened by your defeat...and I shall enjoy that very much.* He let his smile show his true intent. "Shall we let our armies clash?"

She hesitated, a hint of dread on her face, almost as if she could read his thoughts. But then she nodded, her voice brimming with the naive confidence of a feckless mortal. "Yes, let's play."

6

Liandra

Queen Liandra sat before the chessboard, considering her opening move. By tradition, the lighter color always moved first. It struck the queen that this was a fallacy. In truth, Darkness always made the first assault, breaking the peace and drawing the first blood, leaving the ambushed Light scrambling to mount a reply. The thought gave her an interesting insight into the natures of Light and Dark, but this was chess, a game with clearly defined rules. Liandra focused her mind on the checkered board. Darkest ebony inlaid with squares of polished abalone shell, the board rippled with smoky iridescence, an exquisite field of play. Her malachite army stood arrayed against the prince's onyx legion. Knights and monks stood stalwart against dragons and wizards, her lighter color giving her the first move. She'd always loved the subtle intricacies of chess, the challenge of wits and strategies, the ability to see many moves ahead, yet seated across from the prince, a strange anxiety gripped her, as if she'd bet her kingdom upon the outcome of the game. Suppressing the grim foreboding, Liandra considered a range of openings. Finally reaching for her king's pawn, she made the first move.

The queen stared across the chessboard, keen to see the prince's opening. First moves always held a wealth of insights, setting the tone for the game while revealing glimpses of her opponent's hidden nature.

The prince did not hesitate. Reaching for a dragon carved of onyx, he opened with a knight, the trickiest piece on the board.

The move surprised her, something she'd expect from an older, more mature player. "So you have a fondness for knights?"

"A fondness, no, I have nothing but disdain for knights and any piece that does not rule."

Such a brutal reply, yet she soon discovered that it fit his style of play. Instead of building elaborate feints, he attacked from every angle. Showing no regard for his pieces, the prince ruthlessly traded his queen for a mere castle. With such uneven trades, Liandra felt destined for victory, yet somehow the game eluded her. The prince pressed a relentless attack, keeping her off balance. Under the fierce assault, Liandra became overly protective of her malachite pieces, striving to save every one. She knew this was a losing strategy, yet she could not stop herself. Hunched over the board, she sat absorbed in the play, desperate to find a solution. The game became a bloody rout, castles, monks and pawns falling under the prince's brutal onslaught. Malachite figures littered the tabletop with reproach. Backed into a corner, Liandra fought for her life.

Carved chess pieces moved across the board like a silent clash of armies. The queen sought an escape, she sought a stalemate, yet the noose of onyx-carved figures tightened around her malachite king like a relentless destiny. The fire snapped and crackled in the hearth. Intent on the game, not a word was spoken...until he toppled her king.

"Checkmate."

Defeated, the queen sat stunned.

"You look surprised."

Liandra conceded a nod toward the prince. "As the only child of a king, we were reared upon strategy and court intrigue."

"And you see chess as a reflection of life?"

"To some extent."

He fingered her defeated king. "Perhaps you lack an essential quality?"

"And what is that?"

"Ruthlessness." He flashed a feral grin. "An essential quality for a great ruler, but so often lacking in the fair sex."

Anger pulsed through her. "Then you must not know many women."

"I've known countless women...but none that rule."

She met his gaze across the chessboard. "You've met one now." Her voice flashed with steel. "Will you play again?"

"Yes, but not today." He stood and suddenly his smile transformed from sinister to charming, as changeable as quicksilver. "Thank you for a most insightful game. Perhaps we can play again next week?" His smile deepened with murky intent. "Another clash across the chessboard and you can show me how queens rule."

"We would be delighted." Her voice held a daggered edge.

The prince took his leave.

The door clicked closed and relief washed across her. Liandra sagged against the oak-carved throne. Exhaustion claimed her, as if she'd jousted in a tournament and come away battered and bruised. *Defeated,* a headache pounded at the back of her eyes, *and by such an arrogant young man.* The truth rankled. The fire had burned to embers, letting shadows encroach. Shivering against the darkness, the queen considered her time with the prince. She'd learned little of Ur, but she'd gained insights into the man. He was not what he seemed. And he was dangerous. And *he* was in *her* kingdom. Plots within plots, she'd have to double the shadowmen assigned to the prince and his entourage. She needed more information. The loss of the first game haunted her like an ill-omen. Somehow she needed to learn his true game, his true intent...and then she needed to find a way to defeat him.

7

The Mordant

T he messenger was delivered in a canvas sack. At a gesture from the Mordant, the two assassins cut the ties and upended the contents, dumping the young man onto the cold stone floor.

Bound, gagged and blindfolded, the messenger wore the emerald livery of the Rose Queen. Screaming through his gag, he squirmed across the pentacle like a green worm.

"Untie him."

The assassin slashed the rope bonds and then stepped back into the shadows.

Tugging off the blindfold, the young man squinted at the dim light. Spitting the gag from his mouth, he yelled, "How dare you! I'm a royal courier, a messenger for the queen!"

His voice reeked of fear despite his bravado. The Mordant breathed deep, savoring the smell. "Take off your tabard."

"What?" The young man flinched backward, his gaze circling the chamber, his eyes widening in fear. "What is this place?"

They stood in the sanctum beneath the manse. Cold stone vaulted overhead to a smothering darkness. Five braziers lit the five points of the pentacle, yet the shadows held sway. Unbloodied and undedicated, the chamber smelled of mortar and fresh-cut stone...but that would soon change. "Take off your tabard." The Mordant's voice was soothing, reasonable, paternal...almost patient.

The messenger shrank backwards. "Why?"

"Or my men will do it for you."

The young man glanced at the two assassins, a flash of fear across his face. He started to undress, his hands shaking.

The Mordant waited, his arms crossed. *How easy the weak are persuaded*. Breathing deep, he imbibed the scent of fear. "And now your pants."

The messenger retreated a step, his voice laden with panic. "No."

"Do it now and things will go easier for you."

The young man's wide-eyed stare skittered around the unholy chapel, drinking in the menace of the chamber. Pale and shaking, he complied, adding boots and pants to the discarded pile of green. Looking younger than his years, he stood shivering in his small clothes, his skin puckered against the cold.

The Mordant gestured to the pile of green. "Take these to Tembo."

"Don't take my clothes!"

One of the assassins leaped to obey. "Yes, my lord." Oblivious to the young man's protest, the assassin gathered up the clothes and retreated into the shadows.

The Mordant smiled. "They will serve a higher purpose...as will you." He gestured to the remaining assassin. "Prepare him for sacrifice."

"What?" Yelping in fear, the young man leaped to run but the assassin struck like a scorpion. A single well-aimed punch knocked the messenger to the floor. Pinning him to the pentacle, the assassin splayed his arms and legs wide. The young man bucked and fought, raw terror on his face, but he was no match for an assassin of the ninth rank. The final shackle locked into place, chaining the messenger spread-eagle to the floor, an unwilling sacrifice stretched across the pentacle. The assassin drew a dagger from his baldric.

Eyeing the knife, the messenger flinched back against the cold stone floor. "Don't!"

Three quick slashes and the captive's small clothes fell away.

Hot piss streamed onto the floor, adding the first stink of true terror to the chamber.

"Release me!" The young man writhed against his bonds, his face contorted in fear. *"I serve the queen! Release me!"* His screams beat against the chamber, echoing with an eerie refrain.

The Mordant smiled, supping on the young man's fear. "Scream all you want, a fitting chorus for the damned."

"Release me!"

"Come," the Mordant gestured to his assassin, "this one needs time to stew in his own terror." At a gesture, the braziers dimmed.

Darkness encroached...like a living beast.

The young man's screams grew frantic. *"Don't leave me here!"*

Crossing the chamber, the Mordant climbed the stairs, the dark-clad assassin following in his wake. He reached the prison level and passed through the false barrel, stepping into the wine cellar. The assassin closed and locked the doors behind him, snuffing the screams to silence.

Returning to the manse proper, the Mordant strode to the great room. Sunlight streamed through diamond-paned windows, casting light across the marble floor. A gilded chair sat upon a raised dais, serving as a make-shift throne. Behind the throne, a banner of purple silk ran from the vaulted ceiling to the polished floor, the Great Wyrm embossed in gold, a dragon eating its own tail, the imperial symbol of distant Ur.

Twelve duegar and seven assassins fell prostrate to the marble floor.

The Mordant crossed the chamber, his boot heels ringing on stone. Climbing the dais, he took a seat upon the throne. "Rise and tell me what you've learned." He'd sent his minions scurrying through the queen's city, searching for monks and magic and Octagon knights. One at a time, they gave their reports.

The Mordant listened till his anger flared. "You bring me nothing!"

They cringed from his wrath.

"Where one monk has died, others will follow. And those others will bring magic." His voice dropped to a deadly hiss. "I want their magic. *Find*...them."

"Yes, lord." The duegar withdrew half a step, trembling at the Mordant's rage.

"And while you search, I'll have you spread rumors against the queen."

One assassin dared a glance toward his face. "What would you have us say?"

"Spread fear about the coming war...and complain of food shortages."

"But, lord," the assassin spoke in a hesitant voice, "the markets overflow with food. No one will believe us."

How little they understood. "Speak a lie loudly and often enough and it will be believed. Famine follows war and Lanverness still recovers from the Flame War. If the queen's people fear a famine, then they will begin to hoard food. If enough become hoarders, then a food shortage will follow. Lies repeated often enough take on the substance of truth."

"Yes, dread lord. Anything else, lord?"

"Yes." The Mordant savored the secret, a gift from one of his best assassins. "Amongst the lies you shall spread one truth." His grin widened. "Dirty truths are even more effective than lies. I'll brand the bitch with her own morals. The queen considers herself a servant of the Light, yet she bore a stillborn bastard to some unnamed lover. She thinks her sordid secret is safe, but the common people love a good scandal above all else. Add a few embellishments and the tale will spread like wildfire. Whisper a rumor that the queen is a whore, that she bore a bastard, a malformed creature cursed by the gods. Smothered at birth, it was buried in an unmarked grave lest the damning truth be known. Born with a tail and horns, the misbegotten and misshaped babe proves her sins. Such a queen should never sit upon a throne lest the gods shun her kingdom."

His men grinned like slobbering dogs, eager for the task.

"Now go, and do not disappoint."

Bowing low, they scuttled from the room.

The Mordant smiled. He'd loosed the hounds of deceit, sent to spread lies in taverns, inns, markets and brothels. Soon the queen's city would shudder with discontent.

A servant hovered at the doorway. "My lord, the dispatches have arrived."

"Good." The Mordant strode from the throne room, weaving his way to Bishop Borgan's chambers. He found the fat prelate ensconced behind a large cluttered desk. Feathered quills, paring knives, wax sticks, and rows of stoppered ink bottles surrounded him. The tools of his trade, the bishop was an expert at forgery and the art of manipulating wax seals. Carefully rolling a scroll over the heat of a candle flame, he delicately pried the emerald seal from the parchment. "This one is from Prince Stewart."

"Read it." The Mordant settled in a chair, fondling the malachite coin as he listened.

The bishop read the dispatch without inflection.

The Mordant listened. For the turn of an hourglass they worked through a satchel of captured dispatches. Sifting through the details, the Mordant decided which to burn, which to alter, and which to allow through. Wielding nothing more than a pen and parchment, he spun a web of deceit around the queen. Lies etched in ink were so easily believed.

The bishop's quill scratched on parchment as he scribed the Mordant's response.

The Mordant smiled, enjoying the game. The woman styled herself the *spider queen,* such a ridiculous title, yet her webs would soon catch nothing but carefully crafted lies. "Seal it and have Tembo deliver the dispatches. The messenger's tabard will complete the deception. Once you're done with these, I want you to approach the queen and confirm a date for our second game of chess."

"You'll play her again?"

The Mordant flashed a cobra's smile. "The arrogant woman thinks I've come across the seas merely to play chess with her." His smile deepened to a sneer. "As if toy armies moving across a checkered board truly matter. While the foolish woman duels with chessmen, the true game begins."

8

Liandra

Nightmares plagued the queen. Shadowy fiends with daggered claws and glowing red eyes chased her through the labyrinth of her dreams. Three times they nearly caught her, but then a blinding light blazed forth, driving them back. Liandra woke panting, surprised to find herself safe in the royal bed.

Only a nightmare, yet a sheen of sweat dampened her skin.

Rain pattered the window, the droplets bejeweled by the dawn's pale light.

Or perhaps her dreams held a warning of dark tidings. Liandra shook her head against the grim thought. In truth, she'd been unsettled ever since losing the chess match. The loss rankled, she should never have lost that match. The prince of Ur seemed so young, but his eyes held such depths...perturbing depths. And then there was his style of play, a ruthless attack, sacrificing major pieces regardless of convention. She should have won yet somehow the game became a rout, a stunning defeat. *You played the game of princes...and lost.* Liandra pushed the nagging doubt aside.

Rain drummed against the windowpane, becoming incessant.

No sense loitering abed when there was so much to be done. She rang the hand bell for Lady Sarah and ordered a bath. The water was warm and soothing, but she did not dally. Rising from the rose-scented water, her women rushed to attend her. Wielding brushes, paints and powders, they applied her queenly armor. Her dark hair combed and arranged and studded with diamonds, she chose a plush velvet gown of deep purple with dagged sleeves and a tightly laced kirtle of seed pearls. Feminine yet regal, Liandra approved the image in the mirror.

Returning to her solar, she supped on tea and dried fruits while reviewing her morning dispatches. Sorting the scrolls by their wax seals, her gaze fastened on the crossed quill and lightning bolt, the sigil of her shadowmaster. *Robert!* Breaking the seal, she rushed to read his words. *Rhune is more and less than we expected. This new queen rules with feminine wiles, seeking to beguile all supplicants, yet beneath her comely curves lurks a shrewd mind and a keen ambition. She accepts your offer of truce but says it is too soon to commit to an alliance, yet she startled when I spoke of the Mordant. I sense she fears the coming of the Pentacle as we do. Perhaps an alliance will form when the threat becomes more imminent. I suggest you maintain a correspondence with her. Perhaps queen to queen, a military alliance can be forged.* He went on to describe his travels through Lanverness and Rhune, providing factual tidbits mixed with scintillating gossip. Knowing how she craved details, he spoke of the state of the land, the commerce on the roads, the farmers in their fields and the general spirit of her people. Liandra treasured every insight, but she kept returning to his analysis of Rhune. Like a wave breaking on a rocky shore, her gaze struck on *comely curves* and *feminine wiles*. So this new queen was a temptress. Jealousy flared, yet she fought to banish the thought. After all, it was her idea to send Robert to Rhune. She trusted him like no other, her shadowmaster, her confidant, her lover. Shaking her head, Liandra swallowed her unworthy suspicions, striving to be the queen instead of a mere woman. From the crown's perspective, this change in Rhune suited Lanverness. Far better to have a vixen queen on her northern border than a rabid religion. But the woman in her wished Robert was home...and in her bed.

Setting Robert's missive aside to be reread at a later hour, she reached for the next scroll. Liandra steadily worked her way through the dispatches. Finally finished, she perused the ledgers for the royal treasury. Numbers spoke to her, a secret language of profits and losses, a tale of coins loaned, silvers spent, and golds earned. Commerce was the lifeblood of her kingdom and the queen gloried in growing her treasury. Like a vigilant gardener, she tended her investments, pruning some while watering others. All of her investments were in Lanverness, and as her investments prospered, so did her kingdom. She discovered a discrepancy in one of the accounts and made a mental note to determine if it was an honest mistake or a brazen theft. Good treasurers were hard to find. She preferred not to lose her latest lord to the dungeons. Finished with the ledger, she penned a note to the stonemason's guild offering a sizeable bonus for the swift completion of Pellanor's outer walls. War was an ugly and costly business, but she'd learned the value of precaution.

Lady Sarah appeared at the outer doorway. "Majesty, the Lord Sheriff awaits your pleasure."

The queen looked up from her scrolls, startled by how much time had passed. Setting quill and parchment aside, she settled back in her chair. "Show him in."

Her Lord Sheriff strode into her solar like a breath of spring air. Doffing a broad-brimmed hat with a feathered plume, he sketched a courtly bow. Ever the dandy, his long red hair was copper bright, his mustache rapier thin, and his face handsomely chiseled. Clad in a fashionable doublet of dark velvet, her Lord Sheriff cut a dapper figure, yet despite his flamboyant style the queen judged him to be both loyal and shrewd. "Majesty, how may I serve you?"

"We wish a report on our constable force. Are you successful with your recruiting?"

He hesitated, still stung by the conscription of half his force to the Rose Army. "The recruiting...goes well. The Queen's Purse has drawn many to our standard. "

"And are they of good quality?"

"A mixed lot. Many fled the countryside seeking safety in the city. Having tasted life in Pellanor, they wish to remain but they haven't a trade or a skill to earn a decent living. A constable's pay exceeds a laborer's wage, so they'll take the queen's badge and patrol the streets."

"See that they know our laws and cull any bullies. Those who wear our badge represent our good name."

"My men are proud to wear the royal sigil."

"We trust you to keep our streets safe. Peace and safety are the heralds of prosperity."

"May Pellanor ever prosper under your reign."

Pleased with his response, she gave him a gracious smile. "Last we spoke, you planned to recruit the city urchins, offering them coin to serve as lookouts and informers."

"The Flame War brought an outbreak of orphans to the city. If the youngsters earn coin from the Queen's Purse, they're less likely to turn to thievery. And scruffy urchins oft times make the best spies."

"Spoken like one of our shadowmen...instead of a constable."

He flashed a rogue's grin. "Perhaps I've spent too much time with the Master Archivist."

"Lord Highgate does have a subtle mind." She struggled to a keep a blush from rising to her face. "And have you succeeded with the urchins?"

"I've recruited a dozen. They've proven quite clever at worming their way into unexpected places."

"And are they discreet?"

The Sheriff shrugged. "They're boys, eight and nine years of age, but they soon learn the value of a steady meal."

"We might have a task for some of your clever urchins."

He waited.

"We wish to learn more about the Prince of Ur."

He cocked an eyebrow. "Do you suspect him of some wrongdoing?"

She gave him a sharp look. "We are wary and we are cautious, nothing more. The Prince of Ur is a royal guest, an emissary from a very wealthy trading power. He must be treated with all due respect...yet we would know more."

"Surely this is a task for your diplomats and shadowmen?"

"They have their tasks, but fresh eyes can bring fresh insights. We would see what your urchins can learn."

He nodded assent. "Is there anything in particular they should look for?"

The queen hesitated to voice her concerns. "There is something odd about the prince...as if he is cloaked in riddles. We like it not. We would learn his secrets, and thereby, learn the nature of his riddle. Have your urchins keep watch on his mansion in the city and report anything odd or unusual."

"As you command." He bowed towards her, offering a gracious sweep of his plumed hat.

"And, Lord Sheriff, this task must be discreet. You will speak only to us on this matter."

He flashed a rogue's smile. "I welcome any reason to meet with my queen."

The man was a silver-tongued fox...but the queen enjoyed his company. She offered her ringed hand. "Bring us word as soon as you've learned anything. No matter how small or how odd, we wish to hear of it."

He kissed her ring and then retreated with a flourish of his emerald green cape.

The door closed behind him and she was alone. The queen toyed with a feathered quill. She missed Robert, but her Lord Sheriff was a capable man...and a delightful distraction, but the task she'd set him was a serious one. Ur was a powerful trading partner...but the prince was a riddle she had yet to plumb.

Lady Sarah hovered in the doorway. "Majesty, Princess Jemma is here to join you for the midday meal."

"So soon?" Light from the window had crept across the floor, marking the passage of the hours.

"Yes, majesty."

"A queen's work is never done."

Lady Sarah gave her a knowing smile. "And you would have it no other way."

The queen smiled. "You know us too well. Show the princess to our dining chamber." Liandra washed her hands in a fingerbowl, scrubbing away the ink stains, and then entered her small dining chamber. Servants in emerald green livery snapped to attention. One held a chair as the queen took her customary seat at the round table.

The table was set for two, an intimate meal with her protégé. Sunlight streamed through the diamond-paned windows, sending fractured rainbows dancing across the silver plate. Everything gleamed and sparkled, befitting the image of the Rose Court.

Princess Jemma swept into the chamber, dropping to a deep curtsy. Beauty tempered with restraint, her lustrous black hair was captured in a bun, held in place by a net of pearls, but otherwise she wore no adornment. Clad in a modest gown of black velvet, the princess remained in deep mourning. Death had ravaged the royal house of Navarre with the murder of her kin at the poisoned feast, her sorrow and loss compounded by the shocking death of her mother. Darkness reached for Erdhe and Navarre paid a heavy price.

"Come and join us." Liandra's voice held an unfeigned warmth.

The princess took a seat opposite the queen. "It is always a pleasure, majesty."

Servants surrounded the table, offering a simple but tasty repast. Fresh baked bread with churned butter and a savory broth of onion soup. After pouring the wine, the servants withdrew, providing the two royals with a rare privacy. Liandra sipped the soup, impressed with the flavor despite the clarity of the broth. "What word from Navarre?" The queen savored her time with the princess, a chance to discuss commerce and kingdoms with a friend, an ally, and a protégé. Liandra thought of the young woman as her daughter that might have been.

"Jordan and the army march at a steady pace. They hope to meet up with Prince Stewart and the Rose Army somewhere south of the Snowmelt."

The queen nodded, pleased to confirm the reports from her own shadowmen and military aids. "We've had word from Prince Stewart. Coronth is a shattered kingdom, decimated from within by the Flame religion. The people offer no resistance...but they also offer no succor. The countryside is stripped of food as if infested by a plague of locusts. We plan to double the supplies sent north." The queen tore a crust of bread from the loaf, the soft center still oven-warm, fragrant with the scent of rosemary. "Fortunately, our roadways are flush with wagons bearing goods from the Delta's seaport and from Tubor's granaries...but the trade from Navarre has slowed to a trickle."

The princess's face darkened. "A worry of another sort."

The queen's interest quickened. "How so? We assumed Navarre needs the supplies for its own army?"

"The merchant fleet is still at sea." Her words held a sepulcher tone. "Overdue by more than three moon turns."

"Storms?"

The princess shook her head. "If it was only storms, a few ships would have limped home...but my factor writes that the harbor is empty save for fishing skiffs."

Her factor, so the young princess sows her own crop of shadowmen. "And does your factor say why the fleet is so late?"

"No, so I wrote the king."

"And?"

"He sent the fleet north on the advice of Jordan...and the Kiralynn monks."

"The *monks?*" The queen set her spoon aside. "This war is more convoluted than we thought." She pondered the facts. "But why send the fleet north? The north offers no trade."

"Just so." Worry plagued the princess's face. "The merchant fleet is the lifeblood of Navarre."

The queen's concern deepened. "You must ask the king why he sent the fleet north."

"I have...but I've not yet received a reply."

"Then we are left with another riddle."

"*Another* riddle?"

The princess was a shrewd player. "Yes, the prince of Ur has come to Pellanor and we find him wrapped in riddles."

"The marketplace was agog with his grand entrance to the city."

"What do our people say?"

"They speak of bells on his stallion, veiled women riding by his side, and a wagon piled high with treasure chests. The people are enthralled by the spectacle. A mysterious prince comes to their city bearing the promise of lavish wealth and exotic differences. What could be more enticing?"

"Indeed." It sounded like a fairy tale, yet Liandra knew so many fairy tales had dark sides. "What else do they say?"

The princess nibbled a slice of bread. "I've heard talk of a grand banquet to be held at his mansion in the city. The merchants are buzzing like bees to the honey."

"A banquet? How odd."

The princess set her bread aside. "Why is it odd?"

"Because we offered to hold a royal reception for him here at the castle, a banquet followed by a dance, but he demurred, preferring a private meeting." Liandra made no mention of the chess game for the loss still stung.

"That *is* odd." The princess fingered her wine goblet. "Why would a visiting prince decline a royal reception?"

The queen had no answer.

The princess leaned forward, her voice dropping to a conspirator's whisper. "Would you like me to wrangle an invitation to the banquet? Perhaps I could help solve this riddle?"

A chill shivered through the queen. The thought alarmed her...though she could not say why. "No...let my shadowmen do their work." Liandra did not want a possible heir to Navarre anywhere near the prince. "My spies will peel back the riddle and then we'll decide."

"As you wish."

The queen guided their conversation towards matters of commerce, but in the back of her mind she worried about the prince...and the missing fleet. The game grew complicated. She sensed the hand of other players. The queen wondered if they were friends or foes. Questions pounded through her mind. The very fate of Erdhe might depend on these riddles yet she had few answers.

9

Bryce

The Mordant slept and the malevolent evil receded like a foul tide, loosening the chains of his prison. A soul trapped within the Mordant, Bryce clung to his sanity, desperate to find a way to make a difference. Somehow his hellish existence had to count for something. Surely the gods would not abandon him, yet his hopes were few and his existence bleak. Horrified by everything he'd witnessed, he railed against his bonds, but it had little effect. Without the sea's ability to weaken the Mordant, he'd lost the strength to move the smallest finger...yet he had to try.

As an acolyte in the monastery, he'd learned a timeworn saying, *When one door shuts another opens.* He'd lost the sea, an unexpected ally, but another slender hope had come his way...but with that hope came dire need. The Mordant had endured a harrowing sea crossing to stalk a queen. Crouched within his prison, Bryce kept watch through his spy hole while the two met across a chessboard. He'd felt the Mordant loose his Dark will upon the queen, yet somehow she resisted. During the whole of his long captivity, Bryce had witnessed only two people who resisted the Mordant's soul-assault, the cat-eyed man in the bloody cavern and now the queen.

The cat-eyed man had been his friend. Chained in the unholy sanctuary beneath the Dark Citadel, the Mordant had tortured the cat-eyed man, yet somehow he'd repulsed the Mordant's soul-probe. Pierced by a hundred cursed daggers and left to suffer as an offering to Darkness, yet he'd endured. Later, much later, Bryce had found a way to follow a magical thread and speak with the cat-eyed man from afar. He'd hoped to thwart the Mordant by sharing his plans, but that valiant warrior had died, succumbing to his wounds. Now the Mordant fixed his deadly gaze upon the Rose Queen.

Spellbound with worry, Bryce spied through his keyhole as the two met. At first the Mordant was charming and courteous, the Dark threat coiled behind his eyes like a cobra's lethal strike. Bryce railed against his prison, desperate to warn the queen, all to no avail. Crouched in his gray prison, he'd felt their stares cross...and then the blinding flash of light beat against the Mordant, invoking his rage. Hope and fear crashed against Bryce like two competing tidal waves. When the waves calmed, hope bled away while the Mordant's rage remained, annealed to a cold, malevolent hate. The queen had somehow repulsed the Mordant's mental assault, but she seemed oblivious to the threat standing before her. Smothering his rage, the Mordant took a seat across the checkered board. The two played chess like civilized people...but the queen knew not what type of vile monster she battled. The oldest harlequin, an emissary of Darkness, a thousand years of evil hidden beneath youth's stolen facade...played chess. Within his prison, Bryce shuddered, barely able to watch. He could not imagine what terrible fate awaited the queen.

Later, Bryce considered all he'd learned. The Mordant's every move dripped with malevolent purpose. Moon-turns ago, he'd planted assassins within the queen's court, one assassin hidden as a jester, death hidden beneath jovial deceit. But the Kiralynn Order had also entered the game. By spying through the keyhole, Bryce knew that a brother monk had come to the queen's court, proof of her importance, yet the monk had died, murdered by the assassin's foul poison. Plots within plots, Darkness foiled the Light...but where one monk had failed, another would take his place...even if that one was trapped within the gray prison of the Mordant's mind.

Bryce had to try. He had to give meaning to this terrible imprisonment.

And then the gods lent a hand.

The death of the monk brought an unexpected boon. The monk's malachite coin sat on the table nearest the bed. The Mordant kept it close, intending to bond with it, but Bryce knew it would never serve the harlequin, for somehow, while the Mordant fondled the malachite coin, the magic of the focus found its way to his prison. Piercing the gray haze, it formed a bond with Bryce. *A coin from ancient Azreal,* his mind dazzled with the implications. Like an ancient curse that had finally found its mark, the coin had come to the Mordant's hand. Bryce felt it on the bedside table, calling to him, so close but yet so far. He yearned to hold it in his hand, to unleash the magic within. He knew not what it did, but it gave him hope.

But before he could wield it, Bryce needed to gain control of his hand.

Tendrils of thought slipped through his prison. Bryce focused on the Mordant's right hand. He willed his hand to move, like trying to flex a rusty gauntlet. Straining against his bonds, he fought to work his will...but nothing happened. Remembering his time onboard the ship, he sought to rethread the connections between his mind and his flesh. Refusing to be defeated, he kept at it...and felt the smallest finger twitch. Elation thrummed through him.

Sunlight pierced the windows and the Mordant stirred.

Bryce retreated to his prison, dampening his emotions. *The coin had come to him for a reason.* Perhaps the Lords of Light had finally heard his pleas. He'd bide his time and keep watch and find a way to make a difference.

10

Liandra

For the second time, the queen met the prince across the chessboard. Liandra vowed this game would be different. Not only did she intend to win, but this time she'd drill him with questions, seeking to unearth his intentions, his motives, his plans. Before this game finished, she'd peer behind his youthful face and courtly manners to discern his true nature.

The prince entered her solar with a confident smile. Clad in a sumptuous robe of dark purple, his fingers glittered with jeweled rings, a blunt reminder of Ur's formidable wealth. His face was so youthful, the queen guessed his age at twenty-two, a young man just entering his prime, yet every aspect of his bearing screamed of royal privilege. He carried himself with a rare confidence that belied his years. A royal riddle, the prince was intriguing and deeply mysterious despite his youth.

He took a seat opposite her. "Once more we meet across the chessboard."

"We trust this outcome will be different."

The prince flashed a haughty smile, yet his blue eyes remained cold as ice. "Your beauty is exceeded only by your unbridled confidence."

"Unbridled?"

He gave an elegant shrug. "Having lost the first battle, there is no reason to believe you shall win the second."

The queen smothered a tart reply, her desire for victory multiplied.

Light against dark, the exquisite chessboard sat between them, a lavish gift from the prince. Malachite knights, monks, and soldiers stood in straight ranks, ready to battle his phalanx of onyx dragons, wizards, and gargoyles. Chess was a game of wits, patience and strategy, a game the Spider Queen intended to win.

He gestured to the board. "Yours to begin."

"We opened the last game. Shouldn't you take the lighter side?"

"Never." He gave her a courtly nod. "As a gentleman, I'll play the Dark, ceding the first move to the queen."

His words held an unexpected edge, yet the queen accepted the advantage. Besides, green was ever her color. She scrutinized the board, considering her first move. Expecting a bloody conflict, Liandra decided to strike first. She chose a bold move, opening with her queen's knight, setting up a strong attack. "Your gift is an interesting choice, knights against dragons, reality vying against myth."

"Myth or metaphor?" The prince opened with his king's pawn, advancing the gargoyle by one space.

An intriguing reply...and he makes a conservative opening, more proof the prince is layered with riddles. The queen considered the board while plying him with questions. "Myths we understand, but if dragons, wizards and gargoyles are meant as a metaphor then we confess to be confused. What is the message behind your gift?"

His gaze remained fixed on the board, as if consumed by the game, yet the queen refused to let silence reign. "Surely you know the intent behind your own gift?"

"Intent should be discovered, not explained. Why take the mystery out of life?" The prince moved another pawn.

Such a mature answer for one so young. She took a stab at his meaning. "As the Empire of Ur is ever shrouded in myth?"

"Conveniently so."

Liandra moved her queen across the board. Already the game was shaping up to be an epic struggle, a convoluted tangle of moves, so different from the first bloody onslaught. Black evaded green, always slipping away from her traps, as if he was afraid to engage. The prince displayed a devious mind, so different from his ruthless attack of their first game. He played the second game like an intricate dance, delaying the inevitable clash. Move and counter move, the tension built to a fever pitch.

A log fire snapped and crackled in the hearth, releasing a breath of pine. Bathed in the ruby glow of the firelight, they sat across from each other, goblets of wine and platters of cheese long forgotten.

The queen eased back in her chair, forcing herself to take a break. "We are curious about your title, the twelfth-fold prince of Ur?"

"Merely a measure of my nearness to the throne."

"So you have eleven brothers?"

"Hundreds." He flashed a startling smile. "We are legion, for the Emperor has many wives and many more concubines."

A harem, the queen hid her distaste. "So how is succession decided?"

"By deeds, by duels, by the machinations of the harem, by the knife of an assassin, and ultimately, by the Emperor's favor."

"So you've come to Erdhe to set yourself apart?"

"Precisely."

"Or perhaps you've come to evade the assassins?" She could not resist the jab.

"I have no fear of assassins." His dragon took her castle, the first major loss of the game. "I find it passing strange that your lords let a queen rule alone."

"And why is that strange?" Her queen took his pawn, gaining access to his castle.

"When a royal line narrows to a single queen it takes a perilous risk." He shot a pointed glance across the chessboard. "I hear you have but one living heir."

Liandra gave a terse nod, disliking the turn of question. Her hand stole across her empty womb, mourning her lost daughter.

"Another reason women should never rule." He fondled the fallen pawn. "Kings sow their seed across many women while queens risk their life at every childbirth."

"True, yet it does not lessen our ability to rule."

He shrugged. "But it risks your royal line."

Anger spiked her voice. "Unlike Ur, our court is not mired in assassins and duels."

"That is your loss, for such trials winnow out the weak, ensuring only the strong and the worthy wear the crown."

"There is much more to ruling than knives and assassins. We value intelligence and honor in our monarchs, not cunning and deception."

"Spoken like a queen instead of king."

His words struck like an underhanded cut, yet the queen refused to be baited. Liandra fixed her gaze on the board. Crowded with pieces, the game was becoming tricky, feints within feints, plots within plots, so different from their first game...almost as if she played an entirely different opponent. For such a young man, the prince was laden with unexpected mysteries. He played a deep game, a complex game.

"Is Navarre not an ally of Lanverness?"

His question ambushed her, drawing her attention from the board. "Why do you ask?"

"Because the royal line of Navarre is so very fecund. They say the fecund shall inherit the earth."

"Yet Navarre remains a small kingdom while Lanverness prospers beyond all telling."

"If you are truly allies then why does Navarre not share their magic."

"Their *magic?*" Startled, she met his stare across the chessboard.

"How else can the seaside queens bear so many tuplets and live? Yet they do not share this magic with you?"

Magic! His reply spiked her with doubt. It was widely known that the royal line of Navarre was exceptionally fertile...but she'd never considered magic as the key to the riddle.

"You have but one heir. Navarre's magic could strengthen your line, giving you multiple children with a single birth." He gave her a barbed look. "Spare children can be very profitable. Surety for your throne, alliances by marriage to spread your influence to other kingdoms, security for your borders. So much to be had for the getting of a gaggle of children. After all, why conquer kingdoms when you can gain them by marriage?"

His words ambushed her. Flustered, she stared at him, desperate to discern his intent.

He moved his castle, threatening her king. "Check."

So, the conversation is merely a distracting diversion. Liandra forced her mind back to the game. Dark pieces surrounded her king, threatening to hand her a second defeat. While she'd focused on building a subtle attack, he'd slowly surrounded her king, trapping him in a corner. Liandra studied the board. In three moves, he'd checkmate her king, winning the game. Refusing to accept defeat, she scrambled to mount a defense. Out of necessity, she moved her king, evading the check, but he moved his queen, tightening the noose.

He flashed a wolf's grin. "The outcome is evident."

Refusing to concede, she studied the board. Evading would gain her nothing, so instead, she decided to attack. Her father had often said that the best defense was a good offense. Liandra reached for her monk, moving the malachite cleric the length of the board in a diagonal attack. "Check."

Annoyance flashed across his face. "You peck at me like a hen, when you know the game is over."

"We know no such thing." She continued to attack, every move checking his king, driving him backwards. None were killing blows, yet while she attacked, she kept hope alive, keeping his pieces from closing on her king. Relentless, she chased him into a corner. Bringing all of her remaining pieces to bear, she threatened him with a pawn. "Checkmate!" The word was sweet upon her lips.

Rage flashed across his face but was quickly smothered beneath a congenial mask...but his eyes told the truth. Something ominous gleamed in the depths of his eyes, something akin to hatred.

The queen stilled, a rabbit hiding from the hawk's bloody talons, but then the prince smiled and she doubted her own insight.

Reaching forward, he toppled his own king. "A victory for the Queen of Lanverness. That makes one game apiece, the third game will tell the tale." The prince offered her his felled king. "To the winner goes the spoils." He drilled her with his stare. So sharp, his gaze cut her like icy daggers.

Unable to blink, unable to look away, the queen felt assaulted...she felt defiled.

"Will you have more wine?" Lady Sarah blustered into the chamber, a tray in hand.

Light flared behind the queen's eyes. Liandra broke from his stare, her head throbbing.

The prince snarled. Standing abruptly, he knocked the chess pieces across the board. "You shall not win." His voice was a low hiss, a barely audible threat.

The queen struggled to ignore her throbbing headache. "The last game is not even begun."

"This endgame is closer than you think."

"Your arrogance will be your undoing. Even a pawn can topple a king."

He sneered. "Only in myths."

"Myths are metaphors for life; any bard will tell you that."

"Bards and pawns, I'll grant you the riffraff of life, the dross of the back alleys, for they shall never defeat magic and cunning. But then, what does a mere woman know of either? How can a woman ever wield true power?" Turning abruptly, his cape swept across the board, toppling the few remaining pieces. Without a backward glance, the prince strode from the chamber.

The queen remained in her chair, staggered by the prince's parting words. *You shall not win.* She stared at the chessboard. *So many toppled pieces,* the prince left wreckage in his wake.

"Are you well, majesty?" Lady Sarah hovered close, concern on her face. "So sorry to interrupt, but I didn't like the way he was staring at you."

"You did well to interrupt." The queen rubbed her forehead.

Lady Sarah gathered up the cheese platter and forgotten wine goblets. "Will you play him again, majesty?"

"We suspect we are entangled in some game to which we barely know the rules."

"How can you play a game when you don't know the rules?"

"Life often entangles us in the games of others. The real question is learning how to win even if you are blind to the rules."

Lady Sarah gave her a puzzled look. "How do you do that, majesty?"

The queen gave her friend a wan smile. "Know your enemy. Know yourself. And then make your own rules."

"Is that what you're doing?"

"We try." The queen closed her eyes, hoping to dull her headache.

"Can I bring you something?"

"Leave the wine."

"As you wish." Filling the queen's goblet, the lady retreated from the chamber.

The queen sat alone before the toppled chess set, malachite soldiers and ebony gargoyles scattered across the iridescent board. *Two chess games, each as different as night and day.* The prince was far more complex than he first seemed and his barbed talk of Navarre and the precarious nature of her own royal line put her teeth on edge. Some deeper game was at work here. *Magic to quicken a child,* the thought wormed itself into her mind. Plots within plots. Liandra reached for a goblet of red wine. She'd won the second game, but somehow she felt as if she'd lost.

11

The Mordant

The Mordant returned to his manse, seething with anger, cursing the queen. Twice she'd foiled his soul-strike, but he'd defeat her with chains of a different sort. Adding insult to injury, she'd snatched victory from defeat in the chess match. The silly board game mattered not, yet the loss rankled. The thrice-damned woman would soon find herself mired in the true game. Beleaguered with lies, she'd lose her prestige and her precious crown. A sinister smile crossed his face. Retreating to his solar, he sought his magic.

So many focuses, so much magic to choose from. An eon of lifetimes spent seeking magic had brought him a dragon's hoard of focuses. The Mordant craved power, the elixir of the gods. Unlocking the ironbound jewel box, he removed the velvet-lined drawers, sensing the magic within. For centuries, his minions had scoured Erdhe, stealing focuses of every size, shape and description. Despite his best efforts, some remained stubbornly insensate to his touch. He'd left those impotent tools behind, locked in his treasure vault in the Dark Citadel. But many more awakened to his touch. Like a lover he fondled them, courted them, cajoling forth their inner secrets till their magic served his beck and call. He'd brought the most powerful with him. Hidden as a wealth of adornments, the Mordant fondled the rings and armbands arrayed on red velvet, magical focuses fashioned into jewelry. Some held trifling powers, like the ability to light a candle with a snap of his fingers. Such a seemingly trivial magic, yet even this small focus had the ability to captivate the minds of mere mortals. Deception was such a delicious game. To captivate, to dominate, to charm, to control...how he loved to twist mortal souls to the Dark through mesmerizing deceit. A shiver akin to sexual ecstasy ran through him. The Mordant craved the Great Dark Dance.

Choosing among the bejeweled baubles, he clad himself in power.

Of all his focuses, there were two he valued above all others, two that were never far from his hand. One was the red crystal from the

Staff of Pain. The staff itself was a confection of iron fashioned to reflect the menace of a wizard's staff combined with the regal authority of a king's scepter. The Mordant was not above using symbols to dominate, but the staff itself was ordinary iron. The true power resided in the red crystal fixed atop iron prongs. A shard of crimson quartz as long as his middle finger, the crystal held the power of pain, inducing excruciating agony in any foe within sword-striking distance. To wield the crystal, the Mordant merely needed to imagine the torture and his foe felt the affliction. How delicious to watch an unsuspecting enemy drop to the ground and writhe in torment, merely by flexing one's will. The crystal of pain provided a power he'd found extremely useful over many lifetimes. Removing the red crystal from the staff's crown, he placed it deep in his right pocket.

The second focus he cherished above all others offered a far subtler power. He fingered the medallion-shaped cameo carved from bone. The sculpture depicted a two-faced head in relief, a man gazing to the right, a woman to the left. The two-faced relief hinted at the power lurking within. How rare to find a magic that only served a harlequin. Pinning the cameo brooch to his butternut-brown cloak, the Mordant stepped before the full-length mirror...and willed his appearance to change.

His face began to melt. His reflected features danced and morphed, as if a second face sought to escape from within. His nose grew more bulbous, his eyebrows becoming thick and bushy as caterpillars. His blonde hair darkened to black with faint streaks of gray. His chest filled out with muscles and the beginnings of a beer gut. So uncanny to watch the changes, yet he felt only a faint tingling of magic across his skin. The Mordant studied the mirror, focusing on each detail, willing them to change till they matched his memories. Satisfied, his new visage slowly annealed, locking into place.

The Mordant staggered, feeling the sudden drain in power. Magic always took its toll...but it did not take him long to recover.

Straightening, he stared in the mirror.

A face from another lifetime peered back. A man of middling years with sun-weathered skin and salt and pepper hair. He'd chosen the face of a ruthless general, although none now alive would recognize it. His new face had the maturity to be believed without being too memorable. Already clad in tailored clothes of non-descript brown, the Mordant relaxed his stance, slouching to fit the role of a moderately successful merchant. He practiced walking before the mirror, pretending he carried more weight and more years. Beneath the altered image, he wore the vital body of the young monk. Relying on memories from another lifetime, he walked like an older man, his weight centered in his gut.

A pity the cameo could not make him younger, or fitter, or stronger, for the transformation was pure illusion. The Mordant peered in the mirror, studying the changes. The only visible detail that remained the same was the cameo brooch pinned to his cloak. For some reason, the brooch had to remain visible or the illusion would vanish.

Fortunately, the brooch was an oddity that seemed to fit almost any illusion. Cameos were rare, and the quality of the sculptured profile was exquisite, implying a master's hand, but the materials were ordinary bone and brass. The cheap materials belied its priceless value, diverting covetous eyes.

Satisfied with his appearance, the Mordant buckled on a belt with a heavy purse of coins, and then he remembered the malachite coin, his latest acquisition. Acquired from the pocket of a murdered monk, the coin remained a mystery, yet it offered the promise of more power. He fondled the malachite coin, willing it to waken. Determined to keep it close, he lodged it deep in an inside pocket.

Locking the ironbound jewel box with his remaining focuses, he returned it to a larger chest. Locking the chest, he reset the poisoned needle.

Wearing the face of a stranger, the Mordant stepped from his solar.

A snargon of the duegars and two assassins waited for him, all three clad in common street clothes. The snargon's nostrils flared wide, scenting the presence of powerful magic, while the two assassins stood poised to deal with any intruders. Staring with wary eyes, their hands dropped to their daggers.

The Mordant wielded the crimson shard, spiking the three with pain.

The two assassins stiffened, their hands convulsing on their daggers, while the snargon dropped to his knees, groaning in agony.

The pain lasted for only a heartbeat, just enough to prove his true nature. Passwords could be stolen or bought, but the crystal of pain was his to wield.

The snargon climbed to his feet and bowed low. "My lord, the Mordant, what will you have of us?"

"My name is Master Cahill, a wealthy wine merchant, and I'll have you three escort me into the queen's city. Dolf and Corlin, you're to stay a discreet distance away, keeping watch in case you are needed. Tonkin, stay closer, but only speak to me if you scent magic. If the monks dare to draw near, I expect to be forewarned. Otherwise, the three of you are to stay in the shadows, while I weave some magic of my own. It is time to besmirch the queen's good name."

"As you command, my lord."

He led his escort out into the cobbled street. His three shadows quickly scattered, disappearing into the supper-time crowd. The Mordant walked among the queen's people, Darkness cloaked in deceit, and they knew it not. Such a colorful crowd, young and old, rich and poor, busy with their tiny lives. The chaotic jumble grated against the Mordant, so starkly different from the ordered pattern of the Dark Citadel. Studying the sounds and scents of the city's everyday life, he followed the flow till he found a popular tavern, the perfect place to sow his lies. The Mordant smiled, reveling in his role as the Deceiver. The queen thought he'd come to play chess, but this was the true game. He looked forward to an evening of spreading lies. There was nothing quite so powerful as a lie believed. And none were better at selling lies than the Mordant.

12

Liandra

*M**agic to quicken a child.* The thought teased and tormented the queen's mind till she could think of nothing else. Liandra yearned for another child, for Robert's daughter, lost to foul poison, the murderer still lurking within her castle. For Danly's twin sister, murdered in her womb, Danly's birth cord wrapped around her neck in a deadly stranglehold. Liandra had buried two fresh-birthed daughters. The bitter losses still cut like spears to her heart, inflicting wounds that never healed. Four times the queen had swelled with child, and four times she'd carried the babes near to term, yet only one child lived, her firstborn son and only heir...and now he rode to war against the Mordant. As a woman, Liandra yearned for the daughter she'd never had...as a queen, she needed to secure her royal line...and her throne.

In everything else, she'd succeeded, but not this, as if the gods mocked her for being a woman who dared to rule.

Magic to quicken a child. She was still young enough to bear one more babe, one more chance to ease the ache in her heart, one more chance to bring security to her throne. And if the magic could ensure a multiple birth, all the better. As a woman and a queen, it was a chance she had to seize.

But how to do it?

Liandra considered summoning the princess to her solar, but it seemed too formal, too pointed...so she contrived a casual meeting instead. Three days later, her shadowmen brought word that the princess practiced archery in the castle's courtyard, the perfect opportunity.

Sunlight danced across the plush carpet, providing a believable alibi to stroll the castle's parapets. Abandoning the mountain of dispatches heaped on her desk, Liandra set her quill aside. "The sunlight beckons, we shall take a walk on the parapets."

Lady Sarah looked up from her knitting. "Shall I join you, majesty?"

"No, you look content. We shall take Sir Durnheart."

"As you wish, majesty."

Liandra settled a delicate lace shawl across her shoulders, more for adornment than warmth, and swept from her solar. She dismissed her guards save for her knight protector. Sir Durnheart followed at a discreet distance, the hilt of his great blue sword rearing over his right shoulder.

Maulkin, one of her shadowmen, a plain-looking man clad in dark clothing, stepped from an alcove. "This way, majesty." He led her through the labyrinth corridors of her castle and out onto the perfect parapet for viewing the archery butts. Arrows thumped targets with a deadly rhythm, belying the bright beauty of the day. Below in the courtyard, the princess of Navarre practiced with two of her guards...and Lord Cenric. So the forest lord was back from the south. He cut a dashing figure with his broad shoulders and flowing cloak of peacock feathers.

The queen watched from the battlement as they skewered targets with arrows. The princess was good, but the forest lord never missed the target's heart. Their skill at archery was expected, but what took the queen by surprise were the warm smiles and easy comradery that passed between the two. So the princess was smitten with the forest lord...but then half her court swooned over the man, including Lady Sarah. But as she watched, it seemed to the queen that the cat-eyed archer was equally bespelled by the petite princess. What an interesting and unexpected turn of events. Liandra considered how to use the relationship to her advantage.

Princess Jemma noticed the queen watching from the battlement. She smiled, giving a bright wave.

The queen motioned her shadowman near. "Invite Princess Jemma to walk with us on the parapets."

"As you wish." Maulkin strode towards the nearest doorway.

Laughter drifted up from below. The queen watched as the archers reclaimed their arrows, comparing scores. They unstrung their bows and wiped down the staves, the feather-cloaked lord hovering close to the petite princess.

Her shadowman appeared below, interrupting the charming tableau.

Lord Cenric looked up, his strange cat-eyes glinting golden in the sunlight. He offered the queen a nod, the only homage his stiff-necked pride would allow. Turning back to the princess, he won a smile from her face, and then sauntered off like a regal peacock strutting among drab pigeons.

The queen had to admit that the forest lord gave good strut...but he was hardly a proper suitor for a princess royal.

Maulkin returned with the princess in tow.

"So nice to see you enjoying the sunshine, majesty." She gave a graceful curtsy despite wearing a suede jerkin over leather pants. Her mannish garb was distasteful to the queen's sensibilities, but Liandra had to admit that the formfitting leather showed the princess's petite curves to excellent advantage.

"Spring has finally come south. We could not resist a stroll beneath the sun-warmed sky. Walk with us." The queen turned to walk the parapet at a leisurely pace, the princess falling into step beside her. "You are an excellent archer, my dear, but we believe Lord Cenric won the day."

"He's an uncanny shot! I've never seen him miss the target's heart. When it comes to the longbow, there are none better in all of Navarre."

The princess gushed like a love-struck girl. "And do you practice with him often?"

"As often as I can. He's helping me hone my skills."

The queen cast a sideways glance toward the princess. "And are you sure it is the target's heart he's aiming for?"

The princess fell silent, a blush heating her face.

The queen considered her protégé, still so young yet so blazingly competent. "Springtime love can be heady as an elixir," the queen softened her voice, "but never forget you are royal born. The crown is your true destiny."

"The crown of Navarre is a longed-for possibility...not a certain destiny."

So it was as serious as that. The queen decided to take a different tack. "The forest lord cuts a dashing figure. Half my court swoons over him, yet what do you really know of him? He seems...so much older?"

"He is older." The princess's blush deepened, but a stubborn glint shone from her eyes. "And he was married, but his wife recently died of the flux. It's one of the many reasons he answered the Treespeaker's call to lead his rangers to the aid of Lanverness."

"And we remain extremely grateful for that aid...but you seem to know quite a bit about forest politics."

"He talks to me."

"The surest way to win the heart of a quick-witted woman. Your archer does indeed know how to hit the target."

The princess stopped, her face changing from embarrassment to chagrin. "Do you think me a fool?"

"Never that." Liandra's heart went out to the young woman. "But you are young and full of so much promise. We do not wish to see you make a mistake."

"And you think he's a mistake?"

Such a knife-edged question. The queen resumed walking. "Lord Cenric has proven himself to be brave and stalwart. He is proud and carries himself with noble bearing, and he certainly cuts a splendid figure in his peacock cloak...but does he bring Navarre any political advantage besides archers?"

"Always politics." Her voice held a bitter edge.

"Always a queen. If you thought with your head instead of your heart, you would say the same."

"But I *am* thinking with my heart," wonder brightened the young woman's face, "for the first time in my life!"

So it was worse than she thought. "Be cautious. That is our best advice. For love is a poison that eats wits."

Defiance flashed across the young woman's face. "Yet the most capable queen to rule in all of Erdhe nearly bore a love child."

The dagger struck close to the bone. Hearing the words spoken aloud, the queen froze as if ice were armor.

The princess gasped, dropping to a deep curtsy. "I'm so sorry, majesty, that was unkind and uncalled for."

The queen recovered her mask. "Uncalled for, yes, yet it proves you have not lost your wits...or your claws."

The princess blanched pale. "I'm so sorry, majesty, but I'm so confused. There must be a way to serve the crown...and also have love."

Such a heartfelt plea, Liandra ached for the young woman despite her ill-considered words. "That is the riddle, the true challenge for a queen who dares to rule." She beckoned for the princess to rise. "Come, walk with us. We royal women must stick together, for all the world is against us."

The princess fell into step beside the queen. For a while they said nothing. Walking in companionable silence, they gazed from the crenellated ramparts across the bustling heart of Pellanor. Spring brightened the queen's city with fresh leaves budding on trees, herbs sprouting in gardens, and window boxes laden with flowers. Like a new gown, the fresh green color lent Pellanor an air of hope and renewal, but the illusion was marred by the sound of hammers striking stone, proof the defensive wall slowly grew to surround her city. *A walled city.* Liandra had never wanted that for Pellanor...but war changed many things. Another reason she needed a spare heir. "Tell us of this forest lord who has captured the heart of a princess."

Delighted by the queen's prompting, the princess launched into a monologue of archery lessons, long walks, intimate dinners and small kindnesses. The queen listened intently, gleaning insights to the forest lord and his reclusive people. The princess painted a picture of subtle courtship and small delights, yet the queen sensed they'd not yet slept together. Liandra kept her relief to herself, glad that young love had not entirely trampled royal wits and proper decorum.

The princess fell silent. "A copper for your thoughts?"

The queen smiled. "We trust they are worth far more than a mere copper."

The princess waited, an anxious look in her green eyes.

The queen stepped carefully. "It is easy to see his allure, and he is a lord of the forest...but would your father, the king, approve?"

"What do you think?"

"You are his daughter. You know King Ivor better than we do."

The princess looked pensive. "What if you were to write him? To vouch for Lord Cenric?"

A favor for a favor, just the opening she'd hoped for. "We might consider it. You are like a daughter to us and Lord Cenric has done much to aid Lanverness."

The princess brightened. "And his people are gaining acceptance in Erdhe. Just the other day I saw Durin in the market and his golden cat-eyes barely caused a stir."

"How was the mood in the marketplace?" The queen steered the conversation towards commerce and market gossip. As always, the princess provided a remarkable crop of insights. Liandra enjoyed discussing the state of her kingdom with the princess, but when the ideas began to wane, she broached the question close to her heart. "We heard something interesting the other day, that the royal tuplets of Navarre are quickened by magic. Is that true?"

"Yes."

"Yes?" *So the Prince of Ur was right!* The queen's hopes leaped. "Such a small answer for such a large question."

The princess shrugged. "Magic is feared by most people, so while we do not deny it, neither do we trumpet it from the castle ramparts."

"We've always known the royal line of Navarre was extremely fecund...but we never considered magic."

"Most people don't. They can't consider what they don't believe."

"Since the death of Lord Turner, we've come to believe in many things. Those glowing red eyes of the harlequin haunt us still." The queen suppressed a shudder. "We confess that magic seems like a force for evil...but if used to quicken a child, it would be a boon to any woman."

"As heirs to Navarre, we were taught that magic is like a sword, the intent depends on the hand that wields it."

"How does it work?"

"Magic?" The princess gave a light laugh. "You'd do better to ask a philosopher."

"No, the magic that quickens conception, how does that work?" The queen held her breath, hoping, yearning.

"I do not know. It is a closely kept secret held by the king and queen and one other. The knowledge is only passed once the new monarch is chosen and accepted."

The queen listened closely but she heard no guile in the young woman's voice...but neither did she get the answers she so sorely needed. Liandra decided to set subtleties aside and joust straight for the target's heart. "Can this magic be shared?"

"Shared?" The princess paused, turning to face her.

"Magic to quicken a child would be a boon to any woman, but especially to a royal queen...with only one heir."

The princess gaped, her eyes going wide.

The queen dropped her voice to a whisper, her gaze drilling the princess. "Royal to royal, woman to woman, we ask for Navarre to share this birth-magic." The princess started to reply but the queen forestalled her. "We ask this as a queen who has but one heir, an heir who rides to war against the Mordant with his wife, your sister, by his side. The Tandroth line is stretched perilously thin." Iron filled her voice. "We shall not let the Rose line perish from Erdhe." The queen softened her tone, her heart rising to her voice. "That love child you spoke of was sorely wanted, a long-sought daughter of our heart, a babe to fill our aching arms, a spare heir to secure our royal line and our throne. We tell you this so that you know the importance of our request." The queen's voice dropped to a hoarse whisper laden with need. "Will Navarre share this birth magic with your closest ally?"

"Majesty...I so wish it was so."

The queen waited as if balanced on a knife-edge. "Explain."

The princess looked stricken. "From what little I know, this magic is tied to the royal bloodline of Navarre. It will serve none but the freshly anointed monarchs of the seaside kingdom."

"Has it ever been tried with another bloodline?"

"Not that I know of, but..."

"Then it's time to try."

The princess shook her head. "Majesty, it is not for me to say..."

"But you could write the king and persuade him."

"I could, but..."

"Please." Liandra's voice brooked no argument. "Do this as a favor to the queen who has shared so much with you, to a queen who would support your choice of husband."

The princess caught her breath. A look that was both pensive and eager filled her lovely face. "I can try, I can ask, but..."

"Write. Ask. And we shall pray that this boon can be shared."

"As you wish." The princess bowed low and then withdrew.

The queen turned away. Leaning against the parapet, she stared out over her city, yet she saw nothing. *So the Prince of Ur was right, magic to quicken a child.* Such magic would be a godsend to her throne. How she longed for another babe, a chance to secure her royal bloodline, a chance for a cherished daughter, a chance to have a love child with Robert. *But would Navarre share?* Truly, the fecund had a huge advantage in the game of kings...in this too, the Prince of Ur was right. And the Tandroth line had never been fecund. The queen hid her hands beneath the folds of her shawl. *Magic to quicken a child.* Liandra wanted it so badly her ringed hands shook.

13

The Mordant

Wars could be overt, the sting of arrows and the rending of swords, or they could be subtle. Wars of the sword wreaked death and bloodshed on a massive scale, but like daisies growing on gravesites, they were soon overshadowed by life, their horror forgotten within a single generation. Unlike wars of the sword, subtle wars could be everlasting. Wielding words to corrupt hearts and twist souls, subtle wars carved deep scars that lasted for centuries, even eons, indelibly etched in the collective memory. By attacking beliefs, values, and morals, subtle wars collapsed cultures and undermined kingdoms. Wielding lies and deceit, the Mordant waged a subtle war against the queen. The oldest harlequin had come to Lanverness to deepen the Great Dark Divide.

Every morning the Mordant sent his minions scurrying through the queen's city, the duegars sniffing for signs of magic, while his assassins searched for knights in Octagon tabards or monks clad in midnight blue robes. In truth, he did not expect his enemies to be so blatant or so bold...but one should never underestimate the stupidity of others. And while his minions searched for his oldest foes, they also took the pulse of the queen's city, aiding in the subtle war of deceit. Collecting gossip and hearsay from taverns, inns and markets, they listened for lies believed.

There was nothing quite so powerful as a lie believed.

The Mordant savored the game of lies. He'd seeded some of them himself. Wielding his cameo focus of many faces, the Mordant spent many a night venturing into the queen's city. Visiting popular taverns, he planted his crop of lies. Cunning deceits laced with just a hint of truth, he disparaged the queen, mocking her right to rule. Reveling in the game, he rose each morning, keen to learn which of his lies had fallen fallow and which had taken root. The true test lay in the frequency with which a lie was repeated.

Every day at noontime, the Mordant climbed the dais in the audience chamber of his mansion and took a seat upon the throne-carved chair. Bishop Borgan sat three steps below, a scribe's writing tablet perched across his ample lap. At the Mordant's signal, Major Tarq unrolled the map of Pellanor across the chamber's floor. As large as a carpet, the patchwork vellum displayed every street, alley, marketplace and tavern within the queen's city. Bright with colors and glorious detail, the map proved that Pellanor's craftsmen could produce almost anything for a hefty weight in gold. The Mordant considered the coin well spent. His gaze roved the map, surveying the battleground of truth versus lies.

His minions made their way back to the mansion, trickling into the audience chamber. One by one, they bowed before his throne and gave their reports. Major Tarq used a spear to move chess pieces across the map, marking the taverns and marketplaces where the gossip was gathered. The Mordant listened closely. Sifting through the snippets of hearsay and gossip, he searched for echoes of his own lies. Some of his lies died a quiet death, having fallen on stony ground, but others were repeated verbatim, while a rare few gained a life of their own, growing and morphing with embellishments to become glorious tales bursting with colorful untruths. The Mordant relished each success and learned from his failures. He made note of the places where his lies were most readily repeated, fertile ground for future endeavors, and which taverns he should shun. It mattered not if those who first repeated his lies were weak of mind and will, often besotted with drink. Success was measured in how often a lie was repeated, for the more times it was retold, the more conviction it gained. If people heard something often enough, they remembered the words while forgetting the source. It was almost as if the masses believed repetition was a sure sign of truth. The Mordant grinned at the thought. The stupidity of mere mortals never ceased to amaze him. How easily he enlisted the people of Pellanor in their own damnation.

The Mordant listened to each report, formulating his next round of lies.

Finished, he gestured for Major Tarq to take up the map. "Now, bring me the boy."

The major rolled the map into a scroll case and then bowed low before departing the chamber. He returned with two guards who carried a boy between them. Gagged and trussed, the urchin-child struggled to no avail. Carrot-bright hair, with freckles splashed across his face, the boy looked to be eight or nine years old. Dressed in a hodge-podge of soot-stained clothes, he looked poor and underfed, the refuse of the back alleys.

His guards forced the boy to his knees.

The Mordant considered the lad. "My guards think you are a thief, but I wonder if you might be something else." He studied the boy. "Why did you break into my house?" He gestured and the guards released the boy's gag.

The urchin glared at the Mordant. "I was hungry."

"Yet my guards found you sneaking into the wine cellar."

The boy shrugged, but his face betrayed the lie. "Some people hide jewels in their wine cellar."

"So you sought to steal?"

The boy remained sullen.

"Bring him to me."

His guards lifted the boy between them. Carrying him up the dais, they forced him to kneel just below the Mordant.

"Look in my eyes, boy."

Compelled, the lad lifted his gaze.

Unleashing his inner Darkness, the Mordant trapped the boy's stare. Breathing deep, he caught the scent of petty Darkness clinging to the lad's soul. *A lowly pickpocket,* yet minor sins were all he needed to gain access. The Mordant followed the thread of Darkness, burrowing into the lad's mind, delving into his very soul. *A thief, a sneak, a snitch...a spy,* the Mordant delved deeper till he found the image of a dapper, red-haired lord. The boy was bound to the lord, sworn to serve for food and coin. The Mordant plucked a name from the lad's mind. "Who is the Lord Sheriff?"

The boy stiffened.

Released from the Mordant's stare, the boy cringed backwards but the guards held him firm.

"He ain't no one."

The Mordant smiled. "Too late for lies." He gestured to the guards. "Take him to the dungeon and show him what he came to see. He'll make a tasty offering to the Dark God."

"*No! I'll...*"

The guards shoved the gag back into the lad's mouth, stifling his screams. Lifting the boy between them, they carried him away to the wine cellar.

"Bring Dolf to me."

One of his servants rushed to obey.

So the queen seeks to defeat the oldest harlequin with a mere pawn. Such a clumsy move, the woman knew not whom she played against.

Clad in black clothing, his master assassin glided into the chamber like a liquid shadow. "You summoned me, my lord?"

"I've discovered a fresh enemy, a dapper, red-haired lord who goes by the name of 'the lord sheriff'. He's enlisting street urchins to spy on us. We suspect he serves the queen. Such a resourceful lord deserves to be eliminated. Find this red-haired lord and make him disappear. Kidnap him and then chain him to the pentacle in the sanctum. I wish to peel the motives from his mind."

"Yes, my lord."

"And, Dolf, I want this done quietly, as if the man disappeared into smoke. I want his sudden absence to add another layer of unease to the queen."

The assassin flashed a feral smile. "It will be as you command."

Plots within plots, he'd bring the queen to a slow boil. And then he'd see what choice her soul would take.

14

Master Numar

Springtime brought a bounty of green to Pellanor's markets. Master Numar rose at first light, donning the modest robes of an apothecary. The brown robes were only half a disguise, for in truth he was a skilled herbalist. Nestling his focus deep in his pocket, he took up his quarterstaff and made his way to the nearest market. Business at his apothecary shop was brisk. He needed to replenish his ingredients, but more importantly, he sought a harvest of rumors, a way to measure the health of the queen's city.

The heady scent of fresh-grown greens greeted him well before he reached the market. Turning the corner, he was not surprised to find the cobblestone square already crowded, everyone keen to make their purchases before the sun's heat ravaged the leafy produce. Brightly colored stalls turned the square into a maze, the farmers selling everything from honey and eggs, to herbs and vegetables and fresh-churned butter. Sniffing deeply, he caught the fragrant scent of thyme and followed it to a farmer's stall. Thyme was such a delightful herb with so many medicinal uses. Indulging in the sport of the market, he dickered fiercely for two bundles. For him, the dickering was not so much about the coins spent as it was about the respect earned. Friendship and respect bought him more secrets than parsimony, so he played the dickering game, always letting the farmers feel as if their extra coins were hard won. Handing over six coppers with a wink and a gracious smile, he snapped off a fresh sprig and wound it around his cloak pin, a ward against the city's fouler smells. Breathing deep, he enjoyed the sprig's luscious springtime scent. Storing the two bundles in his satchel, he wandered among the stalls looking for hyssop and fennel and other ingredients. While his gaze roved the green bounty, he kept an ear open for gossip. Of late he'd heard foul rumors whispered against the queen, but he'd yet to discover their source. Someone spread slander against the Rose Queen, seeking to turn the people against their monarch. Lies were ever the hallmark of Darkness. He'd come to uncover the trail. A snatch of gossip caught his attention. He began to meander that way but then he noticed an odd snuffing sound at his left side. His hand reflexively delved into his left pocket gripping his focus. Glancing down, he expected to see a dog questing with its nose, seeking interesting scents.

A dwarf with pointy teeth sneered up at him.

Master Numar recoiled from the ugly little man. "What do you want?"

The dwarf hissed, staring at him as if he were something good to eat.

The master brandished his quarterstaff. "Be gone!"

Casting a baleful glare, the dwarf slunk away, disappearing into the crowd.

Master Numar shuddered. Something about the little man was deeply unsettling. Shrugging off the encounter, he pressed deeper into the market. He found a farmer selling flowering fennel and bought a bundle of the feathery leaves, but as he paid for his purchase the master felt a hard stare drilling into his back. Whirling, he spied the dwarf crouched by a table, watching him.

He knows! A cold certainty settled into the master's stomach. The dwarf did not look like a killer, yet secrecy was the master's best defense. He felt the need to run yet he knew it would be unwise to draw more attention. Moving away from the dwarf, he slipped into the thickest part of the crowd. Like a minnow moving among many, he followed the crowd, using them for cover. Keeping his fist locked on his focus, he scanned for the dwarf. Jostling through the market, he waited for his chance. The crowd's movement seemed aimless, a random torture of meandering. Sweat beaded his brow, striving for patience, but then the crowd pulsed near an alley. He fled the market, slipping into the city's shadowy back ways. Racing down the alley, he turned left and then right, taking the path that seemed most evasive. Ducking beneath a shaded doorway, he waited, straining to hear over his racing heart. He expected the clatter of footsteps running behind, but he heard nothing. His back pressed to the door, he kept listening, waiting till his heart slowed to a regular beat.

Still nothing.

Needing to be sure, he crept back to the last corner. Pressed to the wall, he carefully peered around. At first he saw nothing...but then he noticed a furtive movement at the far end of the alley. *The dwarf!* But instead of running, he was crouched down, moving slowly, methodically, his head slewing back and forth...*as if he followed a trail.*

A thread of fear ran through the monk. He studied the hard-packed dirt of the alleyway and saw no tracks, nothing to betray his path, and then he remembered the strange sniffing sound in the marketplace. *My scent! Perhaps the dwarf tracks me by my scent!* The thought evoked a primal fear, the sound of wolves howling in the night. *Perhaps it's just the pungent scent of my herbs.* He soothed his fear with strained logic. Shrugging the satchel from his back, he left it lying in the shadows. Plucking the sprig of thyme from his cloak pin, he tossed it aside and scurried back down the alleyway. Moving quickly but quietly, he sought to leave no trail. He ran blind through the back ways, twisting and turning, seeking to escape.

Five times he tried doors and five times they remained locked, bolted, closed. Trust was scarce in the back alleys...and then he spied a red lantern, the age-old symbol for a house of ill-repute. He hurried towards the lantern. Dispelling any doubts, the iron door knocker was shaped like two lovers entwined. He rapped on the door, wanting to be heard without making too much noise. No one answered. Twice more he knocked.

A bolt slid back and the door eased open. A sleepy-eyed woman in a drab velvet robe peered out. Her brow furrowed. She took one look at him and began to slam the door. "We're closed."

He thrust his foot into the opening. "I just need a room to rest for an hour."

"Get an inn, grandfather."

He flashed a fist full of gold coins. "I'm not paying inn prices."

Her eyes widened. She reconsidered, slowly opening the door.

He slipped inside. "Close and bolt it."

"Are you bringing trouble to this house?"

"I'm bringing gold to this house."

Her avarice won out. She closed and bolted the door.

The master sagged in relief. The small parlor smelled seedy, a mixture of sour ale and cheap perfume overlaying other smells he did not care to name.

The woman gave him an appraising stare. "Yer a bit old for an early morning romp."

"I'm not seeking a romp. I just need a room on the second floor with a window overlooking this alleyway." He held three golds towards her. "Show me to the room, and when I leave, I'll put two more golds in your hand."

She gave him a petulant pout. "Three."

"Done."

Snatching the coins from his hand, the madam scowled, realizing she could have bargained for more. "This way." She led him to a stairway. "You can use Lucinda's room. But if you so much as touch the girl, you'll pay double the golds."

"Agreed." He followed her to a front room. She opened the door without knocking, ushering him into a small bedroom. A girl with hair dyed scarlet red peered from tussled sheets. Instead of looking startled, she looked mildly annoyed.

"Relax, Lucinda, he's just here to look." The woman's voice held a hint of wry amusement. "If you can get the old man to touch you, there's two golds in it for ya."

The master crossed to the window. "I'm just here for the view."

"So you say." The madam lingered by the door, a shrewd look on her face. "I'll leave the door open." Her look turned hard. "Don't leave without paying."

"I won't." The windows were heavily curtained, shielding the daylight. Instead of opening the heavy damask, the master stood pressed to the wall, peering behind the faded curtains. Dirt encrusted the window, tinting the pane brown, but it gave a decent view of the alleyway below. From his angled perch, the master kept watch, his anxious gaze scanning for the dwarf.

"Wouldn't you rather come to bed?"

Striking a suggestive pose, the girl had dropped her sheets, displaying her naked wares. From the stretch marks, he judged she'd already had a babe or two. Such a hard and heartless life, he pitied the girls who thought a brothel was their only choice. "Thank you, child, but there's no need. I'm really just here for the view."

"But Minara said..."

Hearing the pout in her voice, he extended his hand toward her, offering two gold coins. "For you. Keep them for yourself, I won't tell the madam. Now, please just let me keep watch."

She took the coins, planting a tender kiss on his hand.

The delicacy of her kiss surprised him, but he refused to be distracted. "Cover yourself." His words were harsher than he intended. Turning back to the window, he resumed his vigil. Leaning against the wall, he pondered the riddle of the dwarf. In his dash through the back alleyways, he'd recalled a vague rumor in the monastery, something about a creature who sniffed magic. He shuddered at the thought, making the hand sign against evil. Such an ability would make any disguise impossible, destroying the Order's hidden ways. Enemies came in many guises, even dwarves. He wanted to believe the dwarf's nearness to his focus was only a coincidence, but wishful thinking could be dangerous, even deadly. Either way, he needed to know.

For the turn of an hourglass, he kept watch. Just when he thought it was safe, he saw the dwarf slink into the alleyway, his head slewing back and forth, his nostrils flared.

So it's true!

The dwarf crept to the very door of the brothel, sniffing the handle like a dog on a scent. For a handful of heartbeats, he crouched by the door, and then he looked upward, toward the master's window.

The master jerked backwards without disturbing the curtains. *Did he see me?* Counting to a hundred, he stayed pressed to the wall, and then he cautiously peered back through the window.

The little man was gone, no longer by the door.

Puzzled, the master scanned the alleyway. He found the dwarf sitting cross-legged in the shadows, his gaze fixed on the brothel's door like a hound awaiting its quarry.

The master fingered his focus, considering his choices, but magic of his sort should never be wielded lightly. His gaze snapped to the girl. "Does the brothel have a back door?"

She nodded.

"Good." He explained the favor he needed. "Now get dressed and take me to the madam so I can pay her fee. Then show me to the back door." He looked away while she pulled on a faded red robe.

"Come." Her gaze was downcast, her brazen gestures fled.

Clothing transformed her, instead of a wanton whore, she appeared demure, almost shy. Perhaps clothing brought out her true nature, a pity she'd been ensnared by a brothel. The master followed her down the stairs and found the madam waiting for him, her hand extended. He paid the promised three golds. "Thank you for the use of your window. The girl will show me to the rear door."

The madam gave him a lewd look. "Come again, your gold is always welcome."

Anxious to be gone, he said, "I won't take any more of your time."

The girl showed him to the rear door, opening the heavy bolt.

He peered out, blinking at the bright sunshine. Instead of an alley, the door opened onto a narrow bolt-hole, a backdoor escape path threading between buildings. "This will serve." He handed the girl two more gold coins. "Pay the madam your fee and then find another life. You don't belong here."

The girl looked startled as a deer, as if she'd forgotten kindness. Taking the coins, she secreted them in her robe and then dropped a curtsy towards him. "Thank you, m'lord."

"I'm not a lord, child. Now close and bolt the door after me."

He waited till he heard the bolt slide shut and then he hurried down the narrow walkway. Barely more than a shoulder-width wide, the back way stank of refuse and stale piss. He reached the end, the cleft between buildings opening onto a wider alley. Turning left, the master made his way back to the lane that fronted the brothel. Crossing to the shady side, he cautiously peered down the alley. The dwarf was there, crouched in the shadows, keeping watch on the brothel door.

Shifting his own gaze to the door, the master tightened his grip on his quarterstaff, waiting.

Nothing happened.

Perhaps he'd taken too long, but then the brothel door eased open.

The dwarf rose from a crouch, his gaze locked on the door.

"Come again, m'lord."

Hearing the girl's voice, the master took three quick strides towards the dwarf, wielding his quarterstaff in a lightning strike. The dwarf turned, but not fast enough. The quarterstaff struck him a numbing blow on the right shoulder.

The dwarf yelped, falling backwards on his butt, his right arm dangling useless.

The brothel door slammed shut.

The dwarf drew a dagger with his left hand.

The quarterstaff whirled in a blur, striking the dagger from the dwarf's hand. "Whom do you serve?" The master held the quarterstaff in a threatening pose. "Name your master."

The dwarf snarled, flinching away.

"Whom do you serve?"

The little man's eyes blazed with hate. "Not tell you, never tell you."

Impatient for answers, Master Numar twirled the quarterstaff, striking two solid blows on the dwarf's ribs. "Speak the name and you shall live."

"You fight with sticks...the master fights with...pain." Sneering, the dwarf flicked his wrist, hurling a dagger towards the master's face.

Flinching backwards, Master Numar narrowly avoided the blade.

The dwarf used the diversion to scuttle away, running down the alley. The master leaped after him, desperate to stop him. The dwarf was quick, but the quarterstaff's length shortened the gap. Wielding the polished ironwood in an overhand strike, the master landed a solid blow. The dwarf buckled to his knees and then dropped like a heavy sack. Skidding to a stop, Master Numar crouched beside the crumpled dwarf. His hand searched for a heartbeat, but he'd struck too hard. The dwarf's skull was caved in, felled by a killing blow. Struggling to regain his breath, Master Numar slumped beside the dwarf, bitten by regret. "You should have told me the name." Rolling the little man over, he searched his clothing, but found no clue to his master's identity. *Dead and forever silent,* the master knew he needed to get away from the corpse. Seeking the subterfuge of age, he leaned on his quarterstaff, using it like a walking stick, and made his way back to the cobblestone streets.

A magic-sniffing dwarf...and vile lies levied against the queen. Darkness had come to Pellanor. He needed to warn the others. He needed to keep vigilant and unmask the enemy before death came calling to his very doorstep.

15

The Priestess

Forsaking her queen's crown, the Priestess rode south in search of immortality. Leaving Rhune in General Tarmin's capable hands, she traveled to Pellanor in the guise of a wealthy noblewoman. Steffan rode by her right side, her consort bedecked as a wealthy lord. Braxus rode to her left, serving as her handsome seneschal, while faithful Hugo rode point, her steadfast captain of the guard. Her two handmaidens, Lydia and Tara, trailed behind wearing modest attire. Thirty plain-dressed soldiers, loyal swordsmen who'd come with her from the Oracle Isle, surrounded her small party with a protection of sharp steel, discouraging robbers and cutthroats. A pair of pack horses carried two wooden chests, both laden with her womanly wiles. The larger cedar chest held elegant silks, and jewels, and scents, her trappings of seduction, while the smaller rosewood chest held her harvest of deathly delights. Armed with her best weapons, seduction and poison, the Priestess set a fast pace, eager to claim her destiny.

They rode south, passing beyond her small kingdom and into Lanverness. The countryside bloomed bright green in the full throat of spring, yet the signs of war were legion. For every thriving village, the next was burned and blackened, abandoned to crows. For every two fields tilled by farmers, a third lay fallow. The Priestess counted the scars of war. Death and destruction lay like a heavy yoke across Lanverness, yet the queen's people struggled to rebuild their lives. The villagers and farmers put up a brave fight, determined to recover their prosperity, but a far greater danger stalked the Rose kingdom, doomed by the Mordant's attention. Lanverness was fodder for the gods, though few mortals knew it.

They trotted past another burnt farmhouse, the timbers blackened, the roof caved in like a toothless mouth. The Priestess watched Steffan, seeking signs of shame or pride, but he showed neither. Instead, he grew more sullen with every passing league. Brooding beneath a hooded cloak, he kept his face hidden in shadows.

The Priestess matched her stallion's pace to his gelding's stride. "What troubles you?"

He flashed an angry scowl, spitting the name like a curse. "Pellanor."

Nothing more needed to be said. She knew he loathed returning to Pellanor, to the place of his defeat, but every game of power had its price, and this was his. Her own price hung around her neck. Shuddering at the horror of her last scrying, she reached within her bodice to touch the remnants of the Eye. Her most powerful magic sundered by the Mordant, yet she'd refused to relinquish the remnants. She'd had the three pieces of the great moonstone fitted together and bound with a cage of silver wire. An ancient relic entombed in silver, she wore it on a chain around her neck, a memory of power lost and vengeance vowed.

The trip south seemed to take forever, but on a sunny morning they finally gained the outskirts of the queen's city. Scaffolding spider-webbed the city walls, workmen scurrying up and down ladders. The central gate was completed, twin towers proudly supporting a crenellated barbican over a pair of ironclad gates. Flanking the gatehouse, stonemasons troweled a white paste of crushed stone over a crude patchwork of cobbled buildings. The Priestess assumed the white paste strengthened the walls and towers while hiding the ugly patchwork beneath. Glistening white, the finished walls sparkled bright in the sunlight, casting an image of enduring strength and prosperity. "Beautiful," the word came unbidden to her lips, but the walls held a deeper message. Built on cobbled buildings, they bespoke a practical mind hidden beneath beauty's veneer, the hallmarks of a ruling queen. *Well done, sister*, the Priestess flashed a feline smile, appreciating the double entendre.

The ironbound gates stood open, welcoming the flow of commerce. Guards in emerald tabards watched from above, yet they proved oblivious to the hidden threat riding towards them. Following a merchant's wagon piled high with colorful fabrics, the Priestess and her entourage passed through Pellanor's gates without pause.

Steffan spurred ahead, guiding them through the cobbled streets. The queen's city sprawled in every direction, dwarfing even mighty Salmythra. The Priestess stared, impressed by the colorful bustle, yet Steffan knew his way, threading a path through the crowds. He led them unerringly towards the wealthy district, to an upper class tavern bearing the name of 'The Silver Swan'. Lads in gray livery rushed to take their horses. Dust-stained and travel-weary, the Priestess and her entourage climbed the steps to the inn.

Braxus, serving as her seneschal, negotiated for their rooms. Paying extra golds, he secured the entire second floor. The innkeeper, a hooked-nosed man with a bad limp, was lavish in his groveling, insisting on showing the Priestess to her room. "So pleased to have you grace my inn." He gestured towards the staircase. "If you'd come a few moon-turns sooner, we'd not have had rooms available. The city was bursting with refugees from the war, but the queen's blight drove them back to the countryside, taking the very bread from my mouth."

"The queen's blight?" The turn of phrase caught her attention.

"A bloody tithe squeezed from innkeepers to pay for the queen's wall." He ushered her down the hallway to the last room. "They're calling it a folly, saying it will never be finished in time. The queen sucks us all dry with her tithes and taxes. A bloody great waste, if you ask me." He unlocked the door, showing her to a well-appointed room. A large four-poster bed thick with quilts dominated the chamber, a copper washbasin sat in the corner, damask curtains hung on the window. The faint scent of dried lavender provided an unexpected feminine touch. "Saved me best room for your ladyship." Executing a clumsy bow, he handed her the iron key. "Ask for Burt if you need anything."

"I'll be needing a tub and plenty of hot water."

Steffan pressed a gold coin into the innkeepers hand, "And a bottle of your best brandy," as he ushered the man from the room. The door closed and they were finally alone. Steffan kicked off his boots and sprawled on the bed. "Feather mattress and thick quilts, not bad. The rooms are small, but the beds are comfy and the meals are tasty. As I recall, their roast quail is particularly good."

The Priestess removed her travel-stained cloak. "Don't get too comfortable, you're not staying."

"What?" He gave her a sharp-eyed glare.

"Remember why we're here. We're playing against the oldest harlequin, we'll need every advantage. The Mordant expects me, but not you. You're our dagger hidden in the dark."

He gaped at her. "And just what do you expect me to do against the Mordant?"

She bit her lip. "I don't know."

He scowled, "So for no real reason, I'm banished from your side?"

She gave him a coy smile, "Not at night."

Steffan flashed a wolf's smile. "That's more like it." He prowled towards her, but a knock interrupted.

She forestalled him. "Come."

Her men entered carrying her two chests, the cedar and the rosewood, seduction and poison sitting side by side. A parade of servants followed bearing an enormous copper tub and buckets of steaming water. The innkeeper reappeared, flourishing a bottle of brandy and two goblets. Steffan nabbed the bottle, ushering the man to the door.

Her handmaidens came to attend her. Lydia knelt to remove her boots, while Tara added oils and scents to the bath water, creating an alchemy of feminine delights.

Steffan poured himself a large goblet of brandy and then sprawled on the bed, watching as her clothes came off. A lusty smile filled his face, a cat anticipating a bowl of cream.

The Priestess felt his stare, enjoying his rising hunger. She made it a tease, slowly divesting the layers. Naked, she stepped into the tub. Steam rising in curls around her, she gave him a come-hither glance.

Lydia reached for a sponge, but Steffan said, "I'll do that."

Her handmaidens retreated with knowing smiles, closing the door behind them.

Steffan knelt by the tub, lathering the sponge. "Am I truly banished?"

"For your own protection. Surprise is our ally."

He nibbled her ear, caressing her skin with the soapy sponge, lathering all her curves. "Will you really go to him?"

"I must."

The sponge moved down and around, leaving a soapy trail. She groaned in delight. Abandoning the sponge, he gathered her breasts in his hands, the soap making the orbs slick and slippery. "But I'll see you at night."

"Yes." She groaned with pleasure.

"Will you let him touch you?"

He'd never minded before. "It's what I do."

"Must you?" His teeth grazed her nipple, a burst of pain and pleasure.

"You know I must." She reached for the bindings on his trousers, her hands slippery with soap, yet she freed him from the leather. "I'll need all my wiles against him."

He groaned, moving against her. "But will you let him touch you...like this?" Slick with soap, his hand delved down below the water. Finding her hidden gate, he plunged deep.

"Yes!" She arched her back, speared with delight.

He shucked his trousers like a snake shedding skin, and then he was in the tub with her. Sloshing water over the sides, he forced her knees apart. And then he was in her. She shuddered in ecstasy, rocking waves across the soapy water. Her long legs wrapped around him, riding him hard. Lifting her onto his hips, he stood, staying deep inside her. She clung to him, fingernails raking across his back, shuddering with his every stroke. Water droplets fell like rain as they rode their pleasure. He bellowed his ecstasy as they both came.

Stepping from the tub, he carried her to the bed, collapsing on a mound of towels. Wet and slick, he pinned her to the bedding, his voice husky with hidden intent. "Don't go." He tightened his grip. "I don't want you to go. Not to him."

"You know I must. It's what I do."

"Is there no other way?"

"Seduction is my best weapon."

"And poison is the other!" His voice leaped with fervor. "Why not kill him and be done with it!"

"Shhhhhhh," she hissed in warning. "We dare not kill him, not without consent of the Dark Lord. Would you risk our god's wrath?"

"No." His voice was surly but she spied a flicker of fear in his eyes.

"We tread a dangerous path, carving power from the Mordant's shadow."

"Can we keep what you carve?" His gaze blazed bright. "Will there be enough for the two of us?"

"The Dark Lord encourages his dedicates to compete for his favors, but to do that, we must enter the Great Dance. That's the real reason we're here. I'll dance with the Mordant, learn his plans, learn his weaknesses, and then we'll plot our own moves."

"So you'll go to him. You'll bed him." Bitterness laced his voice.

Perhaps he truly loves me, her breath caught at the thought. Caressing his face, she tried to soften the harsh lash of truth. "I'll *always* be the Oracle Priestess, the dark succubus, the queen of sex."

Steffan straddled her, his face fierce with the need to possess. "Then go to him with my scent on your skin and my seed deep in you," and then he took her again and again, rough and hard, as if to brand her with his own mark.

16

Tokar

His brother was missing. Three days missing...which meant he was dead, for no snargon of the duegars would disobey the Mordant. Those who could scent magic knew far better than most the awesome power of their dread lord. Tokar shuddered just thinking of it. The Mordant wore magic like a raiment. Being in the dread lord's presence was nearly overwhelming, evoking a strange mixture of heady ecstasy and slavering fear. Their lord trailed a magical scent that was irresistible, forbidden, indomitable. To Tokar, the Mordant smelled like a god.

No, if his brother was missing, he was dead.

And the dread lord knew it.

The Mordant gave orders to scour the city, to find the monk or the knight who had slain one of his snargons. For Tokar, the order was more than mere duty, it was personal. He swore by all that was Dark that he'd find his brother's killer.

He knew Sorkon had been patrolling the southwest quarter of the queen's city, so that's where he started. Clad in a hodge-podge of ill-fitting clothes, he made his way to the market, searching for the lingering scent of magic.

People jostled against him, hardly noticing him.

He hated this city, so undisciplined, so unordered. In the Dark Citadel he had standing and privilege, a respected snargon of the Mordant's guard, but here, in this soft southern land, he was nothing more than a runtish, deformed man, someone to be overlooked, stepped upon, and ignored. Tokar stood no taller than most men's belt buckles, yet these southerners overlooked him at their peril, for he served a dread lord. When the Mordant revealed his true power, the southerners would tremble, learning their place in the new order. Tokar smiled a hungry grin, flashing his pointy teeth to scare a southern child. The girl ran screaming, a small satisfaction.

Breathing deep, he patrolled the market, seeking the scent of magic. The city was full of smells, the unwashed next to the flower-scented nobles, fresh-farmed greens sold near rotting refuse. Tokar caught the scents of baking breads mingling with soured ale, of flowering vines and reeking chamber pots, yet none of the scents, neither the repugnant nor the delightful, could mask the potent smell of magic. Complex and ambrosial, magic was like no other scent, teasing the mind and waking the imagination. The best snargons could tell Light from Dark, potent from weak, active from latent...and Tokar was one of the best.

For three days he prowled the marketplace, yet he found no whiff of magic. Frustrated, he widened the search, exploring the cobbled streets. Noon-time and supper crowds afforded the best hunting hours. Tokar flowed unnoticed through the throng, breathing deeply...and then he caught it, the unmistakable scent of magic. Just a faint tease, yet it was enough to lead him through the crowd. Like a fisherman reeling in a line, he followed the scent, yet he kept a wary lookout, for he dared not be seen by the magic user. Tokar sought to avenge his brother, not to share his fate.

The scent grew stronger, leading him to his quarry.

Powerful magic, he shuddered at the smell. This quarry was dangerous, a fitting prize for his lord the Mordant.

Tokar dodged in and out of the supper crowd, weaving his way towards the magic. His nostrils flared at the strength of the scent, old and powerful. *Close, too close,* yet he needed to be sure. The scent led him towards two men. One was stocky and muscular, a short sword belted to his side, and the other was old, a white-haired elder in flowing robes of dark brown. The two men were locked in a hushed conversation, walking too close together for him to discern the magic user.

Some might assume the older man carried the magic, but Tokar knew better. Magic was a power coveted by all.

The older man stopped, casting a sharp glance backward.

Tokar dodged behind a fat woman carrying fresh-baked pies. His heart thundering, he hid in the woman's ample shadow, praying he wasn't seen. When no one came hunting, he dared to emerge from behind the woman. The two men were further away, still walking together, seemingly unaware they were being followed. Tokar dawdled, drifting backwards, giving his quarry more of a leash. Magic users were dangerous and he dared not be caught.

His quarry seemed to walk aimlessly, but then they came to an apothecary shop, a white unicorn carved over the lintel. Tokar ducked behind a rain barrel, keeping watch. The two men stood for a while, talking in hushed tones, but then they parted. The swordish one kept walking while the old man entered the apothecary, a cheerful bell ringing as he opened the door.

Tokar waited, crouched behind the barrel, wary of a trap. When neither man reappeared, he stepped from behind the barrel and sauntered past the shop. The scent of magic led to the apothecary... and went no further. Tokar flashed a crooked grin, yet he needed to be sure. Hiding amongst the crowd, he circled around, returning to the rain barrel. Sitting behind the barrel, he kept watch on the shop. People wandered by, some entering the shop, mostly women, but the old man never reappeared. The sun sank to dusk, candles and lanterns adding a warm glow to the cobbled street, yet still he saw no sign of the magic user. Satisfied that he'd run his quarry to ground, Tokar stood, easing a cramp from his leg. "You'll pay for my brother," he hissed the words like a curse. Turning his back on the apothecary, he made his way through the city to the Mordant's manse. He'd found his brother's killer, a powerful magic user, a fitting present for his dread lord.

17

The Mordant

The Mordant reverted to his true colors, choosing dark leathers and a cowled cloak of deepest black. Unlocking his jewel box, he chose his magic with great care. Fondling rings and armbands glittering with gems, his hand passed over focuses endowed with soul magic and deceit. Instead, he sought his battle magics, focuses empowered to attack and defend. Of all the focuses he'd collected over his many lifetimes, battle magic was the most rare and therefore the most coveted. His most powerful weapon, the crimson crystal of pain, he fitted to the prongs atop his iron staff. The staff was designed to evoke the primal fear of ancient wizards, a showy conceit, yet it seemed appropriate for the occasion. Tonight, bedecked in glorious Darkness, he'd confront an ancient foe...and there'd be nothing subtle about it.

"Tell me again what you saw."

The snargon knelt before him. "An old man, dressed in robes of brown and leaning on a quarterstaff. He walked with a swordish man, but it was the old one who smelled of magic. They parted in front of an apothecary shop. The old man went in and never came out."

"And what of his magic."

"Powerful...and very old."

The Mordant grinned, another focus for his trove of power. "Good. You've done well, now come."

The snargon followed like a well trained hound. Clad in power, the Mordant strode from his solar to find a hand-picked cadre of assassins and duegars waiting for him. Wearing dark clothing and bristling with weapons, they bowed low before him.

"Arm your darts with sleep not death. I want this foe taken alive."

He led them to the back of the manse, through the kitchen and out into the back alleyway. Saddled horses waited for them held by grooms. The Mordant mounted a dark stallion. Setting the butt of his staff in a lance cup, he gestured to begin. Krugar, a ninth rank assassin, led the small host through the back alleyways at a swift trot.

Night darkened the sky, thick clouds shuttering a crescent moon, yet there was light in the queen's city. Candles, torches and lanterns held the velvety darkness at bay. The light annoyed the Mordant, as if the queen's city had the audacity to snub the darkness...but where there was light, there were also shadows, and shadows he knew very well.

His men exploited the shadows, weaving a path through the back alleys.

The queen's city slept, still hours from dawn. As expected, the alleyways proved empty. The Mordant caught faint whiffs of fresh-baked bread and stoked iron from a nearby forge, but most of the alleyways stank of piss, sour ale, and rotting refuse. The queen thought her city better than others, but tossed piss pots reeked the same no matter the ruler.

A stray cat bolted in front of his horse.

His stallion shied. Yanking hard on the bit, the Mordant kept his horse in check.

Unchallenged, they threaded their way through the honeycombed streets, moving at a steady trot.

A duegar slipped from a side alley, whistling a warning.

Pulling his stallion to a halt, the Mordant dismounted, tossing his reins to a guard. "How close?"

"The apothecary is two streets over." The duegar grinned, showing teeth filed to points. "You can't miss it, my lord. The shop boasts a white unicorn head carved into the lintel."

"A white unicorn," the Mordant sneered at the conceit, "as if fairy tales will save them." He gripped the Staff of Pain, eager for the confrontation. "And the enemy?"

"All three are inside. The old one is the one you want. Posing as a master apothecary, he has pale white hair and a long beard and goes by the name of Master Numar. He's the only one who reeks of magic."

"And the other two?"

"Younger men, posing as apprentices. They look like they could wield a sword...or a cudgel."

"Nothing my assassins cannot deal with."

"True, my lord."

"Aside from the older monk, have you smelt magic on any of the others?"

"No, lord...though we've not dared to send a snargon into the shop, lest we warn them of our presence."

"Anything else?"

Krugar answered. "I sent an assassin in last night to scout. Two apprentices sleep in a small room behind the shop. The master, the one with the magic, sleeps in a back bedroom."

"The assassin went undetected?"

"Yes, lord."

"Good." The Mordant grinned. "Let's see what type of magic the old man wields." He gestured to the others. "Come." The Mordant strode through the empty streets toward the shop, his black cloak swirling behind, his iron staff in his hand. He relished the coming confrontation, a chance to cower his enemy with magic. It had been a long time since he'd unleashed his power against a monk.

A white unicorn was brazenly carved over the apothecary doorway, as if the mythical creature could somehow hold Darkness at bay. An assassin stepped from the shadows, his voice held to a whisper. "Let me do this for you, lord."

"No, the monk is mine. I want to see his face when we take him, when he realizes he's met his doom."

Bowing, the assassin removed a blowpipe from the pouch at his belt. "Guards are posted at the back in case they try to flee. The front door has a flimsy lock, but a bell is rigged to ring once it opens."

"Deal with the lock, then you and Krugar slip inside. Be prepared to take the two younger men." The Mordant flashed a predator's smile. "Leave the monk to me."

"And the bell?"

"It matters not." The Mordant cast a warning look their way. "Remember, deal sleep not death. I want them taken alive."

The two dark-clad assassins prepared their blowpipes and then led the way. Tokar, the snargon of the duegars who'd tracked the magic user to his lair, stayed close by the Mordant's side. The first assassin picked the lock, carefully easing the door open. A cheerful bell rang a gentle greeting. Silent as cats, the assassins slipped inside. Threading their way to the back of the shop, they crouched near the rear doorway, lethal shadows lurking for prey.

The Mordant glided inside. His face hidden in the depths of his cowled robe, he stood still as Darkness, poised to confront his oldest foe. He held the Staff of Pain in his right hand, a potent magic waiting to be wielded. The snargon crouched low by his side. Like a faithful dog, the duegar's nostrils flared wide, sniffing for magic. The Mordant's gaze roved across the apothecary, everything clean and orderly. Dried herbs hung from the ceiling, spreading a medicinal aroma of bayberry and thyme through the shop. Glass jars filled one wall, a long table ran down the middle, the marble top polished to a shine.

Lantern light flared to life in the back room. Footsteps walked towards them. "Who's there?"

A sandy-haired young man appeared in the far doorway. He took two steps and then the snick of a blown dart took him in the throat. Issuing a strangled gurgle, he fell forward. One assassin caught the lantern, carefully setting it aside, while the other caught the young man. Dragging him away from the doorway, the assassin stuffed a gag in his mouth and bound his hands.

Lantern light illumed the shop, casting a buttery glow across countless jars and bottles.

A voice from the back said, "Simon, who's there?"

The Mordant chose to answer. "I seek Master Numar on a matter of life and death."

"Just a moment."

The Mordant grinned, amazed by the naivety of his foe. Those who dealt in the truth were always too trusting. While he waited, the Mordant summoned the monk imprisoned within the depths of his mind. *Come and witness how I deal with one of your precious masters.* He felt the monk quaking in terror, sauce to his pleasure.

A second light flared in the back followed by more footsteps. An older man appeared in the doorway. Clad in a soft brown robe, his face bore the wrinkles of age, his pale white hair cascading below his shoulders, his beard long and tangled, but his blue eyes flashed sharp and keen. "Who asks for me?"

In the depths of the Mordant's mind, the captured monk screamed an impotent warning.

The snargon hissed at the scent of magic.

The Mordant summoned the Darkness within. He felt his presence grow, as if mortal bonds could not contain his power. His cowl slipped back. A thousand years of evil spilled from his gaze. The crystal in the Staff of Pain awakened, glowing a malevolent red. "Do you not know me?"

The monk flinched backwards. "*You!*"

"I've come to claim my due."

The monk reached for the pocket of his robe. "*Gideon, run!*"

The snargon hissed in warning.

The Mordant pointed his staff at the monk. Loosing a bolt of pain, he imagined a dragon's talon slicing into the monk's stomach, rending flesh, ripping bone, inflicting a terrible agony... and then he willed it to be so.

The monk crumpled to the floor, his face contorted in agony. He gripped his stomach as if seeking to contain his entrails.

A man bearing a cudgel appeared in the doorway. *"Master!"* Rage twisting his face, he leaped to the attack, but the assassins dealt with him. Darts struck the young man in the face and throat, toppling him backwards.

The Mordant kept his will focused on the monk. Deepening the torture, he tightened the dragon's talons, twisting and pulling, imagining intestines ripping like white worms. "Where is your blade bearer? Where is your vaunted champion?"

Pale-faced with pain, his brow beaded with sweat, the monk grimaced, refusing to speak.

"In every lifetime, you send a champion against me, but always he fails. Where is he this time? What guise does he wear? Who wields the crystal dagger?"

The monk convulsed across the floor, but he did not answer.

The Mordant redoubled the agony. "For a thousand years I've waited for this lifetime, for all the pieces to fall into place. This hour is mine. Feel my power, feel my wrath!"

The monk screamed.

"I shall make a gorelabe of your flesh. The dregs of your soul shall serve me and your magic shall be mine!"

"Never!" The monk spat the word. Thrashing across the floor, he grimaced against the agony. *"You...shall...not...win!"* Yanking his right hand from his pocket, the monk punched his fist toward the Mordant. A fireball appeared.

A fireball!

Growing in size, the fireball hurtled towards the Mordant, a sizzling ball of death.

The Mordant had but one heartbeat to react. Reaching for the focus binding his right forearm, he yelled a command. *"Nullo!"*

The fireball struck. Heat raged against his face, fierce as a forge. The fireball punched the Mordant backwards, like being struck by a Taal's fist. His head hammered the wall, hitting hard. Pain bludgeoned him. *Not possible!* The Mordant struggled to remain conscious, but Darkness claimed him, the smell of burnt flesh sizzling the air.

18

The Mordant

The pained dulled and the Mordant awoke. An ugly-faced duegar crouched beside him, peering into his face, his breath foul. "My lord, you live!"

Anger spiked through the Mordant. "Of course I live!" He found himself crumpled against the wall. His head ached but otherwise he seemed unharmed. The Mordant took stock of his surroundings. *Stink of burnt flesh and charred wood,* and then he remembered. *A fireball!* Tightening his fist on the Staff of Pain, the Mordant climbed to his feet. Leaning on the staff, he surveyed the damage. Not a smudge on his dark robes...but the shop was another matter. Timbers were blackened and burned, jars melted to glass puddles. The apothecary shop was burnt to a husk, a testimony to the fireball's fierce heat. Small flames still sputtered amongst the dried herbs. Charred walls reflected a glowing warmth. The fireball had scorched the shop to a blackened ruin. *A fireball!* His defensive spell had worked, shielding himself and the snargon crouched by his side, forcing the fireball back on its maker. *Its maker.*

The Mordant crossed the charred expanse, the crisped floorboards crunching beneath his boots. The hot stench of burnt flesh answered his question. Five charred corpses lay crumpled on the floor. Their skin blackened and burnt, they oozed a foul pink fluid, proof the monk had died by his own magic.

The Mordant snapped his fingers, summoning the snargon. "Find the focus." He pointed to the monk's charred corpse. "I want the fireball."

Tokar knelt, sniffing the corpse, like a pig rooting for truffles. Three times he sniffed the corpse from foot to head. His voice reluctant, he cowered to the floor. "Nothing, lord."

Anger erupted in the Mordant. "It must be there! Pry open his fist."

The monk's right hand was seared to a charred knob. The snargon pried at the blackened fingers. Two broke, leaking more foul fluid, but he got the hand open, revealing a small metal disc.

The Mordant yearned to snatch it up but he had the good sense to wait. Caution was advisable when it came to new-found magic. "Sniff it."

Tokar held the disc to his nose, his nostrils flaring wide. The small man cringed. "Nothing, lord. The magic is dead...or fled."

The Mordant extended his hand. The snargon yielded the focus, cautiously placing it in his lord's hand and then retreating to crouch near the monk's corpse, as if he preferred the dead to the living. The Mordant studied the focus. A small brass disc inset with a quartz crystal, faint rune marks scribed around the edge. At its heart, the crystal was shattered, blackened as if the fireball had consumed its magic, burnt from within. The Mordant refused to be foiled. Magic was the ultimate prize...and he wanted the fireball. Locking his fist around the small disc, he willed the magic to waken, but the focus remained dormant. Anger sizzled through him. His gaze snapped to the snargon. "Tell me what you saw."

Tokar cowered low. "The monk writhed in pain, smitten by your dread magic, but then I smelled the way his own magic flared, hot and potent. The monk's fist shot out and he hurled a fireball. *A fireball,* a terrible burning orb the height of a man. The heat was hellish." The snargon shuddered. "I thought I was dead, but you, great lord, you summoned a shield of magic." Tokar sketched the sign of Darkness, his voice fervent with awe. "The fireball struck, throwing you backwards, but your shield held, refusing the flames. Repulsed, the fireball rebounded, flying backwards it scorched everything in its path. The monk, the assassins, everything consumed by flames. Scorched to char, the monk died by his own magic." The snargon prostrated himself before the Mordant. "Your magic is superior. You wield the magic of the gods." He kissed the Mordant's boots. "You saved me, dread lord."

"No, I did not." The Mordant loosed his anger, unleashing the Staff of Pain.

Tokar gasped, assaulted by a searing agony. Writhing on the floor, he gazed up at the Mordant, his voice a harsh croak. "Why?"

The Mordant intensified the pain, pouring his anger into the small man. Screaming, the snargon's heels thrashed the floor, his back nearly bent double. Froth appeared at his mouth. He clawed at his own throat, his eyes bulging wide and wild. The snargon convulsed...and then lay dead, his open eyes becoming vacant.

"You saw too much." The Mordant placed the fireball focus deep in his pocket next to the malachite coin. Turning, he glided from the ruined shop. Three assassins and two duegars came running like hounds called to the whistle.

Clavis was the first to reach him. The young assassin bowed low. "My lord, how can I serve?"

"Have the guards bring the horses. I want a snargon to search the shop for magic, then remove the duegar's corpse. Leave no evidence save the dead bodies of our enemies."

Clavis hovered at the shop's entrance, his nostrils flared wide at the burnt stench. "Flames roared through the shop...we feared none survived." The assassin's voice held a thousand questions.

"The monk angered me, so I burnt him with a fireball."

The assassin's eyes flew wide, awe tinged with a healthy fear.

"Leave the charred bodies as a lesson to my enemies."

Clavis bowed low. "Yes, dread lord."

The horses arrived and the Mordant swung up into the saddle. Putting spurs to his mount, he galloped through the sleeping city. In his mind, he weighed his encounter with the monks, a stalemate of sorts. His age-old enemy had evaded capture and inquisition, yet the monk paid for his escape with his very life, charred to a blackened crisp by his own magic. And the fireball focus that should have been the Mordant's...appeared to be ruined. Yet with a single lie, the Mordant gained the upper hand, usurping the fear of the fireball by claiming it was his own. He'd gained the fear but not the power. A snarl rose in his throat. In truth, he wanted both. Rumors of his fell powers would spread like wildfire through his own men, bolstering their loyalty...but he'd gained no information, and he'd lost a valuable focus. *A fireball!* He hadn't seen such power wielded in centuries. More proof the monks dared to meddle, entering the Great Dark Dance. Perhaps the blue-robed monks were not as impotent as he thought. Anger surged through him, he'd make the monks pay for this. His legions would ransack their precious monastery, putting every blue-robed monk to the sword. He'd work his will on Lanverness and then he'd ride to their mountain sanctuary, claiming their magic. If the monks dared to let a fireball focus wander below the mountains, what did they keep hidden in their secret vaults? Tantalized by the possibilities, the Mordant laughed, anticipating the power that would soon be his. All of Erdhe would cower before him...and he would rule for forevermore.

In the North

19

The Knight Marshal

No fodder for his sword, the knight marshal slowed to a halt. Death surrounded him. Corpses sprawled in the bloody snow, their sightless eyes gazing at him with reproach. Severed heads, sundered limbs, the slaughtered corpses sprawled along the trail, blood and entrails releasing a terrible stench. It smelled like death, it smelled like victory.

The marshal used a cloak from the dead to clean his sword. Dark as midnight, the black steel glittered cold and keen in the waning light. Dragons coiled on the hilt, runes carved between the runnels, the two-handed great sword thrummed in his hands, hungry for more. A sword of power, a sword of legend, he raised the great blade to the heavens, flush with victory. "I am a god!" His shout echoed against the mountains, a challenge hurled to all of Erdhe. "*I am the God of War!*"

"*War, war, war...*" his words echoed back at him, an eerie refrain.

Sheathing his great sword, he reclaimed his stallion. His warhorse pawed the blood spattered snow, seeking tender shoots of grass among the dead. Taking up the reins, he checked the girth. With the vigor of a much younger man, the marshal vaulted into the saddle, keen for the next battle.

"Osbourne!" The cry came from the hills.

The marshal whirled, seeking the voice. And then he spied a new foe. A lone knight, mounted on a horse, waiting at the crest of the trail.

"*Fight me!*" The marshal roared his challenge.

"Remember your honor!"

Kill! The Dark Sword whispered its siren's song.

The marshal spurred his horse to a gallop, ironshod hooves churning up the bloody snow.

"Remember the maroon!"

Unsheathing the dark sword, the marshal stood in the stirrups. Feeling invincible, he roared his challenge, "*Fight me!*" Holding the Dark Sword aloft, he raced towards this new foe, keen for combat.

The knight stood his ground, his hands empty of weapons, his maroon cloak fluttering in the wind. "Remember the Octagon!"

The marshal felt the Dark Sword thrum in his hands, hungry for heart's blood, hungry for death.

"Remember King Ursus!"

King Ursus, the name shuddered through him, waking memories, his friend and his king, buried in a stone cairn overlooking Raven Pass. Grief pierced him. The marshal slowed his charging stallion, checking his mount to a trot.

Kill! The Dark Sword keened in his mind.

The mounted knight sat unmoving at the trail's crest, hurling words like spears. "Remember King Ursus, remember the maroon, remember Castlegard!"

Names slammed against the marshal, laden with memories. He yanked on the reins, slowing his warhorse to a walk. The stallion fought the bit, but obeyed. Battered by memories, the marshal lowered his sword.

Kill! In his mind, the Dark Sword screamed its hunger, yearning for another kill, but the marshal fought to ignore it. He stared up at the knight...and remembered his friend's name. "Lothar."

"Yes," Lothar nodded, "and you are the knight marshal of the maroon, my friend and my commander."

The marshal slowed his stallion to a halt. He stared at his friend, horrified by what might have been. "I nearly killed you."

"It would not have been easy." Lothar gestured and twenty archers stepped from behind trees, their longbows bent, their arrows aimed at the marshal's heart.

A snarl came from the marshal's throat. He whipped the Dark Sword upward, poised to kill...but something made him hold his ground. Breathing hard, he forced the sword down.

"It's the sword." Lothar held his stare. "Sheath it. I can feel its bloodlust from here."

The marshal came back to himself. He looked at the Dark Sword and then he looked down at his silver surcoat spattered with blood, the octagon sigil nearly obscured by the gore. And then he remembered the battle. Corpses littered the trail. Not just slain, they were slaughtered, chopped to pieces. Butchered, dismembered, as if a monster had come among them, rending limb from limb. A horrible stench rose from the severed entrails. Sickened by the slaughter, the marshal rammed the Dark Sword into the harness riding across his back. The dragon-coiled hilt reared over his right shoulder like a promise and a threat.

Lothar grunted, "Good." He made a gesture and the archers disappeared back into the forest. "Come. You need food and rest and time to remember yourself before you seek another patrol."

"I know who I am."

"Do you?" Lothar gave him an appraising look. "You're the knight marshal of the Octagon, yet you slew all those who surrendered."

Kneelers, the word twisted in his mind like a curse, unleashing a terrible fury. "Kneelers deserve to die."

"That's Darkness talking." Lothar speared him with his stare. "Don't let the sword claim you."

Kill him! The Dark Sword whispered at the back of his mind.

The marshal grimaced, resisting the sword.

"You can fight it!"

The marshal locked stares with his friend. "I *am* fighting it! Else you'd be dead."

20

Nimeria

Sunlight pooled on the crisp white page of vellum, illuminating it with a golden glow. Despite the light pouring through the alcove window, Nim lit eight lanterns and set them in a circle around the desk. For this, her apprentice piece, she'd suffer no shadows to hinder her view. A prudent practicality, the lanterns were also part of the ritual, for they served to keep Darkness from sullying her work while paying homage to the eight pointed star. "*Seek Knowledge, Protect Knowledge, Share Knowledge,*" she whispered the words of the Kiralynn Order.

Taking a seat at the desk, Nim contemplated the infinite possibilities of the blank page. She loved the unbridled optimism of art melded with words, striving to create something of lasting beauty imbued with intricate meaning. Since her very first day in the monastery, she'd been enthralled by the illuminated texts shimmering jewel-bright upon the walls, knowledge writ upon every corridor and hallway. And now it was her turn to contribute to the monastery's works.

The other acolytes sought easy passages to transcribe, but not Nim. She'd searched the old tomes, seeking ancient patterns of intricate knotwork, seeking the pathway to Illumination. She shivered at her own audacity, imagining her masterwork, knowing every detail must be perfect for the ancient magic to take hold.

It began with a blank page of vellum, so smooth, so superior to ordinary parchment, an unblemished canvas awaiting enlightenment. "May the Lords of Light guide my hands." Taking a deep breath, she used a sharp-pointed stick and a straight-edged rod to line and block the page with the faintest indentations, just deep enough to be seen but not deep enough to last. Having blocked the page, she began tracing the complex designs for the great ornamental capital letter and the illuminated armored knights riding forth from a dauntless castle. She planned to add gold embellishment in a cascade of complex knotwork beneath the illuminated letter. The knotwork would frame a gauntleted fist holding a sapphire-blue sword aloft. *Blue steel,* the fabled swords of the Octagon knights, the very stuff of heroic legends, a fitting topic for her first master work.

It took the better part of a fortnight to transfer the intricate details to the virgin vellum, but finally her bold design took form, appearing as faint indentations woven across the page. Keen to bring her design to life, she was finally ready for ink.

Relighting the eight lanterns, she trimmed her best quill to the appropriate shape for the calligraphy's width. Nim opened a bottle of the finest black ink. Pricking her finger, she squeezed a single drop of blood into the bottle, an offering to the gods, a binding to the ink. Only a pinprick, yet she bound her finger with cloth and held it till the bleeding stopped lest she stain the page. While she waited, Nim cast her mind across the chosen text.

The text, like the design, was of her choosing. Nim could have chosen anything from the acolyte scrollaries, from the famed lyrics of Xel the Harper, to the poetry of Keetai, to the philosophies of Aranald, but she'd heard the whispered rumors and seen for herself how the frost owls flew thick as starlings, bearing messages to the mountain mews. It did not take a sworn master to know that dire times had befallen Erdhe. In such times, it occurred to Nim that the heroes and swords of ancient times were sorely needed once more. Drawn to the Sword Codex, she chose a passage on the forging of the first blue steel blade.

In her mind's eye, she saw the passage, not as it was writ in the Codex, but as it would be scribed upon her vellum. She visualized every word, every letter. When she was certain the text was fixed in her mind, Nim took a calming breath and dipped her quill in the gall iron ink.

Setting the nib to the vellum, she began. Script flowed out of her, elegant calligraphy scribed across the virgin page. Once started, she could not stop, breaking only to carefully add more ink to her quill. Each letter was a miniature masterpiece, scribed to exacting standards, yet the letters also held an elegant, seemingly effortless fluidity. The smooth motion of her hand was imbibed by the ink, the words forever captured on vellum. Consumed by the details, by the burning passion of creativity, Nim worked without stopping till she reached the last period.

She blinked as if coming out of a trance.

Lifting the quill from the vellum, she carefully set it aside lest an errant drop mar her work. Stepping back, Nim stared at the whole and saw that it was good.

A good start, her heartbeat quickened, thrilled by the challenge.

Nim forced herself to wait a full day for the text to dry and then she traded black ink for vivid color. Having ground and carefully blended the pigments herself, she'd assembled a stunning pallet from the monastic stores. Vermillion red destined for the castle's rippling banners and the knights' sigils, turmeric yellow for the sun-blazoned castle walls, azurite blue for the sword, smalt for the shadows, and a brilliant malachite green to offset the gold of the knotwork. Using the finest brushes, she painstakingly applied the jeweled colors, bringing the illumination to blazing life.

To bind her work and exult the illumination, Nim planned to add silver and gold. This was the trickiest part, for any mistakes could not be undone, but Nim was determined to exult her work, to make it worthy of the gods. She started with silver leaf beaten thinner than the finest parchment. Nim held her breath lest she tear it. Bent over the desk, she carefully worked the silver detail onto the gauntleted fist and the upraised sword. A rich shimmer of silvery light appeared along the blade. Her breath caught, pleased with the effect, as if the sword were fresh forged.

And then she added the gold. Carefully cutting the gold leaf, she applied swirling curls with stag's glue to the fretted knotwork, weaving golden light among the painted twists and turns, creating a shimmering pathway for the eye to follow. The knotwork pattern she'd chosen was old, very old, something she'd found in a musty tome, a legacy from another age, yet she'd felt compelled to use it. For days she sat hunched over her work, delicately applying the glimmering gold leaf.

And then it was done.

Her hands shook.

She was half afraid to look.

Stepping back, Nim studied her work with an artisan's eye. She could find no fault, no smudges, no ink blotches, no malformed letters, no errant strays of color. Satisfied with the detail, she examined the whole.

Gold and silver leaf shimmered in the lantern light, bringing a dazzling metallic sheen to the piece. Vibrant colors leaped from the page, ensnaring the eye of the beholder and drawing the reader to inspect the stunning details. The raised sword shimmered as if awaiting the hands of a hero. The castle battlements glowed in stalwart sunshine beneath the ornamented capital. The intricacies of the gold-leafed knotwork teased the eye with a convoluted mystery, all forming the perfect framework for the exquisite text, art and meaning indelibly entwined.

Master Adelbart peered over her shoulder.

Nim startled, ambushed by her master's sudden appearance.

For the longest time her master said nothing.

Waiting on his judgment, Nim bit her lower lip, her heartbeat racing to a gallop.

"You chose a text with a True Name?"

"Yes."

"And you found a True Description?"

"I believe so, master." She held her breath, waiting for a rebuke.

"Why this text?"

The words came unbidden to her lips. "Because staunch swords are needed in dire times."

Master Adelbart said nothing.

Unnerved by his silence, she dared a glance at his wrinkled face. Realizing his solemn stare remained fixed upon her work, she snapped her own gaze back to the illuminated vellum, praying he found it worthy.

Finally he spoke. "Nimeria Harpsinger, an untried acolyte with years to live before you reach the age of requirement, yet in this, your apprenticeship piece, you have created a masterwork worthy of the inner monastery."

His praise rang like a bell in her heart.

"As is our custom, a finished illumination is first read aloud by the artisan who brought the text to life." His words turned solemn. "Has this text passed your lips?"

"No, master."

He gave her a piercing look. "You think you are ready for this? You think you are capable?"

Sweat erupted beneath her robes. Under his stern gaze, Nim was no longer so certain, but she yearned to be a true illuminator in every sense of the art. "Let me try."

His gaze gave nothing away. "Despite your tender years, you have the eye and hand of a master illuminator. We shall see if you also have the voice. Bring your piece to the heart of the scriptorium so that your first reading may be heard by all."

Both awed and frightened by the honor, she bowed towards him. "Yes, master."

Master Adelbart withdrew from her tiny alcove, disappearing as silently as he'd arrived.

Nim washed her hands in the basin, scrubbing till she banished every ink stain from her fingers. Drying her hands three times to be sure she would not stain the vellum, she took a deep breath and then carefully lifted her finished work from the desktop. Nim tried not to think about what awaited her in the scriptorium, a trial by fire in front of her fellow acolytes, yet she dared not complain, for she'd brought this challenge upon herself. Holding the vellum as if it were the most fragile pane of glass, she slowly wound her way through the warren of desks and alcoves now empty of acolytes.

Reaching the bright heart of the scriptorium, her footsteps faltered, for the soaring chamber was filled with blue-robed masters. Standing among them, she spied the flowing white beard of Master Tolk, the monastery's venerable Chronicler. Nim paled, for in all her ten years of study, she'd never seen the Chronicler in the acolytes' scriptorium. And now he was here, with so many other masters, to witness her brashness, to witness this trial of her own devising.

Master Adelbart saw her trepidation and smiled. "Come, child, we have gathered to hear the first reading of your newly exulted text."

The gathering parted, opening a path to the central lectern. In a single glance, she knew the blue-robed masters far outnumbered the golden-yellow robes of fresh-faced acolytes. Looking neither left nor right lest her nerves betray her, Nim walked the path, gently placing her finished piece upon the lectern. Sunlight dazzled the gold leaf and lit the silver like a flash of light running along the blade of the illuminated sword. Exulted by gold and silver and emblazoned by sunlight, her work looked worthy to be offered to the gods. Nim gave the piece one last searching glance and then stepped to the side.

One at a time, the masters came forward to inspect her work. Their faces remained still as stone but their stares were keen as swords, seeking flaws. Not one of them said a word. Nim sweated beneath her golden-yellow robes. Her hands clenched behind her back, she darted swift glances at the masters, hungry for their approval.

"How old are you, child?" The Chronicler broke the silence.

Nim's eyes flew wide, astonished to be addressed by the venerable master. "Sixteen."

"Remarkable." His gaze roved the other masters. "Does anyone find fault with this piece?"

None of the other masters spoke.

The Chronicler fixed her with his stare that seemed to touch her very soul.

Nim held his gaze, afraid if she faltered in anyway, she would forfeit her chance.

A hundred heartbeats passed. The Chronicler nodded toward her. "By dint of your own work and by your own daring, you have won your chance. May the Light favor you." He gestured for her to take her place in front of the lectern.

Her hands shook, so she kept them clasped behind her back.

Nim stared down at the illuminated script, drinking in the details just as she'd been taught. She started with the illuminated paintings, the sword, the knights, the castle, imprinting them in her mind like a cherished memory. Finished with the paintings, her gaze followed the convoluted knotwork. In many ways, the intricate knotwork was both a key and a lock. For those without the proper talent, the knotwork was a busy distraction, muddling the mind and obscuring the meaning, but for true illuminators, the knotwork was a pathway to other planes, other possibilities. Following the convoluted curves and knots, Nim felt her mind open like a budding flower seeking the sun. Ensorcelled by the knotwork, her gaze sought the text. She began to read.

"At the turn of an Age, when Darkness held sway and heroes were sorely needed, Orrin, the last great wizard, turned his arcane skills to the forge. By hammer and by rune, he sought to unlock the mysteries of blue ore. After a year of toil, he discovered the key. The secret lay in the sequencing of hammer, heat, and plunging cold, the final quenching forever fixing the properties of blue steel. Never to be melted, never to be reforged, blue ore yielded a wondrous blade forever sharp and strong, but Orrin Surehammer was forging a weapon for the Darkest of times. Into the blade he poured his magic. Rune forged, with coiled dragons sculpted on the hilt, the blade was bound with indomitable strength and fearless courage. Gifted to the Octagon Knights, the sword was called Dragonbane. In the hands of heroes, Dragonbane did many great deeds, but towards the end of his life, Orrin foresaw that Darkness would covet the sword. In secret, he forged a twin to the blade, equal in strength and magic. Binding the blade with enchantments, he hid it to await the most desperate hour. Hidden since that bygone Age, the True Name of the second sword was Invictus, the blade that awaits the Battle Immortal."

Nim's gaze moved from the last period to the illuminated image of the sword. A doorway opened in her mind. An unexpected power rushed through with a roaring that filled her head. Nim stiffened, her hands gripping the lectern. A current of power raced along her skin, a chime sounding in the back of her mind. Her voice changed, deepening with command. Inspiration gripped her. No longer reading, Nim wielded the voice of a summoner, invoking the sword by its true Name. *"Invictus, Invictus, Invictus, by the power of the illumination wrought by my own hand and sealed by my own blood, I summon thee!"*

A blinding flash beat against her, bright as an exploding star.

Nim flinched away, shuttering her eyes against the searing brightness.

She held her breath, feeling the presence of the gods.

When she dared to open them again, the blinding light was gone and so was her illumination. The vellum page was wiped clean, devoid of ink, paint, and metal leafing. Accepted by the gods, only blank vellum remained. But sitting atop the lectern, sitting atop the vellum, was a two-handed great sword, dragons coiled on the hilt, runes incised along the blue steel blade. The sword's name whispered out of Nim's soul. *"Invictus!"*

21

General Haith

Braziers illuminated the command pavilion, dispelling the damp chill. General Haith beckoned the scout towards the map table. "Come. Show us where it happened."

The other commanders moved aside, opening a path.

Clad in chainmail and soiled leathers, the scout bowed low and then shuffled forward. Unshaved and unwashed, the man stank of stale sweat, wood smoke...and fear. His hooded stare skittered around the commanders crowding the pavilion, and then he looked at the map. Slack-jawed, he stared awe-struck at the details inked on parchment.

By any standards the map was peerless, a colorful work of military art captured from the Octagon Knights at the sacking of Raven Pass, but General Haith had no patience for the scout's gawking. "Can you find it?" His voice jabbed like a spear.

Startled, the scout leaned forward. With a shaking hand he traced a path along a narrow pass threading through the Dragon Spine Mountains, stopping at a highland meadow. "Here, m'lord, it happened here."

Too close for comfort. "How many dead?"

The scout met his stare.

For the first time, the general got a good look at the scout's fear-laden eyes. *Haunted eyes,* the general knew that hollow-eyed stare, he'd seen it oft enough in the Mordant's service. Soul-scarred, the scout's eyes were shadowed with nightmares, proof he'd seen something far worse than just death.

Ducking his head, as if to shutter the shame of his gaze, the scout mumbled. "It were horrible, more of a slaughter than a battle."

General Marris snapped. "Speak up! You're here to give a report, not to mumble."

The scout cringed as if lashed, but he spoke louder. "Blood and guts everywhere. More than a hundred, all of them killed." His hand groped at his empty scabbard, as if seeking the reassurance of cold steel. "And they was not just dead, they was butchered. Heads taken, entrails smeared across the snow, bodies torn asunder," he cast a wary glance toward the general, "as if an animal had torn them to shreds, hungry for meat, yet none of them was eaten." He gave the general a dead-eyed stare. "This was not done by no four-legged beast," the scout shuddered, "this were a nightmare come stalking."

"And the enemy?"

"That's just it, m'lord. One horse, one set of enemy footprints. How could one man slay so many?"

The others murmured in disbelief, but the general knew the truth. *So the Dark Sword is unleashed*, yet he kept his face stone-still. "You're sure of what you saw?"

"By the Dark God, I swear it were true, m'lord!" The scout cringed as if expecting punishment. When no blow came, his voice strengthened with conviction. "I didn't believe it myself at first. I know my craft, so I cast about, seeking other footprints. Found them, I did, but they was on the ridgeline, as if they watched the battle yet never took part. No," the scout shook his head, "there was only one enemy...one man to slay a hundred."

"And after the battle, where did this enemy go?"

"He withdrew, mounted his horse and rode back into the mountains."

"And you didn't think to follow?"

Terror flashed in the scout's dark eyes. "No, m'lord, thought you'd want word of the slaughter. Someone had to live to tell the tale."

A murmur rippled through his senior commanders, but the general silenced them with a harsh glare. "You did well."

Relief washed across the scout's face.

"Go and get yourself a hot meal. And tell no one what you saw."

"Yes, m'lord." Bowing low, the scout scuttled from the pavilion.

The general swept his commanders with his gaze, settling on a young centurion. "Hastings."

"Yes, m'lord."

"See that the scout is permanently silenced. I'll have no ill rumors spooking the troops."

"I'll get..."

"No, you'll do it yourself." The centurion stiffened as if struck. "And dispose of the body. The gorehounds are always looking for fresh meat."

"Yes, m'lord." Bowing, the centurion rushed from the pavilion, leaving a grim silence in his wake.

The general surveyed his commanders. "Thoughts? Comments?"

General Marris gave him a keen-eyed stare, but he declined to speak. His aid, Captain Jothson, rushed to fill the void, his voice full of scorn. "The scout lies. One lone man could never slay a hundred. I'll wager the scout deserted this squad and told the lie to cover his cowardice."

"No." General Haith cut off that line of reasoning like an executioner wielding an axe. "Didn't you see the fear riding his eyes? Don't you know that look? Most of you have served in the Bloody Cavern. We've all seen that kind of hollow-eyed stare before...in the bowels of the Dark Citadel."

The others looked away, unable to meet his gaze.

"That kind of fear does not lie. So we need another explanation." His stare circled his officers, prodding them to speak. "Well?"

Commander Trovis spoke first. "There's only one answer. The knights have finally unleashed their magic." His words met no argument. The commander grew emboldened. "I never believed those who said the knights have no magic. Castlegard is steeped in magic, so they must have it, but why wait till now to wield it?"

His answer released a storm of comments. "Perhaps they hoard their magic in Castlegard. Since the war goes badly for them, they've finally brought their battle magic to the fray."

Commander Crull scoffed, "Their king fought and died at Raven Pass. If the Octagon has magic, why did their king not wield it?"

"Arrogance," Major Barker met the stares turned in his direction. "The Octagon Knights never believed Raven Pass would fall, especially since we brought no siege engines against their mighty walls. They underestimated the power of our dread lord. So they left their magic in Castlegard, thinking it was not needed."

"But what type of magic rends men to pieces?"

"Perhaps it was a berserker?"

"A berserker...or a butcher."

"One against a hundred?" Scorn riddled the major's voice. "It must be magic."

Arguments waged back and forth, a storm of disagreement spiked with wild conjecture. General Haith listened more than he spoke. Their ignorance told him much. *So they do not know of the Dark Sword.* The general smothered a smile. Their ignorance pleased him, proving he had another huge advantage over his fellow officers. One did not rise in the Dark ranks based on skill alone. Advantage was needed to evade traps, avoid blame, bind allegiance and climb the ranks on the back of others. The Dark Sword was a dangerous and valuable secret. If his lord, the Mordant, chose not share this plot with the others, then neither would he.

General Marris said, "It must be magic. Nothing else makes sense."

Commander Crull turned his way. "We should send a squad with duegars to confirm the knights brought magic to the slaughter."

General Haith responded with a tight-lipped smile. "Finally a sensible suggestion. Yes, send a squad to sniff the site, but have Trantor choose the duegars." Trantor, his personal snargon, would choose duegars loyal to the general, ensuring he got an accurate report before any of the others.

Commander Crull smirked, reading the underlying message. "As you command." His swarthy face sobered. "In the meantime, I suggest we withhold our patrols and double the guard on our perimeter."

"No." General Haith countermanded the suggestion. "Pressure must be kept on the knights. By order of our lord, the Mordant, the Octagon must be harried to extinction." He glared at his commanders, reinforcing the order. "Double the strength of the patrols. Two hundred should prove more than a match for this foe." In truth, the Dark Sword needed to be fed. Better it be fed at a distance.

"And the perimeter?"

"Triple the guards and double the patrols. We'll meet again once the duegar return with their report." He looked towards his aid. "Summon my horse and my personal guard."

His aid leaped to obey, rushing from the pavilion.

General Haith tugged on a pair of fur-lined gauntlets.

While the meeting broke into knots of conversation, General Marris sidled toward him. "You called for your stallion? You're not sleeping in camp tonight?"

"I've grown weary of mud and muck. I'll sleep in the comfort of a king's bed tonight, such that it is. These Octagon Knights put up a brave fight, but their sense of luxury is shocking. Only a peasant would be impressed." He felt the stabbing suspicion of the general's gaze, but he refused to engage. "I'll be at the wall for the next few nights. Send a messenger with any reports."

General Marris scowled. "And I'm left here to face this riddle?"

"Join me on the wall and put Crull in charge. Crull seems capable enough...and rank doth have its privileges."

General Marris hesitated.

General Haith knew exactly what his second was thinking. Giving subordinates too much power was ever a dangerous risk. The superior officer might avoid danger and blame...or he might be overshadowed and miss the benefits of glory. He waited to see what the general would choose.

"No...I'll stay here for now."

So Crull is competent enough that Marris will not give him a chance to shine, the general stored that observation away for future advantage. "As you wish." He strode from the pavilion's brazier-heated warmth into a biting storm. A bitter wind howled through Raven Pass, sleet mixed with rain. The north hovered on the cusp of spring, trading snow for mud and muck. The general hated this time of year, when the sky wept a river turning the land to mire, bringing misery and sickness, but the timing of this war was not his to dictate. Pulling his dark cloak close, he mounted his stallion, shouting orders to his guard. "We ride for the wall." Putting spurs to his mount, he urged his horse to a gallop. Bowing his head against the teeth of the storm, he rode north through the conquered throat of Raven Pass.

A cadre of a hundred guards raced to keep pace, armor and weapons jangling around him. Even protected by a hundred of his best, the general felt exposed. *The Dark Sword is unleashed!* Such a dangerous gambit, yet he knew the reasons for it. But once unsheathed, the sword would slaver for endless souls. The more it fed, the more it would hunger. The general shivered and not because of the cold. Timing was crucial. He prayed his lord the Mordant would not leave it till too late. Better to spend the next few nights behind stout stone walls. Threats and possibilities thundered through his mind, a calculation of risk and reward. Feeling exposed, the general lashed his stallion to a lathered gallop. The Mordant's promises of power and bounty meant nothing, if one did not survive to reap the reward.

22

Master Rizel

Invictus, the name shimmered like a gong in his mind. Master Rizel carried the great sword aloft, bearing it through the illuminated hallways. Dragons coiled on the hilt, runes inscribed along the sapphire-blue blade, a sword forged at the turning of an Age, a sword forged for heroes. Long thought to be lost, an ancient history verging into legend, yet now it was here, in the mountain monastery, summoned in the most dire of times. *Summoned by a sixteen-year old girl!* Had he not seen the invoking for himself, he would not have believed it, yet the proof was in his hands, real as steel.

A flock of blue-robed masters followed close on his heels. Other masters tended to the swoon-struck girl, bearing her to the healery. The girl was a treasure of another sort, but the sword could not be left unattended. By unspoken consent, he bore the blade from the acolytes' scriptorium, through the illuminated hallways to the doors of midnight-blue. Golden-robed acolytes gawked as he passed, shocked to see a master bearing a blue steel blade, especially one of such magnificence, yet the sword was only half the wonder. Whispers swirled through the monastery, rumors spiced with mystery.

Master Rizel tightened his grip on the sword lest it disappear.

He reached a midnight-blue door. Stepping from the golden-yellow floor onto the midnight-blue, he gained the serenity of the monastery's inner sanctuary. A hushed peace greeted him, a privacy protected by the rule of color. Like the outer hallways, the inner walls were steeped in learning. Calligraphy emblazoned with color illuminated the corridors, every wall brimming with ancient prophesy. He wondered if the founders had envisioned this very day, when the power of illumination came back to the Order. The sapphire-blade shimmered in the sunlight. He carried history in his hands, a legend come calling.

Threading his way through the twists and turns of the hallowed halls, he reached the inner heart of the monastery. Passing through the rune-carved doors, he entered the Great Archive. Vaulted ceilings soared overhead, sunlight pouring through leaded windows. In the monastery's inner sanctum, even the windows bore writing. Text scribed on the clear glass panes cast shadowy words in pools of light, a celebration of learning. Master Rizel breathed deep the heady scents of parchment and vellum, ink and leather, the very bindings of knowledge. Dark wood shelves climbed from the midnight-blue floor to the vaulted ceiling, every shelf crammed with knowledge. The Kiralynn Order preserved and hoarded knowledge from Ages past, history and prophecy sitting side by side. Revered, stored, and studied, scrolls and leather-bound tomes filled every shelf and cubby, a cathedral dedicated to learning.

His footsteps slowed to a reverent hush. One did not lightly disturb the peace of the Great Archive, yet it seemed to him there was no better place to discuss the sword.

Heads turned as he passed. Blue-robed masters rose from their chairs, abandoning their studies to follow the sword. He strode to the heart of the archive, to a large table lit by sunlight, and there he placed the sword. *A sword summoned by an illuminated scroll,* he shivered at the thought, proof the sword should be discussed among the ancient histories.

Monks and masters gathered around, a flock of blue-robed scholars.

He waited till the gathering stilled and then he spoke, shattering the silence. "An Illuminator has come among us."

Gasps circled the gathering. Masters who were usually stone-faced, gaped. Little wonder they looked amazed, for high magic of this sort had not been seen in the monastery for nigh on four hundred years.

"Who?"

"An acolyte, a sixteen-year old girl."

Amazement rippled around the table.

Master Carlisle, a half-blind ancient with pale wisps of white hair haloing his wrinkled face, raised a quavering voice. "We should not be so surprised."

The others stilled to listen.

"The turning of an Age is upon us. Wonders and terrors will abound."

"But a mere child of sixteen?"

Master Carlisle answered. "One of the very reasons we keep the young ones sequestered is so they do not know how much has been lost. We teach them the ways of Illumination and then give them the chance to try. *They* believe it is possible, while *we*, with all our learning, believe it is not. That is why a child has succeeded where so many masters have failed."

"Where is this prodigy of a child?"

Master Rizel answered. "Smitten by a deep swoon after the invoking, Master Adelbart and the others are carrying her to the healery, to the care of Master Garth. High magic always exacts a great toll."

"Why this sword?"

"Master Adelbart said the child was drawn to the Sword Codex. She said the swords of old are needed in the Darkest times."

"Out of the mouths of babes."

"The gods work in mysterious ways."

A murmur of assent rippled through the room.

Master Felix bent over the sword, examining the runes. "I see from the maker's mark, this sword was forged by Orrin."

The masters stilled for all were well familiar with the name of the last great wizard of the Kiralynn Order.

Master Rizel felt their stares fix on him, potent with questions. He lifted the sword so all could see the details. "The sword does indeed bear Orrin's mark. When the Illumination was read in the scriptorium, the child Named this sword in the summoning." His gaze circled the others. "This is *Invictus,* the last blue steel blade forged by Orrin Surehammer."

Many masters blanched pale, recognizing the name...yet not all remembered.

"Forged by one of our own."

"The sword returns to its true home, sent to protect the monastery."

Anger blazed through Master Rizel. "This sword does not belong here! It was never meant to be wielded by a blue robed monk. Knowledge, magic and quarterstaffs, these are our weapons, not steel. This sword belongs in the hands of the Octagon Knights."

Master Felix bristled. "Yet it is here, within our cloistered walls, a boon of the Light."

"It came to us because we hold the sole knowledge of Illumination."

"Exactly!" Felix pounced, his eyes aglow with conviction. "And that precious knowledge must be protected at all costs!"

"At the cost of all of Erdhe? I think not!" His gaze roved the others, finding a mixture of support. "While we dither, Darkness conquers!"

His voice sparked with warning. "Those who serve the Light often fail because they watch rather than act."

Felix countered. "Exactly! We dare not let the last bastion of Knowledge fall."

Rizel glared. "Knowledge unwielded is wasted. We must take the fight to the Mordant. This sword must go to the Octagon." He held the sword aloft. "You are all steeped in history and lore. I trust you recognize the name if not the blade's design? This is *Invictus,*" the name alone sent a chill down his spine, "the sword forged for the end of days, for the Battle Immortal!"

Many monks startled at the revelation, but Felix continued to bluster. "All the more reason to wield it in defense of the monastery!"

Arguments erupted among the gathering, a discord of voices.

Master Carlisle rapped his cane on the table. A startled silence returned. The ancient master gave them a baleful glare. "Arguments will not avail you. While we debate, Darkness acts, Darkness prevails. Summoned by Illumination, this sword, wrapped in legend and prophecy, comes to us at a time when the red comet hangs low in the sky. This sword is a matter of the Battle Immortal, a matter only the Grand Master can decide. May his wisdom ever be guided by the Light."

An uneasy truce prevailed.

"By the Light." Agreement rippled through the gathering. The others began to disperse.

Felix gave him an angry glare, but he quelled his arguments...for now.

Master Rizel stared at the sword, certain in his soul it belonged in the hands of the Octagon Knights, yet Master Carlisle had the truth of it. The sword's fate would be decided by the Grand Master...may his wisdom ever be guided by the Light.

23

The Knight Marshal

Blood-spattered and mud-smeared, the marshal spun to a halt. The battle was over, yet he was not tired...but his armor was covered in gore. He wiped at the filth and found more filth. He no longer had a sigil or a color...unless it was blood and mud, the colors of war. *How fitting,* he flashed a hungry grin, his stare roving the mountain trail. Corpses littered the mud-soaked ground, proof of his prowess. A few twitched and moaned, the dying among the dead, but none dared to stand against him. *Look at their cloaks*...but he nudged the nagging thought aside. Flush with victory, he held the dark sword aloft as if challenging the gods.

Laughing, he roamed the battlefield, seeking a foe.

"*Help me!*" A helmeted soldier crawled through the mud. "*Water! Give me water!*"

A kneeler! Anger flashed through the marshal. In three strides he was on the man, the Dark Sword whispering a keening wail. With single slice he took the head and then hacked the body to pieces. He could not abide kneelers, cowards who refused to fight.

Invincible...we are invincible! The Dark Sword crooned a siren's song in his mind.

The marshal knew the sword spoke the truth. He'd lost track of how many battles he'd won, how many men he'd killed. The battles became a blur of ecstasy, the dark sword alive in his hands like a living legend. Every fight was a thing of beauty, a celebration of slaying. His foes fought as if encased in rusted armor. So slow, so obvious, he anticipated their every move, dealing death with every blow. Wielding the Dark Sword, he moved through the battlefield like a whirlwind, like a scythe...*like a god!*

No enemy blade ever touched him. He emerged from battle without a nick, without a scratch. He did not tire, he did not ache, he did not hurt...he felt young! Yet he was always hungry, and his empty eye socket itched something infernal, like a thousand stinging nettles, but otherwise he felt fit as a stallion, eager for the next battle.

Wield me! Wield me and I will make you a god! The Dark Sword whispered promises drenched in glory. The ichor of victory thrummed in his very veins. He dreamt of battle, he dreamt of war...till he could think of nothing else.

"Osbourne!" A stranger's voice echoed through the green-fledged mountains.

The marshal whirled, spying a lone knight on the ridge top. *A fresh foe,* he vaulted into the saddle, wheeling his warhorse toward the knight.

"Remember the maroon!"

He spurred his stallion to a frothing gallop, keen to fight.

"Remember Castlegard!"

The enemy knight sat mounted on a warhorse yet he did not move. He did not flee and he did not charge, a riddle sitting on the ridge top, a sentinel blocking the trail.

"Remember King Ursus!"

The marshal charged toward the enemy at a full gallop. Standing in the stirrups, he raised the Dark Sword over his head for a two handed cleave.

The enemy never flinched. Empty handed, he sat upon his horse, a battleaxe strapped to his side, the pommel of a great sword rearing over his right shoulder. Gird for war, yet the foe hurled nothing but empty words.

Kill him! The Dark Sword slavered for another soul.

Enraged, the marshal stretched to his full height, the Dark Sword held poised to strike. He'd cleave the knave from shoulder to groin, cutting him in half with one fell stroke.

"Remember your honor!"

So close, he could see the knight's sad eyes and drooping mustache...*a familiar face.*

The marshal hesitated.

The knight raised his shield, a maroon octagon emblazoned on burnished silver. Sunlight reflected on the polished surface, skittering across the marshal's face. Dazzled by the light, he was pierced by latent memories. *Lothar!* The marshal twitched his stallion aside, but it was too late. The two warhorses collided with a thunderous crash. His stallion kept his footing, but the other buckled from the blow. The knight tried to leap clear, but his boot tangled in the stirrup. The knight's horse toppled backwards, throwing his rider to the ground with a bone-jarring crash.

The Dark Sword descended like a scythe, keening for blood.

Wide-eyed, the knight stared up at him, pinned beneath his horse. *"Osbourne!"*

Kill him!

The marshal struggled to slow the blade, a grim tug of wills.

The Dark Blade swept downward, yet he willed the blade's descent to slow...to stop. The sword stopped a hair's breadth from the knight's throat.

Enraged, the Dark Blade keened for blood. **Kill him!**

The marshal yanked the blade away. Struggling to prevail, he roared his frustration at the fallen knight. "Are you afraid?"

The knight did not answer.

"You should be!" The marshal turned aside.

The felled horse whinnied. Snorting with effort, it lumbered to its feet and then shied away, shaken but not harmed.

The fallen knight remained sprawled on the ground, his face ashen, his shield sigil-down in the mud, his hands well away from his weapons.

The marshal turned his horse in circles, carving a path around the fallen knight. "Why won't you fight me?"

"For the same reason you won't slay me."

Memories intruded...unwanted memories. Caught between the sword's desire to kill...and his strange need to spare this man's life, the marshal pulled his stallion to a halt. Such a familiar face, a name flitted in and out of his mind. "Do I know you?"

"Lothar...my name is Lothar...and you are the knight marshal of the maroon."

The words beat against him...but they found little purchase.

"Look at my face, look at my surcoat...we are brothers, we are *friends!"*

The face was familiar...and so was the surcoat. *Lothar*...his friend, his brother-in-arms. Memories came crashing back. And then he noticed the blood. Blood beaded across the knight's throat in a thin hairline slice, a cut that could have taken his head. Horror roared through him, realizing that he'd nearly slain his friend. "Lothar...*run!"*

The knight shook his head, his words coming in a tumbled rush. "You're losing your soul to the sword. Better if you give it up and come back with me. The Octagon needs you. We need the marshal back." Desperation sharpened the knight's gaze. "Come with me. Come back to the maroon."

Memories of brotherhood, of friendship shared, roared through his mind...but they were soon drowned by the Dark Sword's clamor.

Kill him. The marshal shook his head, struggling to quell the command, struggling to hold on to his humanity.

The knight tried one last plea. "Come back to us and lead us to victory!"

Victory, the word roared through his mind like a battle cry, but the Dark Sword gave victory a new meaning. The marshal gripped the peerless blade, his gaze skewering the knight. "*Run,* Lothar. Run if you value your life!"

24

Alric

A bell chimed in the mountain mews. Alric leaped from his pallet, grabbed a lantern and scrambled up the stairs to the tower top. A brisk wind blew in through the open windows, carrying a bone-numbing chill, a gift from the snowbound peaks. Alric reached the tower's crown, shuddering against the cold despite his fur-lined cloak. A great frost owl sat on the central perch. Regal and seemingly impervious to the mountain chill, the owl's snowy-white feathers glistened in the lantern light, its eyes glowing like golden orbs. "You're a beauty." Alric used his soothing voice. The owl bated his wings and the bell chimed again, triggered by the owl's weight, or perhaps by its impatience. Frost owls were uncommonly clever birds, the pride of the mountain mews.

Carefully setting the lantern aside, he pulled on a thick leather gauntlet. "Such a beauty, yet I'll wager you've had a long flight." Alric murmured sweet nothings, his tone mattering more than his words, his voice calm and soothing as a caress. From the pouch at his belt, he took a choice tidbit scavenged from the monastery's kitchen. With his gauntleted hand, he offered the owl a chicken liver. The great owl looked hungry, yet he took the offering with a delicate snap of his curved beak. "There you go. You're home now, safe from your long journey." Alric fed the bird, curbing its hunger. Twice more the bird bated, ringing the bell.

"No need for that, you've got my attention." He fed the bird till it was well and truly settled. Tugging off his gauntlet, Alric stroked the bird's downy chest before working on the leather jess. He checked the embossed mark. *Castlegard,* the name of the great castle shimmered in his mind like a legend. "You've flown a long way, little wonder you're so hungry." With deft fingers, he removed the small bone-carved message tube secured by the jess. "That's it, my beauty." Calming the owl with his voice, he settled the precious tube deep in his pocket. He tugged the gauntlet back on, the leather sleeve rising nearly to his shoulder, a protective sheath against the owl's sharp talons. Tempting the bird with another savory tidbit, he offered his forearm to the great owl. "Come, my beauty, we'll find you a warmer perch."

The frost owl accepted the bribe, hopping onto Alric's forearm.

The perch bobbed in the absence of the owl's weight, causing the bell to chime overhead.

"Whoooooo" the great owl hooted his inquisitive call.

"Just me, my beauty, me and your winged brethren." Taking up the lantern, he carefully carried the owl down the central stairs. Other frost owls slept on their perches, their white feathers glinting in the lantern light. A few stared at him as he passed, watching with their golden eyes. Of late, the mews had been busy, frost owls flying from all parts of Erdhe, bearing messages to the mountain monastery, but this was the first from Castlegard in a long while. He wondered what tidings brought this one so far south, but the message was not his to read.

Finding an empty perch, he settled the great frost owl next to an owl newly come from Salmythra. "There you go." He filled the food bowl, watching to make sure the owl was content, and then he raced down the remaining stairs. A welcome warmth flowed up from the mage-stone floor, heated by the thermal springs, another wonder of the monastery.

Tugging off the leather gauntlet, he plunged his hands into the basin, quickly washing. Raking his fingers through his sandy-blond hair, he straightened his golden robes and tidied the knot of his rope belt. Only an acolyte yet he knew the mews was his true calling. The scriptorium and all its scholarly studies held little appeal. He'd learned to read well enough, and he was even better at maps, but Alric much preferred spending time with the magnificent raptors. The other acolytes could keep the scriptorium with all its musty scrolls, for Alric chased loftier dreams. If the gods favored him, perhaps he'd show an aptitude for magic and gain a chance to wield one of the owl rings. To soar like a frost owl, to fly above the mountain peaks, nothing could be more glorious.

"Whoooooo," an owl hooted as if reminding him to hurry. Golden eyes watched him from the rafters.

Unlatching the door, he stepped from the tower into the brisk wind. Spring came late to the mountains, the lofty peaks refusing to shed their snowy cloaks. Hunched against the biting wind, Alric scurried across the courtyard. Stars glittered overhead in the endless vault of night. The moon had already set, proving the lateness of the hour. Most in the monastery would be fast asleep in their beds, but one master was always assigned to receive the owl-borne messages. Alric fingered the bone message tube tucked deep in his pocket, wondering at its tidings.

The rune-carved door creaked open as he slipped inside. Warmth embraced him, as if he'd stepped into summer. Torchlight glittered in the long hallway, dancing along smooth mage-stone walls. Calligraphy filled every hallway, the elegant script entwined with illuminated knights and castles, a reminder of dire prophecies. Intent on his mission, Alric sped past the calligraphy with nary a glance, making his way to the open doorway.

He heard the soft sound of conversation, proving the master was not alone.

Pausing to straighten his robes, Alric stepped through the doorway. "A frost owl has come to the mews bearing a message from Castlegard."

The conversation shattered to silence. Master Caleb sat behind the desk, parchments and inks scattered across the desktop. Master Athar leaned against the far wall, his eyes widening at the mention of the great castle. "We've not heard from Castlegard in many a moon turn."

"True enough." Master Caleb extended his hand for the tube.

Alric gave him the tube and then hovered by the doorway. Oft times the master needed a runner to take messages through the monastery. As an acolyte owl-keeper, that was part of Alric's duties, but first the message needed to be decoded and read. Standing in the shadows, he watched as Master Caleb opened the bone tube, extracting the small coil of vellum. Reaching for a thick tome, the master thumbed through it with practiced ease, using a cipher to decode the message. His quill scratched across parchment as he scribed the decoded words in a sure and steady hand.

Master Caleb stared slack-jawed, his face turning white as parchment. "The gods save us!"

Master Athar startled alert. "What is it?"

Master Caleb's ink-stained hands shook as he folded the parchment. "It's Castlegard! The mage-stone of Castlegard is failing!"

"*Impossible!*" The word burst from Master Athar like a curse.

Alric sucked a sharp breath, shrinking into the shadows.

"Yet the codes are correct." Mater Caleb shook his head, his voice full of foreboding. "This message must go to the Grand Master." The two masters rushed from the chamber, worry etched deep on their faces.

Forgotten in the shadows, Alric trembled. *How can mage-stone fail?* All his life he'd thought of mage-stone as everlasting. Now it seemed as if the very world crumbled, as if some doom had befallen Erdhe. Perhaps he'd misheard the message, he clung to the notion. Only an acolyte, yet it felt as if the whole world had darkened. Fleeing the monastery, he sought the safety and solitude of the mews.

25

General Haith

General Haith chose to remain behind the walls of Raven Pass. Surrounded by stone battlements and strong guards, the general fashioned the illusion of safety. Spending less and less time in the field, he ordered the maps brought up from the command pavilion and spread across the king's table. Couriers and scouts delivered a steady stream of reports while his aides plotted the positions on the brightly painted vellum. The map told a grim tale. He'd ordered the strength of the patrols tripled, trying to hold the Dark Sword at bay, yet the slaughters never ceased. Markers on the map showed the location of every butchery. Scouts brought fresh reports of patrols slaughtered and hacked to pieces, the ground drenched in blood, yet the scouts swore the enemy left but a single set of footprints. Rumors ran rampant, whispers of a spectral knight mounted on a winged warhorse, an invincible hero summoned from a distant Age. Not a single witness survived to describe this paragon of war, yet the general knew the truth. The rumormongers got it half right. The foe was real enough, a knight of flesh and bone...but the sword he wielded was haunted, a dark nightmare, a drinker of souls, a tool of the Mordant.

Beside him, his aide swore, "By the Darkness, how can this be? What magic do the knights have that enables one man to defeat so many?"

The others did not know and the general chose not to enlighten them. Advantage was needed to thrive in the service of the Mordant, and this was a secret he chose to hoard.

A bedraggled scout appeared at the doorway, bringing word of a fresh slaughter.

Major Ruggar added another marker to the map.

The markers formed a deadly pattern, an arrowhead aimed for the heart of Raven Pass. The general feared his lord had left the timing too late.

"General Haith!" The demonic voice battered against the casement window. *"General Haith!"* Sharp and insistent, it screeched his name like a herald from hell.

Pain spiked his chest, proof a gorelabe was near. General Haith rubbed at the rune scribed above his heart, the ever present mark of his master. His commanders stared at him, fear shadowing their faces, for none wanted to face a gorelabe. "Stay here." The general left the chamber alone. Following the summons, he climbed the stairs, emerging onto the windswept battlement.

"General Haith!" The gorelabe hovered above the crenellated battlements, screeching his name.

Soldiers along the wall fell prostrate, their hands covering their heads as if to avert the horror of the gorelabe's gaze.

The winged monstrosity was different from the last one. Instead of a white-winged albatross, this one wore the fleet form of a red-tailed hawk. A tortured nightmare born of darkest magic, the gorelabe retained the hawk's swift grace while bearing the contorted mouth and eyes of a man. The general studied the fiend, looking for signs of decay. Unlike the vicious gorehounds, who had unnaturally long lives, the gorelabes did not suffer life for long. The soul-corrupted magic that stitched them together could not last for more than a handful of moon turns. He'd seen one putrefy while still alive, the melded flesh fraying at the seams, a fester of sores and rot, but this one looked fresh-made, its red feathers still bright. His lord had been busy. Suppressing a shudder, the general strode towards the malformed creature. "I am here and I serve the Mordant."

The hawk gorelabe flew towards him. Hovering overhead, the creature stared down with its unnatural eyes. *"Prove yourself!"*

He often wondered if the Mordant peered through the unholy eyes of his heralds. Unlacing his surcoat, the general revealed the dark rune etched above his heart.

Wings folding to the attack, the gorelabe swooped low. The general braced himself, half expecting the wicked-keen talons to rake his upturned face, but the demonic bird showed restraint, hovering just in front of his face.

The general quailed inside, but he kept his face stone-cold, knowing any sliver of weakness could be his demise.

The gorelabe spoke in a baleful voice. *"General Haith, it is time!"*

The general's heartbeat quickened. The long anticipated command pierced him to the core, releasing him from the ugly stalemate of Raven Pass.

"*It is time! It is time!*" the gorelabe screeched the words, "*Time for old enemies to die! Time for the conquest to begin! Time for my Dark Kingdom to be claimed! Divide the army and wreak havoc upon Erdhe! You know our will, you know our plans. Take the cavalry and make all haste for the south. Kill the monks, secure their magic, and defile their cloistered halls. The cursed monks shall meddle no more. Their very name shall be erased from the annals of history and all of their magic shall be mine, mine, mine. Ride hard and let the Mordant's will be done!*"

The general bowed toward the malformed hawk. "The Mordant's will be done!"

As if released, the gorelabe began flying in a tight spiral. Its horrid screech changed to an incessant wail, "*Feed me! Feed me!*"

General Haith strode towards the nearest soldier. "Your death will serve the Mordant."

The soldier cringed, his face glazed with fear, but General Haith did not hesitate. Drawing his sword, he aimed for the neck, offering a swift death, but the soldier flinched away. The sword took him across the face. Keening a terrible wail, the half-faced soldier struggled to escape, crawling across the rampart. The general followed. It took two more sword strokes to hack the head from the body, an ugly death, an ill omen.

The gorelabe flew to the corpse. Alighting on the chest, it bent its head, lapping at the fresh-spilt blood.

A terrible silence shrouded the battlement. The cowering soldiers remained so still that the gorelabe's bloody lapping sounded obscenely loud.

The general sheathed his sword, regretting the ugly death.

The gorelabe drank its fill and then launched for the sky. Circling twice, its demonic voice echoed through the pass, "*It is time! It is time! Serve or die!*" With a final screech, it took wing and flew south.

The general kicked the corpse. "Dispose of this." He wiped his sword on the dead man's cloak, disgusted by the show of cowardice. "Feed it to the gorehounds."

Turning on his heel, he strode from the battlement. With renewed vigor, he descended the stairs, returning to the command chamber. His officers snapped to attention, poised like hounds for the hunt. The general raked them with his gaze. "You heard the Mordant's messenger. It is time for the conquest to begin." He turned his gaze to a bronze-skinned commander, a barrel-chested man with dark eyes and a reputation for being ruthlessly competent. The general smothered a sneer, for sometimes competent meant the most expendable.

"Commander Crull, you will hold the pass with half the infantry. If the maroon knights come calling, crush them. Otherwise, keep your force in reserve till the Mordant sends further orders."

The commander snapped a brisk salute, fist to chest. "Let the Mordant's will be done."

General Haith's gaze snapped to General Marris. "You'll take the remainder of the infantry and march south through the heart of Erdhe. Cross the Serpentines, sack Navarre and then strike for Lanverness. But be warned, for your timing must be perfect. You dare not enter Lanverness without the Mordant's command. A gorelabe will bring more orders long before you reach the queen's border."

General Marris raised an eyebrow. "And what are your orders?"

General Haith smiled, his hand on his sword hilt. "I will lead our cavalry south, against our lord's oldest enemy." His gaze roved across his commanders, seeing his own keen hunger reflected in their eyes. "The time of rape and plunder is finally at hand! Take your battle banners south and strike a heart-blow at Erdhe. The Mordant has loosed our swords for war!"

"To war!" His officers thundered their reply, keen for rape, pillage, and power. The conquest of Erdhe had finally begun.

26

Lothar

Rain wept from dingy clouds, adding misery to the damp chill. His maroon cloak was sodden, his armor flecked with rust, yet Lothar dared not stop. He needed distance. And he needed to hide his tracks. Enemies prowled the mountains, and not all of them wore black. Lothar nudged his warhorse forward, keeping to the stream's fast-flowing heart. Ice licked the brook's stony banks, the last raiment of winter. His horse nickered in protest, but the icy water was their best ally, smothering their scent and masking their prints.

Lothar kept his battleaxe unsheathed. Green cluttered the trees, multiplying the places for enemies to hide, but all else was washed to gray by the downpour. Rain dripped from his helm, a steady annoyance. He scanned the hillside for any telltale glint of arms or armor. His nerves set on a knife-edge, he kept a firm grip on his battleaxe. Sir Tyrone's great sword rode the harness at his back, a gift from the marshal, but that weapon remained an untried riddle. Perhaps it would foil the Dark Sword...or perhaps it would shatter in his hands like any ordinary blade, betraying him to his death. Under the assault of the Dark Sword, Sir Abrax's great blue sword had shattered like kindling, a champion of the maroon slain by a deranged squire. And now the knight marshal wielded that same dread sword. Too many dead, too many riddles, Lothar shook his head, cursing his own memories. He'd fallen into a nightmare and did not know how to waken.

The stream wound upwards, flowing around a jumble of rocks and boulders, slowing his horse to a crawl. The downpour lessened to a drizzle, but Lothar was so wet and cold it mattered not. And then he saw the axe marks on the pine tree, the subtle sign of the maroon. Steering his warhorse from the stream, he dismounted. He tugged off his gauntlet, surprised by how badly his hands shook. *Must be the cold.* He fingered the axe cut for sap, relieved to find the mark still sticky, proof the marks were fresh-cut. "We've found our way home." His warhorse stamped and snorted, sending a spray of droplets in all directions. "I know. We both need shelter and food." He gave his horse a reassuring pat and then clambered into the saddle. Taking up the reins, he nudged his weary mount up the hill. The axe marks led to a trail, and the trail led to a mountain meadow.

Light broke through the clouds, banishing the drizzle, but the pale sun offered little warmth, making a mockery of spring.

A pair of scouts with nocked bows stepped from behind a stand of green-skirted saplings.

Lothar raised his battleaxe in salute. "For King Ursus!" The password would surely have changed by now, yet he prayed Rannock had told the scouts to keep an eye open for him.

The scouts stared down their arrows for a tense heartbeat, but then they relaxed their bowstrings and waved him past.

He found the main trail. A river of hoof prints marred the muddy ground. He followed them upward to a second meadow. The smell of wood smoke permeated the forest, teasing him forward with the hope of warmth and food. Riding through a stand of birch trees dripping with rain, he emerged to find the camp sprawled before him. Tents and lean-tos, a patchwork of canvas, branches and shields, crowded the mud-swamped meadow. They looked like an army defeated and dispossessed, until one noticed the bright glitter of steel. Their tents were mere hovels, but the knights kept their armor polished and their weapons sharp. Harried and outnumbered...yet the maroon was not broken...not yet. Flushed with a relentless pride, Lothar straightened in the saddle.

He threaded his mount through the hovels and stone-ringed fires, making his way to the lone pavilion at the camp's heart. Friends and comrades shouted greetings as he passed, but their voices and their stares were laden with too many questions. Lothar answered with a nod and nothing more, saving his answers for the other captains.

As he neared the pavilion, his squire, James, came rushing to his side. The shock in the lad's eyes told Lothar how bedraggled he looked. "My lord, you need warm clothing and food."

"After I see the captains." He swung down from the saddle, every part of him rusted and aching. "See that Stalwart gets a full feedbag after you rub him dry." Handing the reins to the lad, he gave the stallion an affectionate pat. "He's more than earned his oats."

"Yes, m'lord."

Lothar turned to find Rannock waiting for him. A younger man with auburn hair and a muscular build, Rannock was the champion of the morning star and a captain of the maroon...and one of the few who had helped to bury the king.

"I feared you would not come."

Lothar gave him a weary smile. "I nearly didn't."

Rannock's stare widened, but he held his questions. "Come, we've meat and mead and decisions that need to be made."

Lothar ducked beneath the canvas flap, nearly swooning from the welcome warmth. A squire knelt to tug off his muddy boots, while another took his sodden cloak. A thick carpet covered the ground, a rare luxury brought from Castlegard, but the pavilion bore not a stick of furniture. The captains sat cross-legged around a brazier, leaning on bedrolls. He took a seat among them, his gaze roving the circle of faces: Sir Rannock, Sir Blaze, Sir Adelmar, Sir Varlin, Sir Krismir, with a fresh scar marring his handsome face, and Sir Gravis, the old sad-eyed veteran. Their numbers had dwindled, too many of their best left to rot as corpses on unnamed battlefields. This winter war had cost too damn much, yet he feared the reaper's grim toll was not fully paid.

Sir Blaze set a mug of heated mead in front of him and then handed him a bowl filled with savory stew. Chunks of venison and dried carrots swam in the thick broth. *Meat,* Lothar lunged for the bowl. He plied his spoon, wolfing half the bowl before he realized how badly his hands shook. A few of the captains stared, while others looked away.

Rannock nudged him. "Eat. You're half starved."

"Tell me of the maroon."

The others gave their reports, speaking of smaller battles, scarce supplies, and too many wounded.

Lothar finished the bowl and ate another, and in between he sipped the warm mead, sweet as mulled honey soothing his throat. Warmth pervaded him, and he began to feel almost human. Finally replete, Lothar leaned back on a bedroll and met their stares. "I feel your questions."

Rannock began, his face grim. "The scouts you traveled with returned with tales of slaughter. They claim the marshal fights like a whirlwind. They say he defeats hundreds, all of them dying beneath the Dark Sword." Rannock leaned forward his face intent. "*Hundreds defeated by one!*" He made the hand sign against evil, his voice dropping to a whisper. "Is it true?"

"True." He felt their stares. "All true."

"They say no foe can stand against him."

Lothar hesitated. "Also true...so far."

A ripple of murmurs circled the captains.

"When the scouts returned alone," Rannock speared him with his stare, "we feared you dead."

Lothar cupped his hands around the mug of mead. "The marshal refused our aid. So I sent the others away. But I kept watch...from a distance."

"And?"

Lothar considered the question, knowing the canvas walls were thin. "The marshal needs our help no longer. Somehow...," he shook his head as if he still did not believe it, "somehow the Dark Sword leads him to nearby patrols, as if the cursed blade can sense a foe." He stared at the others. "He's making his way west. He'll engage the enemy at Raven Pass."

Rannock and Gravis both gaped, but Krismir, the youngest captain, blazed with intent. "Then we must ride for Raven Pass! We can't let the marshal fight alone!" He stared at the others, seeking support, but none would meet his gaze. Krismir rounded on Lothar. "Give the order! We must ride for Raven Pass!"

So full of courage and glory, yet how little you understand. Lothar shook his head. "We have other orders."

Krismir's gaze narrowed as if sensing a trap. "What orders?"

"I met with the knight marshal. I spoke to him. He orders the maroon to retreat to the east." It was a half-truth. He hoped his friend would forgive him for it. "We're to ride east and make our stands at the bridges and at Castlegard. With the Snowmelt in full spate, the enemy will need the bridges to reach the south."

Krismir refused to be silenced. "We can't let the marshal fight alone."

Lothar's patience snapped. "We have orders!"

Krismir glared, their stares crossing, but the younger man gave way.

Lothar bridled his anger. "No one doubts your courage, but would you deny the marshal this glory?"

Krismir's jaw fell open but no sound escaped.

"He does this for the maroon." Lothar glared at the others. "The marshal risks his life, his very soul, to give us fighting odds."

Gravis understood. He raised his mug, his voice solemn. "To the marshal."

The others raised their mugs and tankards in salute. Flasks of mead were passed and the mugs were refilled many times. The talk turned to small things. Lothar dozed, feeling the tug of sleep combined with safety, but he woke with a fierce need to piss. Too weary to rise, yet the need could not be ignored. Pulling on his boots, he stumbled out into the chill night air. The cold hit like a bracing slap, breaking the groggy grip of the mead. A horse nickered from his left, setting his bearings. He walked in the other direction, knowing the piss trenches were always on the opposite side of the horse lines. A crescent moon gave him just enough light to see by. He found the trench and arched a golden stream to the bottom, groaning with relief. Binding his trousers, Lothar heard footsteps from behind.

He turned to find Rannock waiting for him, a grave look on his face. "You and I, we've shared much. We buried our king at Raven Pass...but we won't be burying the marshal, will we?"

Lothar's voice was raw with the truth. "No."

"The Dark Sword?"

"Aye, it will take him, one way or another." His voice dropped to a harsh rasp. "If it hasn't already."

Rannock gave him a sharp look. "What do you mean?"

The truth hurt. "He barely knew me. He barely remembered."

Rannock looked away, considering. When his stare swung back to Lothar, his face looked haunted. "There's one other thing the scouts said, but I swore them to silence lest it ruin morale."

Lothar waited, knowing what was coming yet dreading the words.

"They said the enemy surrendered, laid down their weapons and fell to their knees...yet the marshal slew them."

Rannock's gaze begged for a lie, but Lothar could not stomach it. "It's true, all true." His voice sounded as if it came from the grave. "I fear we've lost him to the Dark Sword."

Rannock shuttered his gaze, but Lothar had to say the rest. "We dare not meet him on the field of battle."

Rannock stared in disbelief.

Lothar endured the captain's searching gaze.

"How can you be sure?"

Lothar's voice dropped to a hoarse whisper. "Because he damn near killed me." Turning, he walked back through the camp, seeking a way out of the nightmare.

27

Master Rizel

Master Rizel hastened to answer the summons of the Grand Master. Sunlight pierced the windows, illuminating the scripted walls. Climbing the steps, he passed through the gold clad doors inset with lapis Seeing Eyes. A pair of blue-robed monks with quarterstaffs stood on either side, keeping watch. Nodding to the guards, Master Rizel entered the audience chamber. Beneath his boots, the mage-stone floor was painted a rich golden-yellow, making the room welcome to acolytes and outsiders. Halfway across the chamber, a low railing marked the divide, the floor abruptly changing from golden yellow to midnight-blue. Elegant in its simplicity, the divided floor had a profound effect, the place where the outer world met the monastery's inner wisdom. As a young acolyte, he thought of it as the place where inquiry met answers, but as a master, he realized many questions had no answers, as if the gods kept riddles of their own.

More than thirty blue-robed monks were already assembled, most were masters who'd witnessed the invoking. He scanned their faces, noting friends and antagonists. Good debates required at least two sides, but sometimes he thought his adversarial brethren were remarkably shortsighted. He prayed their shortsightedness never hurt the Order...or Erdhe.

Nodding to his friends, he strode to the low railing, the divide between the golden-yellow floor from the midnight-blue. Just beyond arm's reach of the railing, the sword was displayed on a silken pillow. A sword without peer, a sword of legend, forged by the last great wizard. Even the name sounded dauntless, *Invictus*.

He'd heard how fresh-faced acolytes swarmed to the chamber to gawk at the sword. Truth be told, more than a few blue-robed masters had done the same, for such an Illumination had not been accomplished in nigh on four hundred years. Little wonder the monastery hummed like a kicked hive.

The sword's invoking brought hope...but it also brought division.

Factions within the blue argued for seclusion, for the protection of knowledge, for wielding the sword solely in defense of the monastery. In the depths of his soul, Rizel knew the sword was meant to be wielded, but not by a blue-robed monk. The sword belonged in Castlegard, in the hands of a hero. He'd argued vehemently against the seclusionists, trying to sway the others. The bitter debate raged through the hallowed halls for more than a fortnight. Debate and argument were timeworn forms of learning, a way to test the facets of knowledge, yet this debate had gained rancor, adding poison to the discourse. Finally, word came that the Grand Master had made his decision.

Master Rizel sidled next to Master Adelbart. "What word on the girl?"

The master calligrapher looked exhausted, deep shadows lining his eyes. "Nimeria remains locked in a magical swoon, no telling when she'll wake. She's under Master Garth's care."

"Great magic exacts a great toll, it was always so, but Nimeria is young and strong. The young are always so resilient."

Adelbart gave him a grateful look. "May it be so."

"Garth will take good care of the girl. She could be in no better hands." Master Rizel gestured to the blue steel sword. "The others are awed by the sword but they miss the point. This sword is Light-sent, a boon to Castlegard, while the girl, *she* is the boon to the Kiralynn Order, a chance to reclaim the lost art of Illumination."

Master Adelbart nodded. "You see clearly. The scriptorium hums with young scholars, burning oil lamps all hours of the day and night. My apprentices strive to repeat Nimeria's prodigious feat. I envy them their single-minded enthusiasm." His voice held a shadow of worry. "The young are so keen, yet they do not fear the consequences."

"The Light will guide them. Perhaps another Illuminator will rise from among them."

"The Light willing."

Behind them, the great golden doors thudded closed, heralding the start of the audience. The chamber had grown crowded with blue-robed masters, a representation of all points of view. Master Rizel spied Felix and Normath and others of the seclusion faction standing near the great mage-glass window. He acknowledged them with a nod, but there was no debate, for the decision was in the hands of the Grand Master.

The sound of a deep-throated gong shimmered through the chamber, drawing all stares to the blue side of the room.

The Voice stepped from behind the Star Screen, a gray-haired master with a solemn face. Sitting cross-legged, he used a striker to light a flame in the brazier inset in the floor. Incense wafted through the chamber, offering a soothing scent. "The Grand Master sees you, the Grand Master hears you, draw near to hear the words of the Grand Master."

The gong sounded for the second time.

Master Rizel bowed towards the Star Screen and then settled to the floor, sitting cross-legged amongst the scattered pillows. His brethren did the same. Blue-robed monks and masters filled the golden floor, their robes puddled around them like still ponds.

The Voice reached behind the Star Screen and accepted a scroll.

Master Rizel held his breath.

Snapping the scroll open, the Voice read, "Debate rages within our hallowed halls, yet this is a time for action, not words. Ancient prophesies rush to be born. The signs are legion, from the red comet ripping the sky, to the coming of the crystal blade bearer, to the invocation of the blue steel sword. The Battle Immortal is upon us." The Voice scanned the assembly, his words ringing with the Grand Master's authority. "Let there be no debate, the Kiralynn Order is at war."

A murmur rippled through the assembly, but Master Rizel remained stone-still. *The failure of Castlegard's mage-stone,* he does not include it as a sign. Master Rizel pondered why the latest portent went unstated...and then he understood. *The Grand Master does not yet have an answer to the riddle.* The realization struck like a punch to his chest.

The Voice waited till quiet returned before continuing to read. "All of our knowledge, all of our history, all of our magic is but a prelude to this battle. To think otherwise is willful delusion, for the Kiralynn Order already spends our knowledge, our magic, and our dearest life's blood below the mountains. To think we can stand apart is foolish and naive."

The gong's voice shimmered through the chamber.

The Voice held the scroll to the small fire, turning the Grand Master's written words to light.

Master Rizel watched the parchment burn, feeling a sense of great moment, as if the whole world teetered on a nib of a quill.

The Voice reached behind the Star Screen accepting a second scroll. Unrolling the parchment, he read, "An owl has come to the monastery bearing grim tidings from Lanverness. Master Numar is dead and his focus is lost."

Dead! Rizel choked on the news.

Cries of shock and outrage spread through the chamber.

"How can this be?"

"Who killed him?"

"What of his focus?"

The Voice raised his hand forestalling the debate. When silence returned, he read, "Serving as a hidden emissary to the Rose Queen, Numar posed as an apothecary, hiding within the queen's capital city. Our agent found him and two of his apprentices dead within his shop, burnt and blackened, blasted by fire. His focus could not be found."

Burnt and blackened, Rizel closed his eyes, sickened by his friend's harsh death.

A strident voice called from the rear of the chamber. "What of his magic? What focus did he wield?"

Master Rizel answered. "A fireball. Numar wielded one of the greatest battle magics in our arsenal."

A deathly chill seeped through the chamber.

Felix growled, "This is why we need to stay within our walls and protect our own."

Master Rizel snapped, his voice armored with steel. "If Numar died of *fire* then he died *fighting*." He glared at the others. "His death tells us much, for what enemy can best a fireball?"

Murmurs multiplied across the chamber, everyone speaking at once.

The sound of a gong shimmered through the room, demanding silence.

Quiet returned, yet a restless undercurrent remained.

"Heed the wisdom of the Grand Master." The Voice read from a third scroll. "For over a thousand years the Kiralynn Order has stood apart in the fastness of our mountain monastery, yet we are also of Erdhe, our fates forever intertwined. Through the centuries we have striven to thwart Darkness by sharing our knowledge and our insights with the royals of the southern kingdoms, but knowledge alone shall not defeat this Darkest of foes. We stand at the turning of an Age. The decisions we make, the actions we take, shall weigh heavy in the outcome. We dare not be laggards to the battle. Like Master Numar, the Kiralynn Order must enter the fray, risking all. To that end, the invoked sword, Invictus, shall be dispatched to Castlegard with all haste. And the relics of the Star Chamber shall be brought forth to see if any here can wield them. Let this decision be written into the annals. May the Lords of Light protect the Kiralynn Order and save Erdhe from endless Darkness."

"By the Light, let it be so."

The sound of a gong shimmered through the chamber.

The Voice retreated behind the Star Screen, formally ending the audience.

The chamber erupted in debate, but Master Rizel did not listen, lost in his own thoughts. *The relics,* the Grand Master released the relics, the most potent magics stored from another Age. He wondered if anyone alive could still wield them...and then he considered the second half of the Grand Master's decision. The full effect hit him like a poleax. His stare roved across his blue-robed brethren, taking in the divided floor, the Star Screen and the beauty of the illuminated text scribing the walls. The Kiralynn Monastery was his home. It was also the most precious haven of knowledge in all of Erdhe, yet it was no longer protected by seclusion. If the monastery fell, the victory of Darkness would be absolute. In the depths of his soul, he knew it was necessary, yet he shuddered at the risk.

28

Jordan

War drums beat a steady cadence. The army marched north under proud battle banners, the red and blue checks of Navarre rippling in the wind. Jordan rode in the vanguard, her silver armor gleaming in the sunlight. With every passing league, her army gained numbers. They came from villages, hamlets, and farmsteads, with weapons on one shoulder, a sack of provisions on the other, answering the call of their king. Clad in homespun browns, most were archers, but a few bore swords. Doffing their caps at their bonny princess, they swelled the ranks, singing folksongs to the cadence of the drums.

Keeping to the roads, her army marched through villages and rolling farmland, and everywhere the people of Navarre turned out to cheer. Women offered loaves of fresh baked bread, girls blew kisses, while young lads ran alongside the column, hero-worship beaming from their faces. Spirits soared and Jordan swelled with pride, but in the back of her mind a foreboding voice warned that her army got the glory without the bloodshed. War made heroes but it also brought death.

Knowing time was of the essence, she pressed her men for more speed. They crossed the coastal ranges, descending gently rolling hills into flat farmland, marching from Navarre into Coronth. The countryside looked much the same as the seaside kingdom, but the difference lay in the people. The Flame religion was dead, yet the villagers were wary as kicked dogs, watching from behind shuttered windows. Food grew scarce, the farms picked clean like a plague of locusts, yet they met no opposition. Her men kept their weapons close and their senses sharp. Pickets were posted around the camp each night while scouts rode a wide perimeter in every direction.

The leagues passed and Jordan grew increasingly anxious to see Stewart. She longed to take the vanguard and spur ahead, to find his camp and rush into his arms, but the army was her responsibility, the steady tramp of boots weighing on her like an iron shackle. She chided herself for her own impatience, knowing every sword she brought would be sorely needed, but the waiting proved hard. Married for more than four moon turns, yet she'd spent but one night with her wedded husband. One precious night, Jordan burned just thinking of him. Her stallion sensed her need. Tossing his head, he whinnied, biting at the nearest mare. Embarrassed, she settled her horse, hoping her helmet hid her blush.

The drizzling rain turned to mist, the morning sun streaming through the clouds. A scout emerged from the woods, cantering towards her. "Riders approach!"

"Friend or foe?"

The scout flashed a grin. "They're clad in emerald green!"

The Rose Army, joy leaped in her heart. "Sound the conch shells and double the march time, we'll sup with our allies tonight!"

Cheers answered her words. The conch shells blew and the war drums quickened their beat, yet it still seemed a snail's pace to Jordan. Scanning the horizon, she yearned for the first glimpse of emerald green banners.

Leagues passed before she saw them. A troop of thirty knights cantered down the far hillside, arms and armor shining bright. They bore no battle banners but all their surcoats were emerald green, white roses emblazoned on their chests. One in particular caught her gaze. Tall and sure in the saddle, he wore no helm, his dark hair streaming like a banner. *Stewart!*

Her heartbeat quickened and she yearned to set spurs to her mount, yet she felt an entire army watching at her back. Keeping her stallion to a steady pace, she bridled her heart, pulling him towards her with her gaze.

His emerald cloak flaring behind, he galloped towards her with a smile on his face "You're a welcome sight!"

An answering smile blazed across her face. "Navarre brings our bows to the north."

"As the Rose brings our swords." His eyes gleamed bright. "My lady of the seashell!" Touching the brooch pinned to his cloak, he pivoted his stallion in a showy turn to ride beside her.

Their knees nearly touched.

"My husband." She yearned to lean across and kiss him, but too many watched.

His gaze burned into hers. "It's been too long."

"Much too long. The Crimson Keep seems like a dream."

His voice dropped to a whisper. "I miss our hovel in the ruins."

A tarp, a brazier and a bearskin rug, so simple their wedding bower, she flushed remembering, feeling a blush rise crimson across her face. She lowered her head lest the others notice.

His escort mingled with her vanguard, emerald green mixing with the red and blue of the seaside kingdom. Greetings were exchanged, but Jordan heard none of it. "How long till your camp?"

"Only a few leagues." His horse sidled towards her, their knees whispered close.

She longed to kiss him. "Shall we ride ahead?"

"No." His hungry smile told her he wished it otherwise. "Let my men see my bride leading an army." Pride filled his voice. "Let them see what kind of queen I've wed."

His words touched her like an unexpected gift.

"My queen of seashells, you bring welcome swords and bows." He gazed at her with unabashed pride...but then his face sobered. "I got your letters."

Messengers traveled so much faster than armies.

His voice dropped to a whisper. "I'm sorry for your loss."

Jordan paled at the memory of so much death. "The gods sent me visions, but I came too late."

"You answered their call and you saved some."

"Not enough, not nearly enough."

"Don't say that. Every life you saved matters."

She had not written about her mother, a weeping wound too fresh to share. "Have you met the enemy?"

"Not yet. Our scouts watch the Snowmelt. If they try to cross, we'll engage them."

"The river is in full spate."

"A gift from the gods. The Snowmelt is at its wildest in the spring...one of our few advantages. They'll not find it easy to cross."

"And the odds?"

His gaze turned bleak. "Too grim to name."

She understood his reticence. They spoke instead of the war behind them, sharing details of Lingard and Pellanor and Navarre. The leagues passed and they topped a rise. Jordan got her first view of the Rose Army. Canvas tents stretched in neat lines, radiating outward from the central pavilions. Battle banners flew at the heart of the camp, the crossed roses of Lanverness topped by a prince's crown, the emerald silk bright against sun-drenched sky.

Scouts came galloping toward them, their bows raised in greeting. A horn sounded a welcoming note, summoning soldiers from their tents. A cheer rose from the camp, echoed by her own army.

"Shall we?" Stewart waited on her.

Jordan grinned. "Sound the conch shells and greet our allies!"

Behind her, the drums beat a merry rhythm while the conch shells added a voice from the sea. With checkered battle banners streaming overhead, Jordan led her army down the rise.

Soldiers in green tabards poured from their tents. Clashing swords against their shields, they raised a hearty cheer. *"The princess of Lanverness!"*

Hearing her marriage announced by thousands of male voices, Jordan felt her face flame bright red.

The two armies met and embraced. Jordan asked Major Colson to settle the men while she followed Stewart to the central pavilions. Dismounting, she handed her reins to an eager page. Stiff from the long ride, she met Stewart's officers, a blur of fresh faces and new names. She struggled through the introductions, knowing the niceties needed to be observed, but it seemed a torture to stand so near to Stewart yet not to touch.

Finally, Stewart ended her agony, dismissing his officers. "We'll feast tonight, our two armies coming together as brothers-in-arms, but for now...I'd like to be alone with my bride."

His officers flashed knowing grins and a few made ribald comments, but Jordan did not care. Stewart took her arm. A jolt passed through her. "This way, my lady." He led her to the largest pavilion. She gaped in astonishment when she saw it, for two coats of arms adorned the canvas, the emerald shield of Lanverness...and the checkered shield of Navarre. Painted side by side, the two shields were entwined with white roses, a declaration of their marriage...and their love. "How?"

"I had it painted before I left Pellanor, a small gift for my bride." He held the canvas flap aside. "My lady?"

She stepped inside, embraced by the warmth of a glowing brazier. A jewel-colored carpet covered the floor, soft beneath her boots. Two armor stands stood at attention, waiting for sheaths of steel. A table cluttered with maps filled the center. And in the rear, a wide bed covered in furs...but this was no ordinary camp bed. Twice as wide and piled high with furs and pillows, it looked sumptuous...and inviting.

Drawn to the bed like iron to a lodestone, her fingers trailing across the sable fur, "And this?"

"A craftsman made it for me, two camp beds cunningly fitted together." He stepped close. "But I've not yet tasted its true purpose."

A smile burst across her face. "It's true..."

His lips were on hers. His kiss consumed her. She clung to him, her hunger answering his. Armor and clothing became impediments. They tugged at bindings and cursed the buckles, leaving an empty trail across the pavilion. Finally naked, they fell across the bed. Skin against skin, the need roared through them. His fingers found her hot and wet. He trembled above her. "I can't..."

"*Yes!*" She needed no preamble. He mounted her with a deep thrust. She bit back a moan, knowing an entire army listened just beyond canvas walls, yet she could not get enough of him. Clutching him close, she urged him on. All too soon, he shuddered on top. Sweat-drenched, they collapsed on soft furs.

She nestled her head on his shoulder.

He smoothed a wayward strand of hair from her face. "I couldn't wait."

"Nor I." She snuggled against him. "I don't want to ever be parted."

"Nor I from you...but we've a war to wage."

"We'll fight it together." Her fingers traced the scars across his chest and shoulders, a legacy of the last war.

"Yes, but this time we fight the Mordant."

He rolled on his side. Leaning on an elbow, he peered at her as if memorizing the curves of her face. "You must promise to live."

His sudden intensity scared her. "What troubles you?"

"Perhaps the queen's fears have infected me."

"What fears?"

"Her dispatches are full of concerns, about the Mordant's army, about some Prince of Ur who's come to Pellanor...and about the Tandroth line." He stared at her. "I am the queen's sole heir...and my wife rides to war beside me."

Her breath caught, afraid he would order her away, locking her behind castle walls, kept safe like a broodmare. Anger spiked through her. "The Army of Navarre is *mine* to lead." She stared at him, her words laced with steel, a warning and a threat. "We both serve by the sword and I will be nowhere else."

"I know. That's why you must promise to live."

She met his gaze. "By Valin, we will *both* live beyond this war!"

He smiled then. "My warrior bride." Leaning down, he kissed her, gentle at first then deepening to a renewed hunger. They made love a second time. Jordan reveled in his arms, their pleasure magnified by the risk. All too soon, Stewart collapsed beside her, a smile on his face. "It seems the bed is a success."

"But, my lord, we've barely tested it!"

"You vixen!" He rolled on top, pinning her to the furs.

She struggled against him, escaping his hold, a mocking display of resistance. Laughing, she leaped from the bed, but he caught her, pulling her back to the warmth.

A voice from beyond the canvas intruded. "My lord, your captains assemble for the feast."

He pinned her to the fur and claimed a deep kiss. "I'm not done with you."

"My lord," a lad's voice persisted, "the princess's men have brought her things."

Stewart sighed. "Duty calls." He gave her one last kiss and then rose from the bed. Naked, he crossed the pavilion to pour a goblet of wine.

Jordan enjoyed the view, a sheen of sweat glistening across his bare skin, highlighting every manly muscle.

Lifting the wine goblet in salute, he winked at her. "Come."

Yelping in surprise, Jordan yanked a fur across her nakedness, a combination of hasty modesty and reluctance to leave the warmth of their bower.

A tow-headed squire held the canvas flap aside. Two men entered carrying her small chest of clothes. Averting their eyes, they bowed toward the prince and then left the pavilion with knowing grins on their faces.

Stewart pulled on a tunic. "At least the queen will know our marriage is consummated."

"You mean my men will know!" Jordan threw a boot, but he dodged aside, a boyish grin on his face. She felt her face flame red, but in truth she knew there were few secrets in an army camp. They were wedded and bedded, and if the whole camp dared to listen, it would not keep her from her husband's bed. "They're just jealous."

"No doubt." He flashed a conspirator's grin. "But now dinner awaits."

Darkness encroached beyond the canvas walls, proving they'd spent hours in dalliance...yet the time seemed so short to Jordan. They dressed quickly, the scents of sizzling spit-roasted beef invading their pavilion to rouse their hunger. Jordan chose a soft tunic of deep blue velvet over leather pants and knee high boots. Buckling her sword at her waist, she swirled her checkered cloak around her shoulders.

Stewart looked dashing in a surcoat of emerald green, a sapphire blue sword belted by his side. The sword piqued her interest, yet she held her questions for another time.

He offered his arm, a gallant gesture. "My lady."

She took his arm, knowing two armies would be watching.

He led her from their pavilion to a large fire. The captains were already seated in a circle around the crackling flames. The others stood at their approach, bowing to the royal pair, more than a few with knowing grins on their faces. Jordan struggled to contain a rising blush.

Stewart made another round of introductions. His officers mingled with hers, emerald green offset by the red and blue checkers of Navarre. Jordan sat with Stewart on her left and Lord Dane, a handsome man with a rogue's smile on her right. Her own officers were already present, Major Colson, her second, Varnick, the captain of her pike men, Cyril, the captain of her archers, and her friend, Rafe, though he chose to wear leathers instead of the blue robes of his Order.

Wooden plates were passed, piled high with choice cuts of spit-roasted beef ladled with gravy, pan fried onions with spring mushrooms, winter leeks, spring carrots and a crusty flatbread. Squires circled the campfire, keeping tankards full with a frothing dark ale. Jordan tasted the beef, juicy and thick, licking the grease from her fingers. "Do you always eat so well?"

Stewart raised his tankard in salute. "We killed the fatted calf to celebrate your arrival. Eat well, for tomorrow we're back to war rations."

Jordan enjoyed the savory meal and the easy camaraderie. As the ale flowed, the talk turned boisterous, mostly boasts about past exploits on the battlefield or in the bedroom, but none spoke of tomorrow, avoiding the uncertain future. Jordan made it a point to speak with each of Stewart's officers, seeking to learn their true natures. Mathis told the most ribald jokes, Kelso was quiet and steady, but Dane seemed to know Stewart the best, a boyhood companion and sword brother. Jordan refilled his tankard, plying the handsome lord for tales of her husband's boyhood.

Stewart leaned close. "He's a rogue, you shouldn't listen to him."

Jordan smiled, "A rogue, all the more reason to listen! I want to hear everything!"

The campfire crackled, spitting sparks towards a star spangled sky. They laughed and talked, the stories growing more preposterous as the ale flowed. Several of the men sat slumped with their eyes closed, succumbed to the feast. Jordan savored every moment, the good food, the hearty company of honest warriors...and Stewart, near enough to touch.

Soft footsteps came from behind, soft and stealthy.

Jordan whirled, her hand on her sword hilt. She froze, surprised to see a figure robed in midnight-blue. Firelight flickered across his face, her memory supplying a name. *"Aeroth!"*

He gave her a grave nod. "We need to talk."

She got Stewart's attention, watching his eyes widen at the sight of the monk, proof his appearance was unexpected. Rafe saw and joined them. They slipped away from the campfire, leading the monks back to their pavilion. Jordan's stomach churned with foreboding. Aeroth's sudden appearance could not bode well. She'd had one moment of stolen peace with Stewart and the war came calling like a relentless doom.

29

Master Rizel

The tome sat like a dead weight in his arms. He'd found it in a remote part of the Great Archive, high on a shelf, covered in centuries of dust. Long forgotten, the tome was either hidden or misplaced, yet he had no doubt it was a true treasure, a trove of knowledge waiting to be rediscovered. His fingers caressed the leather bindings, so old they were nearly brittle. The ornate silver clasp was tarnished by time, yet the workmanship was exquisite. But it was the name embossed on the cover that signaled its true worth, the name of the last Illuminator to walk the monastery's hallowed halls. Old, so very old, Master Rizel handled the tome with great care, but it felt heavy in his arms. It felt like a desperate risk, it felt like a last resort. One he prayed the Order would never need.

He reached the alcove where the others were assembled. Pouring over mountains of scrolls and ancient tomes, the monastery's brightest minds sought to solve the riddle of mage-stone, to learn why Castlegard's walls were failing and what could be done about it. For more than a fortnight the lanterns had burned bright in the Great Archive, the blue-robed masters working through the long nights, yet the answer remained elusive, as if the riddle were posed by the gods.

A hushed silence prevailed. So engrossed in their studies, no one looked his way when he returned to the alcove. Master Rizel carefully set the ancient tome on the table. He sank into a chair, his eyes aching from long hours of reading. His gaze roved the others, seeking a spark of excitement, but he found none. Most had their noses buried in musty tomes, learned bloodhounds on the trail of knowledge, seeking the solution to a perilous riddle. He cleared his throat, a loud disturbance for the Archives. "Anything?"

Blinking like owls thrust into bright sunshine, the masters looked at him from across the scroll-littered table. Lurinda shook her head, *no*, a subtle but damning gesture echoed by the others. Finally, Master Grimshaw spoke, his gravelly voice tinged with defeat. "There's nothing in the prophecies." Bald as an egg, his skin the color of tanned leather, the master had a blacksmith's muscled build, yet he was one of the most learned scholars of the ancient prophesies. "I've searched the oldest quatrains from the Orb. So many of the dire portents of this time are foretold in the ancient writings. I've found numerous passages dealing with the Mordant being reborn in the southern kingdoms, the fiery comet heralding his rebirth, the start of the Battle Immortal, the claiming of the crystal dagger, yet there is no mention of mage-stone."

"None at all?"

"Not of mage-stone," Master Grimshaw shook his head, "but there is one quatrain that might refer to Castlegard." Opening a thick tome, he read, "*North becomes south as castles fall. Victory balances on the unforeseen blade.*"

Master Olgarth seized the words. "The unforeseen blade could be Invictus!"

"Or it could be the crystal dagger."

"Or some other unknown sword."

Ever the pessimist, Master Rugar groused, "The Mordant's spent a millennia hoarding magic, you can bet he's got a magical sword of his own. Perhaps more than one."

Mistress Lurinda shook her head. "It must mean the crystal dagger."

"It could mean Invictus."

The alcove erupted in argument. Prophesies were ever a messy business, as if the gods only spoke in riddles. The debate raged back and forth, yet most of the arguments were conjecture not solid conclusions. Master Rizel listened with half an ear, his mind worrying the words of the quatrain. *North becomes south as castles fall,* he liked it not. Such an ill-omened portent, he could not conceive of Castlegard, the great enclave of the Octagon Knights, falling. And if the mage-stone of Castlegard's walls could fail...the mage-stone of the monastery might be doomed as well. They needed a solution, a remedy to heal the threat. Endless debate would not avail them. Master Rizel stood, invoking an abrupt silence. "It seems the prophecies are silent on the matter of mage-stone, but what of our loremasters? Perhaps the study of magic holds the answers we seek?"

Everyone's gaze swiveled to Master Vernius. Old to the point of being called ancient, the shriveled loremaster sat puddled in his robes of midnight-blue, yet his gaze was bird-bright. "Mage-stone was ever one of the Order's highest magics, yet that power was lost to us long ago." His voice quavered, as thin as fine parchment, everyone straining to listen. "Much that was written about mage-stone is gone, lost in the great fire of the first century."

Master Rizel's disappointment bit deep, for it seemed all routes of inquiry led to dead ends...or more questions.

"But," Master Vernius raised a single finger, reclaiming everyone's attention, "there is something I remember, a rumor passed down to me by my old master, may the Lords of Light grant peace to his soul."

Everyone leaned forward to listen.

"Master Calipurs told a tale about Master Julian, the loremaster of the third century. He claimed that Julian was obsessed with recovering the lost magic of mage-stone. Julian sent the Zward scouring the southern kingdoms searching for tomes and parchments, seeking to restore what was lost. Julian hoped copies of the Order's writings survived beyond the Southern Mountains, thus evading the fire's obliviating embrace. The same Zward who erased the monastery from the maps of men, searched the length and breadth of Erdhe for writings on mage-stone, and do you know what they found?"

Silence throbbed like an expectant heartbeat, everyone hanging on the tale.

"They found nothing."

Master Rugar gasped in frustration. "That's because scrolls were never taken from the monastery!"

"No, not true." Master Vernius's sharp gaze circled the assembly. "They found nothing because someone else searched for them first."

A shiver raced down Master Rizel's spine. "What do you mean?"

"Three of the searching Zward were brutally murdered and one disappeared, never to be found. When the Zwardmaster investigated the murders he returned with unsettling rumors. It seemed skilled killers searched for those very same scrolls, slaying the Zward in cunning ambushes. Some named the killers servants of the Mordant."

The breath hissed out of Master Rizel. "And you believe those killers found the scrolls, found them before the Zward?"

Master Vernius nodded. "Just so."

The conclusion hit like a sword thrust. "Then the decay of Castlegard's mage-stone may somehow be caused by the Mordant?"

Master Vernius gave the smallest of nods.

A grim silence gripped the assembly.

Master Rizel had to ask the question. "Could this same curse be visited on the monastery's mage-stone?"

Master Vernius shrugged. "Without the lost scrolls, who can say?"

The tension gripping the chamber deepened to an ominous hush.

Master Rugar stirred, anger lashing his voice to indignation. "But the prophecies make no mention of this! They warn of every other dire portent but not the failure of mage-stone! How can the prophecies be so silent on mage-stone?"

Master Grimshaw answered, his voice ominous. "The ending of an Age."

Everyone turned his way.

"We've reached the ending of an Age, when all things are possible...when prophecies are fulfilled, or they become undone." His gaze circled the assembly. "Perhaps the timeline is shifted...and new destinies reign."

His words fell like a doom.

Master Rizel stared in shock, for without the prophecies the Order was blind. He hardened his resolve, reaching for the last resort. "We dare not go blind into the Battle Immortal. To solve this riddle we need to seek one who might remember."

"Remember!"

The word echoed through the gathering, evoking disbelief, and even outright scorn. More than a few masters looked at him as if he'd lost his mind.

Master Grimshaw said, "Explain."

"I found this tome." Master Rizel caressed the time-worn binding. "Written by Gwendolyn, the last great Illuminator. I know not if it was lost or deliberately hidden, for I found it on a remote shelf, covered in centuries of dust."

"A lost tome from Gwendolyn?" Master Vernius leaned forward, "I've not heard of such a thing."

"Nor I, till I found it." With reverent hands, Master Rizel opened the tome to the page marked by the red tassel. The vellum was brittled by age, but the colors gleamed bright, the calligraphy crisp and exquisite, a peerless work of illuminated art. "It speaks of a relic, a relic the monastery keeps hidden within the vaults beneath the Star Chamber." He stared at the others. "If this text holds true, then that very relic may permit us to speak to one who remembers."

Startled gazes circled the table, returning to him with a storm of questions.

"Come and read for yourselves."

One by one, the venerable masters came forward to read the page and study the illuminated images. Nothing was said, but many sharp glances were cast his way. A few offered him a respectful nod, but many more turned pale, as if the text offered only a grim doom.

He wondered if they were right.

Master Grimshaw was the last to read the illuminated passage. "It sounds possible, and Gwendolyn was an Illuminator of great renown...yet there is great risk."

Master Rizel answered. "Dire times require dire measures. And we've exhausted all other lines of inquiry." He said what he knew many were thinking. "And we will surely lose this war if we do nothing."

Master Grimshaw gave him a measured look, his voice a deep rumble. "Who will dare to wield this relic?"

Master Rizel drew a deep breath. "I will. I found the tome, so it seems fitting that I bear responsibility...though I know not if the relic will waken to my touch."

For once there was no debate. "So be it."

Master Grimshaw said, "When will you make the attempt?"

"As soon as I've given my report to the Grand Master. I see no advantage in waiting."

The other masters bowed towards him, a mark of deep respect. Together they invoked the words of the Order. "Seek Knowledge, Protect Knowledge, Share Knowledge, may the Light grant you the knowledge and wisdom that you seek."

Master Rizel heard the worry laden in their voices. In truth, he shared their fears, for magic could be wild and unpredictable. Staring down at the illuminated page, he studied the details, for he'd just bet his life on the obscure passage.

30

Jordan

Night held sway, the camp noises muted to slumbering snores. While the captains sprawled around the campfire, sated from the feast, Jordan and Stewart slipped away, leading the two monks back to their pavilion. The guards snapped to attention as they passed inside. "We're not to be disturbed."

"Yes, sir."

Dismissing his squire, Stewart stoked the brazier, throwing light across the pavilion. "When did you arrive?"

Aeroth replied. "Just now."

Jordan's gaze snapped to the tussled bed and the bits of clothing trailing across the carpet, telltale signs of their earlier lovemaking. Heat flamed her face, wishing there was somewhere else to meet.

Stewart poured the wine, offering a cup to the blue-robed monk. "And my sentries did not notice?"

"None notice the owl, and I would keep it that way." He gave them a piercing look, a reminder of their vows of secrecy made at Crimson Keep. "Do you have a map? And I could use some food."

Aeroth looked weary, his face drawn, his eyes sunken. Jordan supposed being the owl took its toll.

Rafe slipped outside, asking the guards to bring a plate of food from the feast, and then returned to stand by her side.

Stewart unrolled a vellum scroll across the map table, the brightly painted kingdoms of Erdhe illuminated by the brazier's light.

Aeroth stared down at the map, his face grim. "I bring word from the north. The forces of Darkness are marching, no longer content to hold Raven Pass."

A shiver of dread whispered through Jordan.

Aeroth leaned over the map, stabbing a finger at Raven Pass. "The Mordant's forces defeated the Octagon and took the pass, and there they remained, spreading tentacles through the Dragon Spine

Mountains, fighting the maroon knights and pillaging the farmers and holdfasts...until now."

"What of the Octagon?"

"The knights have been waging a winter war, attacking in the mountain passes. They fight valiantly, exacting a stiff toll, but their numbers have dwindled. Their remaining forces seem to be retreating to Castlegard."

Rafe gasped, "They're giving up?"

"They fought valiantly." Aeroth glared at the younger monk, his voice harsh with rebuke. "Their deeds are worthy of a bard's song. Their bravery bought the south time."

"Time we sorely needed." Stewart said, "What of the enemy?"

"The Mordant divides his forces, sending all his cavalry and a herd of Taals eastward along the Snowmelt."

Stewart scowled, "We dare not let them cross the Snowmelt." He stared at the map. "How many?"

"Two thousand or more."

Two thousand, the number echoed in Jordan's mind like a curse. A small army in the south, yet she knew it was only a fraction of the enemy's forces. Little wonder the knights retreated to their stronghold.

"And what of the Octagon Bridge?"

"When I last flew over it, the maroon knights held it still."

Jordan stared at the map, seeing the hard truth written upon it. "We have to hold Eye Bridge." The men looked at her. "With the Snowmelt in full spate, they'll need the bridge to cross. The Snowmelt is the south's best defense. We dare not let it be breached."

Aeroth's words fell like a doom. "You may be too late."

"Why?"

"The cavalry and a contingent of Taals are riding east at a blistering pace. Either they seek to cross the bridge, or they're riding for Castlegard."

Jordan said, "Cavalry without infantry?"

Aeroth nodded, "Except for a hundred Taals."

"Taals?"

"Ogre-like beings, deformed by magic, over eight feet tall and immensely strong."

Stewart cursed, "By Valin's stones, we're fighting monsters as well as numbers?"

Aeroth drilled him with his stare. "You're fighting more than you know. It was magic that won Raven Pass for the Pentacle. Magic blasted the gates letting the horde bring their numbers to bear."

"How do you know this?"

"I have seen the aftermath. As the owl, I flew over the walls of Raven Pass. The stonework is buckled and broken, the great gates blasted to dust. The wall gapes like a toothless crone."

"How?"

Aeroth shrugged. "The Mordant has ever sought magic. Throughout the Ages he's hungered for it, sought it, collected it, ever adding more magic to his hoard. Magic is power, the type of power he craves above all others. Make no mistake. The Mordant will wield every trick, every magic, bringing all his powers to bear to win the Battle Immortal."

"And you have nothing to counter it? It was your magic that helped us retake Lingard."

"Ellis has taken her orb back to the mountains. I bring you knowledge, use it well."

Stewart scowled, a glint of anger blazing in his eyes, but Jordan drew the discussion back to the map. "If the enemy sends only cavalry, then speed must matter. Cavalry alone means a lightning raid. The Mordant must want something dearly...and he wants it taken fast." She looked at the others, watching as the insight hit them. "Cavalry alone will never take Castlegard, so what does the Mordant want?"

Her question fell like a stone into deep water.

Aeroth said, "I like it not. The Mordant does nothing without a reason."

Stewart said, "If he sends only his cavalry, what of the rest?"

"Half their infantry still holds Raven Pass...while the other half marches west."

"*West?*" A shiver of foreboding raced down Jordan's spine.

Stewart asked, "How much is half?"

Aeroth looked grim. "Forty thousand or more."

The number fell like a doom.

Stewart gaped. "*Forty thousand* is *half?*"

Aeroth nodded. "Give thanks to the Octagon, or you'd be facing far worse odds."

Stewart reached for a goblet. Filling it with wine, he took a long gulp.

Rafe asked, "West to where? There's nothing in the west but forest and a few farmsteads."

But Jordan knew the map held the answer. "The Serpentines, they're going to try and cross at the Serpentines." Her voice turned cold. "And then they'll march south...to Navarre."

Stewart stared at her. "Can it be done?"

"The Serpentines are tricky, shifting sandbars changing with every season. Maps of the Serpentines are worthless, the river banks convulse like an angry snake every springtime." She considered tales she'd heard from fisherman chasing salmon. "Much will depend on the Snowmelt."

Stewart nodded, his face grave. "Then our battle plan is set." He turned to Aeroth. "Can you warn the maroon knights and get them to hold the Octagon Bridge?"

"I need food and a day to rest, but yes, I can warn them."

"Good, you'll have both." His finger traced a path across the map. "I'll take all of my cavalry and my light infantry and quick-march to Eye Bridge. We'll seal the bridge, blocking the way south." He turned to Jordan, his face pale. "And you, my dear wife, must take my heavy infantry and your army and find a way to seal the Serpentines."

The weight of the task fell hard across her shoulders...as did the knowledge they'd be separated. "I'll find a way."

Stewart gave her a solemn nod. "We march in two days time."

Two days, yet she kept her face as still as stone.

"Benly!" Stewart called for his squire.

The tow-headed lad appeared, his eyes heavy with sleep.

"Find a quiet tent for Aeroth and Rafe. Bring them food and drink and whatever else they need." Stewart turned to the two monks. "We'll speak more in the morning."

The boy led the monks from the pavilion.

The canvas flap fell closed and Jordan dropped her mask. "*Two days?*"

"We dare not delay in war...or love." Stewart stepped towards her, a deep hunger kindling his gaze. "One more night," his gaze burned into her. "Do you think we might make a child?"

A child in wartime, it seemed so dangerous, so reckless...yet she'd stopped taking the infusion of vigean root days ago, leaving it in her saddlebag as if she too yearned for a child. "Do we dare?"

"How do we not?" Need flashed between them like lightning. He scooped her into his arms and carried her to their fur-tossed bed.

31

Jordan

Morning came too soon. Sounds of the camp intruded, an army preparing for war. Reluctant yet resigned, they left the warmth of the furs. In somber silence, Jordan donned her armor, burnished steel for her body, a facade of stone for her heart. As a wife, she could have cried at their parting, but as a general, she could not. Buckling her sword at her waist, she strode towards the canvas flap, keeping a tight rein on her resolve.

"Wait." Stewart called her back.

She turned, struggling to contain her emotions.

"This is for you." He settled a slender chain around her neck. A gold ring dangled from it. "When we wed at the Crimson Keep, I had no ring to give you." He gave her a soft smile. "Signet rings are awkward under gauntlets, so I had it set on a chain."

She lifted the heavy ring of pure gold. *A signet ring,* etched deep with a royal seal. Encircled by engraved waves for Navarre, the heart of the seal bore the shield of Lanverness surmounted by a petite crown. The meaning lanced her heart.

He closed her hand around the ring. "With this ring you wield authority within Lanverness, a princess of the Rose Court...and my wife."

The stone façade protecting her heart nearly cracked.

He pressed a fervent kiss upon her closed hand. "Take care, my love."

A single tear escaped. "And you." She lunged into him, needing to feel his arms around her. Armor to armor, the steel of war clanked between them. "Armor," she shook her head, her voice wry, "is not meant for love." The brief levity fled her voice. "I miss you already."

"And I you, but this war must be won. Despite the grim odds, I believe we'll find a way."

His voice carried such conviction. "How can you be so certain?"

"The gods spared us for a reason. They saved you from certain death in the monastery and then gave you visions so you could save me from Skarn and his brigands. Second chances are rare. They should never be wasted."

"In war or in love?"

"Both." He kissed her, tenderness tinged with passion. "Do you think we made a child?"

She wanted it to be so, but she also feared it. "Only the gods know."

His voice whispered across her forehead. "Then I'll pray for it."

She pulled him close, but their armor intruded, steel clanking against steel.

He gave her a wry smile. "Duty calls."

They separated. Jordan struggled to regain her stone mask. "Keep safe, my love."

"And you."

Settling her helm on her head, Jordan stepped from the pavilion. For half a heartbeat, sunlight glinted on burnished armor, dazzling her. Two armies waited arrayed on the field, the blue and red of Navarre mingling with the green of Lanverness. Battle banners snapped in the brisk breeze, a jaunty sight were it not for their parting.

Rafe held her stallion. The big warhorse tossed his silvered mane, stamping with impatience to run. The leather-clad monk gave her a leg up and then mounted a bay gelding, riding by her side.

She gave Stewart one last lingering look and then turned her face toward duty. "Let's march!" Jordan gave the order and the signaler blew the conch shell, sending the eerie sound of the sea breaking across the farmland. The war drums answered, taking up their steady beat. Saluting Stewart, she wheeled her stallion toward the north and cantered to the front of the column, answering the call of war.

32

Master Rizel

Master Rizel waited for the sun to reach its zenith, that time of day when the Light held sway and shadows were banished to dust motes. With deep solemnity he opened the narrow rune-carved chest and took up the staff. In ordinary light, it appeared as nothing more than a gnarled quarterstaff, an eight foot rod of polished wood with iron shoddings at both ends, but it was so much more. Few knew it was a relic from another Age, one of the greatest treasures of the monastery. His hands caressed the polished ironwood, straining to sense the magic within. Knots and swirls dotted its length, the wood-grained patterns worn smooth with time, yet he sensed no magic, no arcane spark. The staff remained dormant to his touch. Perhaps his gambit was a fool's errand. Perhaps he'd pay with his life, yet the Order needed answers. They could not go blind into the Battle Immortal.

A knock sounded on the door to his cell. He wanted no persuasions, no eleventh hour arguments, so he ignored it, but the knock persisted, growing louder and more demanding. In a rare flash of anger, he yanked the door open. "Will you wake the dead?"

Ambrose waited on the far side, worry scrawled across his handsome face. "Don't do this."

He ushered his friend inside, closing the midnight-blue door behind him lest others come to dissuade him. "It's been debated and decided and now it must be done."

His friend paced the chamber, raking his hand through his pale blond hair, his gaze darting toward the ironwood staff. "I fear for you. None of the relics have been wielded in centuries. For all any of us know, that could be a simple wooden staff you're holding in your hands, the true relic lost long ago."

The argument hit hard, compounding his nagging fear, but he refused to swerve from his course. "What choice do we have? We've searched the ancient annals and there are no answers!"

"You're taking a terrible risk."

"The red comet sinks low in the sky...and this latest portent cannot be ignored."

Ambrose stopped pacing. "But at what cost?"

"Whatever it takes." The calmness of his words belied the tension coiled like a snake in his stomach. "Time has nearly caught us. We stand on the cusp of a new Age. We dare not let Darkness prevail."

His friend glowered.

Master Rizel parried his look with hard-won conviction. "This was my idea, Ambrose. I convinced the council of the wisdom of this path, so I alone must bear the risk."

"At least take this." His friend pulled a guide's amulet from his pocket, an oval medallion inscribed with a Seeing Eye dangling from a golden chain.

"No."

"But..."

Rizel's voice was firm. "On this the annals are clear. The amulet will negate the magic of the staff." He gave his friend a wan smile. "It's as if the ancient wizards set a price on their magic."

"What price?"

"The price of belief."

"But..."

Rizel forestalled his friend's argument. "A sixteen year-old girl illuminated a blue steel sword, how can we masters dare do less?"

Ambrose slumped in resignation. "Then the gods go with you. May you find the knowledge you seek."

"And you." Embracing his friend, he took up the staff. Pulling his cowled hood over his head as a signal for seclusion, he made his way through the hallowed halls. None spoke as he passed, his ironshod staff clicking a determined rhythm on the polished mage-stone floors. Halls of midnight-blue gave way to floors of golden-yellow. Acolytes stared as he passed, but they kept silent, respecting the raised cowl of his robe. His gaze swept past the acolytes to linger on the calligraphy. The colors dazzled, wisdom writ on every wall. Pride mingled with a fierce sense of protectiveness claimed him. More than just his home, the monastery was the last bastion of knowledge, worth any risk.

Opening a rune-carved door, he stepped out into the bright sunshine. Blue sky arched overhead like a great vast bowl, empty of clouds, clear and cold and keen...but the sky held a fatal flaw, the red comet riding low in the west. The red scar neither rose nor set. It hung night and day, through cloud and sun, an unnatural smear slowly sinking toward the western horizon, a blight upon the sky, a portent of death and destruction. Making the hand sign against evil, he crossed the outer courtyard. Warmth rose from beneath his boots providing a patina of comfort. On the far side a blue-robed master waited for him.

Master Grimshaw lowered his cowl. "So it's now."

"We need answers." Master Rizel shrugged, gripping the staff. "I see no reason to delay."

"And this is the relic?" He gestured to the ironwood staff.

"By all accounts, yes."

"It looks so ordinary." A weighted silence hung between them, an acknowledgement of the risk. "May the Lords of Light guide you."

"May the Light guide us all." Chafing at the delay, Master Rizel took his leave.

Guards rushed to open the outer gates, admitting a frosty breath of cold. Snow crested the mountains, locked in winter's last embrace. His gaze flicked to the sun, hovering at its zenith. Drawing strength from the sunlight, he passed beyond the warmth of the monastery into the mountain vastness.

The great gates emblazoned with Seeing Eyes closed behind him with a deep thud. He felt their stare at his back. The silence of the mountains weighed on him. Alone, he made his way down the ice-slick path, bracing himself on the quarterstaff.

The trail disappeared into a wall of white.

A dense white fog encircled the monastery like a moat of magic, but there was no bridge across this moat, no easy way to pass. An ensorcelled protection from a bygone Age, the Guardian Mist blocked his path, a trial of magic mingled with intent. Master Rizel hesitated at the edge, for he well knew the perils. He'd traversed the sentient fog hundreds of time, but never with such risk, and never with such dire need. Gripping the staff, he sent a heartfelt prayer to Lords of Light, beseeching their favor...but he knew the gods were a fickle lot, helping those who helped themselves. Casting a sharp-eyed stare towards the heavens, he hoped for a sign, but his gaze found naught but the red comet searing the pale blue sky, the symbol of the Mordant. "So be it."

Gathering his resolve, he gripped the staff and stepped into the Mist.

Bright sunlight was instantly shuttered to a murky dimness. The chilly fog strangled him like choking hands. Sounds became muted and smothered, severing his last ties to the outside world. Even the ground disappeared beneath his boots, hidden by the swirling white. Thick, potent, and laden with menace, the Guardian Mist enveloped him, lapping at his face. Resisting the urge to hold his breath, he strode into the white void. A sixth sense warned him to shuffle his feet and test his footing, but he refused to be cowed by fear. Walking boldly, he strode into the Mist, keeping his head held high and his hand locked on the staff, an illusion of confidence.

His gaze sought to pierce the Mist, but he saw nothing but cold white in every direction. The farther he walked, the greater the risk. A shiver raced down his back. Tightening his grip on the ironshod staff, he willed it to waken. The relic proved stubborn, appearing like nothing more than a lowly quarterstaff. Doubts assailed him. Perhaps he'd misread the text, missing some subtle clue. Perhaps Ambrose was right and the true relic was long lost, leaving him holding nothing but an ordinary stick. Or perhaps the tome he found was a lie, the brilliant illumination painted amongst the calligraphy merely a scribe's fantasy. Yet, if a sixteen-year-old girl could invoke a blue steel sword, then surely he could find a way to wield the relic. He clung to his belief, putting his faith in the staff.

Something flitted ahead.

He caught a bright glimpse of golden-yellow, the color of an acolyte's robes, yet he knew it could not be. Tightening his grip on the staff, he plowed a path through the mist, ignoring the illusion.

The flash of golden-yellow came again.

Surrounded by dense fog, his gaze leaped to any color, like a drowning man grasping for a floating log, yet he knew it was false. The Mist toyed with him. Annoyed, he shouted. "I'll not be fooled by your tricks, I've come with solemn purpose."

"*What purpose?*"

The Mist answered with a boy's voice, full of youthful exuberance. The choice of voice puzzled Rizel, yet he answered. "I've come for knowledge long lost."

"*Knowledge...knowledge...knowledge...*" the refrain echoed around him, a chorus of many voices coming from all directions.

He shouted above them. "I seek knowledge to defeat the Dark!"

"*Seek...seek...seek...*" the refrain came like a chant...or a taunt.

Tiring of the ruse, he bellowed, "Show yourself!"

A dead, flat silence was the only reply.

He felt watched, surrounded, the hairs prickling at the back of his neck.

The boy's voice came again. "*What will you risk? What will you dare? What price will you pay?*"

He grasped at the boy's voice, seeking an ally among enemies. "Anything!"

"*What knowledge do you seek?*"

"I seek the riddle of mage-stone. Can it be broken? Can it be healed?"

"Your Order protects knowledge. Have the monks failed their charge?"

Having no answer, he waited, hoping, his heart thumping loud in his chest. The pause was interminable.

"Swear on your life that you seek answers to this one riddle and nothing else."

Answers to one riddle, it seemed such an odd thing to swear. Rizel hesitated. One did not swear lightly to the Guardian of the Mist, yet he saw no other way. "You have my word. I so swear."

The Mist swirled around him, dense and impenetrable, as if the Guardian considered his reply.

The flash of golden-yellow came again, but this time it moved toward him. A boy stepped from the Mist, a fresh-faced acolyte of twelve years, a youth on the verge of manhood. A mop of unruly soot-dark hair threatened to hide his jewel-blue eyes. Pushing the hair aside from his face, the lad quirked an impish smile.

Master Rizel staggered backwards, recognizing his younger self. *"How?"*

"All things are possible in the Mist."

"Why you?"

The lad grinned. "Whom would you trust more?"

Another odd reply, yet before he could frame an answer, the lad said, "Come if you want answers." The boy darted into the Mist, yet he did not disappear, his golden robes shining bright like a beacon in the fog.

Master Rizel hesitated. Following illusions in the Mist was ill-advised, a ploy to lead the unwary to a deadly drop, yet what choice did he have? Gripping the staff, he hurried to follow his younger self.

The boy quickened his pace. Master Rizel rushed to keep up. Wary of a trap, he strained to see through the swirling white, but he saw nothing save the boy.

The lad came to a sudden stop. Turning, he wore a solemn look on his youthful face. "This is where we part."

Confused, Master Rizel looked around, but he saw nothing but white.

The lad's voice dropped to an earnest whisper. "Remember our vows, the vows we took when we gained the blue. Hold to them." His voice dropped to a hush. "And beware, for illusions are real in the Mist. They can hurt you, even kill you." The boy cocked his head, as if listening to another voice. "Hold to your vows!" Turning, he faded into the white.

"Wait!" But the boy was already gone. Master Rizel peered into the white, seeing nothing but fog in every direction...but then the mist began to thin, like a curtain pulled away by a giant hand. A towering cliff face appeared, a vertical wall of granite. Carved into the mountainside were four enormous columns, like the entrance to an ancient temple. An eight pointed star was chiseled into the lintel. Embedded lichen lent the symbol a golden hue. *"The Star Knights!"* The words whispered out of him. The temple was old, the features smoothed and blunted by time and weather, yet the daunting scale was awe inspiring. He'd never seen its like...and he'd never heard a whisper of its existence. *Another illusion!* Yet the Mist must have brought him here for a reason. Intrigued, he strode towards the temple.

Massive columns stood like sculpted guardians, carved from ancient granite. He touched the column's base, surprised to find it stone-firm beneath his hand. If this was an illusion, it was well done. Passing beneath the shaded portico, he saw a door. On closer inspection, it was more of a gate. Battle axes, spears, swords, halberds and maces, the trophies of some long-forgotten war were forged together to form a gate. Rusted weapons of every make and description formed the patchwork barrier. A metal plate with a keyhole bound the two halves together. Impressed above the keyhole was the image of a hand, a Seeing Eye emblazoned on the palm. Rust encrusted the ancient weapons, yet their edges seemed sharp, still thirsting for blood. Peering between the patch-worked weapons, he saw a passageway slanting down, another mystery. He rattled the gate, pushing and tugging, careful to avoid the edged blades, yet the lock held firm. Searching around the columns, he found no key.

"I wonder." Returning to the gate, he set his naked palm against the plate. His hand was a perfect fit. A shiver slid down his back, yet the gate remained locked. *Remember your vows,* the boy's words echoed in his mind. "Seek Knowledge, Protect Knowledge, Share Knowledge."

A chime sounded and the gate clicked open.

A rough-hewn passageway slanted down, tunneling into the mountainside.

In the depths a light glowed sapphire-blue.

Gripping the quarterstaff, he strode down the passage, a gullet descending into the netherworld. He stretched his senses, hearing nothing save his own footsteps. The air was tomblike and cold, smelling of damp stone and sulfur. He dared the descent, a thousand footsteps, yet he seemed to make little progress toward the blue light. Turning, he stared back up the passage, but he saw nothing, the gates swallowed by the gloom. Below, the blue glow never wavered, calling him forward. The cold intensified. With just enough light to see by, he continued downward, ever downward...and then the passage opened into a low-ceilinged cave. Stalactites hung from the ceiling. *Not stalactites,* but massive icicles, as tall as a man. Radiating cold, the icicles were the source of the strange blue light, giving the cavern an otherworldly glow. He drew close to the nearest icicle...and then he saw it. Entrapped in the crystal-clear ice was a leather scroll case. A brass plate on the case held a single word. He craned to read it.

Mage-glass.

A gasp escaped him, a long-lost secret of the Order.

He moved deeper into the cavern, peering into each icicle. Scroll cases were embedded in every one, knowledge preserved in ice. He stopped to read the words. *Arcane armor!*

Stunned, he staggered backwards, gasping in wonder. *Arcane armor was thought be a myth!* He moved among the icicles, reading the names, a litany of lost magic. *Lightning Wand, Amulet of Rain, Ice Bolts, Helm of Destiny, Wand of Healing...*he'd stumbled into a treasure trove of magic, a fabled archive of lost knowledge. Any one of these scrolls could turn the tide of the Battle Immortal. Laughter bubbled from his lips. Giddy with hope, his gaze roved across the feast of possibilities. And then he saw a scroll case entitled *Orb of Prophecy.* He stood frozen to the ground, not believing his eyes. The greatest treasure of the Kiralynn Order, long thought to be lost, was within his reach. The thought staggered him. The Orb was knowledge incarnate. Circling the icicle, he wondered if it truly held the secret of prophecy.

A pulsing light intruded.

Deeper in the cavern, on the edge of darkness, a single icicle pulsed with light.

The distraction annoyed him, yet what if that icicle held an even greater power? Marking the location of the Orb in his mind, he walked towards the pulsing icicle. Blue light spilled across him riddled with freezing cold. He stepped close to the icicle and peered inside.

Mage-stone!

This was the secret he'd come for. Yet compared to the others, mage-stone was a lesser magic.

Shaking his head, he backed away. "You taunt me! You trick me! How can you do this when our need is so great?"

"Great...great...great," his words echoed in the depths.

"Do you want us to lose the Battle Immortal?"

"Immortal...immortal...immortal."

Something stirred in the darkness, a rasping sound.

Master Rizel froze, a premonition of danger slithering down his back.

Time was running short. He needed to decide. He burned for the Orb, for knowledge incarnate...but the words of the boy echoed in his mind. *Remember your vows!* He'd sworn to seek one answer, the riddle of mage-stone. Anger smoldered within him, realizing he'd been tricked by the Mist...yet he'd given his word. His stare roved across the treasure trove, hungry for all the lost knowledge, feeling as if victory was within his reach...yet his word was his bond. A sigh escaped him. Despite the temptation, he would not break his vow...but how to release the scroll from the ice? He circled the icicle, a riddle trapped in a pillar of cold. Tightening his grip on the quarterstaff, he struck a ringing blow. Nothing. Four more blows followed in quick succession. Searching for cracks, he found none. If he could not break it, then he'd have to melt it. He searched the ground but found nothing to serve as tinder. Returning to the icicle, he mulled the puzzle. And then he understood...although he did not like it.

Carefully setting the ironwood staff on the ground, he drew near the icicle. Cold beat against him, yet he set both hands on the ice. A chill shivered through him, so cold it seemed to suck all the warmth from his body, yet he persevered. Running his hands up and down the ice, he slowly caused it to melt. Breathing upon it, his breath frosted to white. Setting his cheek against the dead-cold ice, he willed it to hurry. So cold, his teeth began to chatter, stealing the heat from his body, yet he would not give up.

Water ran in rivulets down the ice.

He grew dizzy, depleted of heat, depleted of life...and then he realized the true price. The ice drew more from him than just warmth. Tapping into his life-force, it drained years from him, yet he refused to pull away. In mute defiance, he hugged the ice close.

A crack echoed through the cavern.

Chilled to the bone, he staggered backwards.

The great icicle broke in half. The point fell to the stony floor, shattering into a thousand shards of glittering ice.

The embedded scroll case emerged from its frozen tomb. Numbed by the cold, he tugged it from the ice. His hands shook so badly he fumbled with the latch. With trembling fingers, he opened the top. A scroll of rolled vellum nestled inside, knowledge long forgotten. Relief washed through him...but then he heard that rasping sound again, this time much closer, like rusty metal dragged over stone. Clutching the scroll case, he peered into the darkness. Something large moved in the depths.

A roar thundered through the cavern, a lick of bright flames scorching the ceiling.

A dragon uncurled in the shadows. Rusty scales and glowing eyes, the beast was a monster.

"Impossible!" the word whispered from him.

The great horned head swung his way, releasing a gout of flames that shot halfway across the cavern.

Master Rizel shook his head, refusing to believe...but then a blast of scorching heat hit him. Heat riddled with the smell of burnt carrion and sulfur, the blast singed his face like forge fire. He staggered backwards, clutching the scroll case. He needed to escape, to get back to the surface...but then he heard the pattering sound of drops. All around him, the icicles began to melt, releasing a rain of tears. Understanding struck, loosing a fresh horror. If the dragon gave chase, the icicles would be broken, melted, their precious scrolls smashed and burnt...all their knowledge forever lost...unless he saved them. A tempting thought shivered through his mind. If the ice melted he might be able to protect the scrolls, gathering them from the dragon's path, assuring the Order's victory over Darkness. A risky ploy, but the prize was tempting.

Remember our vows, the boy's words echoed through his mind.

He'd sworn to seek one answer, yet he could not let the dragon destroy the trove of knowledge.

The dragon roared again, releasing a fearsome belch of flames.

By the light of the flames, he glimpsed a second passageway on the far side...but he'd have to dare the dragon's reach.

Eyes bright as lamps stared at him.

Refusing to think, he snatched up the quarterstaff and ran towards the far passage. "Here!" He bellowed in defiance, drawing the dragon's stare away from all the knowledge enshrined in ice. "It's me you want!"

The dragon roared.

The sound blasted through the cavern, nearly knocking him to the floor. Clutching the scroll case in one hand, the staff in the other, he sprinted for the far passage. Fire belched close, singeing his hair. Darting behind a tumbled boulder, he ran for the passage.

The ground trembled beneath the dragon's weight, proof the beast gave chase.

He reached the passage and ducked inside. The floor slanted upwards, a distant light at the top.

A hot breath raced behind, foul with the smell of brimstone.

He dared a backward glance.

The beast's head snaked up the passage, great golden eyes glinting with malice.

Rizel ran faster.

The dragon roared. The force of the roar knocked him forward like the blow of a battering ram. Bruised and stunned, he hugged the ground, seeking to hide.

Flames roared over his head.

When the heat subsided, he scrambled to his feet and ran for his life.

The passage began to narrow. Behind him, the dragon bellowed, but this time the sound was only wind pushing at his back, not a battering ram. He kept running. The passage turned steep, narrowing to man-height. Ahead, the pinprick of light grew steadily larger. He reached the exit and staggered out into the cool mist. White fog lapped at his face, soothing his burns. Relief washed through him. Flushed with triumph, he lifted the scroll case to the heavens in thanks.

Something snagged his foot.

He stumbled and fell, hitting the stony ground hard.

The scroll case was knocked from his hand.

Horror-struck, he watched as it rolled forward, disappearing from sight.

"Noooo!" He lurched forward, lunging for the scroll...and found himself staring into a deep chasm, a bottomless abyss. Teetering on the edge, he fought to regain his balance, but the scroll was lost, plummeting to the depths. Outrage thundered through him. *"No!"* He shook the quarterstaff at the Mist in defiance. "How dare you! I kept my vow! I took only a single scroll, yet you deny me this *one* answer?" He roared his anger at the Mist, throwing down a gauntlet of words. "Whom do you serve, Darkness or the Light?"

Light flared bright, illuminating the ironwood staff.

Startled, he nearly dropped it.

The quarterstaff revealed its true form. Instead of a simple ironwood staff, he held a golden scepter etched with silver runes and crowned by blue flames. *A true relic!* Spellbound, he stared at it, shocked by the transformation. Regal and bright, the scepter was more beautiful and more commanding than any painting in the monastery. Crowned by blue flames, the scepter projected a nimbus of soft glowing light that surrounded him like a shield...or a beacon.

Emboldened, he held the scepter aloft, calling upon the Guardian. "By the Light of the Ethereal Flames, I summon the King of the Mist! Come and keep your vow!"

He held his breath, waiting, his anger annealing to iron-hard determination.

Sounds assailed him, the clarion call of a battle horn and the distant clash of swords, as if he stood mired on a ghostly battlefield. All around him, spectral figures appeared in the Mist. Wielding swords and spears, they waged some long forgotten war. The details remained hazy, obscured by the fog...but then one figure drew near. With each stride he became more substantial. Tall and regal and clad in ancient armor burnished bright, he wore a winged helm emblazoned with gleaming stars.

The King of the Mist, Master Rizel fought the urge to bow. "So you've come at last."

"Long has it been since one of your ilk sought my council."

Bathed in the light of the staff, the Guardian King seemed real enough to touch. His face was graven with the deep lines of hard decisions, his dark hair tinged with gray, his eyes full of ancient wisdom. He seemed almost mortal, yet he wore the armor of another Age. Burnished to mirror brightness, his silver breastplate bore the eight-pointed sigil of the Star Knights. The pommel of a two-handed great sword reared over his right shoulder like a threat. A vision of martial splendor, Master Rizel struggled not to be consumed by wonder.

"Close your mouth, you gape like a fresh-made squire."

"I'm not accustomed to speaking with kings."

"...or speaking with ghosts?"

"You are far more than that, my lord."

"So you know your lore."

"Else I would not be here. Yet I did not expect to contend with dragons in the depths."

The king gave him an appraising look. "It takes courage to dare the Mist."

"Was the cavern real? Is all that knowledge preserved, or is it truly lost?"

"Knowledge that built and destroyed an earlier Age, yet despite the temptation, you passed the test." The king stared at him. "Why have you come?"

"The red comet is nearly set."

"Even through the Mist, I can feel it burning the sky like a curse. This Age draws to a close. The Battle Immortal will decide the fate of us all."

The question whispered out of him. "How will it end?"

"The future is never set in stone. Much depends on the players. What will you risk? What will you dare? What do you know?"

"Not nearly enough." The master gripped the staff with grim resolve. "An owl has come from the north bearing a dire portent, something we did not foresee, something we cannot interpret."

The king waited, his face somber.

"The great eight-sided castle raised by the Star Knights has stood unmarred for over a thousand years, impervious to weather and war...but now the mage-stone walls are newly chipped, scarred by a passing wagon wheel."

The king wavered, as if fading back into the Mist...but then he solidified, seeming real once more. A grimace rode his face. He drew his sword as if battle was near, the great blade whispering from the harness at his back. "Darkness prevails. The honor of the Octagon is sullied and my line falters."

"Your line?"

"What of the blade bearer?"

"The crystal dagger has gone north of the Dragon Spine Mountains...we've heard nothing more."

"Much will depend on the daughter of my bloodline."

Your bloodline...the knowledge staggered the monk, yet he forced his mind back to the question at hand. "But how can mage-stone fail?"

The king gave him a daggered look. "Have you forgotten so much?"

Master Rizel waited, gripping the scepter. "How can mage-stone be scarred?"

"By failed intent. The mage-stone of Castlegard is imbibed with the honor of the Octagon. The two are inseparable. For a thousand years, steadfast honor has kept the mage-stone adamant. If it fails then the honor of the Octagon is sullied and my line fails."

Insight hit the master like a slap from an iron-gloved hand. *For Honor and the Octagon...Seek Knowledge, Protect Knowledge, Share Knowledge*...these were more than just words, they were sacred vows, the essence of the knights, the essence of the Order. The insight staggered him. Their magical roots ran deeper than he'd ever fathomed.

The king drilled him with his stare. "Look to lore for the answer you seek. The high magics of the ancient wizards were so powerful they sought safeguards lest they fall to the hands of Darkness. So the wizards imbued their greatest workings with purpose, with intent." His voice turned ominous. "Consider the power of words. Betray the intent and the magic will crumble."

Master Rizel said, "I always thought it just a motto."

"Castlegard's words are potent, a creed, a belief, a pledge. Betray the motto and you betray the purpose." The king gave him a searing look. "The crumbling of the great castle proves the intent is soiled if not broken...and I suspect the bloodline is broken as well." His voice turned grim as a grave. "Your Order breaks its oath to me." The king grew in size and menace, appearing more like a wraith than a man. "Keep your vow and restore my bloodline."

A cold wind sprang up, swirling around the monk like a deadly vortex. Master Rizel fought to hold his place against the gathering storm. "Can the magic be restored?"

"Keep your oath! Restore the purpose!"

An angry gust battered against the master, snuffing the Ethereal Flames from the scepter.

With a roar, the king disappeared in a swirl of white.

The wind intensified, snatching at Rizel's hair and robes, stinging his face with cold. Assaulted by the whirlwind, he was harried and pushed. *Keep your vow,* the ghostly words thundered through the fog, coming from a hundred voices. *Keep your vow for the hour grows late.* A dense white surrounded him, stealing all his senses. Prodded and pushed, he stumbled and fell. The golden scepter clattered against the stony ground, but instead of rune-carved gold it was nothing more than a wooden quarterstaff. Locking his fist on the wooden shaft, he staggered to his feet. Blood poured from a cut on his forehead. Harried by the wind, he staggered blindly through the Mist, clutching the staff like a talisman. Beseeching the gods for aid, he stumbled forward and stepped into the light.

Sunlight dazzled him. He fell to his knees in thanks. The vengeful wind was gone, replaced by the stillness of the clear mountain sky.

Ambrose was there, gripping his arm, anchoring him to the land of the living. Behind him stood Master Grimshaw, concern etched on his ebony face. Ambrose pulled him to his feet. "You're alive!" His eyes widened in alarm. "You're bleeding! And burned! What happened in there?"

Master Rizel shivered despite the sunlight. "It's worse than we feared. Somehow Darkness has corrupted the Octagon Knights...and we've failed the King in the Mist."

33

Jordan

The days fell into a relentless rhythm. Riding from dawn till dusk, Jordan snatched hasty meals with her captains and then spread her bedroll around the campfire, always sleeping with her weapons close at hand. At night, she dreamt of Stewart, but her dreams proved unreliable. Most times she dreamt of their last night together, lying entwined on his sumptuous camp bed, other times she dreamt of their wedding bower at the Crimson Keep, but too often she woke with a scream hovering on her lips, plagued by visions of death and bloodshed. Shaking and covered in sweat, Jordan told herself they were only nightmares, only her imagination, yet she fretted over the terrible odds. War was a grim undertaking where numbers mattered. *Forty thousand,* how could the north muster so many? *Ten to one,* the odds hammered her mind. Such impossible odds, yet somehow the enemy had to be stopped. Jordan glared at the heavens, unsure if she should laugh...or weep. Any seasoned general would say the enemy's numbers alone ensured a bitter loss, but the consequences of defeat were too terrible to imagine. Somehow she had to find an advantage, something beyond swords.

Marching to a steady drumbeat, her war host reached the Snowmelt River, the icy-cold divide between the southern kingdoms and the Domain of Castlegard. This time of year, the river glowed like green jade, a sure sign the cold waters swelled with glacier melt. Beautiful yet treacherous, the springtime thaw made the Snowmelt wild and unpredictable, a raging barrier between the north and the south. Needing a better view, Jordan cantered to the nearest hilltop, her officers trailing behind. From the wooded bluff, she gazed upon the river. A broad ribbon of jade-green swirled with white, she watched as treacherous eddies formed and disappeared, small whirlpools compounding the river's danger. As she watched, a felled tree came roaring downstream, tangled branches reaching toward the sky like a desperate hand. The tree was immense, yet it sped by in a few heartbeats, proof of the river's fierce power. And then she saw a sheep, bloated and dead, floating feet up, caught in the river's embrace.

Beside her Rafe whistled, his gaze tracking the dead sheep. "The enemy's going to cross *that*?"

"Not here. Closer to the coast, the curves of the Serpentines tame the river." Jordan considered the stories she'd heard. "They say the curves slow the Snowmelt but they also make the river tricky with sandbars. If the Snowmelt can be crossed, it will depend on the luck of the sandbars."

"Perhaps luck won't favor the Mordant."

"What are the odds of that happening?"

Rafe looked away.

Jordan sighed. "We can't leave it to luck. We've got to be sure." Spurring her horse to a canter, Jordan led her army along the river's southern bank. Conch shells blew and the army hastened their pace, battle banners rippling in the wind. They searched for any place the enemy might ford. Thankfully the Snowmelt remained a wild, unbreachable barrier. Jordan beseeched the gods to keep it so.

She settled her horse to a steady walk. Her gaze kept roving to the north shore. The raging Snowmelt formed a barrier but it was also a divide. Gently rolling farmland cradled the south side, while the north shore held towering fir trees. Wild and dark, a dense old-growth forest swept to the very edge of the Snowmelt, a feral wilderness full of shadows and threats. Jordan peered north, trying to pierce the forest's secrets. Her sixth sense screamed in warning. An entire army could lurk in the dense green and she would not know it. Jordan warned her scouts to keep their longbows close.

Ten to one, the odds kept pounding at her mind. Jordan stared at the river, wondering if the tumbling jade-green water could be an ally as well as a barrier. The river seemed alive, a fast-flowing patchwork of swirls and eddies, yet it seemed to have subtle patterns. Like river-scrawled calligraphy, the frothing white etched a pattern, but it was one she could not read. *A pattern, a message*...the idea teased her mind.

"Rafe, will you do something for me?"

The monk stared at her with fervent eyes. "Anything."

His avid attraction embarrassed her at times, yet she counted him a good friend. "Take a handful of guards and a battle banner and ride hard for the coast. At the mouth of the Snowmelt, you'll find a small fishing village. Tell them you ride on my behalf, for they owe allegiance to the king of Navarre. Talk to the villagers and bring back someone who knows the river's secrets, someone who can read the messages scrawled in the eddies." Her gaze turned to the jade-green water swirled with white. "We need to make an ally of the Snowmelt."

Rafe looked chagrined. "You're sending me away? But I know nothing of rivers or fishermen."

Jordan laughed. "Seek knowledge, protect knowledge, share knowledge! Who else should I send? My scouts can track hoof prints and follow armies, but I need someone who can ferret out knowledge and wisdom. Someone who knows how to ask questions and weigh answers." Her gaze turned serious. "Find me a fisherman who can read the river and knows the Serpentines." Her voice dropped to an urgent whisper. "Else we cannot win."

He bowed in the saddle as if accepting a geas. "I'll find someone for you."

"Thank you." She turned and called ten names, giving them orders to accompany the monk and obey his commands. "And, Rafe."

His gaze snapped towards her.

"Hurry."

He nodded, putting spurs to his mount.

Jordan watched them gallop west, a small knot of men riding beneath a bright battle banner. They carried a slender hope. She prayed she hadn't sent them on a fool's errand. *Ten to one,* the odds were overwhelming, yet if the enemy crossed the river she would not hesitate to order her army to attack. Her gaze clung to the river, wild and wide, praying for aid. If the Snowmelt was not her ally, then she saw no future save death.

34

Quintus

Quintus reached for his quarterstaff, although in his hands it was more of a walking stick than a weapon. His pruning knife was sheathed at his belt, but only plants needed to fear that small blade. As a healer, he'd never taken to weapons training, but in times of war it seemed imprudent to go outside the castle walls without some protection. He grabbed a cold chicken leg he'd pilfered from the kitchen and thrust it deep into a pouch, intending to save it for his midday meal. Straps for his gathering pouches crisscrossed his chest, leather satchels hanging empty at each hip. Divided into numerous pockets, the satchels were perfect for gathering medicinal herbs. With the steady stream of wounded, his supplies were running dangerously low. He hated this war.

His gaze flicked to his frost owl's perch, still empty, a worry of another sort. Snowman was long overdue. A chilling thought gripped him, *what if the masters have no answer?* Quintus shuddered, making the hand sign against evil, refusing to let his thoughts drift to darkness.

Closing the door on the healery, he crossed the great courtyard, assaulted by the sounds of wooden training swords clacking against shields. This latest levy of peasants' sons was so young and so very green, yet they came bright-eyed to the training yard, eager to learn the sword. The veteran knights that taught them were either graybeards or maimed, yet their visible scars mattered not to the young. All too soon they'd don their maroon surcoats and take up sharp-edged weapons, dross for the gristmill of war. As Castlegard's healer, Quintus well knew the terrible toll of war, but he'd also witnessed how steadfast belief could triumph against the worst odds. He would not gainsay the young their starry-eyed invincibility.

Quintus reached the inner gates and found them open for the noontime passage. Giving the guards a friendly wave, he strode between the mage-stone gates. His heartbeat quickened. Like iron to a lodestone, his gaze swept to the right, to the scar marring the mage-stone wall. *Still there.* A cold fist gripped his heart. Every time he passed this way, he surreptitiously checked the scar, always hoping it was gone, nothing more than a delusion...but the scar was always there, the nightmare too true. Mage-stone was supposed to be invincible, impervious to time, weather, and war, yet the great castle was scarred by a wagon wheel. *A wagon wheel,* he shuddered at the thought, as if somehow the very fabric of the world was coming unraveled. Surely the gods would intervene...or perhaps they did not care.

Gloomy thoughts dogged his steps. It did not help that he trod a path through the killing corridor, the walled gorge between the soaring mage-stone battlements of the inner castle and the outer ramparts raised by ordinary stonemasons. Such a grim and terrible place. Desolate of any cover, the corridor was an eerie and ominous place, a stone killing field, a trap designed for death. Even in broad daylight, the corridor gave him the shivers, as if angry ghosts stalked his shadow.

Spying a troop of guards marching ahead, Quintus hurried his steps. Matching their stride, he fell in behind them, grateful for a living escort through the chilling corridors of no-man's-land.

Even at the soldiers' quick gait, the long trek seemed to take forever. Finally he spied the outer gatehouse. Quintus felt a profound sense of relief, glad to be rid of the grim corridor.

Guards in maroon cloaks walked the crenellated battlements, battle banners fluttering overhead. The great ironbound gates stood open, the toothy portcullis raised, and the drawbridge lowered as it often was at noontime. A wagon trundled across, bearing goods from the nearby town. Quintus made sure to hail the guards so they'd know he'd left the castle. His quarterstaff in hand, he crossed the drawbridge, escaping the towering corridors of stone for the bright sunshine of springtime.

Buttercups blossomed on the greensward, clumps of golden yellow dotting the vast carpet of fresh green that encircled the castle. A herd of sheep munched placidly in the distance, keeping the greensward cropped while providing the castle with a steady source of wool and mutton. Shaggy and dingy white, they looked like lazy clouds tethered to the green. The herder boy, Jon, raised a hand in greeting. A clumsy lad, Quintus had set his bones more than once. Replying with a cheerful wave, Quintus stepped off the muddy road to meander south across the vast greensward. Still soggy from the snowmelt, the grass squished wet beneath his boots. The puddled dampness mattered not, for he'd come for the springtime flowers. Like a bee, he fluttered from one crop to the next, collecting cuttings for his satchels. Dandelions sprouted amongst the buttercups, a cheerful flower with so many uses. Harvesting both the roots and leaves, he made sure to leave half the patch untouched to ensure future crops. Leaving the dandelions he moved towards a clump of blood root, stooping to clip the delicate white flowers, a cure for fevers. His satchels began to bulge with cures, but the find that thrilled him the most was the feathery leaves of the yarrow plant. Renowned for its ability to stop bleeding, Quintus was hard-pressed to harvest only half the crop. Carefully stowing the leaves and flowers in a side pouch, he moved on, approaching the forest's edge.

Mighty oak trees towered overhead, sheathed in springtime green. Quintus passed from sunshine into shade, seeking to renew his supply of mosses used to staunch wounds. He stumbled over an exposed root, but caught himself with his quarterstaff. Spying a nettle bush, he stopped to collect leaves for an infusion to remedy colds. Moving deeper into the forest, his gaze roved the shady green looking for more cures. And then he saw them. A thicket of rusty swords reared from the forest floor, their blades sunk deep in the dark loam, marking the graves of fallen heroes. Shields dangled overhead, some moss-covered and dulled by time, but all of them bore the same sigil, emblazoned with the maroon octagon of Castlegard.

He trod hallowed ground, the gravesite of heroes, the oldest Shield Forest of the maroon. Using his quarterstaff as a walking stick, Quintus wandered amongst the shields. So many were freshly hung that they still glimmered silver, reflecting spears of sunlight, undimmed by the ravages of time. As a healer, death was his enemy, but Quintus always found the Shield Forest to be soothing to the spirit, a place of peace where all those who died under the maroon banner were remembered and honored. Surrounded by centuries of heroes, he walked amongst the rusting swords. A warbler burst into song, adding a feathered melody to the peace of the forest. Other birds twittered overhead, bright feathers flitting from branch to branch. Quintus paused to breathe deep the scents and sounds of the forest, overcome with an abiding sense of peace. Somehow the Shield Forest offered a kind of solace, as if death was not the end.

Leaves rustled overhead, strummed by a light breeze, calling him back to his task. Quintus continued his quest, studying the forest with an herbalist's eyes. He spied a clump of mistletoe and used his staff to knock it from the branches. White berries budding among waxy green leaves, he added the mistletoe to his collection.

And then he noticed something odd.

The birdsong had fallen silent, as if a predator stalked the woods.

A shiver raced down his back, *he felt watched.*

Quintus whirled, nearly tripping over an exposed root. Regaining his balance, he brought his quarterstaff to bear in a cross-body block. The staff felt clumsy in his hands, yet he held it with a desperate grip. Sweat beaded his forehead. He scanned the forest, listening, seeking enemy eyes. Every shield and every sword became the perfect hiding place for foes. His heartbeat quickened. Every shadow seemed to hold menace, the peace of the forest suddenly banished.

"Whoooooo."

Golden eyes stared at him.

Snowman glided towards him on silent wings.

Quintus sagged in relief. "It's you."

The great frost owl alighted on the cross hilt of a rusting sword. "Whoooo."

"What took you so long?" The owl had an uncanny knack of always finding him, even in the most unexpected places. "I'm glad you're back. Did you bring me an answer?" Snowman looked lean, as if the hunting had been thin on his long journey north. Quintus fished the cold chicken leg from his pouch. "Here you go." He offered the chicken leg to the owl's delicate grasp. "You need this more than I do." While the owl feasted on chicken, the drumstick clutched in his formidable talon, Quintus checked the message jess. With shaking hands, he removed the small bone tube. A small parchment was coiled inside, but this was not the place. He thrust the tube deep into his collection satchel. "I'll meet you back at the healery."

Snatching up his quarterstaff, he hurried north. Taking a direct path, he saw nothing as he strode through the forest, neither shields, nor swords, nor medicinal plants, his mind fastened on the small message parchment coil in his satchel.

Emerging from the leafy shade, his footsteps slowed, momentarily dazzled by the bright sunlight and the view of the great castle. Slanting sunbeams burnished Castlegard's towering walls to a silvery glow, maroon battle banners rippling in the breeze. Reflections of the battlements shimmered in the deep green moat, casting an image of everlasting might. His heart quailed, for he knew the image was an illusion...unless the message held a cure.

Desperate for an answer, he beat a straight path across the greensward. The hour was later than he thought, he dared not tarry. Sweating, his lungs puffing like a bellows, Quintus was the last to cross the drawbridge before the guards began to raise it for the night.

He followed the others through the stone corridor without speaking a word. So distracted was he, that he did not even check the scar on the inner gate. Rushing across the great yard, he returned to the healery. Locking the door, he unburdened his satchels and then circled the chamber lighting every candle and lantern, seeking to dispel every scrap of shadow. With shaking hands, he reclaimed the message tube and drew forth the coiled parchment. His heartbeat thundered as he dared to look. *It was in code.* Another ominous sign. He unlocked his codex and deciphered the message.

Three times he read the message before consigning the parchment to the candle flame. *"The mage-stone magic is tied to intent. Darkness has corrupted the Octagon. Restore honor to the maroon. Aid comes in the form of a sword."* His hands shook as the small strip of parchment went up in smoke. *Restore honor to the maroon,* the message made no sense. The maroon knights fought with valor. He saw it in the wounded, in the maimed veterans who found ways to serve, in the war-weary knights who returned to the battlefield. Beleaguered and sorely outnumbered, the knights fought a desperate winter war against an evil foe...so how had Darkness corrupted the maroon? And what was he supposed to do about it?

He paced a path across the healery, wracking his mind for an answer to the riddle. "Restore honor to the maroon," he repeated the words of the message, but they made no sense. And then it hit him. *"For Honor and the Octagon,"* the knights' words whispered out of him, hitting him like a lightning bolt. He stood statue-still, his hands shaking, his mind whirling. *Mage-stone magic is tied to intent.* Quintus shook his head at the elegant beauty of it. He'd always thought the words were just a battle cry, a heraldic motto, an inspiring phrase, but in truth they were so much more. Honor was the very bedrock on which the great mage-stone castle was founded. Honor was something the Dark could never understand. Something that could not be faked or mimicked for true honor went bone-deep. He marveled at the elegant wisdom of the ancient wizards. The answer had been right in front of him all along...yet it was also a riddle. How was *he* supposed to restore honor to the maroon...and how exactly had the Octagon's honor been lost?

Only a healer...the knights don't even know I'm a monk! Befuddled, Quintus sat at his desk, watching the candles burn to wax puddles, feeling as if the weight of the great castle had collapsed on his shoulders. Shadows crowded the room as night knocked on his window, yet now that he had an answer, he knew not what to do.

35

General Haith

The *Darkflamme* whispered overhead, snaking against a pale gray sky. Twelve feet of black silk ending in two tails of bright red flecked with gold, General Haith rode to war under the forked battle banner of the Mordant. Clad in armor worthy of the fearsome standard, the general wore the helm and breastplate of the Skeleton King. Treasures hoarded from a distant Age, the helmet was forged like a menacing skull, the breastplate adorned with a skeleton's steel ribs. Forged with arcane runes, silver cast over steel, the ancient armor was a work of high magic. Imbued with raw terror, the armor was fearful to behold. Even his own men shuddered at the sight, keeping their gazes averted. The general grinned, knowing fear was a powerful ally. The relics of Darkness rode to war, a vanguard of nightmares come to reap the souls of Erdhe.

After the gorelabe's message, General Haith had wasted no time in escaping the lethal trap of Raven Pass. Keen to evade the Dark Sword, the general quickly assembled his elite force. He took all the horses, two thousand cavalry followed by a hundred Taals running to keep pace, their spiked cudgels balanced on their meaty shoulders. He'd also brought a cadre of fifty duegars, most of them snargons to ward against the magic of the monks. The stunted dwarves rode behind mounted warriors, carried like baggage lest they slow the force. Over two thousand strong, the cavalry formed the fleet spear tip of the Dark army, an agile strike force shot like an arrow into the heart of Erdhe.

Ironshod hooves thundered behind him in a storm of war. The general was confident in the prowess of his force, yet he kept his most potent weapon in his saddlebag, a gift of magic from the Mordant. His lord spared no weapon to win this war.

General Haith set a hard pace, knowing the timing was crucial. They rode south till they reached the Snowmelt River. Swollen with the spring melt, the river raged white and frothy. Cold and formidable, the Snowmelt denied their way south. Relying on captured maps, the general avoided the raging river, leading his force east towards Eye Bridge.

The Domain of Castlegard held few roads, as if the wild tangle of wilderness was part of the knights' defense. Thick forest shrouded the northern riverbank, the trees bursting with springtime leaves. Sunlight dappled the ground, painting an uneasy mix of light and shadow. General Haith kept his hand on his sword hilt. The forest made him uneasy. Shuttering his view, closing in on all sides, the dense green felt unnatural. He barked orders, sending a vanguard of his best scouts in every direction. He mistrusted the trees, for there were none to contend with in the north. The flat openness of the steppes was his preferred fighting field, where a man could see forever and numbers mattered more than strategy or stealth. Riding through the leafy green, he half expected an ambush hidden behind every towering cedar, but Darkness favored them. His army met no opposition till they reached the bridge.

His scouts brought warning, an armored force guarded Eye Bridge.

Dismounting, the general followed his scouts to a forested knoll overlooking the stone bridge. The sight that greeted him was almost laughable. With only two bridges spanning the raging Snowmelt, the general expected formidable fortifications to protect the crossing, a gatehouse bristling with weapons, perhaps catapults mounted on towers, but instead, the bridge was clearly built for peaceful times. Three graceful arches of stacked stone spanned the mighty Snowmelt, wide enough for two wagons to pass side- by-side. The stone bridge had no gates, no towers, no ramparts of any sort, proving the south was a soft land lulled by peace. Armored soldiers patrolled the bridge but their numbers were not daunting. Felled logs formed a feeble barrier on the road. Desperate for some defense, the soldiers had felled two massive trees, dragging them to form a chevron blocking the northern roadway. The general barked a laugh. "*Logs*, they seek to stop Darkness with logs!" His voice reeked with disdain, amused by the pitiful defense. "Come, I've seen more than enough."

Returning to his army, the general swung into the saddle, barking orders to marshal his forces. He ordered the Taals to the front, a chevron of muscle pitted against a chevron of logs. His cavalry formed behind, the lethal follow-through to the Taals' brutal punch. Snapping his visor closed, he urged his stallion to a fast trot. Battle banners snapped overhead as they rode in deadly silence, a dark pestilence sweeping across the sunlit land. Without preamble, they thundered down out of the foothills and onto the roadway.

Trumpets flared in warning from the bridge.

The enemy scrambled into position, raising shields and spears. A ragged flight of arrows bit the sky. Peering through his visor, the general grinned, defying death. Ironshod hooves pounded the roadway, hurtling towards the bridge. Sharp-tipped arrows plummeted down, scouring shields and armor, but the volley was too thin to slow the dark tide.

The Taals surged ahead, massive brutes wielding spiked war clubs. Bellowing a war chant, they barreled into the roadblock. Putting their muscled shoulders to the logs, the malformed giants pushed, their huge thighs churning forward.

For ten heartbeats, a brutal stalemate prevailed, the massive logs pitted against the monstrous strength of the Taals...and then the logs *moved*.

Pushed by the Taals, the massive logs became weapons.

Men screamed, crushed to death beneath the felled trees.

The Taals pushed harder, shoulders rammed against the barrier, rolling the logs. Screams turned to tortured howls. Rolled backwards, the logs crushed the defenders, opening a gore-strewn pathway to the bridge.

The general unsheathed his sword, spurring his warhorse to a gallop. *"For the Mordant!"*

His vanguard closed around him, shields set and swords lowered. General Haith led a thunderous charge, galloping toward the breach in the log barrier. A few desperate arrows launched from the enemy. Too little, too late, the arrows skittered harmlessly off shields and armor. Trumpets blared a warning and the Taals opened a path to the enemy. The general and his cohort surged past the strewn logs, barreling into the enemy's lines. His force hit like a battering ram. The enemy crumpled backwards, falling beneath ironshod hooves. Bellowing his war cry, General Haith pressed the attack. *"For the Mordant!"* Leaning forward in the saddle, he slew the enemy with sweeping sword strokes. His foes shrank back, cowering at the sight of his ensorcelled armor. Even the most stalwart soldiers hesitated, assaulted by terror. A skilled swordsman, the general reaped every advantage. His sword grew bloody with gore.

His force pushed onto the bridge, but a knot of resistance formed on the left side, stubbornly resisting the Dark tide. At the heart of the resistance, a gleam of silver snagged the general's gaze. Bright armor often marked a senior officer. A hero rallied the enemy, thwarting his forces. The general's gaze narrowed, *cut the head from the snake and it will quickly die*. General Haith angled his warhorse towards the erstwhile hero, cutting his way into the heart of the resistance. *"Fight me!"* He bellowed his challenge towards the silver-clad hero. The enemy turned, his face going slack-jawed. Having gained a good look at the general's armor, the silver-clad hero faltered. Terror widened his eyes. The shiny knight hesitated. Hesitation in battle was death's prelude. Grinning, the general slew him, taking his head with a single swipe of his sword.

All around him, men screamed and died. The enemy retreated, giving way in the wake of his onslaught. *"Fight on!"* General Haith stood in the stirrups, rallying his own men, but the enemy was not yet cowed.

A frantic flare of trumpets summoned more foes to the bridge.

Swords and spears struggled to bar the way, more grist for his reapers.

The press on the bridge thickened, a lethal clash of swords. The dead and the dying multiplied, their bodies trampled beneath ironshod hooves. The Taals pushed forward fighting alongside the cavalry, wielding their spiked war clubs and heaving enemies into the river. The general's vanguard showed no mercy, forging a relentless path across the bridge. Blood soaked the cobbled bridge, weeping red into the Snowmelt.

Horns blared and the fighting slowed to a grind. The enemy surged, desperate to hold the bridge, but the dark tide could not be contained. Standing in the stirrups, the general gave the enemy a good look at his armor. Soldiers flinched away while others dropped their weapons, stricken by a mind-numbing terror. Grinning like death, the general roared his battle cry, cutting a bloody swath with his sword. *"For the Mordant!"*

Echoing his cry, his vanguard spurred forward, taking advantage of the armor's effect. Hacking left and right, they cleared a path across the bridge. And then they were through. Open road loomed ahead. They'd gained the south side of the river.

"Sound the charge!" The general shouted the order and a trumpeter blew a strident blast, summoning his host to a gallop. General Haith put spurs to his mount, leading his army south. Trumpets repeated their blare, calling his men away from the fighting. The general cared not how many of the enemy survived, or if they reclaimed the bridge, what mattered was that his army had crossed the Snowmelt, and now the tender south lay open to him like a whore with her legs spread wide.

The general spurred his stallion to a hard gallop. Beneath the Skeleton Helm, he grinned, flushed with power...and triumph.

Everything his lord had predicted had come to pass. The *Darkflamme* fluttered overhead, snapping like a serpent's tongue scenting the vanguard's next victim. Terror clad in steel, General Haith rode south, keen to claim his prize.

36

The Knight Marshal

Slaying patrols was not enough. Not enough challenge to test his skills, not enough blood to slake his battle lust, not enough souls to satisfy the Dark Sword. He needed more, much more. Consumed by an insatiable need for victory, the marshal rode west. Like a hound loosed to the hunt, he galloped towards the horde. *Souls that wield swords,* somehow he sensed the multitude massed within Raven Pass, a challenge worthy of the God of War.

Twilight dimmed the sky to darkness as he reached the ridgeline overlooking Raven Pass. Campfires lit the pass, tens of thousands of glowing fires strewn the length of the valley. Competing with the very stars, the fires beat back the night with a warm buttery glow, proof he'd found the horde...but he'd expected more. Their numbers seemed dwindled, diminished since the last time he'd spied them from the ridge. Perhaps they'd been decimated by the winter war, or perhaps the army was split, dispersed to other battlefields: either way the marshal found himself...disappointed, as if fate sought to diminish his glory. He consoled himself with the thought that their numbers still qualified as a horde. A smile split his bearded face. He'd come to wage an epic battle worthy of legends. He'd come to prove his prowess against a vast horde. His destiny was finally at hand.

W...a...i...t.

He shuddered as the command whispered through him.

Wait...wait...wait.

Something bade him wait. Something insidious, something more than the Dark Sword.

The marshal snarled like a mastiff straining against a chain. He yearned to wade into the enemy, to test his sword against their numbers. Thirsting for battle, he fought the voice, railing against the prohibition, yet he found himself obeying. Unable to attack, unwilling to leave, he made camp on the ridge top. Wrapped in his bedroll, he spent a fitful night beneath the stars. At dawn's first light, he saddled his warhorse and readied for battle, but once again the voice spoke.

Wait.

The command drove him to a rage yet he could not disobey. Needing to kill something, he ranged the length of the ridge, seeking prey. For nearly a fortnight, he prowled the ridge, hungering for the horde, yet the prohibition held. And then it came to him, a way to outwit the voice.

Deciding to make it easy for his prey, he rode till he reached one of the few trailheads that connected the ridge top to the valley floor. It took him three days of hard toil to scavenge enough wood, but when he finished, the pyre towered over the trailhead like a sentinel. Stuffed with dry tinder, and stacked with enough wood to rise beyond his head by a full arm's length, the pyre was built to burn for days, a great beacon overlooking Raven Pass.

The marshal paced the ridge like a caged lion.

Dark finally came, night blanketing the mountains.

Even the moon obeyed, shuttered by clouds, cloaking the land in deepest darkness.

Using a flint, the marshal lit the pyre. Flames leaped to the tinder and then licked up the dry wood. The blaze became a roaring bonfire, a beacon summoning his enemies to battle. The marshal pried a loose fagot from the fire. Holding the burning branch aloft, he stood at the top of the trail. Backlit by the bonfire, he roared his challenge. *"Fight me! Come and meet the God of War!"*

37

Quintus

Quintus made the rounds, changing bandages, apply poultices, dispensing potions for fevers and pain, but still too many died. The captains had given an entire tower of the great castle over to the wounded, yet the chambers were crowded with the crippled and the ruined. The dead were taken away, wrapped in their maroon cloaks for an honorable burial in the Shield Forest, but all too soon their beds were filled. War was a ravenous beast, consuming bodies at a frightful pace, yet few of the knights ever complained at their fate. Inspired by their stalwart bravery, Quintus worked endless hours, pitting his skills from the monastery against fever, rot, and gaping wounds, striving to save as many as he could. Every loss chipped at his heart, yet he had no time to mourn.

Daylight dimmed to twilight, yet he remained by the bedside of a young knight barely old enough to shave. "*Not my sword arm, not my sword arm,*" Sir Jared muttered the words like a chant, delirious with pain. The delirium hid the truth, for his sword arm was already gone. A mace had shattered the bones to sharp fragments, leaving Quintus no choice but to saw at the elbow. Now he struggled to save the knight from wound fever. A pity the snow was melted, leaving him nothing but damp compresses and tincture of yarrow to fight the fever's heat. He worked through the night, striving to save the young knight. The fever finally broke. Quintus sagged in relief, another knight saved.

A wave of weariness crashed across him. He needed sleep, he needed his own bed, else he'd be of no use to all the others. Too weary to think, he washed his hands in a basin and then made his way from the tower. Stepping into the night air, he breathed deep, the chilly crispness clearing his mind. Night cloaked the great castle, the dazzling spray of stars strewn across the sky. Pausing to admire the celestial beauty, he was struck by the peace of the moment. The great castle slept, hushed by stillness, no sounds of swords clanging, orders shouted, or boots marching. Quintus knew guards kept watch on the towers and walls, yet for a handful of heartbeats, he let himself be deluded by the dream of peace.

The sound of a hammer intruded...a hammer striking iron.

The forge, the thought pierced him. He'd promised the master swordsmith an answer, yet the reply from the monastery made little sense. Since Snowman's return, he'd kept the message to himself, a riddle locked in his heart, yet he needed someone to talk to, someone to confide in. Quintus wasn't sure he could truly trust the smith with his secrets, yet he found his footsteps drawn toward the forge.

Light laden with heat blazed from the open windows. The hammer strokes fell in a measured rhythm like the beating of a steadfast heart. The master swordsmith worked alone, his massive hammer pounding iron.

"Are you coming in? Or have you just come to watch?"

The healer jumped like a thief with his hand on a purse. "You're working late."

"So are you."

Quintus shrugged. "Too many wounded."

"Never enough swords."

They both served Castlegard, though in very different ways. The healer ventured deeper into the forge, watching the smith work the raw bar of iron.

Otto cast a daggered glance his way. "I wondered if you'd come." His deep voice rumbled like clashing boulders. "Your owl's been back for nearly a fortnight."

The truth struck like a punch below the belt, leaving the healer gasping for a reply. "The owl returned...but the message makes no sense."

"Are you a man of your word?"

Quintus replied with quiet dignity. "Yes."

"Then let's hear it."

The hammer pounded against iron, marking a steady cadence.

Quintus considered the message, a riddle scribed in his mind. Deciding to cast caution to the wind, he blurted the words, "*The mage-stone magic is tied to intent. Darkness has corrupted the Octagon. Restore honor to the maroon. Aid comes in the form of a sword.*"

The hammer missed a beat. The swordsmith glared at him, his eyebrows raised like two sooty smudges marked against his bald forehead. "*That's* the message?"

"All of it, I swear."

The hammer resumed its beat, but the rhythm held an angry edge. "How can you restore something that's not lost?"

Quintus sagged in relief. "Exactly! The knights fight a valiant war despite their losses, never wavering against the Pentacle. The Octagon bleeds heavily for the Light." Quintus shook his head. "The message makes no sense."

The smith issued a low growl, his muscles bulging, his gaze fixed on his work. The massive hammer beat a hypnotic rhythm. Stroke after stroke pounded the iron into the anvil, the rod slowly becoming a blade, bending to the will of the smith. Quintus watched, lulled by the sound. Heat beat against him laden with the metallic scents of charcoal and iron. The forge was a primal force, the birthplace of swords. The rod changed shape, flattening to a deadly blade. Quintus swayed on his feet. He began to think the smith would not reply.

"Valiant is not the same as honor."

The words struck a chilling chord with the healer. "I suppose so."

Like a god of the forge, Otto thrust the sword-shaped blade deep into the furnace fire, releasing a breath of red sparks. "Come." Hefting his hammer, the smith stoked the furnace and then strode toward the rear of the forge.

Quintus shook himself awake and then followed the smith to a backroom. Bins filled with iron ore lined one wall, sacks of charcoal and other minerals stacked along another. Footprints crisscrossed the floor, tracking through a thick coating of red dust. The storeroom smelled heavy with the earthy scents of the underworld.

Otto grabbed a torch from the wall and thrust it toward the healer. "Come."

"Why?" Quintus held the torch aloft, following the smith to the rear of the storeroom.

"I need to see for myself." Setting his hammer aside, the big smith put his shoulder to a bin of iron ore...and shoved.

Quintus gasped, for it seemed an impossible load for any lone man to budge.

The swordsmith strained, massive muscles bulging...and then the bin began to move, pushed along the floor like a sledge. The scrape of metal across stone clawed at his ears, and then came to a sudden stop. "This will do." The smith straightened and retrieved his hammer.

"Why are we here?"

"I need to see for myself."

"See what?"

"If mage-stone is truly failing."

Quintus stared, wide-eyed. "You don't believe me?"

"What if the scrape you saw has been there all along?"

"No, I saw it happen. The wagon's axle chipped the stone." Quintus uttered the words, but in truth, he did not want to believe it.

"Let's see for ourselves." The smith hefted the hammer. He struck the wall, iron ringing against mage-stone.

Nothing happened.

Casting a glance toward the healer, the smith gripped the hammer with both fists. He struck the wall again, a resounding hit.

Nothing happened.

A smile burst across the healer's face. "Nothing!" Relief poured through him. "Mage-stone is sound!"

Otto gave him a warning glare. "That last blow was but half my strength. This one will tell the tale."

Quintus sobered, gripping the torch.

The smith broadened his stance, his feet spread wide. Roped with muscles, his arms were as thick as most men's thighs. He held the hammer high, his gaze fixed on the mage-stone wall. Quintus muttered a fervent prayer. Grunting, the smith loosed the hammer, striking a mighty blow. The hammerhead struck a discordant note, an ugly tone. The mage-stone wall chipped. *It chipped!* A palm-sized chunk fell to the floor.

Both men stared, slack-jawed.

Quintus felt dizzy, as if the world were coming undone. "How can this be?"

The smith reached for the sundered piece. "It's as if the magic has fled...leaving ordinary stone."

Both men locked stares. "The castle is not invincible."

Quintus crumpled to the floor, all the strength fled from his legs. "This can't be happening."

Otto growled, "We must warn the captains."

"No." Conviction rode his voice. Quintus was ambushed by the vehemence of his own reply. "We dare not tell them."

Otto gave him a flinty glare. "No? Why not?"

"I told you before, because of morale."

The smith waited as if needing more.

"I've tended the wounded. I know what this war costs. The knights fight against perilous odds. Take morale away from them...and the war is lost."

"But if they don't know..."

"What can they do about it?"

"But..."

Quintus cut him short. "What does it matter unless the enemy brings siege engines against Castlegard?"

The smith's eyes narrowed, his voice begrudging. "True."

"In the meantime, we dare not dash the hope of victory."

The smith gave him a flinty look. "Victory?"

"To believe anything else is to invite defeat."

Otto gave him a thoughtful look. "Just so."

"So the mage-stone will be our secret unless an enemy army comes calling?"

The smith gave a cautious nod. "For now." Setting his hammer aside, he shoved the iron ore bin back into place, hiding the terrible scar. Wiping his shovel-sized hands on his leather apron, the smith growled, "None save me will move that bin."

Quintus believed him.

The smith offered his hand, pulling the healer to his feet. "Now we know it's true, what'll we do?"

"We solve the riddle."

The smith stared at him.

"We restore honor to the Octagon."

"But that makes no sense!"

"Yet we must find a way."

The smith flashed a bitter scowl. "What? A smith and a healer? Are you daft? Sounds like something a hero would do."

Quintus stared, for the smith's words held the ring of truth. "Then we best find a hero."

"Castlegard is full of them."

"Yet mage-stone fails."

The smith made the warding sign, his voice a low growl. "The castle has fallen under an evil star."

The healer pursed his lips, surprised by the smith's superstition. "There must be a way to solve this. Your bellows boys love gossip. Keep your ear to the ground. Perhaps some scrap of rumor will shed light on the riddle."

Otto gave him a doubtful look. "As you say."

Beleaguered by grim thoughts, Quintus left the forge, trudging back across the great yard. Clouds cloaked the stars, the heavy darkness adding to the weight on his shoulders. *Mage-stone is failing,* the words thundered through his mind like a doom. He shared a terrible secret with the master swordsmith, a terrible burden. He'd asked for help from the learned masters of the monastery, but their reply remained a stubborn riddle. *Restore honor to the Octagon,* it seemed like an impossible geas. Quintus knew how to heal bodies, but not how to heal honor...or stone, yet this terrible burden had fallen to his shoulders. Somehow the Octagon must triumph against the

Pentacle, of that he was certain. They dared not lose this war. Staring up at the cloud-shrouded sky, he prayed to all the gods to spare Castlegard and the valiant knights that served the great castle, for without the gods' help, he foresaw nothing but doom.

38

The Knight Marshal

The bonfire crackled a fierce heat at his back, a beacon summoning his enemies to battle. Girded for war, the marshal stood atop the trailhead, the Dark Sword gleaming naked in the firelight, hungry for souls. Dragons entwined the dusky hilt, runes inscribed along the blade. Forged for heroes, the sword was magnificent, the sapphire-blue blade forever darkened to midnight black. The rune-carved blade belonged in his hands, of that the marshal was certain. Beneath his gauntleted grip, it thrummed with power...the power of invincibility.

Light streaked the sky, the first spears of sunrise illuminating Raven Pass, the campground of his enemies, a horde of swords. The bonfire had burned through the night, a beacon and a warning, summoning his foes to battle.

A murder of crows cawed overhead. Circling, the dark cloud settled amongst the pine trees, his feathered heralds come to witness the battle. Further down the trail, he heard the clank of armor. *They're coming.* Footsteps pounded up the steep trail. He glimpsed their banners before he saw their faces. Midnight black embroidered with a golden pentacle, their pennants rippled in the cool breeze. *What color their cloaks?* The marshal pushed the nagging question aside, for colors had ceased to matter. Instead of banners, he sought souls wielding swords, foes to be vanquished in battle, fodder for his blade, nothing more and nothing less.

Broadening his stance, he waited for battle, an eager grin on his sun-weathered face.

The ogres came first, barreling up the steep trail. Malformed monsters, bulging with muscles, they wore leather armor and wielded massive war cudgels studded with steel spikes. Once he would have thought them formidable, but no longer. Now they were merely another foe, fodder for his sword.

The marshal waited, letting them come, letting them spend themselves on the steep slope.

The first ogre lumbered towards him, a massive creature with curved tusks protruding from his lantern jaw. The ground shook at his approach, his cudgel raised for a killing blow.

Kill them all! The Dark Sword whispered its siren song.

The marshal stepped towards the ogre, loosing the Dark Sword in head-high swing. The blade took the ogre at the neck, slicing clean through flesh, sinew and bone. With a single satisfying stroke, he severed the ogre's ugly head. The body crumpled to the ground, gushing blood. He kicked the head, watching it bouncing down the trail. The marshal flashed a fierce grin, serving proof of his prowess.

The enemy ignored the grisly warning. Ogres had immense strength but it seemed they were too dumb to know fear. A pair of tusked brutes tromped up the trail, bloodlust in their tiny eyes.

The marshal leaped to battle. Cut, thrust, and parry, he slew the ogres as they topped the trail. More swarmed up the steep slope, the living taking the places of the dead. Ogres crowded the trailhead, wielding their war clubs while bellowing curses. The marshal slew them all, the Dark Sword feasting on their souls. Corpses piled around him, creating a bulwark of the slain, yet he wanted no defensive barrier, nothing between him and his prey. Leaping over the dead, he attacked the living. The Dark Sword keened in his hands, supping on souls. For every life he took, strength poured from the sword into the marshal's gauntleted hands. Elation thrummed through him, the wild flush of battle lust. The marshal fought like a whirlwind. Flowing from one form to the next, he danced with the Dark Sword, every stoke a fatal blow. Evading a battleaxe, he planted his sword in an ogre's skull, splitting it like a ripe melon. Yanking the blade free, a spray of blood and brains followed the sword's arc like a battle banner. More corpses clogged the trail. The press of ogres slowed, supplanted by men in dark armor. Men were easier to kill, much easier. The ogres died growling...the men died screaming, either way he took their lives and reaped their souls.

Blood and gore slicked the trail, making the footing treacherous. Fighting against three at once, the marshal evaded their weapons while finding their weak spots. His boots slipped on slime. Cursing, the marshal raised the Dark Sword in a defensive parry. The bearded enemy grinned, attacking with a double-bladed axe. The Dark Sword caught the downward stroke. Ordinary steel clanged against the Dark Blade, releasing a horrible shriek. The axe shattered to shards. Empty-handed, the enemy glared wide-eyed, fear etching his bearded face.

Snarling, the marshal struck. The enemy died screaming, spitted on the Dark Sword.

His blade slid like butter from the dead. The marshal whirled to face another foe, but the pace of slaughter began to slow.

Soldiers hung back, lurking behind boulders, unwilling to enter the killing field.

Rage thundered through the marshal. *"Fight me!"* He could not abide cowards. Lifting the Dark Sword, he bellowed his challenge, *"Fight me!"* but the cowards turned and fled, racing down the steep mountain trail.

The marshal started to give chase...but the sword's voice yanked him back.

Wait.

Like a chained dog, he snarled, wanting to finish the kill.

Wait.

The marshal fought the compulsion. He hated the voice, yet he could not disobey.

And then the voice said something that pierced his battle-fogged mind. *The survivors serve as your heralds, giving witness to your prowess.*

The marshal staggered to a stop, staring at the dark blade.

Great deeds deserve witnesses, else they will not be remembered.

The marshal watched the enemy scurry down the trail, taking word of his prowess back to the horde camped below. The Dark Sword had the truth of it. His victories deserved to be remembered...and then he had another thought. A foe forewarned was a foe better prepared to fight. A hungry grin split his face. Let them prepare for his coming. Let them tremble at his approach. He longed for an epic battle, a victory to rival the legends of old.

Soon.

The word thundered through his mind like a boon. Raising the Dark Sword to the heavens, the marshal bellowed his challenge. *"Soon! Soon, I will slay you all!"*

"All,all,all..." the words echoed through the pass.

The crows came calling.

Victorious once more, the marshal stood on the ridge top, surrounded by death.

39

Commander Crull

Commander Crull strode the wall of Raven Pass. The battlement was now his to command. Black banners fluttered overhead, giving proof of the Pentacle's conquest, yet the pass was nothing more than a couple of stout defensive walls and a long valley churned to mud. No gold, no women, and no real power, he'd drawn the short straw. Again. As usual, his commanding officers had taken the plum assignments, leaving him to mop up their shit, but such was service under the Pentacle. He was sorely tempted to take his army south, to seek plunder and glory at the tip of a spear, but one did not disobey a gorelabe and live. Better to bide his time and find a way to serve the gorelabe's orders while seeking his own way to power

"Commander Crull!"

His second, Captain Andrius, strode towards him. Judging from the scowl on his face, the news did not bode well.

Saluting fist to chest, the captain gave his report. "Survivors have returned from the ridge top."

"*Survivors?*"

"Only twenty-eight out of better than two hundred, all of them men."

Suspicion laced his voice. "They survived victorious, or fled?"

The captain bit the word. "Fled."

Crull drew a deep breath, for he could not abide cowardice. It weakened his command and ruined his own chance for advancement. "And the foe? What waited for them on the ridge top?" Smoke from the signal fire still rose from the ridge, like a dark spear stabbing straight towards a leaden sky.

"More than half the survivors saw nothing, fleeing when the others fled, but a handful spew the same story."

"And?"

Andrius hesitated, clearly cautious. "My lord, what they say is impossible."

"I'll be the judge of that."

Andrius nodded, catching the rebuke. "They claim a single knight held the ridge top, butchering the cadre as they crested the trail. They say he slaughtered every Taal, then he killed the officers, working his way through the men. The dead were stacked like battlements around him, a fortification of corpses. The few survivors decided to retreat."

One man, one foe, he'd heard this tale before. Afterward General Haith had ordered the scout quietly murdered. Murdered messengers were a sure sign of importance, but there had to be more to the tale. "Bring the one who brays the loudest before me. Have the others draw lots. One in every four shall be flayed from head to heel for their cowardice, their bodies fed to the gorehounds while the rest watch. I will have no cowards in my command."

"Yes, my lord." The captain saluted and then sped away.

Crull found his gaze drawn to the smoky column rising from the ridge. *A fiery beacon lit in the night,* this foe was formidable...but he was also brazen. This enemy sought battle, he sought a challenge...but he also sought to be noticed, as if fame mattered. *Fame, the empty coin of dead heroes,* his mouth twisted in a contemptuous scowl, just what he'd expect from the Octagon knights. Yet if the scout's tale was true, and murder named it so, then a lone knight had slaughtered an entire cadre of Taals. Such a feat could not be disregarded. It stank of magic, dark magic. He liked it not. Chewing the thought, Crull made his way to the stairs, descending to the king's war room. A single map was spread across the table. General Haith had taken all the captured maps with him save this one, the one map he no longer needed. A masterwork of map making, the brightly painted vellum showed the Domain of Castlegard, every keep, tower and waystation clearly inked among the craggy peaks of the Dragon Spine Mountains. The Spines had proven a warren of death, traps within traps, keeping the Pentacle from bringing their superior numbers to bear. Of late, the death toll had grown horrendous, whole patrols slaughtered. Wooden markers painted red showed the location of every butchered patrol. The markers told a grim tale, a red arrow aimed at the heart of Raven Pass. Crull walked around the table, studying the map from every angle. General Haith had been obsessed with this map, and whatever interested Haith, fascinated Crull. *An arrow aimed at Raven Pass,* the general had looked decidedly relieved with the gorelabe ordered him south. The general's actions indicated the threat was real. And now Raven Pass was his to hold, his to defend, like a bag of angry vipers dumped in his lap. Crull leaned on the table, glaring at the map. If they expected him to fail, if they expected him to die, then his superior officers were sorely mistaken.

A knock sounded on the door.

"Come."

Captain Andrius entered. "I've brought the songbird."

"Good." Crull took a seat at the head of the table. "I'll hear him sing."

The captain ushered a disheveled soldier into the chamber. Sweat stained his jerkin with dark rings, his face grubby with dirt and stubble, his eyes laden with fear. Bowing low, he hovered near the door.

"Captain, shut the door."

Andrius closed the door and stood in front of it, his hand on his sword hilt.

The soldier sidled away, his gaze darting from the captain to the commander.

Crull poured himself a goblet of wine, a rich red leftover from the king's stores. "Tell me what you saw."

"You won't believe me."

"Sing, if you value your life."

The soldier cringed under the threat, but he found his voice. "They sent us to take the bonfire at the ridge." The soldier shuddered. "Tweren't a battle but a bloody slaughter. We obeyed orders, followin' the others up the trail, but when we reached the top, tweren't nothing but death waitin' fer us. Bodies piled chest-high. All the Taals and officers dead. Blood soakin' the trail. No one left to give commands." His voice turned to a whine. "Tweren't my fault."

Crull studied the soldier. "Sing better, or you'll join the flayed."

The soldier paled. Sweat erupting from his forehead, he began to babble. "Nathor was our commander. He ordered the Taals first, followed by the officers mixed with the best swordsmen. The trail was narrow and steep. We heard the clang of blades and the screams but none of us knew what we was facin' till we reached the top. By then the trailhead was slick with blood, bodies piled high, all of them dead, nothin' but corpses, nothin' but food for crows."

"And the foe?"

The soldier swallowed, his gaze darting around the chamber like a rat seeking escape.

Crull impaled him with his stare. "The foe?"

"Tweren't but one, one knight. Swear it's true, m'lord, by Darkness I do." The soldier began to shake. "The others will tell the same. Only one knight, killin' em all, one knight, one demon-damned knight with a bloody big sword."

"I believe you."

The soldier gasped.

Behind him, Andrius betrayed a glimmer of surprise.

Crull swirled the wine. "Tell me about this knight. Every detail, for your life depends on it."

The soldier nodded like a hound desperate to please. "A knight, he were a knight. His armor was bloody, the sigil hid by gore, but I spied his cloak, spied it I did." His voice dropped to a hushed whisper. "It were maroon." He grinned a gap-toothed smile. "A maroon cloak, a bleedin' maroon knight. He were a knight of the cursed Octagon."

Crull waited.

The soldier flashed an idiot grin, as if he expected a reward. Crull's silence wiped the grin from the man's face.

"A big man," the soldier stammered, clearly grasping at details, "with a thick dark beard. Unnatural, he were. He moved like a ruddy demon, as if he could bleedin' sense a sword stroke before it came at him. Nothin' touched him, as if he were made of smoke. Ain't never seen anything like it. Bleedin' unnatural."

Crull swirled the goblet, his gaze fixed on the soldier.

"And..." the songbird struggled for more, "he fought with one of them fancy two-handed great swords, the kind the knights favor."

Crull set the goblet aside. "Tell me more."

The soldier squirmed looking desperate. His shoulders hunched and he bit his lip, but then his eyes brightened. "I remember somethin' now. Somethin' odd. Somethin' about that sword. Yeah, that blade were black. Yeah," he nodded, "and it tweren't just the blood and gore. The blade were black as sin, swear it were so."

"Anything else?"

The soldier fidgeted and scratched but then hung his head. "No, m'lord."

"You can go."

The soldier's head snapped up, his eyes wide with relief. "Yes, m'lord. Thank ya, m'lord." He scurried from the room.

Crull waited till the door closed. "Andrius."

"Yes, lord?"

"Do you believe him?"

The captain's voice was cautious. "You do, m'lord, and in all the years I've served you, you've seldom been wrong."

A wise answer, a shrewd answer, he'd have to keep a close watch on his second. "Kill the songbird. Do it discretely and then return here. We have a battle to plan."

"Against one man?"

"Against a demon."

40

The Knight Marshal

The knight marshal roamed the ridge top...waiting. The enemy no longer sent patrols into the mountains, content to cower in the valley below. The marshal scowled in disdain. With nothing to slay he grew impatient...and the Dark Sword grew hungry. Restless, he turned his horse toward the burnt beacon, the site of his last triumph.

He smelled it before he saw it. The stench struck like a hammer blow to his gut, making him gag. Bloated corpses lay heaped in mounds around the charred pyre. Hacked by sword cuts, their faces bitten and chewed by carrion feeders, the rotting bodies gave off a horrible stench. Grisly body parts lay strewn between the mounds, the ground crisscrossed by animal tracks. Crows cawed, flapping their dark wings in annoyance at his intrusion, but they did not take flight. Leaping out of his way, they hopped from one corpse to the next, pecking at the feast. So many roving crows, the dark-winged birds endowed the dead with the illusion of movement.

Dismounting, the marshal rummaged through the corpses. His armor had grown tight across the chest, his breastplate pinching him beneath his arms. Shedding his breastplate, he searched for another with a better fit. Twice he discarded salvaged breastplates as too small and a third bore a terrible rent straight to the heart. Spying a large soldier lying face down in the mud, the marshal turned him with his boot. Tinged green, the ghoulish head canted at an unnatural angle, nearly severed from the neck, but the breastplate was intact, the armor embellished with gold scrollwork around the pentacle. "Must have been an officer." The marshal knelt, loosening the bindings. The dead officer gave up the armor with a wet sucking sound. A horrid stench clung to it, but the fit was good. Satisfied, the marshal picked his way back to his horse when he spied a massive shield half hidden by an ogre's body. For a heartbeat he stared at it, puzzled. He didn't recall facing such a massive shield, but his memories of battles were often an exquisite blur. Since taking up the Dark Sword, he'd fought without a shield's protection, but a stout shield could be handy against the horde.

The ogre lay like a felled log. Putting his shoulder to the corpse, he shoved the deadweight aside. The shield proved whole and intact, emblazoned with a gold pentacle painted on black. A massive wall shield, it stood five feet tall and nearly four feet wide. Wall shields were aptly named. Made of laminated wood and leather, the rectangular shield had a convex bow to deflect arrows and to keep it sitting upright on the ground, creating a stout barrier. A round metal boss added to the center of the pentacle averted sword blows. Unwieldy and inordinately heavy, such shields were usually used by archers or crossbowmen as bulwarks or screens, but the ogre had converted it to a melee shield, affixing sturdy arm straps to the back. The marshal tested the straps and found them sound. It would take a giant to heft such a shield in battle. Intrigued by the challenge, he slipped his left arm through the straps. Grasping the shield, he lifted, bearing it on his arm like a melee shield. Much heavier than a normal kite shield, yet he found it surprisingly manageable. Unsheathing the Dark Sword, he practiced with the shield. Fighting imaginary foes, he dodged and whirled, striking with the sword, blocking with the shield. He soon found a deadly rhythm and a new balance. Shadows lengthened across the ridge before he spun to a stop.

He wasn't even breathing hard.

He liked the shield. He liked the legendary size of it. The marshal grinned, imagining the terror it would inspire when his foes saw him wield such a massive shield in battle. *A shield befitting the Dark Sword.*

Walking back to his horse, he came across his discarded breastplate, the maroon octagon nearly obscured by blood and mud. For half a heartbeat he hesitated, a memory clawing at his mind, a regret trying to shame him...but then he kicked it aside and walked on. Colors and sigils no longer matter, for he sought only battle, caring for nothing save glorious victory.

Reclaiming his stallion, he swung into the saddle, keeping the shield on his left arm. Already accustomed to the weight and size of it, the massive shield protected his entire left side from boot tip to helm, a formidable barrier. The marshal grinned. War was sweet, providing him everything he needed.

He drummed his horse to a gallop, riding the ridge, eager for the battle to come.

41

Quintus

The flood of wounded slowed from a deluge to a steady rain. Quintus dared to hope for an end to the war. The healery tower began to clear more beds than it filled, but there were still too many wounds to mend, too many terrible injuries to sew shut, too many lives that needed saving. Desperate for help, he drafted three stable lads, a pot boy, and a scullery maid to serve as his assistants. The stable lads proved apt at making and applying poultices, something they'd learned from the master of horse. Quintus taught them how to change bandages and smell for rot and then charged them to work their way through the wounded, starting with the rooms at the tower top. The pot boy proved dumb as a post, but with so many wounded, the healery tower had an endless supply of chamber pots in danger of overflowing, so he kept the lad busy. The real find was Elise, the scullery maid. Graced with nimble fingers, a quick mind, and a compassionate heart, the flaxen-haired lass had the makings of a first rate healer. When the war finally ended, he intended to speak to her about seeking a place in the monastery. Erdhe needed more healers and the girl showed great promise. Perhaps she'd even earn her master's knot, something he hadn't the patience for.

Cloistered hallways filled with illuminated text, some days he sorely missed the serenity of the monastery, but in his heart, Quintus knew he was meant to be a healer not a scholar. His skills were needed in Castlegard.

Washing his hands in the basin, he moved to the next bed, praying the war ended before the bloody tide swept to the very gates of the great castle. *War at the gates,* he shuddered at the thought. With so many wounded, he seldom had time to dwell on the riddle of mage-stone, yet the danger nagged at his mind. *Magic drained from mage-stone,* something he'd always thought impossible. The strength of mage-stone was said to be as certain as sunrise, impervious to war and weather, yet he'd seen for himself what a smith's hammer could to.

Shuddering at the grim thought, he made the hand sign against evil, feeling as if the great castle were under a dark curse.

"Master Quintus, we need you here!" Elise's urgent call drew him across the room. The bearers moved a scout onto an open bed. Elise cut away the man's jerkin, revealing a nasty sword gash in his side. "Hold him." While the bearers pinned him to the bed, Quintus flushed the scout's wound with wine. Screaming, the scout writhed in pain, trying to twist away from the wine's sharp sting, but the bearers held him firm. Working quickly, Quintus cleaned the wound and then smeared it with a dollop of honey, but only a *small* dollop, the healery was running short of honey. Quintus scowled, the healery was running short of everything save wounded. "You can release him now."

Nodding in deference, the bearers moved away.

"One defeating a hundred," the scout raved, tossing back and forth, babbling in the grip of delirium. *"He killed them, killed them all!"*

The scout felt hot. Quintus feared the onset of wound fever. "Elise, dose him with tincture of yarrow." He held a cool cloth to the scout's forehead while the girl ran to fetch a potion bottle.

"Steel shattered like ice, he slew every one!"

The girl returned with the potion. Holding it to the scout's lips, he cajoled him into taking half the bottle. "That should help."

A horn sounded, beating against the healery windows.

Elise muttered, "More wounded."

The horn came again, but this time it was a volley of trumpets.

"No," Quintus stilled, listening, "that's not the call for wounded, that's something else." A sixth sense spurred him to answer the summons. He pressed the potion bottle into Elise's hands. "Try to get more of this in him. We need to quell the fever or we'll lose him."

Elise took his place by the bed. "Where are you going?"

"To learn the meaning behind the horns." Shucking his gore-spattered apron, Quintus splashed water on his hands and then made his way down the tight spiral stairs. He stumbled out of the tower and into the great yard, dazzled by the sunlight. Others were spilling into the yard, bellows boys from the forge, scullery maids from the kitchen, lads in training gear from the practice yard, all pulled by the horns.

Trumpets blared from every tower of Castlegard, ringing against mage-stone battlements. For half a heartbeat, Quintus feared they might be under attack, but the horns did not sound strident, more like a welcome than a warning. He followed the gathering crowd, everyone moving like a tide towards the inner gates.

A deep voice rumbled from behind. "Can you read the horns, healer?"

Quintus turned to find Otto, the master swordsmith, looming over his right shoulder. "No, can you?"

"They blare a welcome for knights returning."

A shiver raced down the healer's spine, an inexplicable feeling of foreboding.

"You feel it too." The smith's voice dropped to a harsh whisper. "Naught's been right since you shared your secret."

Quintus gave the smith a warning glare, but in truth, he felt it too.

"Come, let's meet them at the inner gate." They followed the tidal flow of the crowd.

The portcullis was raised, the great ironshod gates thrown open wide.

The big smith stood beside him, the smell of forge-heated iron surrounding him like a haze. Quintus sniffed his own robes, wondering if he smelled like blood and potions, but he just smelled like himself.

The crowd jostled elbows, anxiously waiting. At first there was nothing to see, just the empty corridor between the inner and outer ramparts, but then Quintus heard the clop of hooves on stone. Anticipation rippled through the watchers. The first riders came into view, but instead of maroon knights in burnished armor, they saw a patchwork of farmers riding mules and nags, tugging milk cows on leads. A bedraggled lot poured through the great gate, villagers, farmers, and peasants, the small folk of the domain. Women carried swaddled babes while small children clutched at their skirts. Youths led goats and herded chickens. Men burdened with stuffed sacks walked like hunchbacks. Pots and pans rattled as they shuffled past, their dust-stained faces bearing a mixture of relief, exhaustion and fear.

Beside him, the smith said, "They've come seeking sanctuary."

Sanctuary, the word had a hollow sound, for the great castle was no longer invincible.

And then Quintus saw the knights riding escort. Many of their faces were familiar, but he saw no captains riding among them. Beneath their helms, most were fresh-faced youths hastily raised to knights or wounded veterans that he'd patched up and sent back to battle. *Farmers seeking sanctuary guarded by the young and the infirm,* the truth sent a chill down his back. Quintus made the hand sign against evil, a dark dread rising in him. The Octagon Knights were losing the war.

42

The Knight Marshal

T he sun rose bloody in the east, not a cloud in the sky, the perfect day for war. The knight marshal girded for battle, tightening straps and buckles, donning breastplate, gorget, and greaves. He set a visored helm of black enamel embossed with gold upon his head, a showy piece yet he liked the fit. Most of his armor was fresh-scavenged from the newly-dead. *Colors,* the thought annoyed him, the word buzzing in his mind like an angry hornet...and then he remembered the phrase. *What color their cloaks?* He remembered the phrase but he could not remember why it mattered. He shook his head against the pesky thought.

Like a snake becoming more, he'd outgrown much of his old armor. Too dented, too tight, too worn, he shed the old, scavenging for something better. The dead gave him everything he needed. Clad from head to toe in armor, he unsheathed the Dark Sword and danced the classical forms, checking the armor's fit. For this battle, he'd suffer no hindrance of any form. Satisfied, he took up the ogre's shield. A golden pentacle shone from its curved front, but sigils mattered not anymore. A spoil of war, the massive wall shield stood five feet tall and nearly four feet wide. Such a shield was not meant to be wielded in battle, yet a dead ogre had converted it to a melee shield, affixing stout arm straps to the back. Cumbersome and heavy, a mere man could never wield it, yet the marshal found it suited him.

Sheathing his sword, he swung into the saddle. The black stallion pranced as if anticipating the glory to come. "Soon." He settled his warhorse and steered his mount along the ridge till he came to a trailhead, one of the few that reached all the way to the valley floor.

He reached the trailhead just as the bloody sun cleared the Dragon Spines, throwing spears of light into the valley below. *Raven Pass,* the narrow valley was infested by the horde. Tents and battle banners and men in black armor cluttered the valley. Their numbers were staggering. The marshal smiled, a fitting test of his prowess. *To defeat an entire army,* he hungered for the glory. This day would be a day of days. Bards would forever sing of this battle, for this fight would be the stuff of legends, when one man dared to defeat an army. A hunger for bloodshed and glory raged through him with the strength of ecstasy.

"Soon," his whispered voice caressed the Dark Sword.

Turning his stallion down the trail, he held his mount to a careful walk. His warhorse fought the bit, tossing his head, but the marshal kept a tight rein. Too steep and treacherous for speed, he forced his stallion to walk lest his horse take them both to a deadly fall. Narrow and winding, the trail snaked its way past boulders and windswept pines, providing a good view of the valley. Down in the throat of the pass, the enemy awoke, lighting campfires and changing patrols. The marshal listened, but he heard no blare of horns, no warning shouts. His foe seemed unaware of the threat riding towards them. The marshal flashed a predator's grin. He'd meet them without fanfare, no trumpeters, no heralds, no battle banners, just an implacable thirst for battle. Soon enough, they'd learn the grim fate they faced.

By midmorning, he reached the valley floor. He lingered in the forested fringe, watching from between the pines. Seeing no signs of ambush, he readied for battle. One last time he checked his armor, tightening straps and buckles.

The marshal lowered his visor, shuttering the world to a narrow slit. He settled the great wall shield on his arm, protecting his left side from heel to helm. Unsheathing the Dark Sword, he brandished the blade aloft and loosed his battle cry. *"For Death and Glory!"*

The Dark Sword answered, hungry for souls. Power roared through the blade, surging into him with the strength of an unchained dragon.

He felt invincible.

He felt the raw thirst of his sword, a siren's song urging him to kill.

He felt as if the coming battle was a stone-carved destiny.

A smile slid across his face, hungry for a feast of souls.

It was time.

Let my destiny begin! The marshal urged his warhorse to a gallop. Racing out of the forest fringe, he rode towards the horde, one warrior daring many. His armor jangled to the chime of war, his steed's hoof beats drummed the ground with a hungry beat. His sword throbbed in his hands, keening for battle. Leaning forward, the marshal pressed his horse for speed.

A blare of horns called a desperate warning.

The enemy awoke to the danger.

Through the narrow slit of his visor, he saw a confusion of soldiers forming battle lines. *So the enemy is not as lax as they appeared,* it was a welcome thought, for he wanted no easy victory. Glory needed to be earned, and he intended to earn it this day.

He galloped closer, yet the enemy proved their discipline. Holding their line, their shields turned outward, they formed a stout wall of steel and burnished leather.

The marshal grinned, *your wall will not avail you!*

And then he heard the lethal whistle of arrows.

The marshal raised the mighty wall shield, holding it above his head and the head of his steed, a feat no ordinary man could accomplish. Crouched beneath the massive shield, he urged his stallion to a hard gallop. A storm of arrows dropped from the sky, all of them seeking one target. Feathered shafts fell like hail, a rain of death surrounding him. Iron warheads punched into his raised shield, hard blows seeking flesh. The archers found their target, but the massive shield held. He rode through the rain of death...and came out the other side, unscathed.

The marshal lowered the shield to his side. Half a hundred arrows protruded from it. Laughter bubbled out of him, teetering on the edge of a berserker's rage. With a single swipe of the Dark Sword, he severed the arrows. Urging his horse to a lathered gallop, he charged across the open ground, closing the distance. Too close for arrows, he saw the details of his foes. Black shields, black armor, they waited with spears, swords, and battle axes, yet he noted how their line bowed slightly backwards, as if they cringed away, fearing his charge. *One against an army,* he must look like a madman...or the God of War incarnate. He roared his battle cry against their armored line. "*For Death and Glory!*"

And then he struck, hitting at a full gallop. His warhorse barreled into their line, knocking men backwards, churning soldiers beneath ironshod hooves. The marshal took advantage of the breach. Wielding both sword and shield, he loosed a fearsome attack. Stroke and parry, he slew every foe around him. The Dark Sword cut like a scythe, lopping heads and severing limbs. The massive shield struck like a battering ram, knocking soldiers senseless. His warhorse kicked, bit, and stomped, adding to the carnage. Soldiers fell like wheat around him. Screams of the dying rose around him like a dirge from hell. A huge ogre lumbered toward him, loosing a head-high swing of an axe. The marshal evaded the axe and then took the ogre's head, a spray of blood spewing from the headless corpse. Sensing a spear thrust aimed at his back, he swiveled in the saddle and knocked it aside, disemboweling the spearman. Cut and parry, he moved with lightning speed, guiding his horse through the fray while the enemy fought as if they were encrusted in ice. The battle became a lethal dance. The marshal anticipated every threat, parried every blow, always finding the sweet spot for a lethal strike. He slew countless foes and the Dark Sword drank their souls. Strength and vigor roared into him. Instead of growing weary, he grew stronger.

He was Death unchained.

He was the God of War.

The battlefield was his.

None could stand in his path. Shields splintered and swords shattered, unable to withstand the Dark Sword. The dead and dying fell like cordwood around him, creating a rampart of corpses. Seeking fresh prey, he urged his horse to a jump, clearing the grisly barrier.

Horns blared across the field, trying to bring order to chaos. Officers screamed commands, desperate to rally their troops. The enemy pulled back, forming a new battle line. Spears bristled towards him, but their iron tips wavered, presenting a hesitant hedgehog. Black-clad soldiers cowered behind a trembling shield wall, their courage shaken.

The marshal leaped from his horse.

Yanking the helm from his head, he tossed it aside, gaining a better view. Helmless, he strode towards them, coming close enough to smell the pungent ripeness of their fear, and then he unleashed the Dark Sword. Slashing left and right, he decapitated their spear tips, turning their weapons into blunt sticks. His foes backed away. Fear bled from their eyes...as well it should.

Battering their impotent spears aside, he weighed into them, attacking with sword and shield. The Dark Sword thrummed in his hands, keening an unquenchable thirst. Heads toppled across the ground. Entrails spilled from grasping fingers. Bones crunched beneath his shield. Severed limbs littered the mud. Screaming soldiers became still as corpses, their blood congealing in empty footprints. The coppery stench of death prevailed. The line broke and crumbled, yet the marshal pursued. With each stroke, he fed the sword, becoming a whirlwind of death.

Horns blared, calling a desperate retreat. Three times the enemy gave ground, retreating to reform their wavering line. Three times he broke their shield wall, dealing death. The marshal never slowed, he never tired, reveling in the glory of war. The Dark Sword was insatiable. Drinking souls, it fed him strength.

The battle began to slow.

The enemy retreated, pulling away from him, opening a wide swath of space, a killing zone filled with nothing but corpses.

No fodder for his sword.

The marshal slowed to a stop, taking stock of his surroundings. Crows circled overhead, soaring on silent wings. The sun was nearly set, throwing long shadows across the dead. He'd fought for the better part of a day, yet he wasn't even winded. Looking behind, he saw a river of corpses stretching towards the eastern ridge, a feast for crows. *Thousands of dead*...yet it wasn't enough.

He turned to face the living.

The Dark Sword still hungered.

The enemy stood in a ragged crescent. Weapons dangling from tired arms, their shields slumped to the ground, they trembled before him. Bloody and battered, they looked exhausted, they looked defeated.

"Fight me!" The marshal tightened his grip on his shield and raised his sword, for he could not abide cowardice. He advanced towards them, but for every step he took, the enemy retreated the same distance, shrinking away. *"Fight me!"* The words roared out of him.

And then they began to kneel. Dropping to the trampled mud, they offered their weapons, prostrating themselves before him.

"Kneelers!" He spat the word, his face twisting to a snarl. He hated kneelers, for they deprived him of his rightful glory. He stalked towards them, fury in his stride.

A few cringed away, but most remained prostrate. Some prayed while others whimpered, but most stayed silent, their faces pressed to the blood-soaked mud.

"Stand and fight!" He roared his challenge, yet they remained stubbornly prostrate, hugging the muddy ground like craven worms. Anger burned through him, igniting a killing rage. The marshal attacked. Hewing heads from bodies, he turned cowards into corpses. The Dark Sword feasted on an endless sea of souls.

The strident sound of a battle horn pierced his mind.

The marshal staggered to a stop.

The dead and dying littered the ground around him. Beyond the corpses, the rest of the army remained prostrate in the mud like penitents awaiting their fate. Contempt snarled his face, but then he saw a lone rider coming towards him. Bedecked in dark armor, his breastplate embossed with gleaming gold, he wore a plumed helm and carried a saber in his gauntleted fist. *A commander, perhaps a champion, come to do battle,* finally a worthy foe for his sword. The knight marshal raised the Dark Sword in salute. "Fight me!"

The enemy rode within five sword lengths and then he reined his warhorse to a stop. For the longest time he sat unmoving, as if waiting for something, but then he slowly removed his helm, tossing it aside. A man of middling years, he had swarthy skin the color of warm bronze offset by dark hair, dark eyes and a dark mustache. A scar rode his left cheek, proof he was no stranger to battle.

The marshal assumed a fighting stance. "Have you come to do battle?"

"I've come to serve."

A snarl rose in the marshal's throat, yet something bid him wait.

"Do you know why they kneel prostrate, accepting death without a fight?"

The marshal waited, statue-still, poised to fight.

"In the north, we serve a god, a god who walks among us. We northerners know what gods do. We well know what havoc they wreck among mere mortals." He raised his saber, gesturing to the field of corpses. "Look around you. Look behind you. How can one man reap so much death lest he be a god? You are the God of Death."

The marshal shook his head. "No, the God of War."

The swarthy man flashed a feral grin. "Even better." Dismounting, he strode towards the marshal. "But true gods need servants. The God of War deserves an army."

Yes, the voice that he thought of as the sword's whispered in his head, *let them serve!*

"I am Commander Crull, leader of the Third Army of the Pentacle," he extended his saber hilt-first, "and I've come to serve a god." He knelt, offering his sword.

The marshal reeled backwards. He'd expected battle, he'd expected death and glory...but never surrender. His gaze roved the battlefield, the endless sea of carnage...and the living army lying prostrate before him.

The God of War must have an army

The words thundered through him. They felt right, they felt fitting. It was as if the voice planted a battle standard in his mind, and it was glorious. The marshal echoed the words of the sword, "The God of War must have an army." He touched the commander's proffered sword hilt. "I accept your service. I expect your worship." He raised the Dark Sword to the heavens. "For I am the God of War!"

His army stood, banging swords on shields, their voices raised in adulation. "*All hail the God of War!*"

In the South

43

The Priestess

The Priestess took the time to prepare. After a long soak in a steaming tub, her handmaidens washed and coiled her raven-dark hair. Naked as a blank canvas, she knelt before her two chests, considering her arsenal. *Seduction and poison,* she'd arm herself with both, one for offense, the other for defense.

She started with seduction. Considering her prey, she chose a sophisticated scent, sandalwood with a touch of thyme. Subtle yet complex, she dabbed the scent in an alluring path down and around her curves. For her face, she added crushed malachite to highlight the depths of her eyes and a hint of ruby coloring on her lips, but otherwise her face needed no adornment. For undergarments, she chose layers of the sheerest silk, soft whispers against her skin. Instead of a gown, she chose a robe of a deep forest green flecked with gold thread, cut low to display her curves without revealing her depths. For jewelry, she wore the sundered Eye bound in silver, a reminder of the bitter price she'd paid, a cold weight dangling between her breasts. Finished, the Priestess gazed in the mirror, considering the effect. Mystery and sexual sophistication gazed back at her, the perfect foil for a thousand-year-old soul.

Satisfied, she dismissed her handmaidens and reached for her poisons. Unlocking the rosewood chest, she opened drawers and sniffed at stoppered bottles, considering her choices. So many ways to death, poison was the most devious of weapons, the subtle kill, tailored to suit each situation, each victim, the perfect weapon for the Priestess. She might have painted a tincture of nightshade on her nipples or toes...but death was not her intent, at least not yet, not tonight. Instead, she sought something with a deliberate method of delivery. A pair of bracelets caught her gaze, coiled serpents adorned with green enameled scales on gold, jewelry of the deadliest sort. Cunningly crafted, they coiled from her wrists to her elbows serving as bracers, but their true bite came from the hidden needles exposed by a secret touch. She pressed the small button, releasing the needles along the serpent's spine. The potency of their barbed bite depended on the chosen poison. A reduction of wolfsbane seemed the perfect choice. Folklore said that wolfsbane was used to slay the hounds of hell, a fitting omen for tonight's prey. Carefully applying the potent mixture, she made sure it was dry before resetting the needles. A predator's smile slid across her face, certain a single prick would cause a heart-stopping death. She raised her arms to the light, admiring her choice. Glittering along her forearms, the serpentine bracers carried enough hidden poison to kill ten men. For something less lethal, she chose a serpent ring, anointing the hidden fangs with henbane, a sleepy alternative to wolfsbane. Armed and dangerous, she was ready to meet the Mordant.

Steffan glowered from the shadows. "Don't go."

She caressed his cheek, aroused by the rough stubble. "You know I must."

Anger burned in his dark gaze.

"Don't be jealous."

"You like me jealous."

His riposte hit home. She gave him a salacious smile, her voice a velvety purr. "In truth, I do."

He gave her a look that declothed her. For half a heartbeat, she thought he might pounce, strip her clothes off and have her in the hallway, but instead he growled and trod away.

She found herself breathlessly disappointed...but she'd set her aim on more dangerous prey. Gathering her resolve, she made her way out into the twilight.

Since palanquins were not used in the queen's city, she had Braxus order a carriage. Serving as her seneschal, he rode beside her with an escort of six guards.

The sun set in a glorious glow of russets and gold. Despite the fall of darkness, the queen's city came alive with lanterns and candlelight.

She directed the carriage to the wealthy section of the city. From scrying in the Eye, the Priestess knew the Mordant came to Pellanor in the guise of a prince of Ur, hiding in plain sight, like a peacock strutting among pigeons. The queen's city was rife with rumors. The markets buzzed with talk of his legendary wealth and excess, yet none seemed to guess his true nature. Darkness hidden in plain sight, no one expected a peacock to have such deadly claws, yet the Priestess knew the truth. She touched the sundered moonstone bound in silver, dangling between her breasts. How dare he break her strongest magic, a gift from the Dark Lord. The loss enraged her, hardening her resolve.

The carriage trundled through cobblestone streets, stopping before a mansion alight with torches. Servants in purple livery rushed to open the carriage door. Escorted by her men, the Priestess approached the doorway, unsure of her reception.

A fat seneschal in rich robes greeted her. "He's been expecting you." With the slightest of bows, he welcomed her inside.

From the scrying bowl, she recognized his pudgy face, a bishop of the Pentacle. In a similar fashion, she knew the slight men lurking in the shadows were assassins of the ninth rank. *Death lurking in the doorway,* the Priestess wondered if it was a pointed message or merely a precaution.

Candlelight glittered overhead yet the shadows lost none of their potency. Greeting the bishop with the barest of nods, the Priestess stepped into the devil's lair.

"He'll see you in the throne room...alone."

Braxus clenched his sword hilt, a protest on his lips, but she forestalled him. "My men will wait here."

"Good." The prelate flashed a serpent's smile, gesturing towards the heart of the mansion.

She followed him through gilded halls hung with traditional hunting tapestries. The mansion's wealthy trappings were no doubt a legacy of the previous owner, but the throne room held none of the deceptive clutter. Lit by braziers, it was empty save for a raised dais and a gilded throne. A silk banner hung from the vaulted ceiling to the marble floor, the only adornment, purple emblazoned with the great golden Wyrm. Beneath the banner, the Mordant sat upon the throne bedecked in false colors.

Half a hundred times she'd watched him in the scrying bowl, yet nothing prepared her for the raw strength of his presence. *So young and so fair of face,* yet Darkness thundered through him like a storm. So much raw power, she wondered that mortals did not feel his true nature and run shrieking in fear. Gathering her own strength, the Priestess dared to meet his stare. Power beat against her, trying to cowl her, yet she stood unbowed, clinging to the knowledge that he was not a god.

He gave her a lazy smile.

She inclined her head. "My lord, the Mordant."

He flashed a predator's smile. "The Dark Whore."

She dared to correct him. "The Priestess of the Oracle."

"Yet your Eye is sundered."

His words struck like a slap. Her anger flared, yet she kept her voice controlled. "You had no right."

"As the oldest harlequin, *all* rights are mine."

She rebuked him with her stare. "The Eye serves the Oracle Priestess."

He gave her a surly stare. "Why? Are you blind without it?"

"The Eye was a gift of the Dark Lord."

"Then let him fix it."

His retort shocked her, a flippant blasphemy, an outrageous arrogance. "You had no right."

"*Power* gives me every right. *Power* is all that matters." He stood, his shadow stretching across the chamber, his voice thundering through the throne room. "For more than a thousand years I have lived! There are *none* who can stand against me."

So he styles himself a god! She wanted to run from his power, she wanted to laugh at his arrogant folly, but instead, she stood her ground. "Then why am I summoned?"

"The Great Dark Dance has begun. Instead of spying on me from afar, you will serve."

Her pride got the better of her. "I ruled my own kingdom."

"You ruled a petty backwater, without significance or power. Far better to serve in the Great Dark Dance."

She stared at him through hooded eyes. "How?"

"You can start by corrupting the men closest to the queen." He flashed a smile. "After all, it's what you do."

"You want me to turn them to the Dark?"

"I want you to add sexual strings to the court puppets." His smile turned sinister. "I've come to alter history, to sow prejudice and deepen the Great Dark Divide. A queen cannot be allowed to rule, especially one that rules so well. I will twist her deeds to infamy. Horror will be heaped on her name so that all of Erdhe will forever shun a woman's rule."

His words chilled her to the core, giving her notice that even the Oracle Priestess would not rule...yet she kept her face a mask. "As you wish." She needed to get away, she needed to reconsider. "I'll begin at once." Nodding to the Mordant, she turned to leave.

"Where do you think you are going?"

"Back to the inn."

He shook his head, a viper's smile on his face. "You will stay in my house, a room has already been prepared." His gaze raked across her, considering her curves. "You will come to my bed when I beckon. And you will use your powers to serve."

Trapped, she was trapped by his power, by his assassins. "What of my men?"

"They can return to the inn to await service."

So he seeks to strip me of my loyal swords. "And what of my handmaidens?"

"Summon them if you wish." Settling back on the throne, he gave a negligent wave. "Your women are of no account."

"Yes, my lord." She turned to leave.

"And *Iris.*"

He knows my true name! Turning, she kept the shock from her face, meeting his shark's stare.

"When I call you to my bed, I expect you to come. Willing or not, I expect you to serve...," a smile broke across his face, "but I think you will like it."

Instead of instilling fear, her power surged within her, a sexual hunger rising to the challenge. "As you command." Seduction laced her voice. She gave him the smallest of nods, and then followed the seneschal from the throne room.

Braxus paced in the entranceway, his hand on his sword hilt. Relief flashed across his face when he saw her. "Shall we go, my lady?"

"I will be staying here, a guest of the prince."

Alarm filled his gaze. She gave him the smallest of nods, confirming his fears. "I want you to do exactly as I say. Return to the inn and bring my handmaidens and all of my things." She drilled him with her stare, making sure he understood.

"Yes, my lady."

"And then return to the inn and await further orders."

"But..."

"You will await further orders."

Anger rode his voice, yet he complied. "As you wish."

She stepped towards him, kissing him on the cheek. With her lips near his ear, she whispered. "*Warn Steffan.*"

He held her close, whispering an answer. "*I'll keep watch.*" Stepping away, he saluted her, and then he was gone.

She turned to the seneschal. "I believe a room has been prepared?"

The portly prelate flashed a rude smile. "Yes, my lady."

His blatant rudeness roused her anger. She was sorely tempted to brush against him, pricking the fat prelate with the poison of her armbands...but she refrained. It was too soon to sow death among the Mordant's servants. Her face composed in a demure mask, she followed him up the gilded stairs to a suite of rooms at the rear of the manse. Large and richly appointed, the inner room was dominated by a four posted bed piled with embroidered pillows and draped with jewel-colored silks.

"If you need anything, Barry will serve you." He gestured to a slight man hovering at the doorway, another assassin clad in servant's purple.

"I need my handmaidens and my things."

"As soon as they arrive." He closed the door.

She heard the lock click.

So he seeks to cage me. Feeling confined, she went to the window. The diamond-paned windows overlooked a walled garden, a bubbling fountain surrounded by statues and topiaries. Opening the window, she leaned out, staring down. She studied the garden, listening to the night. *The shadows moved.* A black-clad assassin stepped into the torchlight. Brazenly staring up her, he nodded, before retreating into the velvety darkness.

So the gilded cage is a guarded prison...yet he dares to call me to his bed! A smile brewed upon her lips, *how arrogant, how foolish.* His powers were formidable, even frightening, but despite his thousand years, the Mordant was still a mortal, still a man, subject to a man's desires. *Desire is the greatest poison!* The Priestess smiled. She'd bide her time till he summoned her, and then she'd ply her powers, clashing her will against his, the sorceress of sex seducing a thousand years of evil. In the realm of the bedchamber, she had no doubt who would prevail.

44

Steffan

The thought of *her* going to *him* ignited a restless rage in Steffan. Unable to sit at the inn, he wandered the streets of Pellanor, but he saw nothing. She'd slept with others before, plying her skills on lesser men, pulling them under her spell. He well knew what she was, the Priestess of the Oracle, a sexual goddess draped in Darkness. He'd watched her hold sway over others, casting her allure on unsuspecting men, but always before it enhanced his pride to know that *he* was her lover. All the others were mere tools, serving her ambition, but *he* was her paramour, her equal in the bedchamber. But somehow the Mordant was different. There should have been another way.

His thoughts ran in circles and so did his footsteps. Steffan found himself returning to the inn, staring up at her window, waiting for lantern light to brighten her room, waiting for her carriage to return...and then he'd feel the fool, and resume walking. He meant to walk away, but somehow he always found himself wandering in circles, always returning to the inn, waiting, watching, like a love-struck swain. He hated himself for showing such weakness yet he could not abandon his vigil.

A carriage thundered down the street, pulling rein in front of the inn.

Steffan slipped into the shadows, watching. He recognized the guards...and then he saw Braxus, but the seneschal returned alone! Erupting from his hiding place, Steffan raced across the street and circled the carriage, staring at the open door...but the carriage was empty. *She stayed with him!* He staggered backwards, but then anger roared through him. His hand sought his sword hilt. Steffan strode through the inn, up the stairway, and down the hall, murder in his gaze.

The door to her room was ajar.

He banged it open and strode straight to Braxus. Whirling the man around, he grabbed him by the lapels and yanked him close, yelling into his face. "Where is she? Why did you leave her? How could you leave her with *him*?"

Braxus gave him a blank look. "Orders."

"She was supposed to come back." Steffan's voice turned to a snarl. "You were supposed to protect her."

Braxus pushed back, hard enough to knock Steffan to the floor. The seneschal stood over Steffan with fists clenched, his normally calm face shattered to rage. "Do you think you're the only one who loves her!"

The words hit like a slap. Jarred from his rage, Steffan's glance roved the room. It was only then that he realized the others were packing. His own anger fled, replaced by the desperate need to know. "What happened?"

Braxus looked away, visibly swallowing his own anger, and then he turned back to Steffan and offered his hand, pulling him to his feet. "She had an audience with him." Before Steffan could speak, Braxus glowered, "Alone." Anger sizzled in the seneschal's eyes, but Steffan sensed it was not directed at him. "I had to wait in the entranceway, wait like a lackey, yet it gave me the chance to observe. The mansion is crawling with capable looking guards and dwarves with pointy teeth. I liked it not."

Steffan didn't care about the guards, he cared about *her*. "What happened?"

"She wasn't in the audience long. When she came out, she was clearly shaken...disturbed. I've never seen her so shaken." His gaze flashed to Steffan. "She whispered a message for you, a warning to stay away. And then she ordered me to bring her handmaidens and all of her things."

"Bring them?"

"He's holding her captive."

An image of the Priestess bound in chains burned through Steffan like white-hot lightning. "*Captive,*" the word snarled out of him.

Braxus sent him a bracing look. "That's why we have to work together. We have to get her back."

Steffan glanced past Braxus, at the two handmaidens folding silks into the cedar chest. "I'm coming with you."

"No, you're not." Steel laced the seneschal's voice. "She said you're to stay away."

Disdain twisted his words. "Stay away and do nothing?"

"*Dead* you are of no use to her. Stay away and *live*...and wait for her plan." His voice dropped to a hard whisper. "I would not be surprised if the Mordant's men are watching the inn."

Steffan gripped his sword hilt, jealousy warring with anger warring with common sense.

"You'd best be gone."

Steffan gave the seneschal a reluctant nod. "I'll be at the Golden Tankard. Come find me when you know more."

Braxus nodded. "I'll find you."

"Swear!"

"I swear."

Pulling the hood of his cloak up to hide his features, Steffan slipped out the door and down the hallway. He made his way to the back of the inn and out into the alleyway. If anyone kept watch, he did not see them. Steffan stayed to the shadows, moving through the back ways. *Held captive,* the words thundered through his mind. He could not imagine her a captive. How he rued her decision to come to the queen's god-cursed city. They should have stayed away, stayed in Rhune, never tangling with the oldest harlequin...but none of that mattered now. Rage engulfed him. By all the gods, he swore to get her back.

45

Liandra

Messengers came from the north bearing tidings of war. The Mordant's forces broiled out of Raven Pass, putting an end to the south's respite. *Bloodshed in the north.* In many ways the war seemed distant, yet the queen felt a nagging threat growing in her court, as if shadows coalesced around her with a strangling darkness. Liandra shivered at the premonition, touching the key hidden in her bodice for reassurance. She missed Robert, she needed Robert, yet her shadowmaster lingered in Lingard. She'd sent dispatches summoning him back to court, yet his replies spoke of nothing but rebuilding the great city-fortress. Something was amiss, another subtle threat cloaked in shadows.

Liandra reached for a quill, setting ink to parchment. This time she summoned him home with no uncertain terms, craving his keen advice as much as his presence in her bed. Melting the emerald green wax over the candle flame, she sealed the parchment. Her royal seal ensured the scroll's privacy and a speedy delivery...but a wax seal was only as strong as the courier's loyalty.

The queen rang the hand bell, summoning her page. "We will see our deputy shadowmaster now." The page bowed and was gone.

Her quill continued to scratch across parchment, sending orders the length and breadth of her kingdom. So many details to ensure prosperity, so many distracting threats of war, the queen felt beleaguered, yet she persisted, no detail too small.

A knock sounded on the door and Master Raddock appeared. Swathed in somber robes of black, her deputy shadowmaster looked like a plump crow with dagger-sharp eyes.

Wielding her feathered quill like a sword, she pointed to a stack of sealed scrolls on her left. "These are for the royal couriers. Have them sent at once. And this," she tapped the single scroll on her right, "is for the Master Archivist. We order this one to be sent by one of our shadowmen. Have him masquerade as a merchant and order him to see the scroll delivered directly to the Master Archivist's hands."

Master Raddock raised a bushy eyebrow. "You do not trust the royal couriers?"

"We have suspicions. It has not yet grown to mistrust."

He took the scroll in question and slipped it into his pocket. "Shall I have the couriers shadowed?"

"It has not yet come to that. And our shadowmen are stretched far too thin as it is. Meanwhile, we have other concerns." She fingered the quill. "Tell me of the prince of Ur."

"Merchants flock to his mansion by day, offering the finest wines and the most exotic delicacies. Rumors say he sponsors the best bards and the most refined courtesans. By night, the mansion hums with lavish banquets, attended by the wealthy and the powerful. The city is agog with the spectacle of his wealth. One cannot pass through the markets without hearing his name spoken. The rumors are reaching mythic proportions."

"So he spins a web of wealth in order to entice." Having twice played chess with the prince, she knew he had a devious mind. Liandra wondered at his true intent. "He courts the wealthy and the powerful...we need names."

The master removed a tattered slip of parchment from a different pocket and began to read. "Duke Anders, Lord Nealy, Lord Wesley, Merchant Gillrod, Merchant Langford..."

The list was long, full of men who had fallen out of favor with her court...and men who still served her court, all of them powerful in their own way.

"Captain Blackmon, Lord..."

The queen interrupted, outrage in her voice, "Captain Blackmon? The captain in our royal guards?"

"Yes, majesty." He fumbled through another sheaf of parchments. "The notes say Captain Blackmon left the prince's mansion with a very expensive courtesan on his arm."

She felt a noose tighten around her. "Continue."

"Merchant Harstow, Lord Saddler, Lord..."

The queen interrupted again. "Lord *Saddler,* our master of coin? We never considered him to be a man for frivolities."

"Yet he attended one of the prince's dinners." He glanced down at his sheaf of parchments, his voice growing hesitant. "All of your small council have accepted invitations from the prince save for Sir Durnheart, Major Ranoth and myself."

"*All?*"

He nodded. "Several have returned more than once."

Her fingers drummed on the desk. "We like it not." She gestured with her quill. "Continue."

A knocked sounded on the door.

"Come."

Her page poked his head inside. "Majesty, your small council is assembled and awaits your pleasure."

"Let them wait." When the door closed, she gestured for her deputy shadowmaster to continue. Master Raddock read the names in a dispassionate voice, a rarefied list of the wealthy, the powerful, the openly loyal...and the quietly disloyal.

The master fell silent.

Liandra pondered the list.

Master Raddock ventured, "There is nothing illegal in hosting dinner parties."

"Nothing illegal, yet everything suspicious." Liandra tugged on the feather quill, considering. "Have your men continue to shadow the prince." She gave him a piercing stare. "Impress upon them that no detail is too small."

He bowed towards her. "As her majesty commands."

Liandra stood, arranging the folds of her silk gown. "Walk with us to the small council."

Her deputy shadowmaster followed half a step behind. The queen swept through the gilded hallways, her mind mulling the list of names. A pair of guards saluted, opening the doors to the council chambers. She strode into the chamber, her loyal lords jumping to their feet. Her gaze raked across them, fresh with suspicion.

One was missing. "Where is our Lord Sheriff?"

Her lords looked at the empty chair as if they'd just noticed it. None had a reply. She looked to her deputy shadowmaster, but he too was silent. It was not like her loyal sheriff to be tardy. Annoyed, the queen took her seat at the head of the table. She looked to Major Ranoth. "We will begin with the war."

A vellum map was spread across the council table. Metal figurines were placed across the map, most of them crowding the north, marking the armies. Emerald green, checkered blue and red, maroon and silver, the armies stood arrayed against the Mordant's horde of black and gold. The major moved the green knight mounted on a rearing white horse, representing Prince Stewart and the forces of Lanverness. "Prince Stewart and the Rose Army are encamped here, just south of the Snowmelt River. At last report, Princess Jordan and the Army of Navarre are here. By now, the two armies should have joined forces. I expect them to make for Eye Bridge, to try and contain the Pentacle in the north." The major gave the queen a grim look. "If the fighting in the north has not already begun...it soon will. War has come to Erdhe."

War again, an ugly nemesis that dogged her. The queen knew the details, having read and re-read the dispatches but she found it instructive to see the pieces move across the map. The war in the north was her most dire concern, yet her mind kept picking at the list of names, like an itchy scab that relentlessly annoyed.

Major Ranoth finished and the others gave their reports. Instead of absorbing their words, the queen found herself listening to their intonation, noting the skittishness of their glances, wondering at their loyalty. Having seen enough, the queen cut the meeting short. "Lord Saddler, we will see you in our chambers."

The portly lord looked puzzled. "May I ask why?"

The queen snapped a reply. "No, you may not."

Flustered, her master of coin bowed low. "As you command."

"We are done here." The queen rose abruptly.

The others sputtered at her abrupt dismissal, but the queen paid them no heed. She swept from the chamber and strode through the hallways, her deputy shadowmaster and her portly master of coin rushing to keep pace.

The queen entered the sanctuary of her solar. Taking a seat in front of the hearth, she arranged the pleats of her gown. Her master of coin fidgeted in front of her, her deputy shadowmaster skulking in the shadows. The queen allowed the silence to weigh heavy. The fire snapped and crackled releasing a breath of cedar. After a hundred heartbeats, she stared at her master of coin, her voice grave. "We hear you have attended the prince of Ur at his mansion."

Master Saddler looked startled at her line of inquiry. "Yes...my wife insisted. The markets abound with rumors of the prince's lavish banquets. Claudia pestered me till I accepted the invitation."

"And was it lavish?"

"Beyond measure."

The queen waited, spearing him with her stare.

Her portly lord flashed beet-red, sweat beading on his bald pate. "Urian brandy flowed like wine, the best musicians, the most exotic dishes, an abundance of everything, and," his voice dropped to an embarrassed hush, "there was even rumors of courtesans in the upstairs rooms."

"And did you enjoy them?"

His voice was shocked. "Majesty, I'm a married man!"

She granted him a small smile. "We meant the dinner."

"Oh." He took a deep breath, regaining his composure. "Majesty, I'm a simple man with simple tastes. It was too much for me."

The queen waited.

He rubbed his hands on his velvet doublet, his voice dropping to a whisper. "In truth, it felt like a bribe. I won't be going back."

Her voice held a dangerous edge. "And were you bribed?"

He flustered. "Nothing untoward was said...it just felt...soiled."

"Did you meet the prince?"

"Such a young man to wield so much wealth."

"What did he say to you?"

"I...don't remember." He rubbed his forehead. "I left with the most terrible headache, probably too much brandy. I won't be going back."

A terrible headache...the queen recalled having a terrible headache the first time she'd met the prince. *An odd coincidence...if one believes in coincidences.* "So you won't be going back?"

"No, majesty."

He spoke the words with iron conviction. Liandra found relief in his loyalty. "Your words please us. Ever our honest lord."

He bowed low, relief on his face. "Did I do wrong to attend?"

"You would do wrong to persist. Such lavishness raises doubts. If any of our other lords favor the prince in any way, we would hear of it."

His face sobered. "Yes, majesty."

"And if you see our Lord Sheriff, send him our way. We wish to speak with him."

His ample brow furrowed. "It's not like the Sheriff to be absent from a council meeting."

Another worry to add to her list. The queen offered her ringed hand. "We thank you for your loyalty and your honesty."

Kissing her ring, he took his leave.

The door closed and she was alone with her deputy shadowmaster.

Master Raddock skulked in the shadows. "Do you believe him?"

"We do." Liandra's voice brimmed with conviction. "He is an honest man. That is why we raised him to a lord. We need more honesty in our court."

"But you mistrust the prince."

It was a statement not a question, yet she chose to answer. "Wealth can be such a slippery seduction. We almost feel as if the Red Horns arise from the grave to threaten our throne again...yet he is the son of an emperor, the emissary of our greatest trading partner. Where the prince is concerned, we must tread with caution."

"What would you have me do?"

"Tell your shadowmen to keep vigil." Her gaze snapped towards him. "You said you received an invitation to one of his banquets?"

"Yes, majesty."

"We want you to accept."

He took a half step backwards. "But I serve best from the shadows."

"Attend the dinner and speak to the prince yourself. Give him a chance to woo you. We need to know his motives, we need to know his true intent, and we need to hear it from the prince himself."

His face turned reluctant. "As you command." Bowing, he turned towards the door.

"And, Master Raddock."

"Yes, majesty?"

"Find our Lord Sherriff, it is not like him to go missing."

"Yes, majesty."

The door clicked closed and she was alone with her thoughts. Liandra stared into the fire, considering all she'd learned, plots within plots. She shivered despite the warmth, feeling threats close around her like hounds chasing a fox.

Footsteps came from the inner rooms. Lady Sarah appeared bearing a tray with tea and fresh-baked scones. "I thought your majesty might like something to eat."

A tempting smell teased a smile from the queen. "Fresh-baked scones with cranberries?"

"Your favorites. Master Carl baked them himself." She set the tray on the table and began to pour a cup.

"At least our baker is loyal."

Lady Sarah set a cup of tea and a scone near the queen. "You have doubts?"

"We always have doubts. Doubts and suspicions, yet we do not have proof enough to act." Liandra tasted the scone, savoring a sweet flaky morsel spiked with tart cranberries, a bite of heaven. "Master Carl has outdone himself."

Lady Sarah took a seat across from the queen. The two women sat in companionable silence, finishing the scones and tea. When the last morsel was consumed, Liandra set her cup aside. "We thank you for the delicious distraction...but we suspect you came bearing more than just scones."

Lady Sarah blanched pale, staring at the hearth. "You know me too well."

The queen sighed. "And you know we must hear whatever it is you have to tell us, for a queen can never be uninformed. Ignorance is a fatal weakness for a crown, especially when that crown is worn by a queen."

"Yet it is hard to say."

"Then simply say it."

Lady Sarah nodded, her face resolved. "I heard a rumor in the marketplace. A terrible, vicious rumor."

Liandra stilled, as if an axe were about to fall.

"They say...," Lady Sarah looked away, taking a deep breath, "they say the queen bore a child to the Dark Lord, a stillborn bastard with horns and cloven hooves. They say the monstrosity proves the queen is cursed and her city damned."

A spear pierced her heart. "Our people...say this of us?"

Lady Sarah gave the smallest of nods, her face stricken with sorrow, her voice a whisper. "I heard it more than once."

"Yet we saved them from the Flame!" Liandra struggled to understand. "Despite the war, prosperity flows like a river to our people."

"Lies, they are just lies."

"Yet our people repeat them." The queen stood. "When lies are repeated oft enough they gain a life of their own." Unable to contain her anxiety, she began to pace in front of the fire. "Why would our people believe such follies, such blatant lies?' The answer hit like a falling anvil. "Unless they have lost the capacity to discern the truth." The thought chilled her like no other.

Liandra paced in front of the fire, her mind working through the maze of small details like a mouse seeking a way out. The details clicked into place with terrifying conviction. "Our crown is under assault. We need help, but not of the ordinary kind." She needed allies who knew how to fight shadows. She needed Robert, but he was still far away in Lingard. Her mind seized on a name. "Master Numar!" The queen strode to her desk. Reaching for a fresh parchment, she dipped quill in ink and began to write. Her quill sped across the parchment. Finished, she melted a glob of emerald wax and affixed the royal seal. "Take this to Master Numar. A monk of the Kiralynn Order, he poses as a master apothecary. You will find his shop on apothecary row in the south side of the city. A white unicorn's head surmounts the door." Liandra pressed the letter into Lady Sarah's hands. "Go to him, but have a care lest you are followed. Bring him to us under some pretext, any minor ailment will do, but bring him quickly and make sure you are not followed."

Lady Sarah's face blanched pale. "Majesty, I fear for you."

"We fear for our life, as well as our kingdom. Bring us the monk, and perhaps he can help divine the enemy behind this vile assault."

"I will bring him, majesty." She dipped a deep curtsy and was gone.

The queen paced in front of the hearth till the fire burnt to embers. Her crown was under assault, she felt it in the marrow of her bones...yet there was so little proof, nothing but outrageous lies and lavish banquets, yet she felt the noose tightening around her, a stranglehold of Darkness. Her gaze came to rest on the scrolls piled on her desk. So many weighty matters vied for her attention. Her army waged a desperate war in the north, while her kingdom was barely recovered from the assault of the Flame, and now she found herself fencing with shadows...yet somehow she felt the shadows posed the greatest threat. A conviction grew in her mind. Somehow she must counter these lies and innuendos. Her mirrored reflection caught her gaze. A cornered queen stared back at her. Liandra stilled, disturbed by her reflection. Image remained one of her greatest strengths. The queen resolved to arm herself with image...and to seek allies against the shadows, to sow truth against the lies. Perhaps the monk could help. Somehow she had to save her people and her crown...before the shadows held sway over her kingdom.

46

Steffan

He'd had no word from her. Nothing but silence since that first night when her carriage returned empty from the Mordant's mansion. He'd pestered Braxus and the others, but they had nothing for him. Not one whispered message from her seneschal, not one hastily scrawled note smuggled by her handmaidens, not one word to prove she still cared...or that she still lived.

Not knowing was driving him mad.

But Steffan was not without resources. In Rhune he'd found unexpected allies, a defrocked bishop and a ragtag cadre of soldiers, all of them veterans of the Flame War. Living in the woods, shunned as outcasts, they'd sought service with the Lord Raven. At first it amused him to keep them at his beck and call, a secret withheld from the Priestess, a dagger hidden in the dark, but then he found their purpose. Unwilling to return to Pellanor without protection, he'd sent them ahead as a secret vanguard. It was time to collect his hidden dagger. Pulling the hood of his cloak up to hide his face, Steffan made his way through the back alleys, threading a path to the shadier side of the queen's city. He found Bishop Tilden waiting for him in the Brass Rose, a shoddy inn where the flash of coin paid for ale, whores, and silence.

"Wondered when you'd get here." The fat bishop had traded his red robes for mismatched leathers. Salt and pepper whiskers studded his jowly face, the stink of sour ale hovering about him like a pesky fly.

Steffan took a seat at the round table, far enough away to avoid the worst of the bishop's stench. Ordering an ale, he waited till the serving wench moved beyond hearing. Setting a purse thick with golds on the table, he pushed it towards the prelate. "Where are the others?"

The bishop snatched the purse, weighing it in his hand, before vanishing it to his belt. A grin split his fat lips. "Good as gold. I'll give you that, Lord Raven, yer always good for gold."

Steffan hissed. "Not that title!" He shot a vile glare at the prelate. "I'm the Lord Darkmoor."

"Yes, m'lord." The feigned look of contrition slid to a sly smile. "Is it that easy to become a lord? Just call yerself one? Snatch a title from thin air and we're all lords?"

Steffan began to wonder if the bishop was addled by ale...or begging for a knife in the back. His hand slid to his dagger, his voice a keen whisper. "If you take my gold then you serve or die."

The bishop struggled to sober. "Sorry, m'lord, I'm your man."

Steffan drilled him with his stare, but this time the bishop seemed truly contrite. "Where are the others?"

The bishop gestured to the far corner. "Donklin, Marks, and Tandon are dicing. Scrobe and Scanlon are spending their pay with a couple of whores upstairs."

"And the rest?"

"Scattered about at different inns. You said we should split up."

"Good." Steffan cast a lazy glance toward the three in the far corner. "Tell me about those three."

The bishop shrugged. "Tandon prefers the halberd but all three are decent swords."

"Who's the best?"

" Donklin, he served as a captain in the fourth brigade."

The fourth brigade, veterans of Lingard...and the sack of Pellanor, Steffan suppressed a snarl at the bitter loss. "Then Donklin will serve."

Bishop Tilden raised a bushy eyebrow laden with questions. "Serve fer what?"

Steffan cut off his inquiry. "I need a sharp sword and a good head for a scouting job."

"A scouting job?" Suspicion salted the bishop's words.

"A rival has something I want."

"We're all wantin' somethin'. Me, I miss my miter and my mace. The war was good to me...till it ended." The bishop shrugged, taking a swig of ale.

Steffan made his decision. "I'll meet you for dinner tonight, an hour past sunset, at the Whiskey Lady, best steak and kidney pie in the queen's city. And I'll stand you a bottle of their best whiskey. The barkeep can tell you where it is." Steffan's voice dropped to a conspirator's whisper. "But come alone, I won't pay for the others."

A grin split the bishop's face. "Now yer talkin'." He hefted a tankard of ale. "Tonight at the Whiskey Lady."

"Tonight." Steffan took his leave of the bishop and then strolled to the back corner, pretending to be lured by the sound of dice. Like the bishop, the three men seated at the table had forsaken the colors of the Flame for mismatched leathers, but unlike the fat prelate they had the sharp, prickly look of soldiers turned hardened mercenaries. Steffan slid a small stack of silver coins onto the table. "I'm looking for a dice game. Mind if I join you?"

A man with a craggy face answered with a shrug. "Silver says you're welcome."

Steffan took a seat at the table, holding the man's gaze. "Donklin of the fourth?"

The craggy man nodded, one hand slipping to a dagger at his belt. "Aye."

"Then you remember the raven." It was a statement, not a question.

Donklin gave a slow nod. "Aye." His gaze narrowed. "There was glory beneath that banner...and loss."

"I seek glory of another sort, but I need swords that serve."

"The army is gone, but your gold got us out of the muddy backwaters. We're here to serve, Lord Darkmoor."

A sharp sword with a sharp mind, just what he needed. "Good, I need..."

The serving wench brought his tankard of ale, silencing the talk. Dark curly hair and a fading figure, she cast her gaze across Steffan's handsome face and the dashing cut of his cloak. Smiling, she leaned towards him, offering a flirtatious wink. "We serve more than ale here, sweetie."

He smothered a scowl, like tasting gutter water after the ambrosia of the Priestess. "Not today."

She brushed against him as she sauntered past, like a cat leaving its mark. "Ask for Marla when you change your mind."

Steffan waited till the wench was beyond hearing. His gaze fixed on Donklin. "I need you to come with me. I've a task for your men but it needs an officer's eye."

One of the others said, "Three swords are better than one."

"Just one for now, I don't want to draw too much attention."

"As you wish." Donklin stood, a tall rangy man, his belt studded with three daggers and a sword. "My blade is yours."

Steffan liked the look of him, a captain of the Flame turned mercenary, the weapons at his belt announcing a hardened man who clearly knew his trade. Pulling up his hood to shadow his face, Steffan rose to leave.

The soldier with the crooked teeth said, "Your silvers, lord."

Steffan could not resist. "Let's bet on it." He reached for the dice, shaking them with the skill of a veteran gambler. "Double or nothing if I roll snake eyes?"

The three men grinned, certain the odds were in their favor.

Steffan rolled the dice. Invoking the Dark power came as easy as breathing. The others stared, intent on certain victory. The dice rattled across the table...landing on double ones.

"*Snake eyes!*" the soldier hissed the words like a startled curse.

Donklin gave him a thoughtful look. "You're lucky, lord."

"Luckier than you know." Coin flowed like water to him, given his skill with dice. "Keep my winnings, an advance on your next payment."

The men grinned at his generosity, raising their tankards in salute.

"Come." Steffan led the captain out of the tavern's musty gloom and into the sunlight. The streets bustled with the noontime crowd. Commerce never slept in the queen's city, legal or otherwise. Donklin stayed within Steffan's shadow, a hand on his dagger, his alert gaze sweeping the crowd.

"Remember this route. You'll need to return this way with your men."

"Aye."

"Tell me of the bishop." Steffan's gaze slid towards Donklin.

His lip curled in disgust. "He's fallen into his cups."

Steffan gave a slow nod. "Ale has addled his wits...and I can't afford mistakes." He saw no protest on the captain's face. "Someone needs to slit his throat and ensure his silence."

Donklin grunted assent.

"He's to meet me at the Brass Rose for dinner tonight, an hour past sunset. It'd be best if you did it before then. Perhaps on his way to the tavern."

Donklin's gaze sharpened. "You set him up."

"A careless drunk is of no use to anyone. You'll find a fat purse of my golds in his belt pouch. Split it among the men, but first take a hefty bonus for your knife work."

"As you say."

Donklin seemed a reasonable sort, not too greedy, not too bloodthirsty, willing to take orders, willing to get his hands dirty, a perfect captain for his band of soldiers turned sellswords. Satisfied with his choice, Steffan led him from the city's shady side to the wealthy quarter. The cobbled streets widened and the houses grew to the size of mansions. Marble facades and glass-paned windows added a glistening sparkle to the streets. The patina of wealth was everywhere, from the grand carriages polished to a shine, to the liveried footmen clad in bright colors, to the elaborate topiaries decorating the walled gardens. Even the smell improved, the reek of piss pots banished to the back alleyways, the front streets perfumed with the sweet scents of flowering honeysuckle and jasmine twining the wrought iron gates.

Beside him, Donklin murmured, "You've picked a wealthy mark."

"Wealthy...and dangerous."

"Never met a wealthy mark that wasn't." Donklin grinned, "Wealth that isn't dangerous don't stay wealthy."

So the man knows his trade. "Yes, but this one's particularly dangerous, like a viper compared to a common woodland snake."

"So I should take care not to get bit."

"If he bites, you die."

Donklin gave him a thoughtful nod, but he showed no signs of balking. "Good to know."

With uncanny ease, Steffan led the captain through the wealthy district. He belonged among the rich. Skilled at dice and lovemaking, he'd spent many a night winning golds from the local lords, or tupping wealthy widows in plush bedchambers, but now he played for higher stakes. An eager grin rode his face. Higher stakes and higher risks, both appealed to the gambler in him.

From Braxus, Steffan knew the Mordant had purchased the late Lord Nealy's mansion. Luck favored the Raven, for Steffan knew the mansion well, having attended many late-night parties with the snobbish lords. Remembering the way, his footsteps threaded a steady path through the wealth-lined streets. "This is the one." They strolled past a magnificent manse with the diamond-paned windows. Walking no faster or slower than anyone else, they sauntered by and then doubled back, lurking behind a waiting carriage while they took a closer look. Crouched by Donklin, Steffan whispered, "There's an alleyway in the back. The rear door opens onto the kitchen. The bedrooms are on the second floor with a wine cellar in the basement."

Guards posing as footmen stood on either side of the main doorway. Clad in purple livery, the great golden wyrm boldly embroidered across their chests, they both wore short swords belted to their sides.

Donklin hissed. "I know that sigil, so your enemy is the prince of Ur!"

Steffan ground his teeth. "He stole something of mine."

"What? Wealth, power, and too many swords?"

"No, a woman."

Donklin's eyes widened. "This is about a woman?"

"Not just any woman, the queen of Rhune."

"The seductress!" the words hissed from the captain.

Steffan gave him a warning glare. "A woman beyond compare. And I will have her back."

"How?"

"For now, keep watch and wait. Have your men encircle the mansion. Keep track of those who enter and leave. Learn how many swords guard the manse. Learn the prince's habits. But most of all, keep watch for the woman. Once we know she's safe, once we know the prince's ways, then we'll craft a plan."

"Fair enough, but we may need more swords."

"Swords can always be bought."

"If you have the golds."

"I'll worry about the golds, you watch for the woman. And take care, lest you attract notice."

The carriage began to move. Donklin drifted away to the shadows while Steffan sauntered down the street. It felt good to give orders again, to have sharp swords at his beck and call. Buoyed with confidence, he lengthened his stride. He'd get the Priestess back and then he'd make his mark, putting his own twist on the Great Dark Dance.

47

Liandra

The queen paced her solar, anxious to speak to the monk. Twilight came and went and still Lady Sarah did not return. Liandra began to fear she'd sent her friend into danger. Ladies-in-waiting were not shadowmen, yet this was Pellanor, what ill could befall her? The queen's imagination ran wild. Finally a gentle knock on the door assuaged her anxiety.

"Come."

Lady Sarah slipped inside...but she came alone, her hooded cloak beaded in raindrops, as if stained by tears. Curtsying, she stepped towards the fire, a hint of rebuke in her voice. "Majesty, you've let the fire burn down."

One look at her friend's pale face and the queen knew something had gone awry. Liandra watched as Lady Sarah added logs to the hearth, stoking the fire to a bright blaze. The queen longed for answers, yet she knew the simple domestic chore served to calm her friend's unease. With the fire blazing, the lady set a tea kettle to brew.

Unable to wait any longer, the queen said, "Tell us."

Lady Sarah sank to the nearest chair, her face pale. "Majesty, I could not deliver your letter." She removed the sealed parchment, setting it on a side table. "I went to apothecary row and found the white unicorn over the doorway, just as you said...but the shop was blackened and burned to a hollow shell."

"Burned?" Fire was a risk in any city, yet Liandra had heard nothing of a major blaze.

"Burned from inside, just that one shop."

Just the one, it stank of treachery. "How?"

"I talked to one of the other shop owners, purchasing a pouch of chamomile tea as an excuse to gather gossip."

The queen waited. "And?"

"Most of the shopkeepers gave me fearful looks, but one talked." Lady Sarah's voice sank to a whisper. "Majesty, they said it was *sorcery*." She cast a fearful look towards the queen. "Fireballs in the dead of night, glowing bright as the sun, but the blaze did not spread, as if it sought a single target and then expired. The next morning, the shop was naught but a blackened shell, everything destroyed." Her voice cracked with strain. "And at the blackened heart, they found four bodies, burnt to char. Whispers say it was dark magic."

Dark magic...in our city, a shiver raced down the queen's spine. "When did this happen?"

"Two nights ago."

As if someone knew she would reach out to the monks. "But who caused the fire?"

"No one knows." Lady Sarah stared at the queen. "They fled...or took their secrets to a fiery grave."

So the monks are dead...or gone into hiding. The queen began to pace, she'd counted on the monks' knowledge...on their aid. *Dark magic in her city,* but it would not be the first time. Memories of Lord Turner's gruesome death plagued her. *An animated corpse capering in the boiling cauldron,* who could forget those glowing red eyes, a nightmare sprung straight from hell. A shudder passed through her. Perhaps another one of those *things* lurked in her city. Magic was the domain of the monks. If only she knew how to contact them. She recalled their web of spies, the way their scrolled messages appeared as if by magic. Perhaps they would approach her; she clung to the hope, for surely Darkness stalked her throne.

The queen rang a hand bell, summoning a page. When the tow-headed lad appeared, she snapped an order. "Summon Master Raddock to our solar."

Liandra continued to pace, a storm of threats in her mind. *If only Robert were here,* she'd sent him a dispatch, summoning him home, but he'd yet to return...or reply, another ominous sign. Liandra felt as if a noose tightened around her.

Finally, her deputy shadowmaster appeared, a rumpled crow in dark robes. "You summoned me, majesty?"

Lady Sarah rose to leave, but the queen gestured for her to remain seated. "Tell our deputy shadowmaster all you learned at the apothecary shop."

Lady Sarah complied. The queen listened to the recounting, sifting through the details, but her conclusion did not change. She rounded on her shadowmaster. "Why have we not heard of this?"

He made a placating gesture. "Your shadowmen are stretched thin. We cannot chase every ill rumor in the city."

Steel laced the queen's voice. "This is one rumor you *will* chase. We need to know every detail of this fire. We need to know who started it. But most of all, we need to know if anyone survived and where they went. And we need to know it now!"

Annoyance flashed across his sallow face, but it was quickly swallowed. "Yes, majesty."

Her anger boiled over. "Now go. Return to us with answers."

He gave her a perfunctory bow and then retreated from her solar. The door clicked shut and the queen continued to pace.

Lady Sarah dared to interrupt, a quaver in her voice. "Majesty, do you truly think it was dark magic?"

Liandra stopped pacing, her ringed hands balling to fists. "We are not sure. We only know that we reached out to the monks for their aid, and now they are dead or fled." Her voice dropped to a harsh whisper. "As a queen, we dare not believe in coincidences. Someone plays a deep game against us. We feel darkness crowding close. Our enemy is several moves ahead, as if he anticipates our every move."

"But who is this enemy, majesty?"

"That is the secret we must discover...ere he turns the game against us."

48

The Mordant

The red-haired lord hung by his wrists, suspended from chains. His once-handsome face was swollen with bruises, his naked torso crisscrossed with cuts. His blood dripped onto the pentacle, a fitting tribute for the Dark God.

The Mordant circled the prisoner, studying the body like a work of art. In the hands of a skilled torturer, pain was a scalpel, exposing the raw soul. His voice was velvety soft, a keen contrast to the sharp blade. "Tell me of the queen. Tell me what she fears. Tell me what she suspects. Save yourself the pain."

He stroked the prisoner with his voice, but the red-haired lord only glowered, remaining stubbornly silent.

"My men caught your boy, the one you sent to spy on me. But the urchin proved of little use. He knew your name but nothing more."

Silence was the only answer.

The Mordant whirled. Wielding the knife like an artist's paintbrush, he slashed the rune-carved blade across the Sheriff's chest in an exquisite arc. Blood spurted in a line, crimson across pale skin, adding to the mosaic of cuts.

The Sheriff jerked like a hooked fish, his teeth clamped shut against a scream.

"Scream all you want, for no one will hear you."

The Sheriff slung from the chain, slick with sweat and blood.

The Mordant smiled. "Pain but nothing permanent. Not yet. I hope you appreciate my restraint."

"You're a monster." The Sheriff spat the words. "And the queen will have your head."

"Will she now?" The Mordant's voice was a soft purr. "Who does she think I am?"

The Sherriff did not answer.

The Mordant considered his prey. So many of the queen's lords had succumbed to bribes, while others fell to sexual favors, but a few remained stubborn like rocks standing against breaking waves. Even their souls proved impervious to his probes, hence the need for more mundane methods like torture. Never before had so many resisted his probing gaze. Their iron defense puzzled him...troubled him...angered him. He hadn't expected the queen to have gathered so many honest lords. "Tell me this, why do you serve her?"

The Sheriff glared, his naked chest glistening with sweat and blood.

"Answer this one question and we are done for the day."

"You would not understand."

"Try me."

"Because *she* serves!*"

The answer made no sense.

The Sheriff barked a rude laugh tinged with madness.

"Explain." The Mordant's voice strained with danger.

"*She* serves her people. The queen brings prosperity and peace, a type of bounty a fiend like you knows not."

His hand snaked out, scoring two more cuts. A flap of skin hung down, exposing raw muscle.

The prisoner grimaced...but he did not scream.

"You'll scream before I'm done with you. You'll scream and beg for death." The Mordant longed to slash the Sheriff's insolent throat, but he fought the impulse. "I will teach you what it means to serve." He flicked a glance to Gron. "Let him hang for another two turns of the hourglass to ripen and then put him in a cell. I need him whole and unbroken or he cannot serve."

The torturer bowed low. "Yes, lord."

"And patch him up. I want him healed to hurt again."

"Yes, dread lord."

Tossing the bloody knife upon a tray, the Mordant strode across the chamber and climbed the stairs. An assassin rushed to open the door. The Mordant passed from the Dark sanctuary into the dungeon, the holding cells for the damned. Haggard faces pressed against the bars, their desperate stares suddenly averted as they caught sight of him. The Mordant breathed deep their scent of fear, a potent aphrodisiac mollifying his anger, but he did not tarry.

Stepping through the wine barrel, he returned to the manse proper. An assassin closed and locked the hidden door, stoppering the scents and sounds of the dungeon. The Mordant climbed the stairs, leaving the wine cellar behind.

Sunlight lanced through the diamond-paned windows, causing him to squint at the sudden brightness. The day was still young, proving the time spent in the dungeons moved at its own intense pace. He stopped to wash the blood from his hands and then made his way to Bishop Borgan's room.

The fat prelate sat behind a desk cluttered with parchments, ink bottles, feathered quills, and sticks of brightly colored sealing wax, the tools of an expert forger.

"Is it done?" The Mordant sat in a chair opposite the bishop.

"Just finished." The bishop handed him a parchment. "Take care lest you smear the ink."

The Mordant studied the parchment. The penmanship was slanted and quickly scratched, conveying a hurried, harried look. An ink stain in the corner added a nice touch, compounding the impression of frantic urgency. The bishop truly was an artist when it came to forgery. The Mordant read the dispatch, carefully considering each word. A smile slithered across his face. "Yes, this will do. I grow bored with the waiting. Send it."

The bishop reclaimed the parchment, carefully affixing a wax seal. "I'll have one of the young ones deliver it."

"Good." His smile deepened, flushed with anticipation. Still aroused from his work in the dungeon, the Mordant added, "Tell Iris I'll have her in my bed tonight."

The prelate flashed a salacious smile. "Yes, lord."

The Mordant strode from the chamber, his purple cloak swirling behind him, the great Wyrm embroidered across his surcoat. Everything was falling into place, all his carefully laid plans. Soon Lanverness would be his for the taking, the keystone to claiming his next lifetime. And then he'd change his colors one last time, revealing the Darkness within.

49

The Priestess

The Mordant summoned her to his bed. An assassin knocked on her door, bringing word of his lord's desire. The Priestess was mildly amused by the choice of messenger, unable to decide if it was merely ironic or a portent of things to come. Either way the date was set. *Tonight!*

Twilight deepened to darkness and still she prepared. The Priestess managed every detail with utmost care, her skill and art roused to a formidable challenge. Seduction was the ultimate poison, leaching into the soul and subverting the will. Tonight she'd ply her powers on a thousand-year-old evil. Such an old soul, such a dangerous foe, but despite his years, the Mordant was still mortal. He was still a man, and men she knew very well. A cunning smile graced her face, anticipating the challenge. A man's needs often trumped his reason. Needs had a way of becoming weaknesses. All men were slaves to sex. The Priestess planned to master the Mordant in his own bedchamber, exacting her own brand of vengeance while chaining him with his most primal need. *The Mordant chained,* the thought alone brought unspeakable pleasure.

The Priestess studied the mirror. She'd given much thought to his seduction. For such an experienced partner, she decided layered mysteries were the key to his enthrallment. She began with layers of scent to tease his senses, tracing fragrant trails across her skin, a rare aphrodisiac leading him on a merry pathway to pleasure. Layers of silk to tease his eye, she chose gowns from her cedar chest, each more diaphanous than the next. Soft and mysterious, the silken layers would entangle his gaze while she slowly revealed her secret delights. And last but certainly not least, she planned on using layers of technique. Methods of delight melded with magic, she'd wield both pain and pleasure, enthralling his mind while ensnaring his senses. Tonight would be like no other. She'd stoke his passion to an unbearable bonfire.

Her handmaidens hovered about, completing the details. Her raven-dark hair was braided into complex rings, a confection designed to slowly unravel. Accenting her eyes with kohl, they dusted her eyelids with crushed malachite and added a tint of ruby to her lush lips, but nothing more. By design, she kept her guise simple yet complex, the perfect conundrum to ensorcell a thousand-year-old soul.

The Priestess gazed in the mirror and a dark temptress stared back, a sultry smile on her face.

Pleased with the effect, she dismissed her handmaidens. Kneeling by her rosewood chest, she unlocked her store of deathly delights. Her gaze caressed the vials of lethal possibilities, considering her choices. She'd answer the summons of the Mordant, bringing seduction to his bed, but not without her best defense. Her serpentine bracelets were too obvious, a ruse she'd never get past his assassin guards. For tonight's prey, she needed something far more subtle, yet carefully controlled, a poison designed as a hidden dagger. Carefully trimming the smallest fingernail on her left hand, she filed it to a razor-sharp edge. Beneath the nail, she painted her most potent poison, a deadly concoction of nightshade, crushed angel's trumpet, and tincture of yew. A single scratch, a single drop of drawn blood and he'd die a most hideous death.

Of course the poison was only a prudent precaution, far better to enslave the oldest harlequin to her will with sex.

Her preparations complete, she settled a silver chain around her neck. The sundered Eye dangled between her breasts, her only jewelry. Bound in a cage of silver wire, she wore the broken moonstone as reminder of her bitter loss, a score that needed to be settled. The oldest harlequin had shattered the great gemstone, stealing the scrying power of the Eye. A gift from the Dark Lord, the Eye was a focus of great magic, but the moonstone was not her only power. Taking a deep breath, she summoned the Darkness within. Power thrummed through her, waking a ravenous need. The Succubus of Darkness, she was the Lover to the Dark Lord. Desire throbbed in her very veins. Seduction entwined with death, she was the very embodiment of pure allure.

Her powers awakened, her deadliest poison hidden beneath her smallest fingernail, the Priestess was armed to engage the Mordant.

Her handmaidens rushed to open the door. She glided down the long hallway, her slippered feet soft on thick carpets. Assassins stared from the shadows but they did not hinder her passage. She'd come to know the Mordant's mansion but she'd yet to breach his bedchamber.

Candles flickered at the hallway's end.

She reached the final door and paused, her stare fixed on the doorknob.

An assassin abandoned his post, rushing to open the door.

The Priestess smiled, more proof her appearance had the desired effect.

She stepped into the Mordant's bedchamber, a soft whisper of silk.

Brightness was her first impression. An abundance of candles lit the chamber with too much light. A large four-posted bed piled with pillows dominated the chamber's heart, yet the Mordant sat behind a desk piled with scrolls, as if her presence was an interruption instead of a carnal delight. The Priestess ignored the not-so-subtle slight, focusing on her victim. Fair-haired and young of face, he hid his age well, until he lifted his gaze. Ancient and fathomless, his eyes radiated implacable power.

Their stares crossed, the air between them crackling with power.

Undaunted, the Priestess glided across the room, dropping to a deep curtsy. "You summoned me, my lord."

"Yes, you may begin." Setting a scroll aside, he leaned back in the chair. Clad in a crushed velvet robe of deep crimson, the open vee at his neck revealed pale chest hairs, yet he remained seated at the desk, sipping a goblet of red wine.

He's going to make me work for it, she smothered a smile, undeterred by his opening sally. "Shall I strive to please you?" her voice was low and sultry and full of suggestion, "Or shall I make *you* please *me*?"

He flashed a serpent's smile. "If you think to compel me, it will never happen."

So the terms are set, like a gauntlet thrown down, yet how little he knows me. Rising to the challenge, she gracefully glided around the room, snuffing candles. Setting the mood, she made it a suggestive game, her fingers slowly sliding up the long tapered lengths...to gently snuff the flames. Smoke rose from her fingertips like a trail of sizzling passion, her polished nails glittering gold in the waning light. One by one she dimmed the candles, leaving just enough light to see by...and just enough shadows to subtly obscure. Passion flourished on the knife-edge between the hidden and the revealed.

She returned to her starting point, standing in front of his desk.

He remained statue-still, yet she felt his dark gaze drinking her in.

Having seduced his stare, the Priestess began to dance. Slow and sensuous, she twirled before him, weaving an enticing trail of scent and silk and seduction. Every gesture held a promise and a tease, a dance of a thousand delights. Her hands molded her curves like the hands of a lover, and then swooped lower, offering a promise of fulfillment. Silk whispered across skin as she slowly shed diaphanous layers. And all the while, her gaze smoldered, never leaving his.

She licked her lips, full of suggestion. One by one, she twirled away each silken layer, turning them into a perfumed lash. Like colored ribbons she wove them through the air, accentuating her every movement. A silken whip snaked out, entwining the Mordant's neck. She gave a suggestive tug, yet he resisted. A flick of her wrist and the silk released him...but it left her scent on his skin, marking him with a tease of another sort. She saw his nostrils flair wide. Twice more she teased him and twice more he refused.

The Mordant remained statue-still but his eyes had darkened, betraying his arousal.

The Priestess reached the last silken layer. Instead of removing it, she made it a cloak, a shawl, a diaphanous curtain. Reveal and hide, she gave him tantalizing glimpses of her naked perfection. Dancing behind the silk veil, she teased and taunted, but never revealed the whole. And as she danced, she slowly unbound her hair. Raven-black tresses cascaded to her thighs. Silken and scented, she used her hair as a second cloak. She danced before him, every glance provocative, every movement a beckoning promise.

Coming to a sudden stop, she gave him a smoldering stare more intimate than touch. Her voice was low and throaty. "Come to me, my lord."

Still he resisted.

For the second time, she licked her lips. "Come and taste my pleasures." She twirled the last silken layer into a lash and snapped it towards his neck.

The Mordant caught the lash. He stood, shrugging his robe from his shoulders. Naked, he revealed his rampant manhood.

She gave the silken leash a tug.

He tugged back.

Dropping the silk lash, she fled for the bed.

The Mordant gave chase.

An animal thrill rushed through her, prey enticing a powerful predator. She reached the bed and knelt with her submissive side bared towards him, pale curves alluring against the dark furs. And then he was on her...in her. Pressing her face-down into the pillows, he took her swift and hard. She let him have his way. When his pace slackened, she rolled. Keeping him trapped inside her, she reversed their positions. Straddling him, she pinned him to the bed and took control.

With excruciating slowness, she stroked his length. A gasp escaped him, proof of her affect.

She plied her powers keeping him rock hard. Painstakingly slow, she rode him up and down, taking his measure. Part pleasure, part torment, she teased and tortured him, but she did not let him come. Deciding to sate her own needs, she indulged her every whim. Tasting, teasing, touching, she used him in every way imaginable. Pain and pleasure came in shuddering waves as she plied him with every trick, every technique. Twice he arched his back, straining with a guttural growl, yet she would not release him, her magic holding him in thrall. Gifting him with uncommon stamina, she rode him through the night. He growled in frustration, but she would not let him reach his peak, exacting a petty vengeance. Lashing him with her hair, she taunted him, holding him on the very knife-edge of climax. His whole body bucked and shuddered beneath her, slick with sweat. Agony and ecstasy became a blur. His eyes became glazed, drunk on sex. The Priestess deepened her hold. Weaving a spell of enthrallment, she set a trap of obsession lodged deep in his soul. Satisfied with the spell, she took her pleasure in a different way. Connected by sex, she unleashed the succubus. Ravenous, she began to feed on his life force...and found herself intoxicated. *A thousand years of life,* she delved into a deep bottomless well of velvety Darkness, brimming with power. *Hers for the taking.* His life force was like nothing she'd ever encountered. So many flavors of Darkness blended together in an ancient brew, she nearly swooned with the first taste. The succubus within reveled at the feast, howling for more. Drinking long and hard, she tapped his strength till she pulsed with magic, a vessel brimming with power, stoked by a heady elixir. Reeling with power, she set the last binding spell and released her victim to his pleasure.

Answering the unspoken compulsion, the Mordant strained upwards like a lunging bull. Thrusting deep, he roared his triumph.

Sodden with sweat, he collapsed back onto the pillows.

The Priestess lay next to her vanquished foe. Power thrummed through her veins, a succubus finally sated. Suppressing a satisfied smile, she nestled her head on his shoulder, her raven hair spread across his chest like a cloak. *Now you wear my colors!* His breathing slowed to a deep sleep, issuing a soft snore.

Restless with imbibed power, the Priestess flicked her gaze to the far window. The dawn's first light probed the curtains. She'd ridden him all night...a night he'd never forget, a night indelibly etched in his Dark soul. Triumph blazed through her. She'd conquered the oldest harlequin. She'd drunk his power and set her obsession deep in his soul. As the Priestess of the Oracle, the Succubus of Darkness, she had no peer. To seal her triumph, she wrote her true name in the sweat glistening on his chest.

A hand snaked out and grabbed her wrist.

Shocked, she tried to pull away, but his grip was iron-hard.

"You thought to master me!" Rage rode his voice. "I *am* Darkness!" He threw her to the floor like a discarded strumpet.

Leaping from the bed, he stood naked over her.

Before she could rise, pain seared through her, as if every nerve in her body burned with fire. Wracked with agony, she convulsed across the carpet. A scream burst out of her. *"No!"* A thousand knives stabbed her, yet no wounds appeared. She tried to crawl away, but the pain followed, doubling in intensity. Collapsing, she bit back a wail. Her limbs twitched and shuddered. Her body convulsed, becoming an instrument of torture. Gripped with agony, she writhed at his feet. *"Stop it! Stop it!"*

His voice dripped with venom. "You sought to seduce me. In this realm, *I* am the Lord of Darkness, *I* am your god...and you are but a trollop bound to my bed. You shall *worship* me!"

Desperate to end the pain, she began to crawl towards her tormentor. She stretched out her left hand, the poisoned fingernail reaching towards him. One scratch, one cut, and he'd die a hideous death, ending her torment.

Pain pounded through her, deepening to an unbearable agony. Feeling as if her insides were being torn asunder, she collapsed to the carpet, clutching her stomach. Consumed by pain, her feeble attempt to poison him fled. Screams ripped out of her throat as she writhed across the floor. She thought she would die, murdered by Dark magic. A keening wail burst out of her, the sound of a wild animal caught in a trap.

The agony intensified. She felt as if she were being flayed alive. Ripping with pain, her screams became muted, smothered to ragged whimpers. Tears streamed down her face, green with malachite. She began to yearn for death...and remembered her fingernail.

The pain stopped.

Suddenly gone, she gasped in surprise. She lay on the floor, shocked by the sweet absence of pain. Smothering a whimper, she froze statue-still lest the pain return. Sodden with sweat, she found herself panting, her body quivering with remembered agony.

"Now you know who is master here." The Mordant nudged her with his bare foot, but she was too weak to rise. His raised his voice to a shout. "Come!"

The door opened and a pair of black-clad assassins rushed to answer their master's call.

"Take this one to her room."

Strong hands grabbed her, roughly lifting her from the floor.

"And, Iris."

The assassins stopped, one of them lifting her head so that she could see the Mordant's face.

"The next time I summon you to my bed, you will come as a mere woman, as a meek woman. You will offer yourself to me and you will take what I choose to give without touching a drop of your power." He gave her a chilling stare. "I like spirit in my horses and my hunting dogs...not my women. Am I understood?"

Her voice was hoarse from screaming, yet she croaked a reply. "Yes, lord."

He made a dismissive gesture and the assassins carried her from the room.

Devastated by the reversal of fortunes, she lay supine in their arms. Insensate like a corpse, they carried her back to her room and dumped her inside the door. She heard the door close and the lock turn, a prisoner once more.

Slick with sweat, she shivered with the aftershocks of agony. She rubbed her eyes, her hands coming away smeared with malachite, kohl, and tears. *Tears!* Humiliated and defeated, the Priestess curled on her side, riven by the ordeal. She'd never known such extreme pain...or such shame. For half a heartbeat, she considered scoring her own flesh with her poisoned fingernail...but then *he* would win. Despair threatened to crush her...but then a spark of outrage glittered in her soul. *She was the Priestess of the Oracle...how dare he treat her this way.* The Mordant's words replayed in her mind. Her thoughts fastened on a deeper profanity...and she began to see his undoing. *How dare he style himself a god!* Outrage shuddered through her. There was but one Lord of Darkness, one Dark God...and he ruled this realm and the next. The Priestess knew their god better than most. Their lord was all-powerful, but he was also a jealous god. Hell hath but one power and that power never shared.

Her voice whispered a hoarse prayer. "My Dark Lord, my Dark God, he dares to rival you. Let me be the instrument of your *vengeance!*"

A second pulse beat between her breasts.

The Priestess stiffened in surprise...and then she remembered the sundered Eye. Wrapped in silver wire, it dangled on a chain nestled in her cleavage. She took it in her shaking hands and breathed upon it. A heartbeat answered. She gasped in amazement, feeling the gathering power within. Instead of three sundered fragments...the Eye was fused together, whole once more. A wild giddiness gripped her. She must have drawn far more power from the Mordant than she'd known, power enough to heal the Eye. A smile lit her face. Draining so much power would have its consequences. She'd tapped deep into the well of his life-force, drawing decades from him, cutting short his unnatural lifespan. He'd not miss it now, but he'd feel her vengeance later, ambushed by the early onslaught of old age. A victorious smile slid across her face. She imagined him bent and riddled by the early assault of old age. The Priestess gripped the great moonstone tight, triumph lighting her face. Fused together by passion and pain, the Eye of the Oracle was whole and unsundered...proof the Dark Lord had not abandoned her. The Great Dark Dance continued but not as the Mordant expected. The Priestess remained a formidable player. The game was far from done.

50

Steffan

Impatient for word of the Priestess, Steffan began to haunt the streets around the prince's mansion. His sellswords kept watch, confirming that she lived, but he needed to see for himself. Midday was always the best time to spy, the cobbled streets crowded with merchants, craftsmen and minstrels come to ply the wealthy for coin. Amidst the bustling commerce, the scents of flowering jasmine wafted down the street, as if the wealthy cast perfume upon the very air. Steffan sneezed, annoyed by the cloying scent. Threading his way through the crowd, he spied Donklin lurking in the shadows of a side street. Sauntering across, he joined the sellsword captain. "What word?"

Donklin leaned against a wrought iron railing twined with flowering honeysuckle. "I'll tell you this," he cast a baleful glance across the street, "yer prince is a cautious fellow."

"Why?"

"The manse is bursting with servants...'cept they ain't no servants, they're veteran swords."

A shiver of foreboding raced down Steffan's back. "How can you tell?"

Donklin shrugged. "The way they stand, the way their stares prowl the streets for enemies, the way their hands hover where their swords should be." He flicked a glance toward Steffan. "Takes one to know one." Plucking a white flower from the vine, the sellsword popped the honeysuckle in his mouth and chewed. Seeing Steffan's stare, he shrugged. "Sweet as honey only chewier." His face sobered. "Tell you somethin' else. The short ones in dark clothing, they're the most dangerous. You best keep away from them. They look small, but they glide like prowling cats and are damned difficult to track in a crowd, disappearing like smoke in the breeze."

The more Steffan heard, the more he worried. "So have you seen the prince?"

"Aye, the prince and the seductress. They come and go at all hours, 'specially at night." Donklin gave him a narrow stare. "Tell you this, whatever yer plannin' it best be outside the manse. Too damn many swords inside to tangle with."

Steffan had no intention of invading the Mordant's lair. "What about the alleyway in back? Anything suspicious there?"

"Plenty suspicious. Two of my swords have gone missing."

A chill shivered down Steffan's back. "Dead or caught?"

"No way to tell, 'cept if we find a body." Donklin spat a chewed flower and plucked another.

Anger riddled Steffan's voice. "I warned you not to get caught."

"And I warned them," Donklin bristled, "but those dark-clad bastards are scary as hell. Best avoid them. I don't post any watchers back there no more. A waste of swords."

Steffan bridled his anger. "Tell me about the woman. When do you see her?"

"Mostly at night, but it's hard to catch a glimpse. The prince's guards shuffle her in and out of waiting carriages, and there's always a couple of those black-clad bastards keeping close watch on her. My guess is the prince has got her on a tight leash."

A tight leash, the Priestess was not the type of woman to be kept on a leash. "Anything else?"

"Yeah, the prince likes to revel, and he spares no expense. Merchants deliver all manner of wine and food during the day. Lordlings and their ladies arrive at night, all decked with velvets and jewels, the carriages coming thick as starlings. Lights blaze from the manse till the wee hours." Donklin gave him a pointed look. "A dapper lordling like yerself might wrangle an invite to the feast. See yer lady fer yerself."

It was a thought, a dangerous thought, yet it appealed to the gambler in him. "I'll consider it." He tossed the captain a purse stuffed with golds. "Pay your men and keep them watching."

Donklin weighed the purse, a smile creasing his craggy face. "Happy to serve."

Steffan ambled out into the street. Falling in behind a troupe of mummers, his gaze raked the manse. So many diamond-paned windows gleaming golden in the reflected sunlight, he wondered if the Priestess peered from one and knew he kept watch. *"Soon,"* he whispered the word like a promise.

Movement at the mansion's arched doorway drew his gaze. Servants in purple tabards poured out, standing tense on either side of the door. Watching them, Steffan knew Donklin had the truth of it. *Dressed like servants yet they move like soldiers braced to meet a foe.*

A magnificent white stallion was led to the doorway, its mane braided with bells, its saddle trappings glimmering with jewels. Stamping and snorting, the stallion showed its spirit, fighting the groom. An excellent judge of horses, Steffan knew the stallion alone was worth a small fortune, the arrogance of wealth on brazen display.

The mummers stopped to gawk.

Steffan lingered behind them, using them as a screen.

The soldiers dressed as servants tensed. Four of the black-clad men flowed out of the doorway. Short in stature, yet they moved like liquid death, taking positions around the stallion.

Steffan held his breath, aware he should walk on, yet compelled to watch...and then he saw him, the fair-haired prince of Ur. He was tall, but his build was ordinary, like a young man who'd spent his short lifetime wielding a quill instead of a sword. His shoulder-length ash-blond hair was neatly trimmed in the latest style. Clad in sumptuous silks, his clothing was of the finest quality, dyed a deep imperial purple, the Great Wyrm of Ur boldly embroidered in gold across his chest. Jewels glittered on his fingers, yet he wore no sword. Swinging into the saddle with practiced ease, he took up the reins and quickly mastered the fretting stallion.

So this is the Mordant.

Fascinated, Steffan studied his rival. The prince mastered the stallion with ease, displaying a clear knack for horsemanship, and he showed excellent taste in tailors, but otherwise he looked quite ordinary. Neither handsome nor physically daunting, his most imposing feature was the richness of his trappings. *A common thrush bedecked in peacock's plumage,* Steffan was not impressed.

A sneer rode his face, *so this is the oldest harlequin, the one who dares to cage my Cereus.* His hands slipped to the throwing dagger sheathed at his belt.

The Mordant was so arrogant, he did not even wear armor. Bedecked in bright silks, he made an easy target. A single well-thrown dagger and Steffan could forever end this arrogant threat.

The Mordant urged his stallion to a showy prance, his servant-guards keeping pace around him.

Steffan sidled forward, drawing closer, angling for a better position. Easing the dagger from its sheath, he held the wicked-keen blade by the tip.

The Mordant drew near, close enough for an easy kill. He looked unaware, a noble out for an afternoon ride.

Steffan took a deep breath, poised to throw.

The Mordant's gaze suddenly snapped towards Steffan.

Their stares locked.

A thousand years of Darkness slammed into Steffan like a thunderbolt, pinioning his soul.

How dare you! The words boomed in his mind.

Steffan quivered, unable to breathe, unable to move. Something Dark reached inside of him, slithering through his soul. He felt raped, he felt violated. Sweat erupted across his skin, the dagger falling from his useless hand, clattering on the cobbles.

I see you. I know your Dark soul. You shall grovel before me!

The Mordant released him, riding past.

Steffan gasped and staggered backwards. Shocked to be alive, he turned and fled, desperate to escape that searing gaze.

51

Liandra

Riddled with doubts, Liandra paced a path in front of the hearth, seeking solutions to half a hundred questions. Dispatches littered her desk, yet the mound of scrolls only raised more problems. Robert remained in Lingard despite her instructions to return with all haste, her Lord Sheriff was missing and no one knew where or why, and now she learned that the monks posing as apothecaries were either dead or fled. *Dead in her city*, yet she seemed the last to know. Frustration warred with rage. She was the Spider Queen, she'd threaded her shadowmen like silk strands through the courts of Erdhe, yet her inquiries brought nothing but riddles. Feeling beleaguered, Liandra tread a path in the wool carpet.

Missing allies, dark magic and dangerous rumors, the problems tightened like a vexing noose. The queen's mind fastened on the last. Someone stirred false rumors against her. A queen needed the faith of her people to rule. "We need to be seen."

"Seen, majesty?" Lady Sarah sat before the hearth, her knitting forgotten.

"To quell the false rumors we need to be seen, to remind our people that we rule and rule well." Liandra considered the possibilities. Pomp and pageantry never failed to impress. "We shall ride out to inspect the city wall. And we shall wear our armor to remind our people that we saved them from the Flame."

Lady Sarah sighed, "Silk is so much easier than steel."

"True, but armor has its own allure, and we need every advantage."

"When?"

"On the morrow, assuming the sun shines. We seek the glitter of steel, not a rusty drizzle."

"I'll get the ladies polishing." Curtsying, Lady Sarah went to rouse the others to their tasks.

Liandra felt her burdens lessened by one, yet so many problems remained. *Dark magic in her city, the monks dead or fled,* she resumed pacing, hounded by a hundred problems, a myriad of questions plaguing her mind. Three times the fire burned to embers, and three times Lady Sarah added logs to the grate, stoking the fire to a roaring blaze. The queen took comfort in the heat and the light, yet she found no answers. Growing weary, she settled in a chair, staring into the flames, worrying a riddle with too many questions and not enough facts.

An urgent pounding startled her. Flustered, Liandra realized she must have dozed in the chair. Still clad in her silk gown, a wool blanket was tucked across her lap. Tugging the blanket aside, she glanced at the diamond paned window. Night ruled the sky, proving she'd slept longer than she thought.

A fist pounded the outer door.

Annoyance spiked through the queen, angered by the rude urgency. "Come, but you'd best have a good reason for your pounding."

The door burst open and her deputy shadowmaster flew in like an angry crow, his dark robes flapping. He ushered a mud-splashed messenger into her solar. Breathing hard, as if he'd run the length of the palace, Master Raddock blurted the message. "Majesty, terrible tidings have come from the north."

His words struck like a slap, yet the queen hid behind a stone mask. "Tell us."

Master Raddock gestured to the boy. Clad in the emerald green tabard of a royal courier, the freckle-faced lad was ghost-pale, his eyes sunken with exhaustion, his clothing rumpled and mud-splattered. "Majesty, they told me to ride hard for Pellanor. I came as fast as I could." The lad wavered on his feet, clearly exhausted. Dropping to one knee, he proffered a battered scroll towards her. "Majesty, the prince is dead."

The words made no sense. "What?"

The boy's voice quavered. "Prince Stewart is dead, killed at the battle of Eye Bridge."

Her heartbeat galloped at wild pace, as if it could outrun the grim tidings. "No, you are mistaken." The voice sounded so calm, so collected, it could not be hers.

The boy extended the scroll towards her. "Majesty, he fell fighting the Mordant's army at Eye Bridge. They said he fought bravely."

"*No, it cannot be!*"

The lad proffered the scroll towards her.

She struck it from his hand, as if it was a poisonous snake.

The messenger gasped, but the queen did not care. Liandra balled her ringed hands into fists, desperately clinging to her disbelief.

Master Raddock recovered the scroll. "Majesty, I checked the seal myself, the message is valid. You must listen to reason."

"*Reason!*" She loosed her rage on the fat crow. "*Who are you to tell us of reason? Are you an anointed queen? Are you a mother?* We cannot lose our firstborn son, our stalwart warrior, our only heir!" She reined in her voice, yet her words cut all the deeper. "If our son dies, our reign will all be for naught!" Liandra was a petite woman, yet her rage was fearsome, a towering wall of denial. She pointed a warning finger at her shadowmaster. "Tell us not of reason, for this cannot be!"

Her shadowmaster cowered before her.

The messenger-boy lowered his gaze, tears streaming his dirty face.

Liandra waited, her ringed hands balled into fists.

Lady Sarah flew towards her. Taking the scroll from the shadowmaster's hands, she opened it with shaking hands. "Majesty," a heavy sorrow laced her friend's voice, "he speaks the truth. It says Prince Stewart is dead."

"*No!*" The words pierced her mind, pierced her heart. "*It cannot be!*"

Someone was screaming, a terrible keening sound.

"*My son!*" The queen fled from reason, shrieking like a banshee. "*By all the gods, it cannot be!*"

Courtiers came and went from her chambers, but she did not care. A flask was forced to her lips, a draught of bitterness, a draught of tears. Liandra swallowed the potion and felt herself fall...like falling into a bottomless well...like falling into forgetfulness. Swallowed by darkness, she welcomed oblivion.

52

Jemma

Another message pouch from Navarre, but this one bore the complex sea knots that marked it of special importance. Once a fortnight, Jemma received scrolls from home, a letter from her father, gossip from her family and friends, reports from her factors, but the sea knots marked this delivery as something more. Locking the door to her room, she made fast work of the knots. Opening the pouch, she peered inside. Nothing...but a message coil.

A message coil! It lay on the table like a coiled snake. Only the most dire messages were sent by coded coil.

Perhaps the king is dead, the thought shook her soul. She shuddered, making the hand sign against evil. The Curse of the Vowels had plagued her family with death, too much death. Shaking her head against the grim thought, Jemma prayed it was not so.

Unread, the message coil waited on the table.

The coiled strip of parchment bore a carefully inked message scribed in a clear hand. The message was false unless read the proper way. She stared at it for a hundred heartbeats but delay would not change the outcome. Taking a steadying breath, Jemma knelt by her cedar chest and turned the lock. Buried beneath her keepsakes and scrolls, she found her message rod. Every royal had one, its twin kept safe in Castle Seamount. Made of turned pine, the two foot rod bore a single nail at one end. It looked insignificant but a rod of any other thickness would yield gibberish. Such a simple thing, yet it was the key to unlocking the royal code. Returning to the table, she pierced the message coil with the nail and slowly wound the parchment strip around the rod so that only the first letter of each word showed beneath the nail head. Concentrating on the task, she refused to read the message until the coil was complete. She reached the end, her hands shaking. Taking a deep breath, she read the message. *"Return home with all haste to wear the crown."*

The coiled rod fell from her hands. *The crown of Navarre...*she was going to be queen! Her destiny came calling, a rush of elation warring with trepidation. *So her father was stepping down.* The passing of the Seaside crown came with a pang of sorrow. Jemma knew her mother's death had struck her father like a well-aimed arrow. She read the words again, resolve pushing away her sorrow. Her long-held dream was nearly at hand, yet with the crown came a daunting responsibility. Jemma swore to all the gods, she would be worthy.

A thousand thoughts hammered her mind. She needed to pack, she needed to return home with all haste...but she also needed to tell the queen. Her thoughts jarred to a halt like a ship hitting a rocky shore. Queen Liandra, her mentor and her dear friend, the one who'd most understand her elation...and her fear, was locked in her own misery, grief-struck by the death of Stewart. *The queen's only remaining son,* her brother by marriage, felled in a distant battle. Jemma worried for the queen, she worried for her sister. So much death, they truly lived in foul times, yet Jemma longed to seek the queen's advice, to share her joy and trepidation.

A knock sounded on the door.

Startled, Jemma tore the message coil from the rod. "Just a moment." She threw the coiled parchment into the blazing hearth, watching to be sure it caught fire, and then hid the message rod in her chest.

The knock sounded again, frantic and insistent.

"Coming." Jemma smoothed her velvet gown. Trying to appear unflustered, she unlocked the door.

Lady Sarah blew into the chamber like a stormy gale. Her normally coifed hair was in disarray, giving the senior lady-in-waiting a wild look. "Princess Jemma, you must help!"

"Is the queen awake? Is she asking for me?" Jemma had spent long hours keeping vigil by the queen's bedside. While the queen slept, the princess spoke of commerce and market gossip, hoping to ignite a spark of interest, to rouse the queen from her torpor, all to no avail.

Lady Sarah paced in front of the hearth. "I'm so worried about the queen. She doesn't talk and now she won't eat. I tell you, I'm at my wit's end! You must help!"

"Can no one get through to her?"

"At first her councilors came, seeking the queen's approval, but she said not a word. She just stared, as if she did not even see them. Now they don't even bother coming. Only the gods know what decisions they're making without her approval."

Jemma swallowed her unease. "And the healers, what do they say?"

Lady Sarah threw up her hands in dismay. "They ply her with potions and tell me to keep her abed. *Abed!* She lays there like a corpse! As if she's the one who died and not her son." Lady Sarah bit her lip, her voice quavering. "It's all coming undone. If only Lord Robert were here. She has to take an interest. She has to wake and be the queen."

"I'll come. We'll find a way to rouse her." Jemma took the older woman's hand, trying to impart a sense of calm. "I've received fresh word from home; perhaps it will spark the queen to life."

"Pray that it does." Fresh lines of worry scrawled the older woman's face. She looked as if she'd aged a decade. "Come. I don't like leaving her for long."

The two women made their way through the castle corridors, a whisper of velvet trailing across the marble floors. Courtiers and lords barely spared them a glance, as if they were both beneath notice. *As if we don't matter,* the thought sent a chill down Jemma's back. They reached the queen's tower and climbed the stairs. Petitioners normally crowded the antechamber, hoping for a word with their monarch, but the outer parlor was eerily empty, silent as a tomb. Jemma shivered at the ill-omen, as if the queen was already dead...or irrelevant.

Sir Durnheart stood guard at the inner door, his great blue sword looming over his shoulder.

Lady Sarah hesitated. "Has she asked for anyone?"

"No, my lady."

The two women slipped inside the queen's bedchamber. Heavy curtains shuttered the windows, turning the elegant chamber into a cave. Jemma blinked against the gloom, her gaze drawn towards the queen. Candles surrounded the great canopied bed, giving off a soft glow. Deathly still, the air was laden with the stringent smells of medicinal potions leavened with the scent of burnt candles. Ladies Martha and Amy kept vigil, sitting by the queen's bed, silent as a wake.

Jemma approached the royal bed. The queen lay stiff and pale as a corpse. Her dark hair was combed, artfully fanned across the silken pillow. Rouge painted her lips, but the false color only heightened the queen's ghastly pallor. Queen Liandra looked like a wraith hovering on the brink of death. Jemma stifled a gasp.

Lady Sarah knelt by the royal bed. Taking the queen's hand, she said, "Majesty, you have a visitor. Princess Jemma has come to seek your advice."

The queen made no response.

A malady of grief, Jemma silently railed against the queen's sad state. "This cannot continue." She looked to Lady Sarah but the older woman had no answers. Jemma's gaze swept across the chamber as if seeking a culprit, finally settling on the table strewn with bottled potions. "Take these away." She pointed to the stoppered bottles as if they held poison. "No more potions, no more milk of the poppy. The queen must regain her wits."

Lady Amy flung a hesitant glance towards Lady Sarah.

The older woman nodded. "Do as she bids. Nothing here has helped."

With a quick curtsy, Lady Amy gathered the bottles onto a silver tray and bore them from the chamber.

"And open the windows, the air smells like a healery instead of a queen's chamber."

Lady Martha hesitated. "But the air holds a damp chill?"

"Then we'll stoke the fire, but let the queen breathe fresh air, not the stale smell of confinement and sickness."

Lady Sarah nodded. "Do as she says."

The women bustled about the chamber, removing the shrouds of sickness and mourning. The windows were thrown open wide, inviting a gust of fresh air and the hearth was stoked for heat. Logs were added to the grate, crackling in the fireplace, releasing a welcome breath of pine. Pillows were plumped and quilts added to the royal bed. The queen lay swathed in fresh comfort...but she did not stir, as if embalmed by grief.

Princess Jemma took a seat by the queen.

Lady Sarah drew the other women from the chamber. She returned to sit by the fireside, her knitting needles clicking a soothing rhythm.

Jemma took the queen's hand, so cold and unresponsive, yet the queen still wore her great rings, symbols of her anointed power. The rings glittered in the candlelight, the great emerald and the golden seal. Jemma well knew that power unused could be lost, stolen by ambitious lords. And the Rose Court was rife with ambitious lords...if only she could waken the queen. She began to speak, talking of small things, observations from the castle, the court, and the markets. She hoped to spark the queen's interest before sharing her news, but the queen remained waxen and still, her stare vague and uninterested. For three turns of an hourglass, Jemma kept vigil by the queen's bed. Having depleted her small talk, she leaned close to the queen's ear, her secret bursting within her. "Majesty, I've had word from home." Her voice carried a fever pitch of excitement.

She waited, but there was no response.

"Majesty, you know how the crown is passed in Navarre. The king and the council choose the heir depending on the needs of the kingdom." Jemma's breath caught on her excitement, a dream and a destiny come true. "I've heard word from the king." Her excitement bubbled to the surface. Longing to confide in her friend and mentor, she leaned close to whisper the words. "I'm to be the next queen of Navarre!"

The queen's gaze seemed to quicken, a spark of life dispelling her vacant stare. Queen Liandra drew a sharp breath as if pricked.

Lady Sarah heard and dropped her knitting, rushing to the bedside.

Jemma gripped the queen's hand, willing her back to life. "Majesty, come back to us!"

The queen took a gasping breath as if surfacing from a perilous dive. Her eyes regained their potent focus. She turned her head on the pillow, her gaze fastening on Jemma. Her voice was a hoarse croak, rusty from long disuse. "Na...varre?"

Joy blossomed in the princess. "Yes, I will be the next queen of Navarre."

"Navarre?" The queen clung to the name as if it was a lifeline.

"Yes, I pray I will rule with all the wisdom that you have taught me, bringing a new prosperity to the seaside kingdom."

Queen Liandra struggled to sit up. "The queen of *Navarre*...he said the fecund would inherit the earth." She stared at Jemma, her gaze as sharp as daggers. "Are you fecund?"

The question ambushed Jemma. "What?"

The queen's voice held a sepulcher tone. "He said the magic of Navarre will make the queen fecund."

Understanding struck. Jemma released the queen's hand. "Majesty, I told you, the magic cannot be shared."

The queen's hand shot out, grabbing Jemma's wrist. "Share your magic! Make us fecund!"

Jemma tried to pull away, but the queen's hand tightened like a steel claw.

"We need an heir, a child of our womb." Liandra leaned forward, her dark hair long and loose, contrasting to the paleness of her face. Her white nightgown hung on her thinning frame, making her look like a banshee sprung from the grave. "Share your magic and we shall have the heir we so desperately need!"

Shock rippled through the princess. "I told you, majesty, the magic cannot be shared!"

The queen's dark eyes held a feverish intensity. "Cannot, or *will not!*"

Fear spiked through the princess. Instead of lucidity, the light in the queen's gaze looked like madness. "No! I cannot!" Jemma recoiled, trying to pull her hand away, but Queen Liandra held tight, fingernails digging into soft flesh.

"Give us the magic and we shall get sons and daughters to replace the ones we've lost! Heirs to secure the Tandroth line! Give us the magic and we shall be fecund!"

Lady Sarah tried to intervene. "Majesty, what are you doing?"

Venom laced the queen's voice. "This one claims to be our friend, our daughter, yet she will not share!"

Jemma tried to the parry madness with reason. "Majesty, the magic is keyed to the royal bloodline of Navarre, it will serve no other!"

"Lies! You spew lies!"

Lady Sarah tried to ease the queen's grip. "Majesty, release her."

The queen bristled. "Do not touch us! We know our mind. We know what we need."

Jemma tried again, her voice a desperate plea. "Majesty, this is wrong and you know it!"

"Wrong!" The queen gave her a scathing glare. "All our life we have served the Light, we have served our people, ruling for the greater good of our kingdom, yet *this* is how the gods treat us? Every one of our children dead? Our noble line ended? Our legacy nothing but dust and ashes?" Her rouged lips curled in an ugly sneer. "If this is what it means to serve the Light, then we...choose...Darkness!" The queen raised her voice to an imperious shout. *"Guards!"*

The outer door banged open and Sir Durnheart rushed in, his blue sword raised in his mailed fists. Two guards with short swords followed close behind him. Seeing nothing but women, Sir Durnheart lowered his sword, a puzzled look on his face. "Majesty?"

"There is a traitor in our midst."

Sir Durnheart raised his sword.

The queen shoved princess Jemma away. "Take this one to the dungeons! Let her rot till she comes to her senses."

Jemma gaped, unable to speak.

Lady Sarah knelt by the queen's bed. "Majesty, you are not yourself!"

"We know our will." The queen pointed an accusing finger towards the princess. "This one betrays our greatest need."

Sir Durnheart hesitated.

Anger spiked the queen's voice. "Obey us!"

Sir Durnheart bowed. Grabbing the princess by the arm, he lifted her to her feet. "Come." He ushered her from the royal chambers.

Jemma stumbled, shocked by the queen's transformation. "That was not the queen."

The knight supported her, his gauntleted hand clamping a firm grip on her arm. "The queen is grief-struck. She is not herself."

But he did not release her. *He did not release her*...Jemma considered running, but the knight kept a firm grip, holding her tight. "What will you do?"

The knight gave her a terse look. "Obey my queen." He hurried her down the corridor, two guards trailing behind, their hands on their swords.

Her mouth gaped. "*The...dungeon?*" The words choked her throat.

Sir Durnheart turned, never loosening his grip. "You two return and guard the queen. Let no one pass till I return."

The two guardsmen snapped brisk salutes and then turned, striding back towards the queen's chamber.

Sir Durnheart tugged on her arm, nearly lifting her from the floor. "Come."

Jemma rushed to keep pace. "Where...*not the dungeon?*"

"No," the knight bit the answer.

"*Then...where?*"

"A distant part of the castle. I'll imprison you with loyal swords standing guard at the door."

Imprisoned! Jemma felt as if a nightmare engulfed her. "This is wrong."

"Yes," the knight gave her a sideways glance, "yet I'm sworn to obey."

Castle Tandroth was a labyrinth of passageways. Jemma lost track of the twists and turns. They left the gilded hallways for shadowy corridors. He took her to a remote part of the castle, his grip firm as steel on her arm. Jemma considered crumpling to the floor, behaving like a deadweight, making him carry her...but such a response had no dignity. She walked in a trance, her thoughts beating against her, frantic with the terrible turn of fate. *The queen is not herself!* Perhaps she should have screamed, yet she knew he spared her the dungeon. For that, at least, she was grateful. Better to avoid attention and wait for a chance to escape. She sagged against him, yet he propelled her up the spiral stairs. So many steps, she lost count.

He reached an oak door. "I'll have food and wine brought. You'll not be ill treated." Opening the door, Sir Durnheart thrust her inside.

Thrust off balance, she tripped and fell. "No!" Jemma lunged for the door, but it slammed in her face. A key turned in the lock, such a damning sound. "*No!*" Her resolve cracked...she beat against the oak door till her hands hurt, a trickle of tears on her face. "*Release me! By all the Lords of Light, release me!*"

Nothing.

The silence beat against her. Jemma slumped to the floor. Her mind bruised, her heart numbed, she turned to face her prison. Dusty and spare, the small tower room was clearly long unused. A narrow bed with a faded quilt was pushed against one wall, a cracked chamber pot sat in the corner, a stool tilting at a drunken angle sat in front of a dead hearth. The chamber held no adornment...and no warmth. A coating of dust across the floor bore the lonely marks of her own footprints...and nothing else, proof the chamber was long forgotten. Biting back a sob, she crossed to the small mullioned window, the only source of light. The air smelled stale, choking her with more proof of her confinement. Desperate for fresh air, she clawed at the window latch. Pushing open the lead-paned window, she gulped fresh air. Standing on tiptoe, she peered out. Her room was in a tower top, nothing but rooftops and battlements below. A sob caught in her throat. *Imprisoned!* Retreating from the harsh view, she left the window gaping open. A cool breeze haunted the chamber with the scent of freedom. Curled on the musty bed, she watched the daylight fade to darkness. At noon-time she'd been offered a crown...at sunset she was a prisoner. The reversal of fortune hit like a hammer blow, as if she'd stepped into insanity. Tears threatened, but she held them back. Jemma shuddered, feeling darkness close around her.

53

The Priestess

Returning from another late night, the Priestess stared from the carriage window, yet she saw nothing. The Mordant treated her like a high-priced courtesan, sending her on assignations with rich nobles and influential lords. She gave them a single night of incomparable sex, dangling the promise of more, and they forfeited their souls to Darkness, working the Mordant's will upon the queen's kingdom. How easily she subverted the queen's loyal lords, but the Priestess despised being used. It left a bitter taste in her mouth, yet the nightly dalliances also served her own purpose, for she needed to feed. Locking her victims in the throes of passion, she unleashed the succubus. Indulging her own hunger, she drank deep from their life essence. Drunk on sex, she left her victims snoring on their beds, her true name written in the sweat on their chests.

Staring out the carriage window at the night-darkened city, a laugh bubbled to her lips. Twenty years from now, Pellanor would be plagued by old men, aged beyond their years by the kiss of a succubus. *A plague of sex upon your city,* her laughter turned to gallows humor, realizing the price of their passion would only be paid if the Mordant let them live. She wondered how many would survive the Mordant's brutal reign, herself included.

Forcing the grim thought away, she breathed in the night air, watching the passing lanterns illuminating the queen's city. In truth, she liked Pellanor, a city brimming with a wealth of opportunities, a plethora of amusements. A pity its rich diversity would not survive the Mordant's rule.

The carriage rounded a corner, turning onto a familiar street. *Nearly back to my prison,* she gripped the handle of the door, tempted to jump, but she knew the thought was foolish. Instead of escape, she'd only injure herself. A pair of dark-clad assassins followed her every move, keeping watch like hungry hounds. Her hand moved to the serpent-shaped armband coiling her forearm, the hidden needles armed with one of her deadliest poisons...but not tonight. Better to wait till her plans were in place.

The carriage slowed to a stop. A dark-clad assassin appeared at the door. Opening it for her, he offered his hand, playing the servant, a snide smile on his dusky face. Ignoring his attitude, she accepted his help from the carriage, as any great lady would.

Guards surrounded her, ushering her into the mansion. Lantern light lit the entranceway, yet the great house was silent. The revelers had gone home, or perhaps the Mordant had gone out, seeking pleasure or purpose of his own devising.

She climbed the stairs, the two dark-clad assassins following close as shadows. She made her way down the long hallway, carpet soft beneath her slippered feet. The door to Bishop Borgan's suite gaped open, candlelight spilling into the hallway. The Priestess despised the fat prelate, but information was a weapon she sorely needed. Loosening her robe to reveal a hint of cleavage, she struck a suggestive pose in the frame of his doorway. She needn't have bothered for the fat prelate had his nose stuck in a mound of scrolls.

"No revels tonight?"

He flicked a bored glance her way. "Not tonight, but there's one planned for the morrow. Wear something special. The Mordant will expect you to mingle with the guests and display your wears."

Like a harlot up for bid, she kept the sneer from her voice, "Of course."

"How did you find Lord Weathering?"

A shrewd man but a fool for sex, "He's eager to serve the prince of Ur."

Dipping a quill in ink, the bishop opened a thick ledger. "Very good."

"And my next assignation?"

The bishop thumbed through the pages, an erudite whorcmaster. "In three nights, you're to go to a Lord Ferdic. The Mordant wants him to propose a writ to double the taxation on taverns. Squeeze the people's pleasures and their hate for the queen will escalate to a bonfire."

Their petty schemes mattered not a copper to her. "In three nights." Having gained the information she needed, the Priestess turned to leave.

"And, Iris," a satisfied smile filled his jowly face, "the Mordant appreciates your ardent service."

She bristled with hate, resenting the use of her true name. "I'm sure he does." The Priestess longed to poison the fat pig, but not tonight. Keeping her face composed, she glided down the hallway to her own suite of rooms.

An assassin rushed to open the door. Without giving him a glance, she crossed the threshold of her gilded prison. The door closed behind her, the key turning in the lock.

Her two handmaidens slept in chairs in front of the smoldering hearth. They'd clearly sought to await her return, but the late hour had caught them. She let them sleep. Shedding her cloak, she made her way to the inner bedroom.

Forced to serve the Mordant, she felt the need to reaffirm her power to kill. Seeking the solace of her poisons, she knelt in front of her rosewood chest, her harvest of deathly delights. Taking care lest she trigger the poison-tipped needles, she unlocked the chest. Easing the lid open...she found it empty!

Empty!

Her heartbeat thundered, her hands shook with rage as she hurriedly opened the small drawers, searching for any scrap of poison. Someone had ransacked her chest, taking her hoard of velvet pouches and stoppered bottles. Even the secret compartments were empty. *Nothing!* They'd taken everything, stealing all her precious poisons! How dare they! A scream of rage ripped out of her. Feeling like a beast declawed, she howled for all that was lost.

Her handmaidens came running. "*Mistress?*"

"Who was in here?"

They trembled in the doorway. "None while we were here."

Lydia paled. "They offered us dinner served in the courtyard," her voice dropped to a repentant whisper, "a chance to be outside."

It was not their fault, but her rage was not easily caged. "Leave me."

They fled to the outer chamber, closing the door behind them.

The Priestess prowled her bedroom like a caged beast. The Mordant defanged her with his every move, chaining her sexuality to his own purpose, stealing her poisons. Rage thundered through her, gradually annealing to a smoldering anger, another score to settle with the Mordant. Thankfully she still had her serpent armbands and ring. Lethal jewelry loaded with enough poison to kill ten men, yet now she needed to hoard her poisonous sting to its best advantage.

She bitterly regretted answering the Mordant's summons. Everything had gone wrong...yet she'd won back the Eye.

The Eye! Her hand slipped to the great moonstone dangling between her breasts. Fused together by searing passion and stolen magic, the Great Eye was whole once more...and the Mordant did not know it. *What he did not know could hurt him.* A smile teased her face.

Shuttering the windows against prying eyes, she went to her cedar chest, delving through her silken finery till she found her silver scrying bowl. Kneeling by the bowl, she filled it with water from a pewter ewer. Releasing the pale moonstone from its wire cage, she fondled the oval stone, marveling at its silken feel, smooth and flawless once more. Whispering a prayer to Darkness, she lowered the ancient gem into the crystal clear water.

The Priestess held her breath, waiting.

Powers clashed. The water spat and roiled, fighting the stone, proof of the moonstone's potency. Darkness prevailed and the water turned inky black, a fitting surface to reflect Dark deeds.

Shrugging off her gown, she knelt naked over the bowl, her raven-black hair cascading down like a shuttering veil. Her breath whispered across the dark water, "Yours to use." She petitioned the Dark God, wondering if he would answer her entreaty despite the nearness of the Mordant. She shivered, anxious with need. "Do not forsake me, Lord."

Darkness answered, surrounding her, enfolding her, impaling her.

Smitten by her god, the Priestess writhed with pleasure and pain, ecstasy balanced on the knife-edge of agony. She bit back a scream as the god delved deep, filling her with Darkness, and then the divine presence withdrew.

"Thank you, Lord." Her voice trembled with smoky pleasure, a succubus fulfilled.

Brimming with power, she cast her will upon the Dark waters. "Show me Steffan." Images appeared on the mirror-dark water. She found him asleep, his dark hair tousled, the sheets twisted around him as if he fought in his dreams. He slept alone...and that pleased her. She watched his restless sleep, watched him toss upon the sheets, and then she entered his dreams.

By swearing an oath to her, he'd opened himself to the power of the Eye.

Wielding the moonstone, she slipped into his dreams. *Steffan, hear me!*

How? Where?

She felt his eagerness...and his puzzlement. *Here, love, in your dreams. Think of me and I am here.*

The link was uncannily strong. He thought of her naked in his arms...and she was there. More than any dream she'd ever entered, this felt like reality. She could almost feel the strength of his need as he nuzzled her neck. *I need you.*

*So this was how he imagined her. *You need to think.* She drew back from him, lest passion cloud his mind. Steffan reached for her, but she evaded him. *No, we need to talk. We need to thwart the Mordant.*

Fear blasted through his mind, banishing all thoughts of passion. *He saw me!*

His fear was contagious. *He saw you?* She had hoped to keep him hidden, a dagger in the dark.

I kept watch outside the mansion. It was noontime, the street was crowded. I was one among many, yet his stare locked onto me like an arrow shot in the dark.

A sense of foreboding gripped her. *He saw you, yet he let you live?*

He more than saw me. His gaze invaded me! She felt his frustration, his fear. *It felt like rape.*

Her own fear festered. *Steffan, you are but a youngling in the eyes of Darkness, a fresh-sworn dedicate still living your first lifetime. If the Mordant plumbs your mind, he will rape you of every thought, every intent. You must stay away from him.*

I'll not leave you.

She felt his conviction, she felt his love...and the strength of it stunned her. The Priestess nearly lost control of her magic. Love was something others dreamt of, something always denied her, for passion was her true domain...yet Steffan's dream did not lie. Caught off guard by the strength his love, the Priestess struggled to bridle her emotions and keep her wits. *It was a mistake to come here, a terrible mistake. The Mordant deems himself a god. He will not share power. He will not suffer us to live unless we serve. You must keep your distance, yet I need your help to escape.*

How can I help?

A wave of dizziness washed across her, she felt her power fading. Unwilling to forfeit this chance, she struggled to keep the link. *In three nights I'll be sent to service Lord Ferdic. Get Braxus and the others and plan an ambush. Slay the Mordant's men and have horses ready. We'll flee the city and then cross an ocean to escape the Mordant's reach.*

Her power was stretched too thin, the link began to waver. *I cannot stay! In three nights at Lord Ferdic's. Be ready!*

I'll be there...

Steffan's image vanished, severing the link. Exhausted, the Priestess slumped to the carpet, reeling with dizziness. Speaking through dreams drained so much more power than mere scrying, yet a smile rode her ruby lips. The power of the Great Eye was hers once more...and in three nights she'd escape the Mordant's greedy grasp. The oldest harlequin had stolen her poisons, but not her magic, proving he was not infallible. A smile graced her lips. Succumbing to sleep, she dreamt of Steffan, glorying in her own Dark prowess.

54

The Mordant

The traitor fell prostrate before him, his arms spread wide in abasement. He'd turned this one in a single soul-searing gaze, proving the queen did not have as many loyal lords as she thought. The Mordant finished reading the scroll and then set it aside. The petty Darkness of the man's soul called to him, a tool waiting to be used. "Tell me of the queen."

The traitor rose to his knees. "The queen is felled by grief. She's taken to her bed, closeted with her women, ignoring her counselors and all matters of state."

"Good." The Mordant fondled the malachite coin, tumbling it between his fingers, a latent power destined to serve his will...just as all of Erdhe would soon serve. "While the woman wallows in grief, much ill will be done in her name. See Bishop Borgan before you leave. He has a stack of scrolls for discreet delivery to those lords turned to the service of Ur."

"Yes, my lord."

"Now tell me of the other matter."

"The princess?"

"Yes."

"I was not privy to the scene, but I heard whispers from some of the queen's lesser women."

"And?"

"It seems Lady Sarah took it upon herself to withhold the queen's dosage of poppy milk. Released from the poppy's entangling dreams, the queen woke to find the princess seated beside her. Perhaps the poppy milk addled her mind, for rumors say the queen flew into a rage and ordered the princess imprisoned."

Imprisoned, the Mordant savored the word, *so the queen takes the first step towards Darkness.* How easily the woman succumbed, yet the Mordant savored the triumph. Plots within plots, he'd despoil the arrogant woman's soul, pushing her towards Darkness while turning allies against allies. Divide and conquer was ever the first rule of Darkness. A satisfied smile slipped across his face. "Imprisonment is but the first step. Set your own men to guarding the princess. Her death is of the utmost importance."

"Her death?"

"Yes, but the timing must be right. When the queen awakens, she will seek your advice. You must push her towards further atrocities."

"The queen's women are stirred like angry hornets buzzing a nest, refusing all admittance to the royal chambers."

The Mordant made a dismissive gesture. "They're only women."

"Yes, my lord."

"The queen will gainsay them. She will strive to reclaim the reins of power, and when she does, she will need her loyal advisors. You will be waiting to serve her."

The traitor smiled. "And how will I advise her?"

"The queen wants something from the king of Navarre, something she believes she desperately needs. To gain this boon, she will need to barter with coin of equal value. Advise her to hold the princess's life in ransom against her need."

"Ransom?"

"Yes, advise her to barter the life of the princess for the magic of Navarre." The Mordant fondled the malachite coin. "And when Navarre refuses, as they must, you will advise the queen to follow through on her threat." The Mordant flashed a sinister smile. "Remind her that anything less would be a blatant show of weakness. In a land brimming with kings, queens dare not be seen as weak. Weakness will topple a crown, especially if it is held by a woman." His voice hardened. "The queen must make good on her threat, and the execution must be done in public."

"In public?"

"A public execution will compound the sin and will enrage Navarre to war. Allies fighting against allies, the queen will be forever branded as a corrupt ruler, a woman scheming for war merely for the sake of her empty womb. Her very name shall be reviled, eternally cursed in the annals of Erdhe, a lasting warning that women are not meant to rule." *And the Great Dark Divide shall be served, enacting the will of the Dark God.* Tendrils of ecstasy shuddered through the Mordant, proof of the Dark Lord's pleasure.

The Mordant stiffened as the Voice of the Dark God boomed through his mind, dangling the ultimate promise. *Everlasting life is within thy grasp...all of Erdhe shall cower before thee.* The Mordant savored the words, *everlasting life!*

As if coming out of a trance, the Mordant snapped his gaze back to the traitor. "Go...and work my will upon the queen. Keep a sharp watch lest she stray from the plan. And secure the princess, the pawn in our game."

Bowing low, the traitor retreated, closing the door behind him.

The Mordant fondled the malachite coin. The schemes of centuries would finally bear their Dark fruit. Everything was falling into place. It was only a matter of time.

55

Jemma

A key turned in the lock. Jemma startled awake. Dark and cold and dusty, her strange surroundings puzzled her...and then she remembered. *Imprisoned!* For half a heartbeat she considered feigning sleep, but the chance was soon lost. Lantern light pierced the darkness, and with it came a familiar face.

Startled to see her friend, Jemma leaped from the bed. "*Lady Sarah!*" Her gaze fixed on the older woman. "Have you come to free me?"

The lady slipped into the chamber, her arms full of bedding and the swaying lantern. Lady Amy followed, struggling to carry two baskets.

Their burdens betrayed the bitter answer. "Oh." Jemma considered dashing for the open door...till Sir Durnheart appeared. The knight shut the door with his heel and then dumped a load of kindling by the cold hearth.

Jemma sank back to the bed, numbed by the bitter truth.

Lady Sarah clucked like a mother hen. "It's so chilly in here, you'll catch your death of cold." Latching the window, she bustled about, dusting and setting the chamber to rights. Lady Amy set a loaf of bread, a bowl of fresh churned butter, and a flask of mead on a blanket beneath the window, as if she were laying a picnic for a summer day. Sir Durnheart knelt, kindling a fire in the hearth. The blaze soon sprang to life, releasing a welcome heat.

So they'd come to gild the prison. Still clothed, Jemma sat perched atop the musty bed, her hands clasping her knees, watching her friends turned captors.

The knight moved from the hearth to the door, blocking any chance at escape.

Lady Amy approached, her face chagrined. "We've brought fresh linens for the bed."

"Let me go and I'll save you the trouble."

Lady Amy stared at her shoes. "We're only trying to help."

In her heart, Jemma knew she spoke the truth. Her friends had spared her the horror of the dungeons, but everything about this was wrong. "You know this is not right."

Lady Sarah looked chagrined. "We cannot disobey the queen."

"But the queen would not want this."

"Yet she ordered it." Lady Sarah's voice turned gentle, even pleading. "Let us make the bed."

Jemma stood and moved to the corner. Her back to the wall, she watched in sullen silence as the two women stripped the dusty bed and remade it with fresh linens and a thick comforter. Finished with the bed, Lady Amy set the lantern on the hearth mantle and then gathered up her empty baskets. The two women turned towards the door.

"*Wait!*" Jemma stepped from the corner, suddenly afraid they'd leave without answers. "I have to know what's happening."

Lady Sarah nodded. She gestured to Lady Amy. The knight escorted Lady Amy from the chamber, closing the door behind them. The lock did not click, but Jemma was certain the knight stood guard beyond the door. She stared at her friend. "You must let me go."

Lady Sarah looked stricken. "We serve the queen."

"But this is lunacy!"

The older woman sighed. "This is the milk of the poppy, this is the madness of a mother's grief, this is a queen with too many burdens. All or none, the queen is not herself."

"Then release me!"

"I cannot gainsay the queen more than I already have."

"I'll sneak out of the castle and leave Pellanor. I swear I'll return to Navarre and forget this ever happened."

"It's too late for that."

Something in her tone gave warning. Jemma drew a sharp breath. "What do you mean?"

Lady Sarah sank to the bed, looking weary beyond her years. "After ordering your...," she struggled with the word, her mouth twisting in distaste, "arrest, the queen was so agitated that Healer Crandor insisted on dosing her with more of his potions, but instead of calming her, the queen became agitated, flying into a wild rage. Her majesty ranted about you and Navarre, screaming about the need to bear a child." Lady Sarah stared at Jemma, regret filled her brown eyes. "It was grief, or the potions speaking, but the damage is done."

"Damage?" Jemma did not like the sound of this.

"We were trying to protect you and the queen." Lady Sarah made a feeble wave. "We sought to keep her majesty secluded till she came back to her senses, but others heard the rant." The older woman took a deep breath. "We brought you here to spare you from the dungeons, but now you must stay for you own protection."

"*My* protection?"

"Others who love the queen less might obey her commands to the letter. They're looking for you."

A chill shivered down Jemma's back. *So the dungeon remains a very real threat,* her heart jolted to a wild gallop. She struggled to marshal her thoughts. "Who knows I'm here?"

"Only we three. We'll keep you hidden, we'll keep you safe. And when the queen comes to her senses this will all be put to rights."

Jemma prayed for it to be so, but prayer was rarely enough. "Can you not smuggle me out of the castle?"

The lady gave her a warning look. "Don't press me to disobey my queen more than I already have."

Stalemate, she knew Lady Sarah walked a thin line between duty and honor. Jemma reached for the other woman's hand, offering a gentle touch of thanks. "I'm sorry. You've done so much for me, but this is hard."

"Hard for us all." Lady Sarah stood. "I must get back to the queen. I fear to leave her unattended." She gave Jemma a beseeching look, her voice a mixture of concern and contrition. "Keep safe. I'll return when I can." With a nod toward the princess, she exited the chamber.

The key turned in the lock, a damning sound.

Still a prisoner, but at least her cage was more comfortable. She went to the small window and watched the dawn rise across the castle, but the light brought no cheer. Madness stalked the queen, and somehow Jemma had been caught by it, snared by a web of insanity. She feared the consequences, for herself...and all of Erdhe.

56

Steffan

Steffan dreamt of her, but this time it seemed so real, so much more than just a dream. Naked, she came to him, lush and ripe, her raven-dark hair cascading to her hips. He swept her into his arms and carried her to his bed. Her scent was intoxicating, desire suffused with mystery. *"Cereus!"* he whispered her name, his voice laden with hunger. So tempting to have his way with her, to ease the throbbing ache in his loins, but he knew the sweet delay would only heighten his pleasure a thousand fold. A skilled lover, he decided to make her beg for it. Trailing kisses down her throat, his hands worked their own magic.

A sound intruded.

He longed to remain, to quench his desire, but a sixth sense warned him to be wary.

Reluctant to leave her arms, yet he swam awake.

He woke to an empty bed. Lying warm beneath the quilt, his manhood still rampant, his sleep-drunk gaze roved the night-darkened room. Nothing seemed amiss. Steffan rankled his nose at the room's stale smell. *Piss pots and stale ale,* the smell disgusted him. Despite pockets full of gold, he'd taken a cheap room at a dodgy inn in the city's shadier side and told no one where he stayed, not Braxus, not Donklin, not even the Priestess when she came to visit his dreams. Her words of warning no longer fell on deaf ears. He'd crossed stares with the Mordant...and lost. Steffan knew he dared not be found. He shuddered at the memory of those probing eyes flaying his soul. Coming to Pellanor was a perilous mistake. Better to take ship to a foreign shore and start their own Dark Dance. At least the Priestess had a plan. One more night of hiding in this dank hole and then he'd snatch Cereus from the Mordant's guards and carry her far beyond his foul reach. Steffan smiled, thinking of their future together.

The sound came again, a subtle scratching at the door.

Perhaps it was mice, or a petty thief, yet it paid to be cautious. His hand slipped beneath the pillow, seeking his throwing knife.

The door burst open.

A pair of dark-clad men leaped through the doorway. Crouching on either side of his bed, they glared like hounds on a tether.

Servants of the Mordant, Steffan's heartbeat hammered. *Two against one,* he tightened his grip on his throwing dagger, yet he kept it hidden, attempting bluster instead. "What are you doing? *Get out!*" He made his voice a shout, hoping to draw others, though he knew it was a weak ploy. Denizens of the shady quarter tended to flee rather than fight. *"Get out!"*

A dark-robed figure appeared in the doorway. "There you are." The Mordant stepped into the room, a nightmare come calling.

Steffan edged backwards, his head against the wall, the knife hidden beneath the quilt. "How did you find me?"

"Darkness has its own scent." The Mordant's nostrils flared wide. "Only a youngling, yet your soul brims with it."

Steffan locked his stare on the Mordant's lips, trying to avoid the deadly snare of his gaze. "What do you want?"

"You should have asked that question when you first saw me. You should have dropped to your knees and begged to serve a higher Darkness."

Steffan stammered an answer. "I...didn't know."

"Didn't you? Then why were you spying?"

Sweat erupted across his skin, bearing the stink of fear. Sometimes the truth served better than a lie. "The woman...I want the woman."

A sneer curdled the Mordant's lips. "*A woman?*" His voice solidified with certainty. "The succubus."

Steffan nodded, his throat desert-dry.

"Your desires betray you, proving you are as stupid as you are weak."

Steffan hurled a reply. "I'm a Dedicate of the Dark Lord."

"A youngling of little value."

Steffan tried a desperate gambit. "I have a Dark Gift."

The Mordant flashed a skeptical smile. "What gift?"

"I'm skilled with dice. I never lose. With me in your service, you'll never want for gold."

"Yes, I see your worth," the Mordant gestured to the dingy room, "a youngling cowering in a flea-ridden inn."

Desperation made him indignant. "I'm sworn to the Dark Lord! My soul is his!"

"The Dark Lord rules in Hell." The Mordant's voice struck like a slap. "*I* rule here. I'll send him your soul when I'm done."

Death grinned at him. Steffan did not hesitate. He hurled the knife, aiming for the Mordant's jugular.

A dark-clad assassin sprang to action, his hand snaking out like a toad's tongue.

Steffan stared, slack mouthed.

The dagger pierced the assassin's outstretched palm, impaling him like a nail through flesh, yet he did not scream.

Steffan erupted from the bed, running for the open window.

Pain caught him. His legs crumpled. Steffan fell face-first to the dingy floor. Impaled by a sharp pain, as if a sword skewered his back, he stifled a scream.

"How dare you!" The Mordant's voice was a harsh hiss.

The agony doubled. A scream ripped out of him. His right hand flailed backwards, reaching for the sword, but he found nothing...yet the blade turned, grinding through bone and flesh. "*No!*" Steffan howled in torment, like nothing he'd ever endured.

The agony stopped.

Steffan clung to the floor, panting like a dog, afraid to move.

A boot nudged his side. "Look at me."

Afraid to comply, terrified to disobey, he rolled over.

"Look at me."

Steffan lifted his gaze.

The Mordant stared down at him. "Your thoughts are mine." Darkness slammed into him, a scythe ripping through his mind, flaying his thoughts, skewering his soul.

57

Jemma

The light faded to dusk and still no one came. Jemma paced her prison, walking from the bed, to the door, to the lead-paned window. Every time she reached the door, she pressed her ear to the solid oak to listen, but heard nothing. Every time she reached the window, she stood on tiptoes to look out, seeing nothing but a lethal drop to the battlements below. *Nothing,* she bit her lip in frustration. In all her childhood fairy tales, imprisoned princesses were always rescued by handsome knights, but she feared no one would come for her. A missing princess, yet few would know. She assumed her own guardsmen were imprisoned. If the queen dared to imprison a princess, then she'd not hesitate to imprison her guardsmen from Navarre. Jemma only hoped they were well treated. Her lord father would be expecting an answer to his letter, but Navarre was a long way away and it could easily take at least a moon-turn before her own letters were missed. Her best hope was Cenric, but the forest lord had gone south to help his people settle in the queen's gift. *Her handsome archer,* she sorely missed him, but the cat-eyed forest lord came and went from Pellanor like a windborne leaf. She prayed for his return, certain he'd search for her, but she knew it could be a moon-turn or more before he made his way back to the queen's city. *A moon-turn,* it seemed like forever. She fondled the bracelet he'd given her, hand-carved beads of polished wood, each bead bearing a different leaf pattern. Her fingers sought the hemlock leaf, knowing it was his clan. They'd only had stolen moments together, archery lessons in the castle yard, a gallop through the sun-dappled forest, a campfire dinner under diamond-bright stars. Cherished memories turned to longing. Despite their many differences, Jemma could not get enough of his touch. If only he'd come for her.

Dusk dimmed to night and still no one came.

Her worry deepened. It was not like her friends to abandon her. *But are they my friends?* The question nagged at her. Perhaps something was wrong. At least last time they'd brought ample food, a picnic basket brimming with delicacies, a feast fit for a queen. Jemma nibbled on a piece of sharp cheese. Adding a log to the hearth, she stoked the fire, bringing a blaze of welcome warmth to the small chamber. For the sixth time she tried to pick the lock with the slender knife, to no avail. She swore she'd have someone teach her the trick once she escaped. Who knew lock picking was a skill she'd need as a princess.

A princess, soon to be a queen, yet she sat here imprisoned.

Frustration and worry gnawed at her, yet she sat impotent within her cage. Snatching up the wineskin, she crawled into bed, hiding the slender knife under her pillow. Sipping the wine, a good merlot, she watched the firelight, waiting for someone to come.

Jemma woke with a start.

A tap, tap, tapping came from the window. *It must be a bird,* for the tower was too high for anything else. The chamber had turned cold, the fire burnt to embers. Jemma burrowed beneath the cover's warmth, trying to reclaim sleep.

Tap, tap, tap, the noise was insistent.

Night darkened the small windowpane, the embers in the hearth giving a faint light.

Tap, tap, tap, the noise came again, an annoying sound that would not let her sleep.

Jemma reached beneath her pillow for the slender eating knife. The knife was short and the blade dull, but it was the only weapon she had. Clutching the small knife like a dagger, she slipped from beneath the quilt's warmth and crept toward the night-darkened window.

Tap, tap, tap, it sounded like metal on glass.

Curious, she crept along the wall, trying to stay out of the window's sight, her bare feet silent on the cold stone floor. She reached the window and tried to peer out but the glass was mirrored by darkness, reflecting the hearth's feeble glow. Pressed to the wall, she waited, but the tapping did not return. Curiosity warred with caution...and curiosity won. She reached up and opened the latch. Throwing the window wide open, she stepped in front, the knife held at the ready.

Nothing.

The window framed a cloudy night, nothing but chilly darkness beyond her lonely tower.

A key rattled in the door to her prison.

The princess whirled, her heartbeat hammering. *Lady Sarah!* But then she realized it was too late for the lady. A chill of foreboding shivered down her spine. Jemma tightened her grip on the small knife, praying the key would not fit the lock. Barefoot and vulnerable in her night shift, she edged away from the door.

A scraping sound came from behind her.

A deadly chill gripped her. Feeling a predator's hard stare, she whirled to face the window.

A black thing crouched on the windowsill. Arms and legs bent like a spider, it grinned at her with a man's face!

A scream burst out of her.

The door banged open and someone grabbed her from behind. A soft cloth drenched in bitterness pressed against her face. She screamed but the cloth only pressed harder, muffling her outrage. Hairy arms held her tight, pressed against a man's broad chest. Jemma struggled, bucking against her assailant, but the man held her firm.

"That's it, princess, scream all you want, twill make the potion work all the faster."

Too late, she tried to hold her breath. A tingling numbness invaded her body. She tried to fight back, to slash at him with the knife, but her efforts grew feeble, the knife slipping from her fingers to clatter useless to the floor.

Laughter rumbled deep in her assailant's chest. "That's it princess, sleep tight. Where you're going, none will ever find you."

58

Liandra

Liandra swam in and out of darkness. Her mouth tasted bitter...and so did her heart. *Stewart,* she flinched away from that throbbing pain as if it were a white hot coal. Avoiding the worst hurt, her mind skittered to other matters, fastening on the princess of Navarre. A memory pierced her, the shocked look on the princess's sweet face. Another memory assailed her. *The fecund will inherit Erdhe.* A desperate need shivered through the queen, all the pieces falling into place. As the sovereign queen, Liandra needed Navarre's magic for the sake of her kingdom, for the sake of her unborn children, for her lost heir, for her very soul. Confined by silken sheets, she thrashed against her bonds, screaming commands. *"Bring us the magic! Give it to us!"*

More bitterness poured down her throat.

My son!

She welcomed the mind-numbing darkness, yet nightmares chased her into the depths. Someone tried to remove her royal rings, but she fought against them, screaming for the guards. Clutching her rings in tight fists, Liandra retreated back to her dreams, clinging to the fog of not-knowing, but the others intruded, prodding her with words. *Words, what do words matter when our only son is dead?* Fleeing the nightmare, she looked for Robert, needing the comfort of his arms, but when she turned upon the pillow, she found herself embracing his corpse, his dead lips pressed to hers.

Screams poured out of her.

Liandra woke screaming and they forced more bitterness down her throat.

She plunged back into a dense fog. At first she found it comforting, a place where reality could no longer harm her, but then she began to feel hunted. The feeling grew to a terrifying dread. She caught a sideway glimpse of a malformed creature made of inky darkness...and Liandra knew it hungered for her soul. Relentless in its pursuit, it bore a face that was both familiar and strange. *Eternal damnation,* the shadow scared her enough to face reality, but when she tried to wake, Liandra realized she was lost. The fog became a trap, a quicksand of the mind, slowing her thoughts, sapping her will, locking her in nightmares. She ran through a mirrored maze, a thousand versions of her own face staring back at her, each one bearing a different emotion. Terrified, accusing, desperate, a spectrum of emotions beat against her, all of them pushing her towards the dark hunter. In the blink of an eye, the images changed, showing the malformed creature. *She* became the shadow! Darkness stared back at her, and it wore her face. Liandra screamed, yet no one heard.

Locked in a maze of nightmares, it was weeping that pulled her back.

The sound of a woman weeping honest tears.

Clinging to the sound, Liandra struggled awake and found herself in the royal bed.

"Majesty, you must come back to us." Lady Sarah knelt by the bed, gripping the queen's hand, tears dampening the velvet quilt.

Liandra's stare roved her bedchamber, noting the black crape hung in mourning on the casement windows. Sorrow pierced her heart. The queen woke to a mother's grief, harsh and biting. "So...it's...true."

Her voice was a hoarse croak, yet Lady Sarah heard. "Majesty!" She gripped the queen's hand as if to anchor her in the present. "Majesty, stay with us! It's all coming undone. You are sorely needed."

"No...more...poppy." Her voice was hoarse with disuse.

"No, majesty, no more."

Liandra struggled to sit up, surprised by her weakness. Even her mind felt groggy, too tired to ask a myriad of questions. "How...long?"

"Nearly four weeks."

Four weeks, it seemed like the blink of an eye...it seemed like an eternity.

Her ladies-in-waiting came flocking, plying her with soup and tea. The queen let herself be pampered, slipping in and out of sleep. At first a few spoonfuls filled her stomach. Refusing more she fell asleep only to wake with a ravenous hunger. "We wish to rise."

They washed her, and combed her dark hair, and dressed her in a maroon gown of softest velvet. Helped from bed, she sat in a chair by the hearth, supping on onion soup, fresh-baked scones and slivers of trout. Her body still felt feeble but her mind sharpened like a knife to the whetstone. "Tell us of our son."

Lady Sarah bit her lip.

The queen was insistent. "Tell us."

Lady Sarah nodded, her voice soft with sorrow. "They say he died bravely, fighting to hold Eye Bridge."

So it was true, a part of her had hoped it was just an evil dream, yet this time she refused to flee the truth despite the pain. Binding her heart with iron bands, she chose to be the queen not the mother. "His body, do they bring it back to Pellanor?"

"Majesty, I do not know."

Liandra chewed the scone, but the taste had fled. She set the dish aside. "And what of his wife, the Princess Jordan?"

"Majesty, I do not know."

"And our court, what can you tell us of our court?"

Lady Sarah flinched away as if scalded.

Alarms sounded within the queen's mind. "When I woke, you said it was all coming undone. What is coming undone?"

Lady Sarah paled.

"You must tell us, for we are queen."

"Majesty, so many things have gone wrong." Lady Sarah shook her head, despair in her gaze.

"Tell us of our court."

The answer came with great reluctance. "Save for three of your most loyal lords, your courtiers no longer come calling to your chambers."

Ice impaled her heart. *A queen ignored is no longer a queen.* Stricken by a mother's grief, she'd imperiled her crown. Liandra gripped the arms of her chair, and then she remembered her royal rings. *Perhaps it was not a dream.* The queen's stare fixed on her friend. "We dreamt that someone sought to remove our royal rings?"

"Yes."

So it was true, they sought to steal her power. "Who dared?"

"Lord Canning, but even in your grief, you fought against him. Sir Durnheart evicted the craven from your chambers. He has not returned."

The last lord raised is the first to turn against us. Liandra tightened her grip on her rings. "Sir Durnheart shall be raised to a baron for his actions...and *Lord* Canning shall become deeply acquainted with our dungeons." The queen struggled to master her rage. "Now tell us of our loyal lords. Who can we count upon?"

"Sir Durnheart rarely leaves his post, even sleeping outside your chambers."

"Such staunch loyalty shall not be forgotten, and the others?"

"Lord Saddler comes calling every other day and Master Raddock haunts the outer chambers at random hours, always asking for you."

Her loyal goldsmith raised to a lord and her deputy shadowmaster. "So we retain the loyalty of coin and shadows. What of Lord Robert?" Liandra found herself hungry for any word of him.

Lady Sarah slumped. "Nothing, majesty."

Nothing, the word beat against her, raising nightmares. *If Robert has not come, then perhaps he too is dead.* Her heart quailed at the thought...but something inside her refused to believe it. *If he has not come, then we are surrounded by conspiracy.* The queen straightened in her chair. She would not yield her throne without a fight. "We need information and then we need to act. Summon Master Raddock to attend us." She glanced toward the nearest mirror, dismayed by the haggard women reflected in the glass. "But first we need to look like the queen. Attend us."

Her women surrounded her, plying their skills. The queen traded her soft velvet gown for shimmering silks of emerald green with a narrow waist and dagged sleeves lined with glittering cloth of gold. Her raven-black hair was teased into an elaborate confection, studded with diamonds and topped with a glittering crown. Jewels draped her neck, a great emerald dangling among her cleavage. But her face required the most work, carefully painted to erase years and mimic rosy health and a brimming vitality. The queen studied her reflection. Her women had accomplished much, yet the mirror was not entirely fooled. Liandra knew she would have to complete the illusion by dint of her own personality.

Lady Amy returned from the outer chamber. "Your deputy shadowmaster is here."

"Good, send him in. Lady Sarah, stay close, the rest of you are dismissed." The queen stood. Deliberately turning her back to the outer door, she faced the hearth, basking in the fire's warmth.

The queen heard the door open, and she heard him enter, and then she heard his footsteps pause. Summoning steel to her gaze, she turned in time to see a startled look dart across his face. Clearly he'd expected a bedridden woman, not a jewel bedecked queen. She extended her ringed hand. "We are pleased by your loyalty."

Never a courtier, yet he fell to his knee and kissed her royal ring. "Majesty, it is good to see you well!"

"We have been abed too long." She gestured for him to rise. "Past time we reclaimed our royal duties." The queen struck at the heart of the matter. "Tell us of our court."

The pug-faced shadowmaster told her what her ladies would not. "Majesty, your lords scramble to find an heir."

An icy dagger spiked her heart, yet she kept her face stone-still. "So they count us dead already."

"No, but they fear a war instead of a smooth succession."

Stiff backed, she stared at him. "The naming of an heir remains the royal prerogative of the ruling monarch."

"True, but with Prince Stewart dead, and you taken to your bed, they feared an empty throne."

"They bury us before we have died."

"Majesty," exasperation rode his voice, "if you will not name an heir, then you must get one." He pulled a rolled parchment from the pocket of his robe. "I've drawn up the terms of ransom. You need only sign it and I will see it sent by the swiftest courier."

"Ransom?"

"Yes, for the Princess Jemma. If you will not name an heir, then you need the magic of Navarre to get one. Surely the king of Navarre will lend his magic to ransom his daughter."

"Ransom?" Her mind stumbled on the word.

He looked at her as if she'd lost her wits. "Yes, you ordered the princess arrested, demanding Navarre relinquish its fertility magic."

The queen remembered confronting the princess, but *ransom?* It seemed such a vile and repugnant measure, yet the game of thrones was not for the faint of heart.

Her shadowmaster pulled a second scroll from his pockets. "And this is a writ for her death."

"Her *death?*"

"As queen you can rescind the order at any time, but by signing it Navarre will know you are serious. Only if they believe your intent will they pay the ransom."

Events were galloping widely out of control. She'd been locked in mourning for far too long.

Her shadowmaster set both scrolls on her desk. Dipping a quill in black ink he turned, extending it toward her. "Your signature, majesty, and I will see your will done."

She stared at the quill, shocked that it had come to this.

When she hesitated, his voice became a goad. "Majesty, you dare not show weakness."

Weakness, his words held a kernel of truth, yet his proposal seemed too vile. As if in a trance, the queen found herself walking towards him. Accepting the quill, she sat at the desk. Smoothing the parchment flat, she intended to read both documents, but the words swam before her eyes. *How had it come to this, ransoming friends and threatening allies?* Revulsion shivered through her. *This was not her way, this was not right...this was Darkness come calling.* She stared at her deputy shadowmaster, realizing how large his hands were, a hulking brute beneath black robes. Setting the quill aside, she stalled with a question. "What of our Lord Highgate?"

"He remains in Lingard."

"But we summoned him home."

Master Raddock shrugged, a hint of annoyance creeping into his voice. "Then he has not arrived."

His words did not ring true. "And what of our Lord Sheriff?"

"He has not been seen."

"But we ordered you to find him."

"Shadowmen combed the city searching for him, but he was not found." Leaning on the desk, he picked up the quill, pressing it into her hand. "Majesty, your heir is of paramount importance. The Rose Throne must be secure. If you will not name an heir then you must get one. Let me help you. Merely sign the documents and I will see your will done."

She stared at the quill as if it were a viper. *Merely sign the documents and her soul will be forever damned.* Liandra recalled the malformed creature in her dreams...her face on the shadow. Stifling a gasp, she saw her deputy shadowmaster in a new light. *Not a loyal lord, but a dire threat.* She took the quill from his hand. "You are right, the crown must be secure, but we grow weary. Leave these for us to sign. We shall read them tonight and then sign them on the morrow."

For half a heartbeat, she thought he would protest, but instead he bowed towards her, "As you wish," and strode from the royal chamber.

The door closed and the queen felt a small measure of relief.

Lady Sarah hovered at the inner doorway.

The queen gestured for her. "Come."

Lady Sarah crossed the room, her face pale. "Majesty, you aren't really going to sign those?"

The queen stared at the coiled scrolls. "This was a trap." Standing, Liandra carried the offending documents to the hearth. Placing them deep in the fire's heart, she watched the parchments curl to black, their treachery consigned to smoke. "We suspect the tentacles of this trap reach far beyond our disloyal shadowmaster. Master Raddock has been corrupted. Our loyal lords are missing and our enemies draw close. We are besieged with threat."

Lady Sarah's breath caught. "Master Raddock a traitor?" She sank to the chair. "Will you order him arrested?"

"Not yet. We dare not tip off our enemy before we muster our own offense."

"What will you do?"

"First tell me of the princess." Liandra dreaded to ask, yet she needed to know.

Lady Sarah was hesitant. "You ordered her sent to the dungeons."

To the dungeons, so that foul memory was true. In her deepest grief, she'd struck at a dear friend, another bitter mistake.

"But we knew you did not mean it."

Hope kindled within the queen.

"We spirited her away to a remote part of the castle."

"We?"

"Myself, Lady Amy, and Sir Durnheart."

She gave her friend a reassuring smile. "You three have done your queen a great service, sparing her from a grievous mistake." Liandra stood and began to pace, plans churning in her mind. "The princess must be released and safely spirited back to Navarre, removing an important piece from the chess game. Once returned to Navarre, she cannot be used against us."

"Majesty."

"But her escort must be loyal, her safety is dear to us."

"Majesty," the anguish of her friend's voice pierced her musing, "the princess is missing!"

"Missing?" Fear spiked the queen.

"I've been taking her food at night. I swear no one knew save the three of us, but someone must have followed. When I went to her room the other night, she was gone!"

A chill gripped the queen. "Then our enemy has her."

"But who is the enemy?"

That was the true question. A question she did not yet have an answer for. It troubled her more than she cared to admit that the princess, the sheriff, and Lord Robert were all mysteriously missing, more proof she played against a dangerous foe. But of one thing, the queen was certain. "We must seize the offensive before we are ringed with enemies." She glanced at the window, but the light was already fading, another day lost. "On the morrow, we shall don armor and ride out into our city." Plots within plots, her mind spun a battle plan of details. "We shall ride out on the pretext of inspecting the city walls, but in truth, we must be seen by our people. They must know we are their sovereign queen. With the people securely behind us, we will then deal with our disloyal lords and take back our court." Her gaze fixed on Lady Sarah. "Discreet messages must be sent to our stable master so that our white stallion is ready for us at noon, bejeweled and beribboned for a stately ride. Our armor must be polished to a silvery shine and Sir Durnheart must assemble an honor guard of loyal men. We must have trumpets and royal banners...yet the preparations must be made with the utmost secrecy. Assemble the others, for we have much to plan." A fresh resolve rippled through her. The queen stood within the light of the hearth, eager for the battle to commence. The Rose Throne was hers, and by all the gods, none would take it from her. "On the morrow, we shall take the offensive, and flush our true enemy into the light."

59

The Priestess

The third night finally arrived. Anxious to make her escape, yet the Priestess took her time preparing. Soaking in a great copper tub set before the blazing hearth, she indulged in a last luxury. Small purple buds floated in the water, adding the soothing scent of lavender to the rising steam. Her handmaidens washed and combed her long raven hair. Clean and scented, the Priestess rose from the water, shedding droplets across the carpet like a spring rain. Still wet, she reached for the great moonstone necklace, settling the silver chain around her neck, needing to feel the gemstone against her skin. A potent magic throbbed between her breasts like a second heartbeat. A smile lit her face, knowing the favor of the Dark Lord was still hers, a secret weapon hidden from the Mordant.

Her handmaidens dried her with soft towels and then plaited her hair into rings and added kohl and crushed amethyst to accentuate her eyes. Painted and coiffed, they helped her dress. The Priestess yearned for her riding leathers and knee-high boots, but the plan dictated she dress as a courtesan, so she chose a diaphanous confection of purple silk with a long slit reaching to mid thigh. The slit offered a tempting tease to male eyes, but in truth it gave her ease of movement. When the time came, the slit would allow her to straddle a horse, an important practicality hidden beneath allure.

The Priestess stared into the mirror, satisfied with the kohl-eyed seductress who stared back. She merely needed her serpentine armbands to complete the hidden sting of the ensemble. The last of her poisons, she kept both close at hand, the armbands and ring sitting on a table near the tub, gold and enamel gleaming in the firelight.

The outer door banged open.

Startled, the Priestess and her women drew back.

The Mordant and two dark-clad assassins strode into her chambers. "Good, you're dressed." His stare snapped across her without any sign of interest.

The Priestess reached for an icy calm. "Why do you invade my privacy?"

"You have no privacy in my house." The Mordant wore the purple and gold of the Prince of Ur. "Now come, I have something to show you."

She tried to delay. "I'm preparing for Lord Ferdic."

"He can wait. Now come."

It was a command not a request. Her poisoned armbands sat coiled upon the table, a lethal weapon, yet she dared not draw attention to them.

Reluctant, she followed the Mordant out into the hallway. The two assassins trailed close on her heels. The Mordant strode ahead with an implacable stride, leading her down the hallway, down the marbled stairs, and back towards the wine cellar.

"The wine cellar?"

"You'll see."

They descended the stairs to the small wine cellar. A lounging guard snapped to attention.

"Open it."

The guard moved to an enormous wine barrel inset in the wall. He did something with the tap, and then the front of the barrel swung open, revealing a hidden door. Opening the door, he released the fetid stench of a dungeon. The Priestess froze, fearing a trap.

The Mordant stepped through the doorway. "Come."

Assassins hovered at her back, herding her forward.

She had no choice but to follow.

The Priestess stepped through the wine barrel into a dungeon. Torchlight sputtered in the dank gloom. Cells lined the walls, hopeless faces pressed against iron bars. The dungeon reeked of piss and fear. Somewhere a child sobbed.

"Come."

A guard opened a second ironbound door.

She followed the Mordant down the rough-cut stairs. An earthly chill embraced her. Torchlight glittered below. The stairs opened onto a vaulted chamber, shadows lurking in the corners. A great pentacle was inscribed across the floor, braziers glowing at the five points. *A chapel to Darkness,* she felt the thrum of power.

A single sacrifice dripped blood upon the pentacle. Handcuffed, wearing nothing but a soiled loincloth, he dangled from chains, his toes barely touching the stone floor. Partially flayed, his body was crisscrossed with welts, burns and cuts, a litany of torture writ upon his skin. Dark-haired, he moaned, his face swollen, one eye-socket empty and weeping gore.

Steffan! She screamed his name within her mind. So beaten, she barely recognized his handsome face. Stifling a gasp, the Priestess struggled to appear icy-calm. Fingernails piercing her palms, she stood statue-still.

The Mordant walked towards his victim. "I found this youngling in my city."

The Priestess kept her gaze locked on Steffan, counting every cut, every wound, every injury.

The Mordant circled Steffan as if studying a work of art. "This youngling reeks of Darkness," the Mordant's nostril's flared wide, "yet he did not come and abase himself before me. He did not come to offer homage."

Steffan's handsome face was ruined, his body broken beyond repair, she quailed to see him so.

"Instead, the youngling had the effrontery to spy on me. So I followed his Dark scent. I found your paramour-champion cowering like a cockroach in a flea-ridden inn." The Mordant stopped circling, his gaze swiveling back to her. "I looked into his eyes and delved his soul. Do you know what I found?"

The Priestess kept her stare fixed on Steffan, mourning his pain.

"I gazed into his soul and I found *your* name writ upon it."

Her name, *her* fault.

The Mordant strode towards her, blocking her view. He grabbed her chin, lifting her face, forcing her to meet his gaze. His stare thundered into her. "You sought to escape your liege lord." Rage licked his voice. "You, a mere woman, sought to thwart the oldest harlequin."

She longed to shred his face with her fingernails, to rip out his eyes and gouge his skin, but she had no poison, and her magic was no match for his. Swallowing her rage, she fought to keep her face a stone mask, refusing to answer.

"There will be no escape." His gaze drilled into her. "You shall serve for as long as you are useful." His hand slid down to her throat. "Even unto eternity." His grip tightened with cruel intent. "Do you understand?"

"You dared to harm a Dedicate."

The Mordant barked a laugh. "There is nothing I will not dare. That is why *I* am the oldest, the strongest, the one destined to rule. That is why *you* serve." His grip tightened. "Do you understand?"

"Yes."

"Louder." Locked in a choking hold, the Mordant forced her to her knees.

Barely able to draw breath, yet the Priestess knew not to fight back. She choked out an answer. "Yes."

His grip tightened.

Her vision began to darken.

She felt death draw near. Just when she thought she would succumb, he released her.

Gasping for life, the Priestess rocked back on her heals. Her throat ached from his chokehold. She remained on her knees, drawing deep breaths, yet she refused to bow her head, offering a subtle defiance. She stared at him, her hatred etched deep in her soul.

For the longest time, he stared at her, as if studying an insect beneath his boot.

She kept her face stone-still, her gaze fixed on the Great Wyrm embroidered on his surcoat. Tension coiled between them. She thought he would strike her, but instead he strode past, his boots ringing on stone. "Lord Ferdic will be here within the hour." His voice was dismissive. "You will service him in your chambers. And if he desires your handmaidens, they will serve as well. Do not disappoint."

She heard his boot steps climb the stairs, but the door did not close. Remaining on her knees, she listened for his arrogant stride. When he did not return, she rushed to Steffan.

Assassins kept watch from the shadows, but they did not interfere.

Drawing close to him, a sob escaped her, stricken by his ruined body. *"Beloved."* He reeked of blood and sweat and seared flesh, all the scents of torture. Needing to touch him, trying not to hurt him, she stroked his face with a feather-soft caress.

One blue eye flickered open. He stared at her, confusion and pain melting to astonishment. *"Cereus!* Is it really you?"

"I'm here, beloved."

Anguish filled his face, "I tried to fight him but..."

"Shhhhhh." Her finger caressed his bruised and battered lips. "It will be all right." She sought to calm him, to soothe him. "I can take away the pain. I can make it better." His body was broken beyond repair, his life essence nearly dwindled to nothing. The Priestess quelled her own rage, her own sorrow, focusing on his needs. "Think of me, think of you and me, lovers entwined forever." She kissed him softly on the lips, tenderly at first. Her kisses deepened. She worked her magic upon him. Enthralling him with seduction, she took away his pain, trading agony for pleasure and passion. Steffan kissed her back. Wakened by her touch, his body shook with ardor. He strained towards

her, yet she felt his life force waver, growing threadbare-thin. There was only one way to save him. *"Remember me! Remember us!"* She kissed him deeply. Enfolding him with passion, she used her succubus powers, draining the last of his life force.

Tears streaked her face...and then it was done.

He hung lifeless from the chains.

Dead, yet a smile graced his battered face, a victory against the Mordant.

She took one last look, memorizing every wound inflicted on his body, a bitter debt to repay, and then she turned and walked away. Her assassin guards followed like relentless shadows.

The Priestess refused to shed anymore tears lest she give the Mordant any satisfaction. Walking with regal poise, she crossed the sanctum, putting on a stone-hearted face. She nearly reached the stairs when she heard it.

Chains rattled behind.

A flare of Dark power trickled down her back.

"Cer...eeee...us!"

She turned. Steffan's corpse still dangled from the chains, but his face was smiling. His eyes glowed bright red like twin lanterns lit by Hell. *"I...will...find...you!"* His words whispered through the chamber, a promise from beyond the grave. Before she could respond, the red light of his eyes flared bright as oil-soaked torches...and then the light was gone, snuffed out by Darkness. The power withdrew. Nothing but a butchered corpse remained, dangling from the chains like battered meat...yet she knew with certainty that Steffan would live again, granted a new life by the Dark Lord.

"In another lifetime," she whispered the words like a promise.

Turning her back on the corpse, she climbed the stairs, passing through the dungeon and into the manse. In the marbled hallway, the Mordant spoke with Bishop Borgan, but neither man looked her way, as if she were beneath notice. The Priestess climbed the stairs as if in a trance. Her assassin-jailors trailed her to the door of her suite but they did not follow inside.

"Lock the door and let no one enter."

Her handmaidens gasped to see her, but she ignored their entreaties.

"Lock the door and tell me when Lord Ferdic arrives. We'll be receiving him here tonight."

The Priestess paused long enough to don her serpentine armbands and ring. Gold glittered on her forearms, coiled like serpents, the poison needles carefully hidden beneath enameled scales. Armed with poison once more, she retreated to her bedroom. Locking the door, she removed the silver scrying bowl from her cedar chest. The Priestess dared not scry on the Mordant, but she could watch the others. She found herself keenly interested in the fat bishop and the dark-clad assassins. Once woken, a woman's hatred was a dangerous scourge. Plots within plots, she'd find a way to exact vengeance for Steffan...for a woman's broken heart never forgets...and never forgives.

60

Liandra

The queen traded silk for steel. Her women worked in silence, for there was something solemn about donning armor, a ceremony of deadly intent. Liandra much preferred the comfort of glamorous silk, but during the Flame War she'd come to appreciate the value of burnished steel. Polished to a slivery glow, she'd discovered that armor multiplied a monarch's ability to inspire steadfast courage and loyalty. Clad in armor, she'd stood atop her castle ramparts, a beacon against doubt, a relentless hope against hard odds. She'd won the Flame War and now she needed to reclaim her people and her court, a battle of wits and image against a shadowy foe. Anger brewed within her, bolstered by steel. Her courtiers sought to ignore their sovereign monarch, such a travesty could not be allowed. She would have their fealty or their heads. Trading silk for steel, she donned the image of an invincible queen.

Her women fluttered around, tightening greaves and gorget. A gold-hilted short sword was buckled to her side, an emerald cloak affixed to her shoulders. Liandra studied herself in the mirror. Glimmering glorious in reflected light, her silver armor melded to her curves, enhancing her womanly form, a warrior queen once more.

"Will you have the helm, majesty?"

The crowned helm was tempting, another image of royalty, but Liandra preferred her people to see her face and her dark mane of lustrous hair. "No, we'll have nothing come between us and our people."

"Then, majesty, you are ready." Lady Sarah dropped to a deep curtsy, a puddle of bright silk. "You are magnificent."

Her women all dropped to curtsies, admiration mirrored on their faces.

Touched by their devotion, the queen gestured for them to rise. "You have all done well. Be of good cheer, for we ride not to war but to purposeful image." Liandra cast a parting glance in the mirror. She needed to reassert her power and then find those who were missing. She'd spent too long mired in grief.

Sir Durnheart strode into her chamber. A handsome hero in armor, the hilt of his blue steel sword rearing over his right shoulder, he dropped to one knee. "Majesty, you are a vision."

His reaction pleased her. "Our knight protector, you are as gallant as you are loyal." She gestured for him to rise. "Is everything prepared?"

"Ten loyal guards stand ready outside your chamber. Another twenty will be waiting in the courtyard with the horses."

"Good. We'll ride north through the city to the outer gate, circle the wall, and return from the south. The more people who see us the better. On our return to the castle, we'll keep all our guards in attendance till our disloyal lords are dealt with. Those who will not swear fealty will face the dungeon or the headsman's axe."

"Yes, majesty." He saluted, his gauntleted fist pressed to his silvery breastplate.

"Then let us begin." The queen strode from her solar to the outer antechamber.

Ten guardsmen snapped to attention, their burnished breastplates embossed with twin roses.

Behind her, Sir Durnheart snapped an order. "Salute the queen!"

The guardsmen drew their swords and held them aloft, crossing them in a ringing archway.

Liandra gave the guardsmen a gracious smile, appreciating their gallant gesture. She marched beneath the crossed swords, Sir Durnheart following behind. Her smile deepened, enjoying the martial splendor.

Armor and swords held their own powerful mystique, adding a swagger to her step. The queen found herself taking longer strides than she ever would in jewels and silks. She pondered the difference, enjoying the boldness, wondering if armor made men rash as well as bold.

Liandra led her loyal men down the long marbled hallway, a clank of arms and armor following behind. Her forebears stared down from gilded frames, paintings of her royal ancestors keeping watch on the castle. She wondered if her ancestors would be scandalized to see a queen in armor, yet Liandra would wield any image to protect her throne.

A clatter of footsteps approached up the long marble stairs.

Master Raddock appeared, huffing from the long climb, a bevy of guards in emerald tabards following in his wake. "Majesty, you must return to your chambers." Her dark-robed shadowmaster blocked the way forward.

"*Must* is not a word used with princes." The queen's anger sparked. "We know what you've done. Drop to your knees and swear fealty or pay the traitor's price."

He gave her a surly smile. "Madam, it is you who do not understand. Return to your chambers at once."

"*Guards!*" The queen's voice barked with command. "Arrest this traitor and escort him to the dungeons."

Swords whispered from scabbards. A pair of emerald-cloaked guards stepped from behind the queen, their swords leveled at the shadowmaster's heart. "You heard the queen, yield or die."

Raddock flashed a sinister smile. "It is you who will die!" He made a hand gesture and a pair of soldiers in emerald tabards leaped from behind him. Swords drawn, they engaged the queen's guards. Steel clanged against steel in the marble hallway as men fought for their very lives.

The queen stared, shocked by the fighting.

Sir Durnheart yelled, "Protect the queen!" He gripped her arm, pulling her backward, while more of her guards rushed to join the fray.

Shouting above the clamor, the queen sought to end the conflict. "Lay down your arms and stop this madness! Surrender and you will be spared!" but her words had no effect. More soldiers in emerald tabards forced their way up the stairs. Among them were short men garbed all in black. The queen watched horrified as the dark-clad men darted among the clashing soldiers, wielding knives and slashing hamstrings. The marbled hallway became a bitter battlefield, blood spraying the gilded walls.

Sir Durnheart pulled her backward, one gauntleted hand gripping her forearm, the other holding his blue steel sword at the ready. "Fall back! Protect the queen!"

Outnumbered, her loyal guards died screaming before the queen's very eyes, consumed by the onslaught.

When only two loyal guards remained, Sir Durnheart released her. "An honor to serve you, majesty." He gave her a heartfelt look revealing a smolder of unspoken passion.

His look pierced her heart, for she'd never suspected.

Sir Durnheart stepped close, his voice a fervent whisper. "I'll hold them as long as I can." Turning, he strode towards the onslaught. "*Run,* majesty!"

As the last guards died, Sir Durnheart leaped forward, unleashing his blue steel sword.

Liandra knew she should run, knew she should seek the safety of the hidden passageways, but she could not bear to leave him. Unable to turn away, her gaze locked on her gallant knight, praying for him to prevail.

"*For the Queen!*" Roaring his battle cry, Sir Durnheart attacked. The swing of his blue sword spanned the width of the hallway, holding the enemy at bay. He fought three at once, slicing heads from bodies and arms from shoulders with a single stroke of his sapphire blade. Blood fountained and men screamed, releasing the stink of death. The blue blade became a blur. Swords shattered and chainmail cut like leather. Sir Durnheart fought like a whirlwind, he fought like a champion. None could stand in his path. The enemy fell before him like wheat before the scythe, dying beneath the blue steel sword. Cut and parry, he pushed the traitors back, forcing them all the way to the marbled stairs. Victory was within his grasp.

And then the clangor suddenly stopped.

Sir Durnheart teetered at the top of the stairs.

For half a heartbeat, Liandra feared he was wounded, but then he turned towards her, elation lighting his handsome face. "We won!"

Relief rushed through her. She stepped towards him. "Our champion!" Corpses littered the hallway, yet she threaded a way through them, needing to be certain he was not wounded. "Are you hurt?" She searched his face.

"Not a scratch." A grin beamed across his handsome face. He hefted his sword aloft. "They were no match for blue steel."

"Blue steel in the hands of a champion." Her golds were never better spent. "You saved us. You were magnificent!"

He hefted his blue steel sword. "You gave me a magnificent blade."

For half a heartbeat, their stares locked, sharing the elated of victory...but then the ugly truth of the battle struck the queen. Betrayed by her shadowmaster, ambushed in her own castle, Liandra surveyed the dead and dying. "And Raddock? Where is the turned-cloak traitor?" She did not see the dark-robed shadowmaster among the dead. *All the dead wear emerald green,* the swift brutality of the battle remained a shock. "We did not expect an open rebellion." And then she spied one of the dark-clad men lying dead among the corpses. "Our enemy is bolder than we thought." The hallway stank of death and dying. Corpses stared at her with accusing eyes. This battle seemed her fault, a checkmate she should have foreseen, a trap she should have avoided.

Sir Durnheart hovered protectively at her side. Blood dripped from his blue steel sword, yet his voice was tender with concern. "Majesty, you should return to your chambers while I seek more loyal swords."

She stared at the dead as if they held an unplumbed riddle.

"Come," he sheparded her back towards her chambers.

They nearly reached the door when a voice rang out. "*Stop!*"

The queen turned to find Raddock standing at the top of the stairs with six of the dark-clad men at his back.

"So the traitor returns." The queen faced him across a hallway strewn with death. "It seems you are a coward as well as a betrayer."

"I serve a higher power."

"*A higher power?*" His words made no sense, yet she sought to draw him out.

He strode towards her, his hands held wide in supplication, yet his a face was a surly threat. The dark-clad men kept pace with Raddock, staying close like bodyguards, yet they bore no swords, only knives sheathed at their belts. "I did not want to go to him, but you insisted."

"*Him?*"

"I found power in his gaze."

Sir Durnheart raised his blue steel sword. "Come no closer lest you seek death."

Raddock came to a stop three sword-lengths away, but a sneer rode his thuggish face. "You think a sword makes you powerful? You've no idea what true power is."

The queen gave him a scathing look. "Who is this enemy you serve?"

Footsteps rang on the marble floor.

Raddock's sneer evaporated, his dark eyes betraying a flicker of fear. "See for yourself." Stepping aside, he bowed low, opening a pathway down the hall.

A lone man approached. Boot steps rang on marble as he strode amongst the dead. His hooded cowl was drawn forward, hiding his face with darkness. Cloaked from head to toe in deepest black, he appeared as a faceless silhouette, yet he conveyed a sense of power and menace, his floor-length cloak swirling around him like an embracing shadow.

A sense of foreboding slithered down the queen's back.

Beside her, Sir Durnheart stiffened, his blue sword raised as a warning and a threat.

The cloaked stranger stopped five sword-lengths away. Pale hands bejeweled with rings reached up to draw back the hooded cowl.

A gasp escaped the queen. "*You!*"

"Checkmate." The Prince of Ur had traded imperial purple for darkest black. A subtle smile rode his ruddy lips but his ice-blue eyes were implacable. "I told you I would win the last game."

The queen knew better than to bandy words with a viper. "*Kill him!*"

Sir Durnheart leaped to the attack.

The black-clad men moved faster. Lightning-quick, they raised narrow tubes to their mouths and blew.

Sir Durnheart gasped. Twisting in mid air, he crumpled to the floor, armor clattering against cold marble. Her knight fell well short of the prince, his blue steel sword falling useless from his gauntleted hand. Groaning, Sir Durnheart turned towards her. His gaze sought hers, his eyes stricken with pain. Blood frothed at his mouth, darts riddling his throat and face. "*Run!*"

His dying word jolted her from shock. Liandra leaped for the door.

She rushed inside her solar, slamming the sturdy oak door behind her. Her hands shook as she rammed home the iron bolt. Her heartbeat hammering, she backed away from the door, shocked by the enemy, shocked by Sir Durnheart's death.

"*Majesty!*" a plaintive whisper at her back.

The queen whirled.

A dark-clad stranger held Lady Sarah to his chest, a knife threatening at her throat.

Another ambush, two of her women were slumped on the floor, puddles of unmoving silk. The others cowered on the far side of her solar, fear on their faces.

The queen gasped. "*How?*"

Lady Sarah answered. "He came in through the window."

The casement window stood open, yet her solar was at the top of the tower. The answer made no sense.

The dark-clad intruder spoke. "Unbolt the door or she dies."

"Don't hurt her." The queen sidled away from the door, yearning for the safety of the castle's hidden passageways.

Lady Sarah stifled a gasp, a drop of blood at her throat.

"Last chance, unbolt the door or she dies."

"Don't harm her." The queen could not risk her friend's life. Moving back to the door, she drew the heavy bolt and then stepped away.

The door eased open and four black-clad men poured in. Short in stature, yet they moved like liquid shadows. They moved like *assassins*. A shiver raced down the queen's spine. How little she knew this enemy.

The dark-robed prince strode into her chambers. Raddock, the traitor-coward, lurked at his back like a surly shadow.

At first, the prince did not even bother to look at her, as if she was insignificant. His ice-blue gaze roved the chamber, lingering for a moment on her desk. "Did you sign the documents?"

"What?" For a nonce, the queen was confused, her mind fixed on death and swords...but then she remembered the ransom note and the death sentence. "*You?*"

He finally deigned to look at her, a smirk in his gaze.

"Why?"

"To give you a chance to willingly darken your soul."

Her soul, his answer chilled her, yet it also evoked a glimmer of stubborn pride. "We burnt them. Navarre is our staunch ally. You shall not turn us against the seaside kingdom."

He stared at her, as if his ice-blue gaze could pluck the truth from her mind. "No, you did not sign them." A predator's smile curled his lips. "Pity. I would have enjoyed raping your soul."

His stare released her.

Liandra staggered back a step, a sudden headache threatened at the back of her eyes.

"It matters not in the end. Bishop Borgan does an excellent imitation of your signature. I doubt the king of Navarre will note the difference." His smile broadened. "No one else has."

The scope of the plot staggered her. "King Ivor will not believe it."

"The ransom note?" the prince shrugged, "Perhaps not, but his daughter's head in a basket will surely prod him to action."

The breath hissed out of her. "You would not dare!"

"Your puny mind cannot fathom the extent of my dare." He looked at her as if she were an insect beneath his boot. "Don't worry, everything will be done in your name." His smile deepened. "A royal execution ordered by the Queen of Lanverness."

"*Why?*" The question hissed out of her.

"Because you dared to rule." His gaze turned knife-sharp, his smile raw with hatred. "I shall heap a memory of hate and horror upon your name such that people will forever loathe the rule of a queen. History shall remember you as a woman driven by her empty womb, a bloody-handed queen who ran amok with power, lusting for more. Your name shall be lasting proof that men should forever hold dominion over women."

"So it was you all along!"

"Now you begin to understand the magnitude of the game."

"You sullied our name with lies!"

"I am the Prince Deceiver."

"Why?"

"For the Great Dark Divide." He seemed to relish her confusion. "The Dark Lord sows hatred by three great commandments, divide by sex, divide by beliefs, and divide by race. First among these is divide by sex, for by pitting men against women it sunders mortals nearly in half, the greatest single divide. Sowing simple deceits, the Great Divide drives people to commit acts of atrocity for no greater reason than "difference." By invoking a Great Divide, I exult the power of the Dark Lord, perpetuating his will." Shadows coalesced around the prince. He seemed to grow in stature, his voice becoming magnified, a terrible vision of dark dominance. "By invoking a Divide, I work my will upon Erdhe, forever changing the past, the present, and the future! By invoking a Divide, I become a *god*." His gaze transfixed her, a fathomless stare laden with Darkness. "Kneel, woman, for in me you see the true power of Darkness made manifest."

The truth struck like a fist to her stomach. *"The Mordant!"*

"Invoking my True Name shall not avail you."

"But why meddle with my kingdom when you have an army great enough to conquer Erdhe?"

A sneer rode his lips. "Killing is easy. Taking a life pleases the Dark Lord but it garners the least of his favors. Others wield swords, while I wield lies, rewriting the past, corrupting the present, twisting the future." He loomed above her, a terrible vision of cruelty. "*Kneel*, woman, for you are in the presence of a god."

She felt compelled to kneel, to cower before him...but something in her spirit rebelled. Liandra balled her hands into fists. Fingernails driving into her palms, she dared to stand erect, lifting her stare to his. "We shall never kneel to you...for we are a queen."

His hand lashed out, striking her face.

The blow knocked her to her knees.

"Woman! You are nothing!"

Pain ripped through her, as if a wild beast clawed at her stomach. Liandra looked down, expecting to see a slavering wolf feasting on her insides, but she saw nothing. The pain intensified. Crumpling to the floor, she sought to stifle a scream, but it burst out of her. The pain turned to agony, as if she were being ripped apart. She felt teeth ripping at her skin, strong jaws gnawing on her bones. Her sweat ran like a river. Liandra writhed upon the floor, clutching her midsection, screaming in agony.

The pain stopped.

Her heart thundered, afraid to move. Sopping with sweat, she shuddered upon the floor. *No blood,* she stared at herself, surprised to be whole and alive.

"I'll not kill you...yet." The Mordant's voice was smooth as velvet. "Far better to let you witness the sullying of your name and the corruption of your legacy, a torture befitting an arrogant woman who dares to call herself a queen." The Mordant snapped his gaze to one of the dark-clad assassins. "Dolf, Scarlin, with me, the rest of you keep watch till sleep claims the castle. If the queen gives you any trouble, start killing her women." The Mordant strode from her chamber, the traitor and the two assassins on his heels.

The queen lay on the floor, sundered by all that had happened, admonishing herself for so many mistakes. *Checkmated by the enemy.* She hadn't expected bloodshed in her halls...she hadn't expected *the Mordant.* Shivering, she made the hand sign against evil, yet it brought her no comfort. Liandra longed to disbelieve, to imagine any other foe, but the proof was too convincing, too devastating. *The Mordant,* her mind floundered on his name, a legendary nightmare come calling. How could a mere mortal hope to best the Mordant? She shuddered, stricken by the deaths of Sir Durnheart and her loyal guardsmen. And then she remembered the apothecary-monk burnt by fire...and the monk brutally beheaded in her very castle. She gasped at the depth of his plotting, how his schemes had burrowed like tentacles into her kingdom, and she had not known. *She had not known,* yet something he said came back to her. *Till the castle sleeps,* her mind fastened on the phrase like a light in the dark. If he needed to wait till everyone slept, it meant he did not own her castle...not yet. It meant there was still hope.

The queen stood. "We need to see to our women."

A dark-haired assassin glided towards her.

She stiffened, remaining statue-still, uncertain of his intentions.

He snatched her ceremonial sword from its sheath and then gestured the queen towards her women.

Liandra went to them, but she kept a watchful gaze on the assassins. Determined to grasp at any hope, she would bide her time. She would wait and she would watch, spinning her own plots. A smile flickered across her face, recalling how she'd defeated the Mordant at chess. *He can be beaten.* The memory offered only the faintest hope, yet she clung to it. Liandra vowed to all the gods that somehow she would find a way to foil the Mordant...or die trying.

61

The Mordant

The Mordant sent the traitor and two of his assassins to clear the throne room. Cloaked in black, he waited in the shadows, fondling the malachite coin. Evicted guards dribbled from the throne room casting curious glances his way but none uttered a word in protest. The palace roiled with confusing rumors. Some whispered the queen was dead. Others swore a brutal assassination attempt had been foiled leaving the queen in hiding and the royal tower bloody. Everyone knew the knight protector was slain, a fact that seemed to lend truth to both rumors. The Mordant smiled. Listening from the shadows, he sipped the rumors like a fine wine, savoring the confusion. Instead of danger, the chaos created opportunities. Most palace guards did not know what to believe or whom to fight, so they obeyed the first authoritarian figure that came their way. In this, as in other things, the traitor served his purpose.

Raddock and the two assassins emerged from the throne room. "All clear."

Indulging a whim, the Mordant entered the throne room alone.

So this is the throne room of the Rose Queen. Corbelled vaults of glistening white stone soared overhead, the side walls studded with diamond-paned windows reaching from the checkerboard floor to the vaulted ceiling. Gold fretwork embellished the windows with roses, swords and scrolls. Braziers stood between the windows, standing guard against any shadows. Sunlight poured through the windows, filling the throne room with a glittering brightness, yet the abundant Light could not hold sway against Darkness. The Mordant strode the length of the chamber, his dark cloak sweeping across the checkerboard floor like a stealthy conqueror. He found the throne room shockingly small and mundane compared to his great basilica in the north. The architecture bespoke wealth rather than power, the embellishments simpering rather than fearful...yet he liked the checkerboard floor. Black squares set against white, as if all of Erdhe were nothing more than a game board. The illusion amused him. The Mordant crossed the board to mount the dais. A confection of gold roses, the Rose Throne was far too feminine for his tastes. He'd have it melted down and design another. Perhaps he'd order a new throne carved from a massive black crystal. He'd heard whispers of a wondrous new discovery across the Western Sea in the deep mines of the Tarmack Mountains. Smoky quartz crystals the size of a plow horse, he'd send his MerChanters to fetch one. He imagined a throne carved from a single smoky crystal, something dark and imposing, massive and powerful, befitting an immortal emperor.

Cloaked in black, the Mordant sat upon the Rose Throne contemplating the Great Dark Dance.

The sunlight dimmed to gloom. Rain pelted the diamond-paned windows, streaking tears down the glass as if the heavens wept. *And well they should,* for all of Erdhe was nearly his.

How easily all of his enemies fell before him. The monks in Pellanor were dead, charred by their own fireball. The Rose court fell prey to seduction and corruption, enacting laws and taxations penned by the Mordant. The queen foolishly allowed herself to be captured rather than killed, becoming a pawn in the game, a puppet awaiting fresh strings. The princess of Navarre had proved an unexpected boon, another pawn awaiting execution, an enticing sacrifice that would forever damn the queen in the eyes of Erdhe. In the north, the Dark Sword was in play, yielding a cunning revenge, while his armies poured from Raven Pass, poised to conquer the south. His only setback was the fall of the Dark Citadel, a loss he still did not understand. A surprise attack by the upstart knights, he'd reclaim the Citadel once the south was secured.

He imagined the map of Erdhe in his mind, every kingdom bearing his stamp.

Soon all of his enemies would bow before him.

In the meantime, he had histories to rewrite and a future to corrupt.

He'd dangle the queen in front of her people, letting her garner the blame for the pain and chaos that was to come. The Mordant smiled like a hungry serpent, enjoying the game of deceive and ruin. How he loved the Great Dark Dance. Power surged through him, a boon from his god. The Mordant rose from the throne. Pulling the hood of his robe forward, he hid his face as he crossed the checkerboard floor, for it was not yet time to come out of the shadows.

Epilogue

Kath prowled the deck of the *Sea Sprite,* scanning the ocean for enemy ships. To the west, the sea stretched to forever, a rolling gauntlet of gray waves flecked with white teeth, the birthplace of fierce storms. To the east, angry waves battered against towering black cliffs, a forbidding shoreline full of rocky traps and treacherous whirlpools, offering death to unwary ships. If the sea turned hostile, they'd find no safe harbors along the basalt cliffs. The *Sea Sprite* threaded the dangers, sailing between the vast ocean waves and the sinister coastline, yet to Kath's mind, the most lethal threats were the MerChanter raiders, relentless predators prowling the sea.

A rogue wave slapped the prow, sending a frothy spray shooting over the railing. Kath flinched away but the spray caught her, more rust for her chainmail. She licked the salty tang from her lips. At least for now, the sea seemed empty of ships. Three times they'd fought the great triremes, the raider ships bearing down on them like hungry sharks, their oars churning the ocean to a fearsome beat. Kath fervently hoped she never saw another trireme in her entire life, but it would have been a comfort to spy the colorful sails of the Navarren fleet, to know they weren't alone. It seemed forever since they'd set sail from the Dark Citadel. Ambushed by MerChanter raiders, the *Sprite* had long since lost sight of the other merchant ships. Kath wondered how they fared. Alone, the *Sea Sprite* limped south, bearing a legion of battle scars.

Sailors climbed the rigging, sewing canvas patches on the mainsail. Tattered sails beat against broken spars, the checkered canvas straining against a crisp wind. Kath lingered by the ship's figurehead, the prow blackened and burnt, scorched by fires. Bloodstains leached into the deck, becoming part of the ship. The north exacted a bitter toll. Sometimes she wondered if they'd ever escape.

Blaine made his way towards her, the hilt of his blue steel sword rearing over his right shoulder. "See anything?" He kept a firm grip on the railing.

"Only waves."

He scowled, "I'm sick of them too."

Somehow Kath had escaped the ravages of seasickness. She thanked the gods for their favor. "Looks like you finally got your sea legs."

"My legs belong on land."

"Just so." Kath knew her painted warriors felt the same. They'd endured much to follow her south.

His gaze turned west. "It's getting lower in the sky."

She followed Blaine's stare towards the red comet, a searing scar hanging low above the roiling ocean. "I know." Tension riddled her shoulders, feeling trapped on the ship while the Mordant worked his will upon the south, yet there was nothing she could do to hasten the voyage. Her hand gripped the crystal dagger, beseeching Valin's aid. Time was growing late.

"I wonder what we'll find when we finally reach Navarre."

Kath gave him a sharp look, wondering if he'd guessed her fear. Many a night she woke sodden with sweat, dreaming they'd come too late to the south...too late to stop the Mordant. She'd seen the horrors of the Dark Citadel...and they haunted her. In her worst nightmares, the south became the north, a land of cruel barbarity, everyone enslaved to the Mordant's will. A shiver raced down her back. Kath made the hand sign against evil, shunning the vile visions. "The gods will lend a hand," but her words held little conviction.

Blaine gave her a sour look. "If the gods are in this fight, I wouldn't know it."

She parried his pessimism with a stout reply. "The Navarren fleet came north."

He gave her a disgusted look that said he wasn't sure the sea voyage was a good thing.

She supposed from his perspective it seemed an ill-turn, yet to Kath it was a god-given boon, the only way to escape the winter's bitter grip on the Dark Citadel, the only way to follow the Mordant south and bring her army to bear. But they hadn't escaped yet and if they came too late it would not matter...and she did not know how the other ships fared. The harsh truths nagged at her, multiplying her worries.

Blaine leaned on the railing. "I was meant to wield a sword, not wallow on a ship."

She heard the bitterness in his voice. "Yet even aboard ship, your sword made a great difference."

He gave her a thoughtful look. "In the Citadel, something happened...," but then he fell silent, as if mulling his words.

For half a heartbeat, she thought he would say something more, but then the lookout sang a warning. "*Isles to the port side!*"

A hearty cheer rose from the *Sprite's* crew.

Startled by the sailors' response, Kath gazed to the left, straining to see, but all she found were white-capped waves. "Do you see it?"

Blaine shook his head, "No."

Puzzled, she made her way back to the aft deck, climbing the stairs to stand by the captain. "What is it?"

Juliana flashed a dazzling smile. "The Orcnoth Islands!"

The name meant nothing to Kath.

"A safe port and a warm welcome! The Orcnoths owe allegiance to Navarre!" Juliana pointed to the southeast. "See how the waves break against the rocks like a white banner against the sea, a sure sign of land. And beyond the Orcnoths, the sea color brightens from dusky gray to warm turquoise." Juliana grinned, clapping Kath on the back. "The sea color never lies, my friend. We're nearly home! We've done it! We've escaped the north!"

Escaped the north, the words echoed in Kath's mind like a long-held promise. She gripped the railing and stared south. Now that she knew what to look for, she saw the low-slung isles, little more than rocky crags topped by green pasture. Beyond the isles, she noticed how the southern sea gradually brightened to a welcoming turquoise. *Nearly home,* though it was not Kath's home, she felt a welcome warmth spread through her, for it truly meant they'd escaped the north. Her gaze was drawn to the west. The red comet still lingered on the horizon, not yet set. For once the comet gave her hope, a reminder that the outcome of the Battle Immortal was not yet decided. Kath gripped the crystal dagger, keen to make a difference. Perhaps the gods had not abandoned them after all.

APPENDIX

LANVERNESS

Lanverness is an old kingdom, steeped in tradition, often relying on its wealth of natural resources and the shrewdness of its rulers to grow in prosperity and influence. Never fecund, the royal line of Lanverness has been forced to branch out several times over the centuries. The Rose Throne is currently held by the Tandroths. The Tandroths nearly lost the throne when the last king of Lanverness, King Leonid, failed to produce a male heir. The king survived a revolt and forced his noblemen to accept his only daughter, Liandra, as the heir to the Rose Throne on the condition that she marry a peer of the realm. Liandra is the only queen to rule a kingdom of Erdhe. Under Queen Liandra's stewardship, Lanverness has become the wealthiest kingdom in all of Erdhe.

The symbol of Lanverness is two white roses crossed on a field of emerald green. The seat of their power is Castle Tandroth, rising from the heart of Pellanor, the capitol city.

QUEEN LIANDRA TANDROTH, ruler of the Rose Throne, also known as the White Rose of Lanverness, also known as the Spider Queen

> -her husband, **PRINCE-CONSORT DONALD TERREL**, chosen from among the noble families of Lanverness, Lord Terrel was raised up to be the Prince-Consort to the queen on condition that he forsake his name and his lineage. He died in a hunting accident shortly after the birth of his second son. The heraldry of house Terrel is a red unicorn rearing on a field of green.
> -their children:
> **PRINCE STEWART**, heir to the Rose Throne, promoted to general of the Rose Army, wields a blue steel sword
> **PRINCE DANLY**, spare heir to the Rose Throne, a condemned traitor
> **PRINCESS ASELYNN**, died at birth
> **UNNAMED PRINCESS,** died at premature birth, some consider it murder by poison

-her councilors:

>**LORD ROBERT HIGHGATE**, the Master Archivist, the queen's shadowmaster, right hand to the queen
>
>**MASTER RADDOCK,** deputy shadowmaster serving the queen, was once a condemned thief, rescued from the dungeons by the Master Archivist
>
>**SIR DURNHEART,** the Knight Protector, raised to a knight after the Red Horn rebellion, wields a blue steel sword named *Loyalty*
>
>**LORD TURNER**, a former member of the queen's council, boiled alive for treason, a harlequin of the Dark Lord
>
>**LORD SHELDON**, the Lord Sheriff, leader of the constable force of Lanverness
>
>**MAJOR RANOTH,** promoted after the rebellion, he serves as a military advisor to the queen
>
>**LORD SADDLER,** a goldsmith raised to a lord after the rebellion, the Master of Coin on the queen's council
>
>**LORD RICKMAN**, the Lord of Mines, responsible for the ruby, emerald and iron ore mines of Lanverness
>
>**LORD CENRIC,** a cat-eyed archer, he sits on the queen's council when he is in Pellanor, leader of Clan Hemlock, his loyalty is to the Treespeaker and the Deep Green, he wears a cloak of peacock feathers
>
>**LORD CANNING,** newly appointed Treasurer
>
>**LORD GRANGE,** newly appointed Royal Scribe
>
>**PRINCESS JEMMA,** princess of Navarre, a Royal J, wayfaring with the queen to learn the way of multiplying coins, sits on the queen's council as the representative from Navarre

-her ladies-in-waiting:

>**LADY SARAH JAMESON**, a distant cousin of the queen, principle lady-in-waiting to the queen
>
>**LADY MARTHA**, a lady-in-waiting to the queen
>
>**LADY AMY**, the youngest of the queen's ladies-in-waiting
>
>**LADY LINDSEY,** a lady-in-waiting to the queen

-other members of the court:

SIR CARDEMIR, fifth son of the Duke of Graymaris, the seahorse knight, sent by the queen as an emissary to the Kiralynn monks, murdered by the Mordant's treachery

FREDERINKO, an emissary from the Empire of Ur, a chained servant of the twelfth-fold prince of Ur, come to the Rose Court bearing gifts, sent to prepare for the prince's arrival

MASTER FINTAN, an emissary from the Kiralynn Monks to the Rose Court, mysteriously murdered in the queen's castle

CAPTAIN BLACKMON, captain of the queen's guards

HEALER CRANDOR, a master healer of the Rose Court

LORD NEALY, once a lord on the queen's council, he fell from favor and was banished from the queen's presence, owns a wealthy mansion in Pellanor

MAULKIN, a shadowman serving the queen

MASTER CARL, master baker in the royal kitchens

LADY CLARA SADDLER, wife to Lord Saddler

DUKE ANDERS, a former member of the queen's council, resigned several years ago after many arguments with the queen

LORD WESLEY, a peer of the realm

LORD FERDIC, a minor peer of the realm

LORD WEATHERLY, a minor peer of the realm

THE PEOPLE OF PELLANOR

MASTER NUMAR, a master of the Kiralynn Order and a skilled herbalist, he is posing as the master of an apothecary shop, The White Unicorn, in Pellanor

SIMON, a monk of the Kiralynn Order serving as an assistant to Master Numar

GIDEON, a monk of the Kiralynn Order serving as an assistant to Master Numar

MINARA, the madam of a back alley whorehouse

LUCINDA, a young prostitute working for Minara

BURT, the innkeeper of The Silver Swan

MERCHANT GILROD, an influential merchant in Pellanor

MERCHANT LANGFORD, an influential merchant in Pellanor

MERCHANT HARSTOW, an influential merchant in Pellanor

MARLA, a serving wench at the Brass Rose tavern

THE ROSE ARMY

PRINCE STEWART, heir to the Rose Throne, General of the Rose Army, wields a blue steel sword
-his officers and soldiers:

> **LORD DANE,** eldest son of the Duke of Kardiff, fostered to the Rose Court at a young age, a sword brother to Prince Stewart, second in command of the Rose Army, the symbol of the Dukes of Kardiff is a rearing griffin
> **KELSO,** serves as one of Prince Stewart's commanders
> **MATHIS,** serves as one of Prince Stewart's commanders
> **MAJOR BATTON,** a commander of the Rose Army
> **OWEN,** a soldier captured by the Flame, becomes a royal guard to Prince Stewart
> **CROCKER,** a scout captured by the Flame, becomes a royal guard to Prince Stewart
> **CRISPIN,** a soldier captured by the Flame, becomes a royal guard to Prince Stewart

LINGARD

Lingard is a fortress citadel, the second greatest fortress in Lanverness. The heraldic seat of the Rognalds, staunch supports and loyal lords serving Queen Liandra. Their symbol is an iron fist on a field of yellow-gold.

BARON ROGNALD, a peer of the realm of Lanverness, a friend and staunch supporter of Queen Liandra, the ruler of Lingard, he is slain by treachery
-his officers, soldiers, and servants:

> **LORD RONALD ROGNALD,** eldest son of Baron Rognald, commander of the south gate of Lingard, heir to Lingard
> **CAPTAIN LEONARD VENGAR,** captain of the guard for Lingard
> **DASCHEL**, seneschal to Baron Rognald

KURT, a soldier sworn to the baron, friend of Vengar
SANDRA, a whore in Lingard, friend of Vengar

THE MORDANT

With over a thousand years of life, the Mordant is the oldest of the harlequins. Imbued with Dark power, he is the god-king of the north, the ruler of the Dark Citadel. He wields the Staff of Pain, an iron scepter with a red crystal at the top.

The Mordant's time-worn seat of power is Dark Citadel, a forbidding fortress-city in the far north. Perched atop three hundred foot cliffs that overlook the Western Ocean, it is built upon a huge monolithic boulder. The tiered city has nine layers spiraling upward around the central stone monolith. Each layer holds a distinct class of people, with the poorest at the bottom and the palace of the Mordant at the summit. The stone monolith contains steps leading to a cave that underlies the Dark Citadel, an ancient sanctum to the Dark God, a source of Dark power.

The Mordant's domain also includes the steppes, a vast sea of grass that serves as a desolate greensward for the Dark Citadel, a barren killing field that becomes the anvil of winter. The northern steppes are divided from the south by a dark wall studded with ten Gargoyle Gates.

The domain also includes the Pit, a massive crater with near vertical glass-sheer walls. Slaves live within the Pit, toiling within the Mordant's iron mines. Female slaves are forced to serve as whores for the Mordant's army. Residual magic in the Pit results in the massive abnormalities of newborns. Two new sub-races have been born and bred in the Pit; the Taals, an ogre-like sub-race with massive strength and limited intellect, and the Duegar, also called the Hounds of the Mordant, dwarves with the ability to scent magic.

The symbol of the Dark Citadel is a gold pentacle emblazoned on a field of black. The Darkflamme is the Mordant's personal battle banner, twelve feet of black silk ending in two silken tails of bright red flecked with gold, creating the illusion of darkness on fire

SERVANTS OF THE MORDANT
> **BISHOP BORGAN,** a bishop of the Pentacle serving as the seneschal to the Mordant, a master forger

MAJOR TARQ, commander of the Eighth Fist, a cadre of elite guards from the Dark Citadel, sent south to serve the Mordant

DOLF, a master assassin of the Ninth Rank, posing as a manservant to the Mordant

ROLO, a senior snargon to the duegars

FREDERINKO, formerly a chained servant of UR, the eunuch was kidnapped by MerChanters and then turned to Darkness by the Mordant, he serves as an emissary to the Rose Court

DOMINIC, an assassin disguised as a jester, gifted to Queen Liandra by Frederinko

CASTOR, a duegar disguised as a jester, gifted to Queen Liandra by Frederinko

TOKAR, a snargon of the duegars

SORKON, a snargon of the duegars, Tokar's brother

KRUGAR, an assassin

CLAVIS, an assassin

GRON, a torturer

HOLDOR, a master assassin of the Ninth Rank

CAPTAIN GARVER, a guard captain from the Dark Citadel sent south to serve the Mordant

CORLIN, a master assassin of the Ninth Rank

BARRY, an assassin

CRIMSON, a concubine from the Dark Citadel

AMBER, a concubine from the Dark Citadel

SABLE, a concubine from the Dark Citadel

ARMY OF THE PENTACLE

GENERAL HAITH- High General of the Army of the Pentacle, witness to the beheading of the Mordant in his prior life

GENERAL MARRIS- General of the Army of the Pentacle

TRANTOR, a snargon of the duegars, serves General Haith as his personal snargon

MAJOR RUGGAR, military aide to General Haith

COMMANDER CRULL, second to General Marris

CAPTAIN JOHNSON, aid to General Marris

COMMANDER ANDRIUS, second to Commander Crull
MAJOR BARKER, serves under General Marris
COMMANDER TROVIS, serves under General Haith
CENTURIAN HASTINGS
VOLTRAN, chief handler of the gorehounds
BRUTHUS, Master Torturer

THE ORACLE PRIESTESS

The Priestess is the ruler of the Isle of the Oracle, the guardian of the sacred well, the wielder of the Eye of the Oracle. She rarely uses her true name, but often goes by the name of Lady Cereus, a name given to her by Prince Razzur of Coronth. Beyond the Oracle Isle, she takes the phases of the moon as her symbol, gold on a field of purple. After the collapse of the Flame religion, she claims the southwest corner of Coronth for her queendom, establishing a capital in the ancient city of Rhune. She assumes the name of Queen Selene, the Lady of the Moon. Silverspire is her castle.

Hidden in depths of the Great Southern Swamps, the Isle of the Oracle is an ancient wellspring of Darkness, a place of power where the Dark Lord reaches through the Veil to touch his dedicates. At times of great prophecy, the Dark Lord releases his priest or priestess into the kingdoms of Erdhe to participate in the Great Dark Dance.

-her servants and soldiers:
> **GENERAL TARMIN,** a major of the Flame Army, sworn to the service of the Priestess and promoted to the general of her army, he commands her forces in Rhune, a lover to the Priestess
> **LORD STEFFAN,** formerly the Lord Raven of Coronth, goes by the title of the Lord of Darkmoor, a dedicate to the Dark Lord, lover to the Priestess
> **BRAXUS,** a lover to the Priestess, serves as her seneschal, also a skilled sword
> **HUGO,** captain of the guards, a lover to the Priestess
> **LYDIA,** dark-haired handmaiden to the Priestess
> **TARA,** blonde-haired handmaiden to the Priestess

LORD STEFFAN, formerly known as Lord Steffan Raven of Coronth, the true power behind the Flame War, a dedicate of the Dark Lord with the power of dice. After the defeat of his army at Pellanor he travels to Rhune to reunite with the Priestess. Once again he becomes her lover and ally, scheming with the Priestess to regain a position of power in Erdhe.

-his servants and soldiers:

> **BISHOP TILDEN**, a former Bishop of the Flame, a refugee from the war, he leads a band of solders turned mercenaries, he secretly takes serves with Lord Steffan
>
> **CAPTAIN DONKLIN,** a former captain of the 4th Brigade of the Flame Army, a veteran of Lingard and Pellanor, a leader of Bishop Tilden's band of mercenaries
>
> **CAPTAIN MARKS,** a former captain of the Flame Army
>
> **TANDON,** a former soldier of the Flame, expert with the halberd
>
> **SCOBE**, a former soldier of the Flame
>
> **SCANLON**, a former soldier of the Flame

NAVARRE

The youngest kingdom of Erdhe, Navarre was founded less than four hundred years ago by a daring adventurer, Alaric Navarre, who rescued the youngest daughter of the king of Coronth from a band of sea pirates infesting the Orcnoth Islands. Gaining the king's confidence, and his daughter's hand in marriage, Alaric earned a freehold of land running along the Western Ocean where he later established his kingdom. His domain includes the Orcnoth Islands.

While defeating the nest of pirates, Alaric discovered a long-forgotten focus. The magic of the focus renders the royal house very fecund, enabling the queens to bear six to ten children in a single pregnancy. After using the magic, both the king and the queen become sterile. The focus is the secret strength of the royal house of Navarre, the bedrock for the succession to the throne. Alaric abandoned the convention of primogeniture, declaring that all of the tuplets have an equal chance to the throne. He instituted the practice of Wayfaring, a type of fostering where the heirs develop their greatest interests, striving to become excellent at a skill, a knowledge, or a trade, so that they can bring this knowledge back to Navarre and thus enrich the kingdom. After the Wayfaring, the King, together with the royal council, chooses the successor to the throne based on the talents, skills, and temperament that best fit the needs of the kingdom at the time. Navarre is well known for its uncommonly wise rulers...but with every great boon there is also a cost, the hidden focus brings with it the Curse of the Vowels.

The symbol of Navarre is a white osprey soaring on a checkered field of red and blue. The seat of their power is Castle Seamount, perched on a rocky outcrop on the edge of the Western Ocean. Navarre has always had close ties to the sea.

KING IVOR NAVARRE, the eighth ruler of the kingdom of Navarre
    -his siblings:
      PRINCE IRWIN, died of poison, believed to be a victim of the Curse of the Vowels

PRINCESS INGRID, fell from the rigging of a ship and died, believed to be a victim of the Curse of the Vowels

PRINCESS IRIS, accused of murdering her two siblings, exiled to the Orcnoth Islands, she murdered her guards and then disappeared

PRINCE ISADOR, Commander of the Army of Navarre, advisor to the king, nearly fell victim to the Curse of the Vowels, murdered at the poison feast

PRINCESS IGRAINE, Counselor to the king, court historian, tutor to the Royal Js, murdered at the poison feast

PRINCE IAN, Royal Bowyer, advisor to the king, murdered at the poison feast

PRINCESS IVY, Captain of a royal merchant vessel of Navarre

-his wife, **QUEEN MEGAN**, a princess of Tubor
-their children known as the Royal Js:

PRINCESS JEMMA, Wayfaring with the Queen of Lanverness to learn the way of multiplying coins

PRINCE JUSTIN, Sent wayfaring to become a bard, he receives permission from the King and Council to travel to Coronth to try and overthrow the Pontifax, also known as the Dark Harper

PRINCESS JORDAN, Sent wayfaring with the Kiralynn monks to learn the art of war, she is felled by the treachery of the Mordant. Healed by the monk's magic, she gains visions of prophecy and returns to Navarre. She is the sword sister to Kath of Castlegard

PRINCE JARED, Sent wayfaring with the Octagon Knights to learn the way of the sword, he is murdered by loyalists to the Flame

PRINCESS JULIANA, Wayfaring with Navarre's merchant fleet to learn the way of the sea, merchant captain of the *Sea Sprite*

PRINCE JAMES, Wayfaring in Tubor to learn to become a vintner

PRINCE JAYSON, Wayfaring in the Delta to learn the secrets of a new water wheels

his retainers:

MARY, Prince Ian's wife, murdered at the poison feast
GARTH, Princess Ivy's husband
SIR LEON, an older knight, serves the queen on market days
MATILDA, a wise woman, an herbalist, a midwife, and a fortuneteller, a friend to Queen Megan
MASTER SIMMONS, the royal healer

CREW OF THE *SEA SPRITE*

JULIANA, Princess of Navarre, a Royal J, captain of the *Sea Sprite*
MARCUS, First Mate
SOOTHBY, Second Mate
WREN, lookout
JANGO, a sailor

THE ARMY OF NAVARRE

MAJOR COLSON, veteran major of the Army of Navarre
RAFE, a monk of the Kiralynn Order, a friend and advisor to Princess Jordan
CAPTAIN VARNICK, captain of the pike men
CAPTAIN CYRIL, captain of the archers

CASTLEGARD

Three hundred years after the War of Wizards decimated the kingdoms of Erdhe, a group of knights banded together to protect the southern kingdoms from the ravages of the north. They claimed Castlegard, the great mage-stone castle left empty after the War of Wizards, as the seat of their power. Adopting the shape of the great castle as their symbol, they became known as the Octagon Knights.

To bolster their cause, the knights were ceded land running along the length of the Dragon Spine Mountains. Stretching from Castlegard all the way to the Western Ocean, this land became known as the Domain. A series of castles, keeps, and walls were built along the Dragon Spines, allowing the knights to control the mountain passes and deny access to the southern kingdoms. The Domain also includes the only iron ore mine in all of Erdhe to yield blue ore, the rare ore required to forge the knights' fabled blue steel swords.

As a sworn brotherhood of elite knights, the candidates forsake their lineage and their past when they win their maroon cloaks. Their symbol is a maroon octagon emblazoned on a silver shield.

KING URSUS ANVRIL, King of Castlegard and the Knights of the Octagon, Lord of the Domain, bearer of a great blue sword named *Honor's Edge*.

      -his wife, **QUEEN PHYLA**, died giving birth to their only daughter

      -their children:

PRINCE ULRICH, First-born son of the king, a sworn knight of the maroon, former commander of the wall at Raven Pass, bearer of a great blue sword named *Mordbane*, slain at Raven Pass

PRINCE GRIFFIN, Second-born son of the king, a sworn knight of the maroon, former commander of Dymtower, murdered at Raven Pass

PRINCE GODFREY, Third-born son of the king, a sworn knight of the maroon, former commander of Shieldhold, murdered at Raven Pass

PRINCE TRISTAN, Fourth-born son of the king, a sworn knight of the maroon, slain while leading a patrol into the steppes

PRINCE LIONEL, Fifth-born son of the king, a sworn knight of the maroon, former commander of Cragnoth Keep, murdered at Cragnoth Keep

PRINCESS KATHERINE, Sixth child of the king, also known as the Imp or Little Sister or Kath. As a female, the Octagon symbol of Castlegard is forbidden to her. Instead she uses the Anvril's ancient heraldic symbol of a red hawk attacking with talons outstretched on a field of white. The wielder of the crystal dagger, Kath travels into the far north with a small band of companions, seeking to slay the Mordant. After being tested in a trial by combat, Kath is hailed as the **Svala,** the war leader of the Painted People.

KATH'S COMPANIONS

DUNCAN TRELOCH - a master archer with ties to the Deep Green and Navarre

SIR BLAINE - a knight of the Octagon who wields a blue steel great sword named *Stonecutter* by the Painted People

SIR TYRONE- a veteran knight of the Octagon with skin the color of ebony, often referred to as the 'black knight', a hero slain at the battle of Cragnoth Keep

ZITH - a master monk of the Kiralynn Order, father of Bryce, loses his left forearm to the gorehounds

DANYA - a young woman who sought sanctuary in the Kiralynn Monastery with her mountain wolf, **BRYX,** she is called a 'Beastmaster' by the monks and a 'Beastspeaker' by the Painted People. She is locked in a healing coma after expending her magic to help take the Dark Citadel.

ARMY OF THE OCTAGON KNIGHTS

SIR OSBOURNE, The Knight Marshal of the Octagon, right hand of the King, a one-eyed man with a scar-crossed face, he wields a saber as his weapon of first choice, but then takes up Sir Tyrone's great sword from the signal tower of Cragnoth Keep.

SIR LOTHAR, knight-captain of the Salt Tower, wields a battleaxe, close friend to the knight marshal

SIR ABRAX, knight of the maroon, champion of the sword, guard to King Ursus, he wields a blue steel sword named *Protector,* slain

SIR RANNOCK, knight of the maroon, champion of the morning star

SIR BLAZE, knight of the maroon, champion of the mace

SIR BORIS, knight-captain of Holdfast Keep, slain

SIR VARLIN, knight-captain of Dymntower

SIR KRISMIR, knight-captain of Shieldhold

SIR KILGAR, knight-captain of Cragnoth Keep, wounded

SIR DALT, knight-captain of Ice Tower, slain

SIR GRAVIS, knight-captain of Sword Keep

SIR ODIS, knight of the maroon, champion of the lance, slain

SIR ADLEMAR, knight of the maroon, champion of the claymore, wields a blue steel claymore named *Stalwart*

SIR TRASK, knight of the maroon, champion of the battleaxe, assigned to Cragnoth Keep as a punishment posting, slain at the battle of Cragnoth Keep

SIR TYRONE, knight of the maroon with skin the color of ebony, often referred to as the 'black knight', a companion to Princess Katherine, he was slain at the battle of Cragnoth Keep

SIR RAYMOND, branded as an unmade-knight of the Octagon, exiled from the Domain of Castlegard on penalty of death, sworn to serve the Mordant, slain

SIR BROCK, wounded knight

SIR KEIFER, wounded knight

SIR ZAKERY, maroon knight

SIR TRADON, maroon knight

SIR MALVOY, a fresh-sworn knight of the maroon

SIR DEVLAN, a fresh-sworn knight of the maroon, died of battle wounds
SIR SPARLIN, maroon knight died of battle wounds
SIR CORBIN, a slain knight of the maroon
SIR TANCIL, a slain knight of the maroon
SIR MARIN, a knight of the maroon
SIR AMBROSE, a knight of the maroon
SIR WINTON, a knight of the maroon
SIR VARDINE, a knight of the maroon
SIR MELLOT, a knight of the maroon
SIR TOWLIN, a slain knight of the maroon
HADRIAN, master archer of the maroon, slain at Raven Pass
BENFORD, master archer of the maroon
BALDWIN, senior squire of the maroon, squire to King Ursus
MARTYN, squire to the knight marshal
TARGIN, a scout of the maroon
BARTLET, a scout of the maroon
BRANNOCK, master scout of the maroon
JAMES, squire to Sir Lothar
ORRIN SUREHAMMER, legendary Master Swordsmith of the maroon, first forger of blue steel blades, some believe he forged magical abilities into his blue steel blades making them destine for the hands of heroes
OTTO, the current Master Swordsmith of Castlegard's forge, responsible for the forging of all blue steel weapons
QUINTUS, the master healer of Castlegard
ELISE, scullery maid turned assistant to healer Quintus

THE KIRALYNN MONKS

Founded over two thousand years ago by a group of scholars, knights, and wizards, the Kiralynn Order has always presented an enigmatic face to the world, a face that is open yet closed. One hundred years before the start of the War of Wizards the monks withdrew from the southern kingdoms, retreating to their monastery hidden deep in the Southern Mountains. As if erased from the minds of men, the monastery's location disappeared from the maps of Erdhe. The memory of the Kiralynn monks has slowly faded, becoming little more than legend and myth. Yet select rulers of the southern kingdoms still receive scrolls sealed with the symbol of the Order. History has proven that these scrolls contain an uncanny prescience. Kings ignore the advice of the Order at their own peril.

The symbol of the Kiralynn monks is a Seeing Eye in the palm of an Open Hand. Their seat of power is their mountain monastery. The motto of the Order is "Seek Knowledge, Protect Knowledge, Share Knowledge".

THE GRAND MASTER, the leader of the Kiralynn Order, his/her identity is a closely guarded secret
-monks and initiates of the Order:
> **MASTER RIZEL**, a Master of the Order
> **MASTER GARTH**, a Master Healer of the Order
> **BRYCE**, an initiate of the Order, he studied to take his vows to become a monk and a healer but was subsumed by the Mordant's Awakening, becoming a prisoner in his own mind
> **MASTER AEROTH**, an ambassador monk sent to the kingdoms of Erdhe
> **MASTER ZITH**, a Master of the Order, accompanies Kath as one of her companions, he is the father of Bryce, he lost his left forearm in the battle with the gorehounds
> **RAFE**, a sworn monk of the Order, he has worn the blue for five years, sent with Princess Jordan of Navarre
> **MASTER YARL**, a master of the Order, an expert with a quarterstaff, sent with Princess Jordan of Navarre
> **MISTRESS ELLIS**, a master of the Order

MISTRESS LENORE, a master of the Order

MASTER ADELBART, master of calligraphy, teaches acolytes in the scriptorium

MASTER TOLK, the Chronicler of the Order, a venerable elder

MASTER CARLISLE, half-blind master, a venerable elder

MASTER FELIX, a member of the seclusionists

MASTER NORMATH, a member of the seclusionists

MASTER GRIMSHAW, scholar of ancient prophecies, friend to Master Rizel

MISTRESS LURINDA, scholar of lore

MASTER RUGAR, scholar

MASTER VERNIUS, the loremaster for the Order, a venerable elder

MASTER JULIAN, dead master to Vernius

MASTER AMBROSE, friend to Master Rizel

MASTER CALEB, decodes messages from the mews

MASTER ALTHAR, friend of Master Caleb

MASTER FINTAN, an emissary from the Kiralynn Monks sent to the Rose Court, mysteriously murdered in the queen's castle

MASTER NUMAR, a master of the Order serving as a hidden Wanderer in Pellanor, a skilled herbalist posing as an apothecary, he owns the White Unicorn apothecary shop

SIMON, a hidden monk serving Master Numar in Pellanor

GIDEON, a hidden monk serving Master Numar in Pellanor

GILBERT, a monk of the Order serving as a hidden Wanderer in Pellanor

ASTER, a monk of the Order serving as a hidden Wanderer in Pellanor

NIMERIA HARPSINGER, sixteen years old, golden-robed acolyte studying under Master Adelbart in the scriptorium, longs to be an Illuminator

ALRIC, a golden-robed acolyte serving in the mews

THE ZWARD

The Zward are sons and daughters of Kiralynn monks who choose to serve by the sword instead of the scroll. An ancient and secret order, they serve the will of the Grand Master. Their symbol is a small silver ring emblazoned with a fist holding an upright sword.

THADDEUS TOKHEART, also known as Thad, a captain of the Zward
DONAL, a sworn member of the Zward
BENJIN, a sworn member of the Zward
MARCUS, a sworn member of the Zward

The MERCHANTERS

An ancient seafaring people, the MerChanters are the scourge of the oceans, born and bred upon the high seas. The self-styled Sea Lords claim no land as their own. Nomadic raiders, they rove the oceans in their great triremes, pillaging the coastal kingdoms for food, women and plunder. Their absolute leader is the Miral. Their weapon of choice is the trident. The MerChanters have a long-standing alliance with the Mordant. Little is known about the MerChanters other than rumors steeped in terror.

THE MIRAL - Absolute ruler of the MerChanters
LORD ASKAL - A MerChanter Sea Lord, captain of the *Dark Fin*
TORMUND - First Mate of the *Dark Fin*
BALTHAR- a MerChanter raider aboard the *Shark*
GALLWAX - a MerChanter raider, First Mate aboard the *Shark*
CORWAY- a MerChanter raider aboard the *Shark*

THE DEEP GREEN

The Deep Green is an ancient power reborn from the ashes of the War of Wizards. Rising from the ruins of a great city, the forest grows with frightening speed. Trees at the heart of the forest are giants, growing to more than thrice the height of normal trees, while the dense tangle of underbrush forms a nearly impenetrable barrier. The forest protects its own, a race of people with golden cat-eyes. Calling themselves the Children of the Green, the cat-eyed people live within the boundaries of the forest in a confederation of clans under the leadership of the Treespeaker.

Outside of the forest, the cat-eyed people are shunned as evil abominations, said to be born from the perverse mating of man with animals. The cat-eyed people are persecuted across the kingdoms of Erdhe, and often put to death by the 'white-eyes'.

THE TREESPEAKER, as old as the forest, she is a seer, a witch, the embodiment of the power of the Green. As the leader of the clans, she wears a cloak of snow-white swan feathers.
-her clan leaders:

> **CENRIC**, leader of Clan Hemlock, he wears a cloak of peacock feathers, volunteers to lead a war party to Pellanor
>
> **AGATHA**, leader of Clan Aspen, she wears a cloak of blue jay feathers. She leads a faction that opposes dealings with the white-eyes
>
> **BRAN**, leader of Clan Ash, he wears a cloak of raven feathers
>
> **CAMILA**, leader of Clan Maple, she wears a cloak of orange kestrel feathers and is a member of the faction that opposes dealings with the white-eyes
>
> **DEREK**, leader of Clan Redwood, he wears a cloak of red woodpecker feathers and is a member of the faction that opposes dealing with the white-eyes
>
> **CONRAD**, leader of Clan Spruce, he wears a cloak of brown thrush feathers

LANA, leader of Clan Oak, she wears a cloak of golden finch feathers

-her people:

JORAH SILVENWOOD, a ranger of Clan Cedar, killed in the Mordant's fire

RONAH, a ranger of Clan Hemlock

JENKS, a patrol leader of Clan Hemlock

MARTYN, an attendant to the Treespeaker

ALWIN, a ranger of Clan Hemlock

THE PAINTED PEOPLE

An ancient people, forgotten by most of Erdhe, the Painted Warriors are the descendents of escaped slaves and runaway soldiers. Living in the shadow of the Dark Citadel, the Painted People have forged a fiercely independent warrior culture that spans a thousand years. Outnumbered and poorly equipped, they strike back at the Pentacle in lightning raids across the steppes, reaping steel and armor from their enemies. They make their home in a secret labyrinth of caves hidden in the Ghost Hills. Deeply spiritual, they invoke the power of nature by tattooing their faces with the images of beasts and birds, a spiritual melding of man and animal. Divided into dens depending on their tattoos, they are guided by the Ancestor, a shaman of mystical memories, and lead by a Council of Leaders made up of representatives from all the dens. A secret and forgotten people, few in the southern kingdoms have ever heard of them.

THE ANCESTOR- Also known as the Keeper of Memories, the Old One. The Ancestor is always a woman, following a matriarchal line of mystical seers that stretches back for nearly a thousand years. As the spiritual leader of the painted people she is respected and revered but she does not rule as a queen. Instead she serves as a guide to the council of leaders.

VALDUR- a Taishan of the mountain lions, lost on a vision-hunter on a quest in the southern steppes. Attacked and left for dead by soldiers of the Pentacle, a patrol of Octagon knights found him and took him to Castlegard where he died in Kath's arms.

THE SVALA - After being tested in a trial by combat, Kath of Castlegard is hailed as the Svala, the foretold war leader of the Painted People.

ROYCE- warrior leader of the mountain lions, leader of the Council

THERA- leader of the ravens, master healer

BRANT- leader of the boars

FANGGOLD- warrior leader of the wolves

RINGOL, warrior leader of the foxes

MERRICK, a raven-faced healer, second to Thera

CORWIN, painted warrior, hunts with Blaine

TOMKIN, painted warrior, hunts with Blaine

THE MAROON BAND

A brotherhood of painted warriors who claim the honor of protecting the Svala. Survivors of the original eighty warriors who witnessed Kath's trial at the Gargoyle Gates and then formed the vanguard for the attack on the Dark Citadel, they call themselves the Maroon Band. Their symbol is a tattered strip of maroon cloak tied to their right bicep. Their strips of maroon come from the extra length of Kath's maroon cloak, given to her by Blaine after the battle with the gorehounds. Led by Bear and Boar, they have become the personal guard to the Svala.

BEAR- a bear-faced warrior assigned to guard Kath, he refuses to reveal his true name, adopts the name of Bear and becomes Kath's personal guard and friend, wields a sword
BOAR- a boar-faced warrior assigned to Kath, refuses to reveal his true name, adopts the name of Boar and becomes Kath's personal guard and friend, wields a mace
TORVEN- eagle-faced warrior patrol leader
SIDHORN, eagle-faced warrior
TINGOLD- a wolf-faced scout, hunts with Blaine
GRENFIR- an owl-faced warrior
RUTHGAR - boar-faced warrior, hunts with Blaine
TANGOR- a hawk-faced warrior
PREN, a bear-faced warrior
CLEMIT- a wolf-faced warrior
VIN- an eagle-faced warrior
TARLY- a boar-faced warrior
BRIN- a wolf-faced warrior
BRINGOLD- fox-faced warrior
GRIFF, lion-faced warrior
TANGOR, a badger-faced warrior
TORKIN, a wolf-faced warrior
TANGAR, a hawk-faced warrior
TOMLIN, a wolf-faced warrior

TALBERT, a badger-faced lad, son of a maroon band warrior who died taking the Dark Citadel, he becomes a squire to Kath, adopted by the maroon band
CONIT, a badger-faced lad, son of a maroon band warrior who died taking the Dark Citadel, he becomes a squire to Kath, adopted by the maroon band

THE WOLF BAND

A band of wolf-faced warriors who have formed a den and are sworn to protect Danya.

NEVEN- the leader of the wolf band, a wolf-faced warrior hand-fasted to Danya.
BALTHUS- wolf-faced warrior

CORONTH

The kingdom of Coronth was long ruled by one of the oldest royal families in Erdhe. Tracing their lineage back to before the War of Wizards, the Manfreds struggled to maintain their kingdom despite the aftermath of chaos and famine caused by the magical war. Their descendents ruled in an unbroken line for over a thousand years until a preacher of the Flame God brought a new religion to the capitol city of Balor. Enthralling the crowds with the miracle of the Test of Faith, the Pontifax gained a rabid following. In less than a year, the new religion consumed the kingdom, making the Pontifax more powerful than the king. Ruling from the pulpit, the Pontifax declared that only a true believer of the Flame God could wear the crown of Coronth, forcing the king, his wife, and all of his children to submit to the Test of Faith. When the searing flames consumed the royal house, the Pontifax became the spiritual and secular ruler of Coronth.

The symbol of house Manfred was a golden lion rearing on a field of blue. The new symbol of Coronth is a golden flame on field of red, the symbol of the Flame God. The seat of power is the capitol city of Balor.

THE PONTIFAX, the supreme spiritual and secular ruler of Coronth, also known as the Enlightened One, beloved of the Flame God, died in a test of faith
-his priests and counselors:
> **THE KEEPER OF THE FLAME**, Senior priest of the Flame, leader of the Confessors of the Flame, he becomes the ruler of Coronth and the leader of the faith after the death of the Pontifax, he remains in Balor
> **LORD STEFFAN RAVEN**, was the Counselor to the Pontifax, the leader of the Army of the Flame, the power behind the Flame War, his personal symbol is a black raven on a blood-red field, after his army is defeated in Pellanor he goes by the name of Steffan of Darkmoor.

RADAGAR

Over five hundred years ago, fierce warriors from a distant desert kingdom followed the caravan route north and invaded Erdhe, carving out a vast new kingdom named Radagar. The proud conquerors maintained their desert culture, with the king and the royal houses taking many wives. The harems spawned an abundance of royal princes, all competing for the Cobra Throne. Treachery and poison became the tools of succession. Over time, the royal in-fighting caused the once great kingdom to dwindle in size and stature. The kingdom is now a shadow of its former size and strength. Radagar is known as a purveyor of mercenaries, poisons, and aphrodisiacs.

The symbol of Radagar is a red coiled cobra on a field of pea-green. Their seat of power is the capital city of Salmythra. The king of Radagar is known as the ruler of the Cobra Throne.

KING RAZZUR, the king of Radagar, the ruler of the Cobra Throne, he attained the throne by assassinating his half-brother King Cyrus. A proud descendent of the desert-born conquerors, he is the leader of House Razzur, his personal symbol is a black scorpion a sky-blue field. As king, his royal symbol becomes a red coiled cobra on a field of pea green.
-his lords:
>**GENERAL XANOS,** general of Radagar's mercenary army
>**HAMID,** seneschal to King Razzur

The Front Cover artwork was done by the Australian artist, Greg Bridges. Greg's artwork has appeared on the book covers of many well-known fantasy authors. Thanks to Greg for the front cover, the spine, and the fabulous rendering of the Dark Sword used in the interior of the book. To see more of his art or to contact Greg, visit his website at http://www.gregbridges.com/

The Maps and the Back Cover blurb was done by a graphic artist from Oregon, Peggy Lowe. Her illustration of the two maps helps to bring the kingdoms of Erdhe to life. Peggy can be contacted at her e-mail address, peggy@portfoliooregon.com

The dragon used in the illuminated D was hand drawn by Karen Azinger.

Look for **The Battle Immortal,** the seventh and final book in *The Silk & Steel Saga* to be published by October 2015.

ACKNOWEDGEMENTS

Another giant step towards finishing my epic saga! My dream of Erdhe continues, and like all my other books, it takes a lot of people to make this saga come true. First and foremost, to my husband Rick, who is always keen for the next adventure and always believes no matter the odds. To my best friend and sword sister, Danae Powers, who listened from the very first chapter. To my alpha and beta readers who continue to cheer for my books, Mike, Nick, Bill, Peggy, Diane, Bob, Mary, Christine, Ruthie and Gina, your enthusiasm means so much to me. To Greg Bridges for the totally awesome front cover and the book spine. To Peggy Lowe, graphic artist extraordinaire, for the back cover, the two maps and the logo, well done! To Robert Owen Williams for corrections. To Deborah Sanders for the eagle-eyed proof read. To all of my readers around the world who are eagerly following the saga, I write for you. And to my mom, for everything, I so hope you know.

Other books by Karen L Azinger

The Assassin's Tear- Explore the medieval kingdoms of Erdhe, raid the tomb of the first emperor of China, and unravel the enigma of Dark Space in this collection of fantasy and science fiction tales from the author of *The Silk & Steel Saga.* The two signature stories, *Prophecy's Twist* and *The Assassin's Tear,* are set in the fantasy realm of Erdhe and are a prequel to *The Silk & Steel Saga. Prophecy's Twist* discovers the dark deceit that started the War of Wizards, forever changing the kingdoms of Erdhe. *The Assassin's Tear* follows the exploits of a petty thief whose ambition leads him to unravel the dark secret of the Mordant's Citadel. *The Emperor's Shadow* is an international thriller in the style of Indiana Jones, combining the power of superstition with archaeology in a desperate attempt to end World War Three. *A Man's World* is a post-apocalyptic adventure set in Australia where coal miners discover all the rules have changed. *Pieces of the Truth* is a time travel story where a young physicist discovers a forgotten truth. In *Snakes and Ladders,* Lynn Gallant sets out to shatter the glass ceiling by taking a walk to the dark side of New Orleans. In *The God Planet,* universal dreams spark a religious frenzy, summoning humanoid kind to the riddle of Dark Space.

ABOUT THE AUTHOR

KAREN L. AZINGER has always loved fantasy fiction, and always hoped that someday she could give back to the genre a little of the joy that reading has always given her. Eleven years ago on a hike in the Columbia River Gorge she realized she had enough original ideas to finally write an epic fantasy. She started writing and never stopped. *The Steel Queen* was her first book, born from that hike in the gorge. Before writing, Karen spent over twenty years as an international business strategist, eventually becoming a vice-president for one of the world's largest natural resource companies. She's worked on developing the first gem-quality diamond mine in Canada's arctic, on coal seam gas power projects in Australia, and on petroleum projects around the world. Having lived in Australia for eight years she considers it to be her second home. She's also lived in Canada and spent a lot of time in the Canadian arctic. She lives with her husband in Portland Oregon, in a house perched on the edge of the forest. She is hard at work on the seventh and final book of *The Silk & Steel Saga, The Battle Immortal,* estimated to be published by October 2015. You can learn more at her website, www.karenlazinger.com or at her Facebook page for The Steel Queen. She loves to hear from her readers!

www.ingramcontent.com/pod-product-compliance
Lightning Source LLC
Chambersburg PA
CBHW060417030726
47495CB00003B/614